REVENANT

Carolyn Haines

REVENANT

MIRA

MIRA

ISBN-13: 978-0-7783-2417-1
ISBN-10:   0-7783-2417-6

REVENANT

Copyright © 2007 by Carolyn Haines.

MIRA and the Star Colophon are trademarks used under license and registered
in Australia, New Zealand, Philippines, United States Patent and Trademark
Office and in other countries.

www.MIRABooks.com

Printed in U.S.A.

For Alice Jackson—

We had some fun when the Mississippi
Gulf Coast was a reporter's dream.

ACKNOWLEDGMENTS

I can never write about newspapers and journalists without thanking my parents, who drew me into the profession they loved. When I was so small I had to stand on a wooden box, I disassembled the slugs of hot type to be melted and reset for the next edition of the paper.

My parents, Roy and Hilda Haines, burned with the passion of true journalists, and they passed that love to me.

In my life I've been privileged to know many fine reporters and editors. The Sellers family in Lucedale gave me my first paid job at a weekly at the age of seventeen. Leonard Lowry, Fitz McCoy, Elliot Chase, Sarah Gillespie, Robert Miller, Fallon Trotter, John Fay, Buddy Smith, Rhee Odom, Tom Roper, Gary Smith, Ann Hebert, Jim Young, Doug Sease, Bill Minor, Elaine Povich, Ronni Patriquin Clark, Jim Tuten, Lee Roop, B. J. Richey, Phil Smith—each one of them helped me down the road toward becoming a better reporter and also helped me recognize my limitations.

Newspapering gave me opportunities that few young people ever see. I owe the people I worked with many thanks.

As always, I owe thanks to my critique group, the Deep South Writers Salon: Renee Paul, Alice Jackson, Susan Tanner, Stephanie Chisholm, Gary and Shannon Walker and Aleta Boudreaux.

My agent, Marian Young, is the best. And the editorial staff at MIRA can't be beat. Thank you, Lara Hyde, Valerie Gray and Sasha Bogin.

I'm knocked over by the terrific cover and the hard work that Erin Craig put into creating a design that conveyed so much of the story. This book has been a terrific experience from beginning to end.

Thank you all.

1

A seagull swooped low over the white, man-made beach of Biloxi. The midmorning sun was bright, and I squinted against the glare of the sparkling Mississippi Sound. The water held potential. An *accidental* drowning wouldn't be a bad way to go, and it would be so much easier on my parents than suicide. My BlackBerry buzzed against my waist, disrupting the constant whisper of the water, the promises of numbness and sleep. I turned back to my truck and checked the number. The newspaper. I was late again.

A discarded coin cup clattered across the parking lot. Casinos, the new Mississippi cash crop. The Gulf Coast was second only to Las Vegas for gaming, a point of pride for those who saw growth as the only indication of progress. The garish casinos, complete with parking garages and hotels, were a blight, built by people who'd forgotten a storm called Camille and the damage of two-hundred-mile-per-hour winds. Talk about a gamble—putting huge floating barges in the Mississippi Sound. It was 2005, and thirty-six years had passed since Hurricane Camille wiped out the Gulf Coast. But Mother Nature, like a guilty conscience, only feigns sleep.

Of course, mine was the minority opinion in a town that had finally seen the promise of two cars in every garage fulfilled by the economic boost brought by the lure of the one-armed bandits.

It was only March, but already the hurricane experts were predicting a bad year for 2005. In a different place and time, I might have wanted to see the list of construction materials used on the hotels and new condominiums that crowded the coastline. If the construction was not up to standards, a Category Five hurricane, like Camille, could be death and destruction. In the past, that would have caught my professional interest, but not anymore. I was done with all of that.

I drove to the newsroom of the *Morning Sun,* ignoring the hostile glances of my coworkers as I went into my office and closed the door. They'd converted a conference room to make my office and indentations from the heavy table were still in the carpet. My desk and computer were at the end of the room beside the long narrow window that reminded me of a fortress. If the Injuns, or the liberals, surrounded us, I'd have a place for my shotgun. The paper's policy would be to shoot on sight.

My telephone rang. "Where the hell have you been? It's almost ten o'clock. We're running a daily newspaper here, Carson, not a magazine."

In my three weeks of employment, nothing had happened that warranted my presence at the paper at eight. "Sorry, Brandon," I said. "I was busy contemplating suicide, but I'm too much of a coward to carry through with it. So, what's going on?" I fumbled through a desk drawer for an aspirin bottle. Perhaps I should have apologized to Brandon Prescott, the publisher, but I didn't care for him or my job.

"Drop the pity party, Carson. We don't have time for it. They're bulldozing the Gold Rush. When they started scraping up the parking lot they found a grave with five bodies in it. It's the biggest story of the decade. Joey's already there. I want you over there right now. And what the hell good is that pager unless you turn it on!"

Brandon was steamed, but there was always something that had his blood pressure at the boiling point. Lately, it was me, his prize. He'd dragged me out of the gutter and put me in a suit and an office with an official press badge. If I were a better person, I'd be grateful.

"I'm on the way," I said, surprised at the tingle at the base of my skull. My reptilian brain felt a surge. Five bodies buried at one of the most glamorous—and notorious—nightclubs along the Gulf Coast. It could be a big story. In the '70s and '80s, the Gold Rush had been the pre-casino gathering place of the Dixie Mafia and the late-night party place where the young and beautiful of all social strata came to be seen. It was even possible someone had pushed up the tarmac and uncovered Jimmy Hoffa. After all, it was the Mississippi Gulf Coast. Anything was not only possible, but it was also probable.

I walked out of my office and was met with the baleful glares of six reporters. They already knew about the bodies, and they'd been hoping it would be their story. By rights, it should have belonged to one of them. But I had the big name and I got the choicest scraps Brandon tossed. I walked out into the March sunshine, hoping the bodies were either very old or very fresh.

Once upon a time, driving along the Mississippi Gulf Coast had been a pleasure. Miles of lazy, four-lane

Highway 90 hugged the beaches where there were more migratory birds than fat sunbathers. With the advent of gambling in 1992, all of that changed. Sunbathers were already on the beach, even though the March sun had barely warmed the water above sixty degrees. For at least a mile ahead the traffic was almost at a standstill. If I didn't get to the Gold Rush soon, the bodies would be bagged and moved. In an effort to calm down, I turned my radio to a country oldies station. There was always a chance I'd catch a Rosanne Cash tune.

Instead, I got Garth Brooks and "The Dance." There had been a time when I agreed with the sentiment expressed in the song. I'd changed. There were very few experiences worth the pain. I flipped off the radio and took a deep breath. Traffic started moving, and in another fifteen minutes I was at the club.

Police cars and coroner vans lined the sandy shoulder of the highway, lights no longer flashing. Clusters of men in uniform stood whispering. Biloxi Police Department Deputy Chief Jimmy Riley sat behind the tinted windows of an unmarked car. It would have to be a big case for Riley to put in an appearance.

Mitch Rayburn, the district attorney, was also on the scene, and I'd made it a point to know as much as possible about him. Mitch was smart and ambitious, a man dedicated to protecting his community. There'd been tragedy in his past, but I didn't know the exact details. Yet. What I saw was a man sincere about distributing justice. So far, he seemed to play a straight hand, which would be a definite detriment to his future political ambitions.

Detective Avery Boudreaux did everything but stomp

his foot when he saw me pull up. Avery disliked reporters
in general and me in particular. We'd already had a run-in
over a stabbing at a local high school.

"Hi, Avery," I said, because I knew he'd rather swallow
nails than talk to me. "I'll bet the bulldozer operator was
shocked." I started toward the edge of the shallow grave
and heard Avery bark an order to stop.

"Let her go," Mitch said. "We're going to need the newspaper's cooperation."

I almost turned around in shock; Mitch was being amazingly cooperative. Then I figured the crime scene had
already been molested by a bulldozer. I could hardly do
more damage. The area was at the far back corner of the
lot. Stumps and the damaged stalks of vegetation indicated
that it had once been a shady, secluded spot.

I looked down into the grave. It was my lucky day.
There was no flesh left, only smooth, white bones.
Delicate in the bright sun. Five skeletons, five rib cages,
five spinal columns embedded in dirt. All of the skulls
were intact, the pelvises riding over femurs and tibias.
They'd been laid side by side with some gentleness, it
seemed. The connective tissue in the joints had disinte-
grated, so when the bodies were moved, they would fall
to pieces. Whoever had buried the bodies had assumed the
asphalt would protect them, and they'd been right, for a
good number of years.

I caught Joey's eye. He was standing about twenty feet
back with his digital Nikon dangling from his hand. He
nodded. I stepped in front of Avery, effectively blocking
him. Joey rushed forward and fired off several shots before
two cops grabbed him.

"Damn it, Mitch." Avery thrust me to the side. "I told you we couldn't trust her!"

"It's better to let the public know," I said. "Speculation is far worse than knowledge."

"Except for the families of the victims." Avery's mouth was a thin line. "I should arrest both of you."

I didn't let his words register. Brandon Prescott ran a newspaper that thirsted for sensationalism. I knew my job, and even when I didn't like it, I knew how to do it. There was very little of my old life that I'd held on to, but I was a damn good journalist. I got the story.

"Any idea who the bodies might be?" I directed my question to Mitch. He waved at the cops to release Joey. The photographer dashed for his car to get back to the office.

"Not yet," Mitch answered.

"Wouldn't you know, they were just so inconsiderate. They didn't carry any identification into the grave with them. Can you believe it?" Avery glared at me.

"That's a great quote, Avery," I said. "Very professional."

"That's enough, both of you." Mitch's mouth was a tight line. "There are five dead people here. Let's focus on what's important. Avery, we need to cooperate with Carson. We're not going to be able to keep the media out of this." He pointed to the highway where a television news truck had stopped. "That's our real problem."

"Do you have any idea who the victims are?" I asked Avery again, this time in a more civil tone.

"As soon as we get the medical examiner to give us a time frame for the deaths, we'll start going through missing-person reports." Avery was watching the television news crew as he talked.

"When we know something, we'll call you, Carson," Mitch promised. "I'd personally appreciate it if you didn't run the photo of the remains."

He'd effectively ripped my sails. The photo was needlessly graphic, and he knew I knew it. I hadn't been in Biloxi long, but Mitch had grown up here. He knew the score. "Talk to Brandon," I said. "You know I don't have a say in what gets printed and what doesn't. Have something good to offer in exchange."

"We wouldn't have to negotiate with Prescott if you hadn't set it up for the photographer." Avery shook his head in disgust.

"Who owns the Gold Rush now?" I watched the television reporter being held at the edge of the parking lot. My time was running out.

"Alvin Orley sold it to Harrah's about five years ago," Mitch said. "It's been empty for about that long. I think the casino corporation is going to build a parking garage here."

"Lovely. More concrete." I looked around at the oak trees that lined the property. With the bulldozers already at work, they were history. "Never let a two-hundred-year-old oak stand in the way of more parking space."

"Why in the hell did you come back here if Miami was such a paradise?" Avery asked.

I looked him dead in the eye. "I guess when my daughter burned to death and I fell into a haze of alcoholic guilt, wrecked my marriage and got fired, I thought maybe I should leave the scene of my crimes and come home to Mississippi. Biloxi was the only paper that would hire me." Avery didn't flinch, but he had the decency to drop his gaze to the ground.

"Alvin's still doing time in Angola prison," Mitch said, breaking the strained silence. "I want to personally ask him some questions. I'm going to talk to him this afternoon. You could ride with me, Carson."

I felt the sting of tears. It had taken me more than two years after Annabelle's death to be able to control my crying. Now I was about to lose it again because a D.A. stepped out of his professional skin and offered me a ride to a Louisiana prison. I was truly pathetic.

"Thanks. I'll let you know." I turned away and walked back to the shallow grave. The five skeletons were lying side by side, heads and feet in a row. I had no idea what had killed them, whether they were male or female, how old they were or why they'd been killed. For all of the things I didn't know, I was relatively certain that they'd been murdered. The skeletons were perfect. Lying under the asphalt, they'd been safe from predators and animals that normally disturb skeletal remains. I knelt down beside the grave for a closer look.

Avery was watching me, alert to my possible theft of a femur or maybe a scapula. I examined the bones, stopping on the left hand of the first victim. I couldn't be certain, but it seemed that a finger was missing. I looked at the next body and saw the same thing. Then again on the third, fourth and fifth.

"Hey, Avery," I called. "The ring fingers are missing on all of them."

He came to stand beside me, his black eyes assessing me, and not kindly. "We know," he said. "And that's something we'd like to keep out of the paper."

I couldn't keep a photograph from Brandon, but I could

keep this information. At least for a day. "Okay," I agreed, "until tomorrow. After that, I can't promise."

"The M.E. said the fingers were probably severed," Avery said. "It might be our best clue for catching whoever did this."

I nodded, still glancing at the bones. Something else caught my eye. Beside each skull were the remains of some kind of material, and beneath that, plastic hair combs. "Look at that," I said. "Nobody wears hair combs like that anymore. What are the odds that all five bodies would have had combs?"

"These bodies have probably been here at least twenty years. I've got somebody checking records to see if we can find out when this parking lot was last paved."

"You figure they're all women?" I asked, feeling yet again the tingle at the base of my skull.

"If you jump to a conclusion, Ms. Lynch, please don't put it in print. There are fools out there who believe what they read in the newspaper."

"Thanks, Avery." I was almost relieved to have him back to his normal snarly self.

"I'll stop by and talk to Brandon," Mitch said. "And you can decide if you want to ride to Angola with me. We could get there by three, back by seven or so."

"Thanks. I'll think about it." When I glanced toward my truck, I saw that Riley had returned to his desk job. The forensics team had done its work and was bagging the bodies. I'd seen hundreds of the black, zippered bags, but they still left me feeling empty. Would the families of the victims find peace or more horror? I got in my truck and eased into the moving traffic jam that was the highway.

2

Instead of going to the paper, I detoured to city hall. Biloxi was an old sea town. Fishing was once the heart and soul of the settlement, and the preponderance of business development was right along the water on Highway 90 or on Pass Road, which paralleled the coast through two counties. The population was French, Spanish, Yugoslavian, German, Italian and Scotch-Irish with a smattering of Lebanese. The Vietnamese were the newcomers who had earned an uneasy place in the fishing industry. The population was predominantly Catholic, a fact that figured into how the gravy train of state funding was distributed for many years. With the power base situated in the Protestant delta, the Gulf Coast sucked hind tit. The casinos changed all of that. The coast now had the upper hand. King Cotton and the rich planter society of the delta were passé.

Highway 90 still had remnants of the gracious old coast I remembered. Live oaks sheltered white houses with gingerbread trim and green shutters. There was an air of serenity and welcome, of permanence. I drove through one such residential area and then turned onto Lemuse where city hall was located.

When I asked for the records of building permits issued in the 1980s, I discovered that Detective Boudreaux's minion was one step ahead of me. A police officer had just copied those documents. They were right at hand, and I read with interest that a small addition had been built onto the Gold Rush in October 1981. The parking lot had also been expanded and paved. The five victims had to have been murdered prior to that. I had a place to begin looking and I sped back to the paper.

The newsroom had fallen into the noon slump. Only Jack Evans, a senior reporter, and Hank Richey, the city editor, were still at their desks, and I hoped they wouldn't see me. They were journalists of the old school, and like me, they'd found themselves employed in an entertainment medium. I slunk past the newsroom to my office and was almost there when I heard Jack yell.

"What's wrong, Carson? Vomit on your shirt?"

I couldn't help but smile. Jack was awful, and I liked him for it.

"I just need a little nip from that bottle I keep in my desk." It wasn't a joke.

"How bad was it?"

I shook my head. "More strange than gruesome."

"Mitch is talking to Brandon right this red-hot minute. I hear Joey got some good shots of the skeletons." Jack grinned. "Mitch will have to trade his soul to keep Brandon from printing that."

"I warned him." I sat down on the edge of Jack's desk. He was a medium-built guy with a head of white hair and a face that tattled all of his vices. In Miami I'd worked with a top-notch reporter who reminded me of Jack. We'd once rented a helicopter to cover some riots. It had been both harrowing and exhilarating.

"So, what did you see?" Jack asked, patting his empty shirt pocket where his Camels had once resided.

When I'd first started as a journalist, this was a game that had honed my eye. "Five skeletons, all uniform in size, buried side by side. I'd say they died around the same time because of the dirt and the decomposition, and also because the parking lot was paved in 1981." I frowned, thinking. "There were hair combs beside each skull, which would indicate female gender." I looked at Jack and decided to risk trusting him. "Not for Brandon to know, but their ring fingers were missing."

"A trophy taker," Jack said, leaning forward. "This is going to be a big story, Carson. If you play it right, you could climb back up on your career and ride out of this shit hole." He shook his head, anticipating my question. "I'm too old. Nobody wants a sixty-year-old reporter. But you could do it."

I felt the numbness start in my chest. My precious career. I stood up. "If I wanted a real career, I wouldn't be in this dump." I realized how cruel it was only after I'd walked away. Well, cruelty was my major talent these days.

I grabbed a notebook off my desk and headed to the newspaper morgue, a type of library where newspaper stories were clipped and filed. The murders had to occur before October 1981, so I started there with the intention of working backward through time. October 31, 1981. The front-page photo was of children dressed in Halloween costumes. It was still safe to trick-or-treat then.

Mingled with the newspaper headlines were my own personal memories. I'd been a junior at Leakesville High School that year. I'd met Michael Batson, the first boy I'd ever slept with. He had the gentlest touch and genuine kindness for all living creatures. Now he was a vet, married to Polly Stonecypher, a girl I remembered as pert and impertinent.

The microfiche whirled along the spool. It gave me a vague headache, but then again, it could have been the vodka from the night before. I stopped on a story about Alvin Orley, the former owner of the Gold Rush. He was handing over a scholarship check to the president of the local alumni group of the University of Mississippi. I calculated that was right before his involvement in the murder of Biloxi's mayor. I noted the date on my pad.

Cranking the microfiche, I moved backward through October. It was at the end of September when I noticed the first photos of the hurricane. Deborah. It had been a Category Three with winds up to 130 miles per hour. She'd hit just west of Biloxi, coming up Gulfport Channel. Those with hurricane experience know it wasn't the eye that got the worst of a storm, but the eastern edge of the eye wall. Biloxi had suffered. There were photos of boats in trees, houses collapsed, cars washed onto front porches. It had been a severe storm, but not a killer like Camille. In fact, there were only two reported deaths. I stared again at the story, my eyes feeling unnaturally dry.

The D.A.'s brother, Jeffrey Rayburn, and his new bride, Alana Williams Rayburn, had drowned in a boating accident September 19. The young couple had been headed to the Virgin Islands for a honeymoon when they'd been caught in Hurricane Deborah.

The boat had been found capsized off the barrier islands a week after the storm had passed. Neither body was recovered.

The mug shot of the bride showed a beautiful girl with a radiant smile and blond hair. Dark-haired, serious Jeffrey was the perfect contrast. They were a handsome couple.

In a later edition of the paper I discovered a photo of the funeral, matching steel-gray coffins surrounded by floral arrangements. The slug line Together In Death made me cringe. The newspaper had a long and glorious history of sensationalism. As I studied the photo more closely, I saw a young Mitch Rayburn standing between the coffins. I recognized the grief etched into his face, a man who'd lost everyone he loved. I understood how he'd become a champion for justice as he tried to balance the scales for others who'd suffered loss.

I turned my attention to another short story about the tragic drownings. There was a quote from Mitch, who said that radio contact with the boat had been lost during the storm. As soon as the weather had cleared, search-and-rescue teams went out, but they found only the damaged sailboat.

"The coast guard believes that Jeffrey and Alana were swept overboard and that the boat drifted until it hit some shallows," Mitch had said. "I appreciate all of the efforts of the coast guard and the volunteers who helped. I can only say that I'd never seen my brother happier than he was the day he set sail with his new bride."

On more than one occasion, my mother had accused me of being incapable of sympathizing with others, and maybe she was right. I felt little at the deaths of a newly married couple, but for Mitch, the one left behind to survive, I felt compassion. Survivor's guilt would have ridden him like a poor horseman, gouging with spurs and biting with a whip. I knew what that felt like. I lived with it on an hourly basis. I wondered how Mitch managed to look so rested and drug free.

I pushed back my chair and paced the small room, consumed with a thirst for a drink. At last, I sat down and spooled the microfiche backward. Mid-September gave way to stories about the Labor Day weekend, and then I saw the front-page story in the September 3 edition. No Clues In Disappearance Of Fourth Coast Girl. I scanned the story, which was a simple recounting of all the things the police didn't have—suspects, theories or physical evidence of what had happened to Sarah Weaver, nineteen, of d'Iberville, a small community on the back of Biloxi Bay, where fishermen had resided for generations. It was a tight community of mostly Catholics with family values and love of a good time. In 1981, the disappearance of a girl from the neighborhood would have been cause for great alarm.

What the police did know was that Sarah was a high school graduate who'd been going to night school at William Carey College on the coast to study nursing. She disappeared on a Friday night, the fourth such disappearance that summer. She'd been employed part-time at a local hamburger joint, a teen hangout along the coast. She was popular in high school and a good student.

There were several paragraphs about the panic along the coast. Fathers were driving their daughters to and from work or social events. The police had talked about a curfew, but it hadn't been implemented yet. Two Keesler airmen had been picked up and questioned but released. Fear whispered down quiet, tree-lined streets and along country club drives. Even the trailer parks and brick row subdivisions were locking doors and windows. Someone was stalking and stealing the young girls of the Gulf Coast.

I studied Sarah's picture. She had light eyes—gray or blue—that danced, and her smile was wide and open. Was she one of the bodies in the grave? I couldn't imagine that such information would be any solace to her family. If they didn't know she was dead, they could imagine her alive. She would be forty-three now, a woman still in her prime.

In my gut, I felt it was likely that she was the fourth victim. But who was the fifth? There'd been no other girls reported missing, at least not in the newspaper, prior to the paving of the Gold Rush parking lot. I'd go back and read more carefully, just in case I'd missed something.

I took down Sarah Weaver's address and skipped to the beginning of the summer. It didn't take me long, scrolling through June, to find Audrey Coxwell, the first girl to go missing, on June 29. This story was played much smaller. Audrey was eighteen and old enough to leave town if she wanted. She was a graduate of Biloxi High and a cheerleader. She was cute—a perky brunette.

Her parents had offered a reward for any information leading to her recovery. I noted their address.

In the days following Audrey's disappearance, there was little mention of her in the paper. Young women left every day. She was forgotten. No trace had ever been found of her. The reward was never claimed.

On July 7, I found the second missing girl, Charlotte Kyle, twenty-two, the oldest victim so far. The high school photo of Charlotte showed a serious girl with sad eyes. She was one of five siblings, the oldest girl. She was working at JCPenney's.

This story was on the front page, but it wasn't yet linked to Audrey's disappearance. The newspaper or the police hadn't considered the possibility of a serial killer on the loose. This was 1981, a time far more innocent than the new millennium.

I scanned through the rest of July. It was August before I found Maria Lopez, a sixteen-year-old beauty who looked older than her age. In her yearbook photo she was laughing, white teeth flashing and a hint of mischief in her dark eyes. There was also a picture of her mother, on her knees on the sidewalk, hands clutched to her chest, crying.

My hand trembled as I put it over the photo. I could still remember the feel of the strong hands on *my* arms, dragging me away from *my* house. My legs had collapsed, and I'd fallen to my knees inside my front door. A falling timber and a gust of heat had knocked me backward, and the firemen had grabbed me, dragging me back. I'd fought them. I'd cursed and kicked and screamed. And I'd lost.

The door of the newspaper morgue creaked open a little and Jack stood there, a cup of coffee in his hand. "I put a splash of whiskey in it," he said, walking in and handing it to me. He closed the door behind him. "Everyone knows you drink, Carson, and they also know you haven't contributed a dime to the coffee kitty. The second offense is the one that will get you into trouble."

He was kind enough not to comment as my shaking hand took the disposable cup. I sipped, letting the heat of the coffee and the warmth of the bourbon work their magic.

"Carson, if you're not ready, tell Brandon. He's invested enough in you that he won't push you over the edge."

"I can do this." Right. I sounded as if I were sitting on an unbalanced washing machine.

"Okay, but remember, you have a choice."

I started to say something biting about choices, but instead, I nodded my thanks. "Where'd you get the bourbon?"

"You aren't the only one with a few dirty secrets." He grinned. "What did you find?"

"Four missing girls, all in the summer of 1981, before the parking lot was paved."

"And the fifth?"

"I don't know. Maybe she was killed somewhere else and brought to Biloxi."

"Maybe." He put a hand on my shoulder. "Mitch wants to see you. He's waiting in your office."

I drained the cup. "Thanks." By the time I made it out of the morgue and into the newsroom, I was walking without wobbling.

3

I studied the back of Mitch Rayburn's head as I stood in my office doorway. He had thick, dark hair threaded with silver. By my calculation he was in his mid-forties, and he wore his age well. His tailored suit emphasized broad shoulders and a tapered waist. He worked out, and he jogged. I'd seen him around town late in the evenings when I'd be pulling into a bar. He used endorphins, and I used alcohol; we both had our crutches.

"Carson, don't stand behind me staring," he said.

"What gave me away?" I asked, walking around him to my desk. He had two things I like in men—a mustache and a compelling voice.

"Opium. It's a distinctive scent."

"If I'm ever stalking a D.A., I'll remember to spray on something less identifiable."

He stood up and smiled. "I'm ready to go to Angola. Want a ride?"

I shook my head. "I have some leads to work on here, but I'd appreciate an update when you get back."

"I didn't realize I was on the newspaper's payroll."

I laughed. "How did it go with Brandon?"

"He's holding the photo, and thanks for not mentioning the missing fingers."

"You're welcome. I'm not always the bitch Avery thinks I am."

"You got off on the wrong foot, and Avery has a long list of grievances with the paper that date back to the Paleozoic era. Give him a chance to know you. He likes Jack Evans."

I plopped in my chair and motioned him to sit, too. "I went back in the morgue and found four missing girls from the summer of 1981."

Mitch's face paled. "I remember..." His voice faded and there was silence for a moment. "I was in law school that year."

Beating around the bush was a waste of good time. "I read about your brother and his wife. I'm sorry."

His gaze dropped to his knees. "Jeffrey was my protector. And Alana...she was so beautiful and kind."

Loss is an open wound. The lightest touch causes intense pain. I understood this and knew not to linger. "I think four of those bodies in the grave belong to the girls who went missing. I just don't know how the fifth body fits in." I watched him for a reaction.

"I'd say you're on the right track, but it would surely be a courtesy to the families if we had time to contact them before they read it in the newspaper."

Brandon would print the names of the girls if there was even a remote chance I was right. Or even if I wasn't. I thought of the repercussions. Twenty-odd years wouldn't dull the pain of losing a child, and to suffer that erroneously would be terrible. "Okay, if you'll let me know as soon as you get a positive ID on any of them."

He nodded. "We're trying to get dental records on two of the girls. There were fillings. And one had a broken leg. Of course, there's always DNA, but that's much slower."

I noticed his use of the word *girls*. Mitch, too, believed they were the four girls who went missing in 1981 and one unknown body. "Okay, I'll do the story as five unidentified bodies. Brandon will have my head if he finds out."

"Not even Avery Boudreaux could torture the information out of me," he said, rising. "Thanks for your cooperation, Carson." He stared at me, an expression I couldn't identify on his face. "I think we'll work well together. I want that."

I arched an eyebrow. "Just remember, nothing is free. My cooperation comes with a price. I'll collect later."

As soon as he cleared the newsroom, I picked up the phone and called Avery. I told him about the girls, and that I was voluntarily withholding the information for at least twenty-four hours. His astonishment was reward enough. I got a quote about the investigation and began to write the story.

It was after four when Hank finished editing my piece. I left the paper and headed to Camille's, a bar on stilts that hung over the Sound. The original bar, named the Cross Current, had been destroyed by the tidal surge of Hurricane Camille. The owner had found pieces of his bar all up and down the coast, had collected them and rebuilt, naming the place to commemorate all that was lost in that storm.

The bar was almost empty. I took a seat and ordered a vodka martini. It was good, but Kip over at Lissa's Lounge made a better one. There had been a bar in Miami, Somoza's Corpse, that set the standard for martinis. Daniel, my ex-husband, had taught the bartender to make a dirty martini with just a hint of jalapeño that went down smooth and hot. The music had been salsa and rumba. My husband, with his Nicaraguan heritage, had been an excellent dancer. Still was.

A man in shorts with strong, tanned legs sat down next to me. His T-shirt touted Key West, and his weathered face spoke of a life on the water.

"Hi, my name's George," he said, an easy smile on his face. "Mind if I sit here?"

I did, but I needed a distraction from myself. "I'm Carson."

"I run a charter out of here, some fishing, mostly sightseeing."

I nodded and smiled, wondering how desperate he was. I hadn't worn a lick of makeup in two years, and sorrow lined my face. I looked in a mirror often enough to know everything that was missing.

"I moved here in 1978, out of the Keys," he said. "I don't like the casinos, but they're a good draw for business."

"The coast has changed a lot since the casinos came in." I didn't want to make small talk, but I also didn't want to be rude.

He settled in beside me. "I lost the *Matilda* in '81. My first boat."

Storms interested me, and the weather was a safe enough subject. "I was inland then. Was it bad?"

"Deborah hit Gulfport, but we got the worst here in Biloxi. The *Matilda* was tied up in the harbor. I had at least ten lines on her, plenty to let her ride the storm surge. Didn't matter. Another boat broke free and rammed her. She took on water and sank right in the harbor." He shook his head. "She was sweet."

"I guess you had plenty of warning that the storm was coming. Why didn't you take her inland?"

"It was a fluke. Deborah hit the Yucatan, lost a lot of power and looked like she was dying out, but she came back strong enough. I really thought the boats could weather it. Never again. I take mine upriver now. I don't care if it's a pissin' rainstorm."

"Was there much damage?"

"Washed out a section of Highway 90. Took a few of those oak trees." He shook his head. "That hurt me. Funny, I've had a lot of loss in my life, but those trees made me cry." He sipped his beer. "Life's not fair, you know. I lost my wife two years ago to cancer. She was my mate, in more ways than one."

I knew then what had drawn him to me. Loss. It was a law of nature that two losses attract. "My dad's told me stories of storms that came in unannounced. At least now there's adequate warning."

He nodded. "We thought it was petering out. After it hit Mexico, it just drifted, not even a tropical storm. Looked like if it was going anywhere, it'd drift over to the Texas coast. Then, suddenly, it reorganized and roared this way. Caught a young couple on their honeymoon. The storm just caught 'em by surprise." He looked at me. "Enough doom and gloom. Would you like to go out when I take a charter?" he asked.

To me, boats were floating prisons. I shook my head but forced a smile. "Thank you, but I'm not much for boats or water. I'm afraid you'd regret your invitation."

"Then how about dinner?"

I hated this. How could I explain that I had no interest in the things that normal people did? "No, thank you."

He looked into my eyes. "Sometimes it helps to be around other people."

"Not this time," I said, putting a twenty on the bar and gathering my purse. "Vodka helps. And sleeping pills." I walked out before I could see the pity in his eyes.

It was dark outside and I got in my pickup and headed east on Highway 90. The stars in the clear sky were obliterated by mercury-vapor lights and neon. The coast was a smear of red, green, purple, pink, orange, yellow—a hot gas rainbow that blinked and flashed and promised something for nothing.

I drove past the Beau Rivage, the nearly completed Hard Rock casino, the Grand, Casino Magic and the Isle of Capri. Once I was on the Biloxi-Ocean Springs Bridge, I left the glitz behind. Ocean Springs was in another county, one that had refused to succumb to the lure of gambling. My house was on a quiet street, a small cottage surrounded by live oaks, a tall fence and a yard that sloped to a secluded curve of the Mississippi Sound. I'd forgotten to leave a light on, and I fumbled with my keys on the porch. Inside a strident meow let me know that I was in deep trouble.

The door swung open and a white cat with two tabby patches on her back, gray ears and a gray tail glared at me.

"Miss Vesta," I said, trying to sound suitably contrite. "How was your day?"

A flash of yellow tabby churned out from under a chair and batted Vesta's tail. She whirled, growling and spitting. So it had been one of those days. Chester, a younger cat, had been up to his tricks.

I went to the sunroom, examined the empty food bowl, replenished it and took a seat on the sofa so both cats could claim a little attention. They were as different in personality as night and day. Annabelle had loved them both, and it was my duty not to fail her. They were the last tangible connection I had to my daughter, except for Bilbo, the pony. Daniel hadn't even tried to fight me for them when we divorced.

I thought about another drink, but I was pinned down by the cats. Today was Thursday, March 12, Bilbo's birthday. He was twelve.

I wasn't prepared for the full blast of the memory that hit. I closed my eyes. Annabelle's hand tugged at my shirt. "Carrot cake," she said, grinning, one front tooth missing. "We'll make Bilbo a carrot cake. And he can wear a hat." We'd spent the afternoon in the kitchen, baking. I'd made a carrot cake for Annabelle, and a pan of carrots with molasses for icing for Bilbo. Together we'd gone to the barn to celebrate. Daniel had come home early from his import/export business and had met us there, his laughter so warm that it felt like a touch. He'd brought a purple halter, Annabelle's favorite color, for Bilbo, and it was hidden in a basket of apples.

Chester's paw slapped my cheek. He was after the tears, chasing them along my skin.

I snapped on a light and got several small balls. The cats had learned to fetch. North of Miami, we'd had twenty acres for them to roam. When I moved to Ocean Springs, I decided to keep them inside, safe.

When the cats tired of the fetch game, I wandered the house. I'd painted the rooms, arranged the furniture, bought throw rugs for the hardwood floors, hung the paintings that I treasured, stored all the family photographs and stocked the pantry with food. It was the emptiest house I'd ever set foot in. When I'd first graduated from college and taken an apartment in Hattiesburg, I'd had a bed, an old trunk, some pillows that I used for chairs, a boom box and some cassettes, but the house had always been full of people.

The fireplace was laid, and I considered lighting it, but it really wasn't cold, just a little chilly. The phone rang, and I picked it up without checking caller ID. It could only be work.

"Hey, Carson, I wanted to make sure that you're coming home this weekend. Dad's got the farrier lined up to do the horses' feet."

Dorry, my older sister, was about as subtle as a house falling on me. "I'll be there. I already told Mom I would."

There was a pause, in which she didn't say that I'd become somewhat unreliable. "Today is Bilbo's birthday," I finally said. "I forgot."

"We'll celebrate Saturday," she said softly. "He won't know the difference of a few days."

Dorry was the perfect daughter. She was everything my mother adored. "The horses need their spring vaccinations, too." I sought common ground. "I'll see about it. Dad shouldn't be out there since he's on Coumadin."

"I know," Dorry agreed. "Mom's terrified he'll get cut somewhere on the farm and bleed to death before she finds him."

My father was the sole pharmacist in Leakesville, Mississippi. The drugstore there still had a soda fountain, and Dad compounded a lot of his own drugs. He was also seventy-one years old and took heart medicine that thinned his blood.

"I'll take care of the horses. It's enough that he feeds them every morning."

"You know Dad. If he didn't have the farm to fiddle around with, he'd die of boredom, so it's six of one and half a dozen of the other."

"Will you and Tommy and the kids be there Saturday?" I was hoping. When Dorry was there, my parents' focus was on her and her family. She had four perfect children ranging from sixteen to nine. They were all geniuses with impeccable manners. Her husband, Dr. Tommy Prichard, was the catch of the century. Handsome, educated, a doctor who pulled off miracles, Tommy's surgical skills kept him flying all over the country, but his base was a hospital in Mobile.

"I'll be there. Tommy's workload has tripled. He has to be in Mobile Saturday. I think the kids have social commitments."

I was disappointed. I wanted to see Emily, Dorry's daughter who was closest in age to Annabelle. "I'm glad you'll be there."

"Mom and Dad love you, Carson. They're just worried."

I couldn't count the times Dorry had said that same thing to me. "I love them, too. I try not to worry them."

"Good, then I'll see you Saturday."

The phone buzzed as she broke the connection. I took a sleeping pill and got ready for bed.

4

The ringing telephone dragged me from a medically induced sleep Friday morning. I ignored the noise, but I couldn't ignore the cat walking on my full bladder. "Chester!" I grabbed him and pulled him against me. "Is someone paying you to torment me?"

He didn't answer so I picked up the persistent phone and said hello.

"Where in the hell are you?" Brandon Prescott asked.

"In bed." I knew it would aggravate him further.

"It's eight o'clock," Brandon said. "I believe that's when you're supposed to be in the office."

"As I recall," I answered, my own temper kindling, "when I took the job, we agreed there wouldn't be rigid hours."

"I expect you to be on time *occasionally.* That isn't the issue. The newspaper has been swamped by families calling in, wondering if the unidentified bodies are someone they know. We need a follow-up story."

In an effort to spare four families, I'd worried a lot of others.

Brandon continued. "I want you to go to Angola and

talk to Alvin Orley. He might have an idea who the bodies are."

"Mitch went yesterday. I'll call him and do an interview."

"He's the D.A., Carson. That means he doesn't want us to know what he found out."

I gritted my teeth and said nothing.

"Besides, even if you get the same information, we can put it in a story. Quoting Rayburn about what Orley said diminishes the power. And the Orley interview will open the door for Jack to do a roundup of a lot of the old Dixie Mafia stories. It'll be great. So head over to Angola. I got you a one-o'clock appointment with Orley. You can call in and dictate your story."

I hung up and rolled out of bed. Hank would be righteously pissed off. Brandon was the publisher, but most of the time he acted like the executive, managing and city editor. He meted out assignments and orders, totally ignoring the men he'd hired to do the job. I called Hank at the desk and let him know where Brandon was sending me.

"I'll call whenever I have something," I told him.

"Jack's already working on the old Mafia stories." Hank's voice held disgust. "Never miss a chance to drag up clichéd images from the past. We're running an exceptional tabloid here."

I made some coffee, dressed, ate some toast and headed down I-10 West toward New Orleans. Before I reached Slidell, I took I-12 up to Baton Rouge and then a two-lane north to St. Francisville and the prison.

Alvin Orley was serving twenty-five years on a murder charge in the slaying of Rocco Richaleux, the mayor of Biloxi at the time. Alvin didn't actually pull the trigger, but he hired someone to do the job. He and Rocco had once been business partners in the Gold Rush and a number of other establishments that specialized in scantily clad women, booze, dope and gambling. Rocco's political ambitions ended his affiliation with Alvin, and once elected, Rocco decided to clean up the coast, which meant his old buddy Alvin. Rocco ended up dead, and Alvin ended up doing time in Angola because the murder was carried out in New Orleans. It was a good thing, too. A jury of his peers in Biloxi might not have convicted him. Alvin had ties that went back to the bedrock roots of the Gulf Coast. And he was known to even a score.

Angola was at the end of a long, lonely road that wound through the Tunica Hills, a landscape of deep ravines that bordered the prison on three sides. Men had been known to step off into a hidden ravine and fall thirty feet. The steep hills were formed by an earthquake that created the current path of the Mississippi River, which was the fourth boundary of the prison. During its most notorious days, Angola was a playground for men of small intelligence and large cruelty. Inmates were released so that officers on horseback could chase them with bloodhounds. Manhunt was an apt description. But times had changed at Angola. It was now no better or worse than any other maximum-security prison.

I stopped at the gate. Angola was a series of single-story buildings. Decorative coils of concertina wire topped twelve-foot chain-link fencing. Hopelessness permeated the place. After my credentials were checked, I went inside to the administration building.

Deputy Warden Vance took me into an office where

Alvin waited. He'd been in prison since he was convicted in 1983, more than twenty years ago. In the interim he'd lost his hair, his color, his vision and his body. He was a small, round dumpling of a man with a doughy complexion and Coke-bottle glasses. He sat behind a desk piled with papers. Two flies buzzed incessantly around him.

"I've read some of your articles in the Miami paper," he said as I sat down across from him. "I'm flattered that such a star is interested in talking to me."

"What do you know about the five bodies buried in the parking lot of your club?" I asked.

"Mitch Rayburn asked the same thing. Yesterday. You know I remember giving a check to an organization that helped put Mitch through law school. Isn't that funny?"

Alvin's eyes were distorted behind his glasses, giving him an unfocused look. I knew the stories about Alvin. It was said he liked to look at the people he hurt. Rocco was the exception.

"Mitch had a hard time of it, you know," he continued, as if we were two old neighbors chewing the juicy fat of someone else's misfortune. "He was just a kid when his folks died. They burned to death." He watched me closely. "Then his brother drowned. I'd say if that boy didn't have bad luck, he'd have no luck at all." He laughed softly.

My impulse was to punch him, to split his pasty lips with his own teeth. "I found the building permits where a room was added to the Gold Rush in October of 1981," I said instead. "The bodies were there before that. Sometime that summer. Do you remember any digging in the parking lot prior to the paving?"

"Mitch told me that it was the same summer all of those

girls went missing," Alvin said. "He believes those girls were buried in my parking lot after they were killed. Imagine that, those young girls lying dead there all these years."

"Do you know anything about that?"

"No, I'm sorry to say I don't. My involvement with girls was generally giving them a job in one of my clubs. It's hard to get a dead girl to dance." He laughed louder this time.

"Mr. Orley, I don't believe that someone managed to get five bodies in the parking lot of your club without you noticing anything." I tapped my pen on my notebook. "I was led to believe that you aren't a stupid man."

"I'm far too smart to let a has-been reporter bait me." He laced his fingers across his stomach.

"You never noticed that someone had been digging in your parking lot?"

"Ms. Lynch, as I recall, we had to relay the sewage lines that year. Construction equipment everywhere, with the paving. I normally didn't go to the Gold Rush until eight or nine o'clock in the evening. I left before dawn. I wasn't in the habit of inspecting my parking lot. I paid off-duty police officers to patrol the lot, see unattended girls to their cars, that kind of thing. I had no reason to concern myself."

"How would someone bury bodies there without being seen?"

"Back in the '80s there were trees in the lot. The north portion was mostly a jungle. There was also an old out-building where we kept spare chairs and tables. If the bodies were buried on the north side of that, no one would be likely to see them. Mitch didn't tell me exactly where the bodies were found."

I wondered why not, but I didn't volunteer the information. "The killer would have had to go back to that place at least five times. That's risky."

Orley shrugged. "Maybe not. On weeknights, things were pretty quiet at the Gold Rush, unless we had some of those girls from New Orleans coming in. Professional dancers, you know. Then—" he nodded, his lower lip protruding "—business was brisk. Especially if we had some of those fancy light-skinned Nigras."

Alvin Orley made my skin crawl. "Do you remember seeing anyone hanging around the club that summer?"

"Hell, on busy nights there would be two hundred people in there. And if you want strange, just check out cokeheads and speed freaks, mostly little rich boys spending their daddy's money. The lower-class customers were more interested in weed. If I kept a book of my customers, you'd have some mighty interesting reading."

He was baiting me. "I'm sure, but since you have no evidence of these transactions, it would merely be gossip. I'm not interested in uncorroborated gossip."

"But your publisher is." He wheezed with amusement. "There was a man, now that I think about it. He was one of those Keesler fellows. Military posture, developed arms. He was in the club more than once that summer."

"Did you ever mention it to the police?"

Orley laughed out loud, his belly and jowls shaking. "You think I just called them up and told them someone suspicious was hanging around in my club, would they please come right on down and investigate?"

Blood rushed into my cheeks. "Do you remember this man's name?"

"We weren't formally introduced."

"I have some photographs of the young ladies who went missing that summer. Would you look at them and see if any are familiar?" I pulled them from my pocket and pushed them across the desk to him.

He stared at them, pointing to Maria Lopez. "Maybe her. Seems like I saw her at the club a time or two. I always had a yen for those hot-blooded spics." He licked his lips and left a slimy sheen of saliva around his mouth. "Nobody gives head like a Spic."

"Maria Lopez was sixteen."

"Maybe her mother should've kept a closer eye on her and kept her at home."

"Any of the others?" I asked.

He looked at them and shook his head. "I can't really say. Back in the '80s, the Gold Rush did a lot of business on the weekends. College girls looking for a good time, Back Bay girls looking for a husband, secretaries. They all came for the party."

I stood up. "Why did you decide to pave the parking lot, Mr. Orley?" I asked.

"It was shell at the time. I was going to reshell it, but the price had gone up so much that I decided just to pave it."

"Thank you," I said.

"Be sure and come back, Ms. Lynch. I find your questions very stimulating."

He was chuckling as I walked out in the hall where a guard was waiting. Alvin Orley's conversation was troubling. If the parking lot was shell, it would have been obvious that someone had dug in it. Orley wasn't blind, and he wasn't stupid.

Once the prison was behind me, I tried to focus on the

beauty of the day. Pale light with a greenish cast gave the trees a look of youth and promise. I stopped in St. Francisville for a late lunch at a small restaurant in one of the old plantations. It was a lovely place, surrounded by huge oaks draped with Spanish moss. Sunlight dappled the ground as it filtered through the live oak leaves, and the scent of early wisteria floated on the gentle breeze.

I was seated at one of several tables set up on a glassed-in front porch. I ordered iced tea and a salad. The accents of four women seated at a table beside me were pleasantly Southern. They talked of their husbands and homes. I glanced at them and saw they were about my age, but beautifully made up and dressed with care. Manicured fingernails flicked on expressive hands. Once, I'd polished my nails and streaked my dark blond hair with lighter strands.

"Oh, here comes Cornelia," one woman exclaimed to a chorus of "Isn't she lovely?"

I looked out the window and my heart stopped with screeching pain. A young girl with flowing dark hair skipped up the sidewalk. She wore blue jeans and a red shirt. For just one second, I thought it was Annabelle. My brain knew better, but my heart, that foolish organ, believed. I half rose from my chair. My hands reached out to the girl, who hadn't noticed me.

The women beside me hushed. A fork clattered onto a plate. A woman got up and ran to the door as the young girl entered. She pulled her to her side and steered her away from me as she returned to her table.

I sat down, waited for my lungs to fill again, my heart to beat. When I thought I could walk, I left money on the table and fled.

I drove for a while, trying not to think or feel. At three o'clock I had no choice but to pull over, find a pay phone— because reception was too aggravating on my cell—and dictate my story back to the newspaper. Jack volunteered to take the dictation, and I was glad.

"I've got about thirty inches on Alvin Orley's illegal activities," he said as he waited for me to think a minute. "I even got an interview with one of his old dancers. She said most all of them had to have sex with him to keep their jobs."

I gave him my story, the gist of which was that Alvin failed to notice his parking lot was dug up. It wasn't much of a story, but it would be enough for Brandon.

"Hey, kid, are you okay?" Jack asked.

"Tell me about the fire that killed Mitch's parents."

"I forget that you didn't grow up around here. I guess I remember it so well because at first blush everyone thought it was arson. Harry Rayburn was a prominent local attorney who defended a lot of scum. Everyone jumped to the conclusion that an unhappy client had set the fire."

"It was an accident?"

"That's right. Electrical."

"Both parents died, but the boys escaped?"

"Mitch was just a kid, and he was on a Boy Scout campout. Jeffrey was at baseball camp at Mississippi State University. He was still in high school but scouts were already looking at him. From everything I heard, it was a real tragedy. The Rayburns were sort of a Beaver Cleaver family. Mrs. Rayburn was a stay-at-home mom." He sighed. "The house went up like a torch." He hesitated. "Sorry, Carson."

"It's okay," I said. "I asked."

"I covered it for the paper, and I was there when Jeffrey got home from State. He'd picked Mitch up at Camp DeSoto along the way. It broke my heart to see those boys standing by the smoking ruins of what had been their home."

"You're positive there was no sign of arson?" I could have read Alvin Orley wrong, but I thought he'd hinted that Mitch's luck was bad for a reason.

"None. That fire was examined with a fine-tooth comb. It was accidental."

"I'm headed back to Ocean Springs. Tell Hank to call me on my cell if he needs me."

"Will do, Carson. Drive carefully."

I was tempted to get off the interstate at Covington and revisit some of my old haunts. Dorry and I had both shown hunter-jumper. Covington, Louisiana, had hosted some of the finest shows of the local circuit. Dorry had always been the better rider; she rode for the gold. I was more timid, more worried about my horse. I smiled at the full-blown memory of both my admiration for, and my jealousy of, her.

When I went to visit my parents, I'd be able to see Mariah and Hooligan, our two horses, as well as Bilbo, the pony. Both horses were close to thirty now, but they were in good shape. Dad took excellent care of them, and Dorry's daughter, Emily, groomed and exercised them. She was the only one of Dorry's children who liked animals, and truthfully, the only one that I felt any kinship with. At twelve, she was only a year older than Annabelle would have been. Had we lived close together, I believed they would have been famous friends.

I checked my watch and stayed on the interstate. I'd spent enough time on memory lane. I needed to get back to Ocean Springs. There were a few loose ends I wanted to tie up before the weekend, and Mitch Rayburn was one of them. He'd promised to call. There was also the matter of the four missing girls. I'd have to run their names in Sunday's paper, but it would look better for everyone if I could quote Mitch or Avery. I wrote leads in my head as I sped down the highway toward home.

Dark had fallen by the time I pulled into my driveway. My headlights illuminated the shells that served as paving. If someone buried even a rabbit under the shells, I'd notice that they'd been disturbed. Much less five human bodies. Alvin Orley was either blind or lying, and I was willing to bet on the latter.

The cats were glad to see me. The truth was, Daniel would have made a better home for them. It was my selfishness at wanting to cling to that last little piece of my daughter that had made me insist on keeping them. I fed them, and somewhat mollified, Vesta settled on my lap as I went through my phone messages. My mother had called twice, Dorry once, Daniel once and Mitch Rayburn once. I called Mitch back.

"We got a positive identification on the bodies. Or at least four of them. You were right, Carson."

I took no pleasure in that. "We'll run the story Sunday. Any idea who the fifth body might be?"

"Not yet. Did Orley tell you anything?"

"I didn't find out squat except that Alvin Orley belongs in prison. He's a vile man."

"He still manipulates from behind prison bars," Mitch cautioned. "He's not a man to piss off."

"Don't worry, I try to keep my personal opinion out of print."

He laughed. "Brandon must be bitterly disappointed."

Mitch knew Brandon well, yet he didn't let it bother him. "Did you find any leads to the girls' killer?"

"The missing fingers. The hair combs. We have leads we're pursuing."

"I wonder why he stopped killing."

Mitch hesitated. "That's a good question. Maybe he moved on, found a new location."

"Have you checked the MO with other locations?"

"Nothing so far, but this was twenty-odd years ago." He sighed. "I'm going to go for a jog and hope that self-abuse will shake something loose in my brain."

"Sweat some for me," I said. "I'm going to listen to some country music and drink something with ice and olives in it."

"You're too classy for me, Carson," he said, laughing as he hung up.

5

I took a long, hot bath, eventually realizing that I couldn't scrub Alvin Orley off my skin or out of my consciousness. Contamination by proximity. He was like a virus, a nasty one. I dressed, opened a can of soup for dinner, then headed for the public beach.

In truth, it wasn't much of a beach, just the eastern shore of the Bay of Biloxi. Front Beach Drive curved along the water, the homes of the wealthy perched like dignified old guards upon the embankment. Many were set back off the road, telling of a time when lawns were purchased with playing fields for children in mind. Huge oaks shaded the houses and the road. It was early for a Friday night, and the road was quiet. The city had cracked down on the teenagers who liked to park and party there. To the north, it was cocktail hour at the Oceans Springs Yacht Club, a Jim Walters-looking building on stilts. To the south, the water undulated to the Mississippi Sound, passed between Horn and Ship Islands and finally mingled with the waters of the Gulf of Mexico.

I sat on a low stone wall and listened to the shush of the

water. Instead of being comforting, it was unsettling, and I took off my shoes and walked in the cold sand. March was warm enough to tempt the flowers out, but the wind off the water at night was still cool. The stars on this stretch of beach, undimmed by competition with the casinos, were brilliant. I walked for an hour, then got in my truck and headed for Highway 57 and the lonely road to Lissa's Lounge, a honky-tonk of the old school.

When I was a child, the only points of interest along the highway had been a bridge over Bluff Creek where teenagers swam on hot summer days, the Home of Grace for alcoholic men and Dees General Store. Until the past ten years, most of the land in north Jackson County had been owned by the paper companies. Now there were subdivisions cropping up everywhere. The huge tracts of timber had been clear-cut one final time and sold to developers. Horseshoe-shaped subdivisions with names like Willow Bend and Shady Lane jutted up on treeless lots.

Along the interstate, a large tract of land had been claimed to preserve the sandhill crane, a prehistoric-looking bird that was near extinction. The rednecks resented the no-hunting rule in the preserve, so they regularly set fire to it. So far, the score was 2-0 in the birds' favor. Last fall, two arsonists had drunk a bottle of Early Times and set a hot fire that swept out of control. They watched the blaze begin to chew through the woods and thought it was great fun, until the wind changed. *Sayonara,* motherfuckers.

Lissa's was tucked back off the highway on Jim Ramsey Road. It was an old place where folks had come to dance and drink for decades. Lissa Albritton was in her sixties, but she didn't look a day over forty-nine. She was at the door every Friday night taking a three-dollar cover charge and checking the men's asses when they walked by. She was a connoisseur. "That man sure knows how to pack out some denim," she'd say when she saw something that caught her fancy. If the man walked by close enough, she'd cop a feel.

There were plenty of classier bars in Ocean Springs and along the Gulf Coast, places where women wore black sheaths and pearls and men wore pinstripes and ties. The coast had a highly developed sheen of sophistication these days. That's why I preferred Lissa's.

The karaoke duo, the Bad Boys, was rocking the bar by the time I got there. They were twin brothers, Larry and Leon, in their fifties with professional voices and day jobs as mechanics.

Lissa waved me in. "No charge, Carson. They've been waiting for you." Her blond hair was swept up and sprayed so righteously that not a strand dared to wilt. I pushed through the door and disappeared in a haze of cigarette smoke.

"Hey, Carson," the bartender called out as I made my way to the bar. "Leon's been looking for you. He has some requests for 'Satin Sheets.'" He handed me a martini and a wink. "This one's on me. You should have been a queen of country. Like Jeanne Pruette."

Kip was a good guy and a primo bartender. Lissa knew his value and paid him well. I took my drink and found a table against the wall, letting the smoke and darkness fall over me like a cloak. I found a crushed pack of Marlboros in my purse and lit one. It was Friday night, my weekly nod to another of my vices.

The patrons at Lissa's were evenly split between men

and women. Everyone wore jeans. The thinner women wore tight shirts, often with some decorative cutout that strategically revealed an asset. The older, heavier women wore the same thing with a much different effect. The men were lean and muscular and often silent. They drank hard, danced hard and worked hard. I was willing to bet not a single one of them failed to sleep hard when they finally clocked out. I envied them that.

"Carson Lynch, report to the microphone."

I finished my drink, signaled for another and went to the stage. Leon handed me the mike. "Satin Sheets" was an old classic, a song of too much money and not enough love. It wasn't my theme song, but I admired the crafting. I sang it with heart, and when I got back to my table, there were two martinis waiting on me.

Leon sang a waltz and then a two-step and I watched the dancers. One middle-aged couple quartered the dance floor, each move synchronized. They stared into each other's eyes as if no one else existed. I smoked another cigarette and sang "Take the Ribbon from My Hair" when Larry motioned me back to the stage.

Instead of a drink, there was a note at my table. "You're four up in the credit department." I smiled at Kip. He knew I had a long drive home.

"Care to dance?"

The man was tall and handsome. He wore a black cowboy hat and he had the confidence of that breed.

"I don't dance," I said.

"I can teach you."

"Another time, maybe." Dancing was part of another lifetime.

He put his hand on a chair. "Mind if I sit?"

I did and I didn't. I liked men. I enjoyed talking with them, laughing with them. I especially liked confident men; they had the balls to charm. But it always came down to expectations, and I was always a disappointment.

"You can sit down, but I'm not dancing and I'm not going home with you."

He smiled. "You sure I was going to ask?"

"No. I just don't want a misunderstanding when liquor has clouded your memory or your judgment."

We talked while I sipped my martinis and smoked three more cigarettes. His name was Sam Jackson, and he ran cows and grew hay above Saucier.

"I'll bet you're the only woman in here drinking a martini," he said, sipping a Miller Lite. "You don't really belong here."

"I don't really belong anywhere." I ate the last olive.

"You sound like you're from here, though." He studied me. "We've talked about grass and cows and horses and weather. I don't know anything about you."

"I'm a reporter for the Biloxi newspaper."

He put his beer down. "Working on a story?"

I shook my head. "I like Leon and Larry. I like this place. No one knows me and no one bothers me. Kip makes a martini just the way I like it."

"I'll make you a bet," he said, leaning forward, a hint of a smile in his eyes. "I'll bet you that eventually you dance with me."

"How much?" I asked.

"Oh, just one dance," he said. "Then if I don't step on your toes, we might try it again."

I couldn't help but laugh. "How much do you bet?"

"I'll bet you a day-long ride on a goin' little mare when I move the cows in another few weeks."

"How did you know I rode?" I asked.

"Same way I know you dance," he said. He pushed back his chair, tipped his hat and left. I watched him for a moment as he was stopped by a redhead and led the way to the dance floor. He swung her into a two-step.

I collected my two remaining cigarettes and left. It was almost midnight. Time to go.

Clouds gathered in the south, and as I reached the truck, they rushed the moon. The night was suddenly black. I was glad for the darkness and the fact that no other cars were on the highway. I'd eaten very little all day, and I realized I was hungry. Carbohydrates. And fat. Maybe a chocolate shake, too. It would help prevent a hangover tomorrow. I drove over the Biloxi Bridge toward the glowing neon of gambler's paradise. There was a Wendy's that stayed open late.

I'd just picked up my order of a burger, fries and a shake when I heard the sirens. There were 137 law officers in the Biloxi PD. It sounded as if half of them were traveling at a high rate of speed down Highway 90. Blue lights sped by. I fell in behind them, hoping no one would question a black Ford pickup at the end of a caravan of squad cars.

They pulled into a lot beside the beach where earlier in the day tourists had sunned and swum. A public pier stretched out over the water, disappearing into the night. Police officers jumped from their vehicles and ran on the weathered boards, their footsteps pounding. I followed at a sedate walk. No one stopped me or asked any questions.

The pier was about a hundred yards long and was used primarily for fishing, although I wouldn't eat anything caught so close to shore. Officers had high-beam flashlights and were searching the old boards. There was something else there, too. I could catch glimpses but not enough to get the whole picture.

"Put someone on the beach," Avery Boudreaux called out. "Block everyone off. No one comes on this pier, you got it? No one. Particularly no media."

"Yes, sir," two officers said and headed in my direction.

I tucked my head and walked past them as if I belonged there. I kept walking. When I was close enough to catch a glimpse in an officer's light, I stopped. My stomach coiled, threatening revolt. I took a deep breath.

"Shit!" Avery exclaimed as he came to stand beside me. "How in the hell did you get out here?"

"Just lucky, I guess." My voice strained for control.

He took my elbow and steadied me. "Don't you dare mess up my crime scene," he said.

"I won't," I promised.

"And don't go any closer!"

"I won't."

"Are you okay?"

I nodded.

"Stay out of the way and don't move. Mitch will be here any minute. He can take care of you." He released my arm and went to talk to two officers.

I stared at the dead girl. She slumped on a bench, blood pooling around her hips and slowly dripping onto the pier.

She looked as if she was smiling, but it was a trick of death. The rictus of her face was a strange imitation of the slash that had opened her throat.

She was naked, except for the bridal veil that floated softly in the chill breeze.

6

Standing in the shadows, I leaned against the rail and listened to the water. Out here, away from the beach, it was calmer. A boat bobbed about a half mile offshore, the lights swaying with the gentle swells. I took some deep breaths and conjured up a mental image of the humiliation I'd suffer if I fainted or threw up. I'd seen death wear a number of faces, but this girl was so young. Her body bore the beginning of a summer tan. Bikini tan lines. A pretty blue-eyed blonde. Somebody's baby girl.

The breeze off the water was steady, and it lifted the gossamer veil in lazy drafts. Lace fluttered against her pale face. It was a beautiful veil with a band of seed pearls forming the delicate headpiece.

The police officers were busy setting up portable lights. No doubt Avery was watching me, but I moved a little closer. When the floodlights came on, I was able to check the girl's left hand. The ring finger had been severed. I turned away, horrified by what I finally understood.

Mitch arrived. He talked to the policeman working the sign-up sheet for all law-enforcement officers on the scene.

He moved on to Avery, talking in a terse whisper. At last he came to me, his face registering only annoyance.

"How the hell did you get here?"

"I followed the squad cars. They hadn't set up the perimeter yet."

"Carson, this is strictly off-limits." In the glare of the lighting two policemen had rigged, I could see the white around the corners of his mouth and nose.

His anger stabilized me. "Take it easy, Mitch. I couldn't write anything until Sunday's edition even if I wanted to. I'm not going to jeopardize your investigation. I want this person caught as badly as you do."

"As you so succinctly put it, you don't have control over what's printed. Brandon Prescott rules that paper, and he doesn't give a damn about this investigation."

I couldn't argue that. "I don't tell Brandon everything and you know it. As long as I'm kept in the loop." It wasn't a threat; it was just a statement of fact. I'd worked well with the Miami PD. I often knew more than I printed, until the time was right. "I've figured out the hair combs," I told him. "Bridal veils. They attached the veils to the victims' hair. Those five dead bodies were buried with bridal veils."

"I can't believe this is happening." He turned so that his profile was to me.

I noticed then that Mitch was sweating, and his pasty color had nothing to do with anger. He was deeply affected by the murder. "But why would someone kill four, probably five, women in 1981, stop for twenty-four years and then start killing again?" I spoke more to myself than Mitch, but my words made him look at me. "It's because we found the bodies." I saw that Mitch thought the same thing.

"We have to stop him," he said.

"You're assuming it's a man, or do you have evidence?"

He hesitated. "That was an assumption."

"An easy one to jump to," I agreed. Women killed other women, but not often with the trappings of nudity and a bridal veil. Also, the killer would have had to be pretty strong to restrain a young woman and slice her throat so deeply with one stroke. I wasn't a forensics expert, but it certainly looked like a clean stroke to me.

"The ring finger's missing," I said. "Jack says he's a trophy taker."

"Jack's not a forensic profiler. I wouldn't print that," Mitch snapped.

"Okay," I said. "I won't print it. But what are the cops thinking?"

"We *thought* we were working a crime that was twenty-four years old," Mitch said with a hint of bitterness. "Carson, I'd like to keep you in the loop, but I need to know that you'll work with us. Even when it means holding out details."

Brandon would skin me alive. That wasn't so bad, but there were ethical considerations. Brandon paid me to do a job that included digging up facts that no one else had. A story that the police were looking at a killer who took fingers as trophies—and this killer was current, not some cold case from another century—was a big deal. I had to figure out my obligations. "There are people's lives at risk here. My job is to keep the public informed."

He took a long breath. "I know that, but panicking the public won't protect anyone. In fact, printing too much detail could screw up our chances of catching this guy."

"I don't intend to do that." There was a fine line to walk between informing the public and damaging an investigation, and it was a boundary that had to be redrawn with every case. The problem was that both the police and the newspaper wanted to be the one to draw it.

"And what does Brandon intend?"

It was a good question because we both knew the answer. A panic would be right up Brandon's alley, especially if the *Morning Sun* was leading the charge. I didn't say anything.

"If Brandon gets hold of the words *serial killer, trophy taker* or anything similar, it will be blown way out of proportion, and you know it."

I wasn't certain that the facts could be distorted to seem worse than they were. In all truth, however, I couldn't argue Brandon's reliability, or lack thereof. I shifted the topic. "Do you think this is a copycat killer or the original?"

He took another breath. "If I talk to you freely, will you promise to work with me?"

I nodded. "We're off the record, until I say otherwise."

"The detail of the missing fingers on the five corpses was never released to the other media. If this is a copycat, that person had privileged information."

"Either the original killer, a police officer or—"

"You," he said. There was no hint of teasing in his face. "See how easily facts can lead to an illogical conclusion?"

"I have to go to Leakesville tomorrow." I wrote my cell phone and my parents' phone number on a slip of paper that I dug from my purse. "Call me by five o'clock. I have to have my story by six for the Sunday paper. And I have to tell Brandon about this girl. I won't mention the finger."

I looked out at the dark water. "I'll wait until daylight to tell him. I'm not responsible for what he does from there. What about the television station?"

Mitch thought over my offer. "I'll call you," he promised. "You know the television cameras will be here any moment. They'll know that a girl has been murdered. Nothing else."

I nodded. "Was there any identification on the girl?"

"Nothing. Just that damn bridal veil."

"Do you *think* it's the same killer?"

"I can't draw a solid conclusion and I'm not willing to speculate. Talk to Avery later on, when he isn't so busy. He's a smart man, and he'll be as honest with you as you let him."

"Okay." It was tenuous footing for establishing a relationship with the detective. I was working in the shadow of Brandon Prescott and I understood that.

"Now leave," he said. "We've got to bag the body and take her some place where we can help her."

He spoke with such tenderness that I blinked back the sting of tears. The help he offered was in capturing the person who'd killed her. Cold comfort, I knew from personal experience.

I walked down the pier, thinking it was so much longer than when I'd first walked up it. When my feet touched sand, I turned and looked back. There was a halo of bright light and the movement of bodies. Had I not known better, I might have thought it was a party.

The population of Leakesville hadn't changed in the past fifty years. Folks died, children were born, some moved away and others moved back. The county itself had fewer than twenty thousand residents, the city about three thousand. The courthouse centered the town, a common enough configuration, except in Leakesville there was the sense that time had stopped.

I drove around the square, looking for evidence that it was 2005, not 1970. Two old men whittled beneath a magnolia tree. They wore bib overalls and spit tobacco on the grass. Crows, brazen in the warm sun, walked over the courthouse lawn, acting as if they owned it. Across the street, Bexley Mercantile was doing a good business. A man with an excited young boy was picking out a bicycle. Birthday, probably. I remembered the thrill of examining the bicycles at Christmas, telling Dad which one I wanted Santa Claus to bring. I'd loved the Bexley and Mr. Clancy, the owner. Everything a girl ever needed could be found in that store.

My dad's pharmacy was on Main Street, a corner store that sold hairspray, deodorant, makeup, fire-ant poison, dog collars, a few Parker Brothers games for the occasional birthday present, greeting cards, Russell Stover candies, rubbers and prescriptions. There was also a soda fountain and a spinning bookrack that held everything from Harlequins to John Irving. I'd grown up working the soda fountain. When business was slow, I'd sit at the counter, drink a cherry Coke and read. I'd developed broad literary tastes and a voracious appetite for fiction.

When I pushed open the door, a bell jangled and Gertrude Mason let out a happy bark of laughter. "Look what the dogs dragged up," she said, coming out from behind the counter to give me a hug. "What about a Coke float?"

I'd found another source of sugar in my vodka, but I didn't want to hurt her feelings. "Sure. That sounds great."

"Carson's here!" she sang out to my dad. He was in the back of the store, typing away on an old computer. Gertrude was the only alarm system Dad had when the store was open, and it worried me. Folks would kill over a handful of Xanax or Oxycotin. I walked to the back and took the step up to where the pharmacist worked on an elevated platform. He could survey the whole store from his perch.

"Carson, I'm glad you're here. You're not sick, are you?"

I shook my head. "Just came to say hi." That was a lie. Mitch Rayburn and the deal I'd made were troubling me.

Gertrude brought my drink. "Here you are," she said, handing me the concoction in a real glass with a long-handled spoon.

I took a bite of the ice cream and sipped the Coke through a straw. "Just as good as I remember," I said, and it was.

My father poured yellow capsules into a blue pill counter and counted them out, five at a time. I watched his hands work with speed and efficiency. "Dad, have you ever made a deal that seemed good but might not be?"

"We're not talking about marriage, are we?" He arched his eyebrows, and I was caught by a gut punch of pain as I realized how white his black eyebrows had become.

"Nothing like that." I studied his face. The firm cheeks that I'd once loved to touch before he shaved were sagging. There were dark pouches under his eyes. My father was seventy-two, and for the first time since I could remember, he looked his age.

"I've made some bad deals. I swallowed the losses. But that's not what you're talking about, is it? This isn't financial." He frowned.

"No, it isn't financial." I didn't want to talk about it

anymore. My father was a man of pure ethics. He didn't make deals. He would tell me what I already knew—that I'd compromised my professionalism. "Never mind," I said.

"What are you up to, Carson?" Dad asked.

"I'll bet you've never asked Dorry that question once in her life," I said, aware too late of the bitterness in my voice.

"I never needed to," my father answered, and instead of bitter, he was sad.

Mariah had given up her favorite pastime of jerking the reins out of my hand and jumping fallen trees, ditches, pieces of farm machinery or anything that happened to be in her path. In her golden years, she was a more sedate— and safer—mount. In her youth, she'd been a firebrand of action. Though Dorry was the better rider, Mariah was the bolder horse. She loved to jump. Once, she'd jumped out of the arena in a flat class and gone through the warm-up field taking the jumps. I probably could have stopped her if I'd tried harder, but she loved it so.

It was a warm afternoon, perfect for a ride, and I let her amble through the woods that went down to the Leaf River. The trail was overgrown now, the sun dappling through the leaves of water oaks and red oaks, the white blossoms of the dogwood giving it all a magical feel. Wildflowers bloomed in purple and yellow abundance along the sandy path, and it was too early for the deer flies that made life a torment for man and beast during the hot summer months.

For a brief time, I was sixteen again, a child of sunshine and lazy afternoons. Mariah and I made our way to the river, a brown ribbon that had once been the main thoroughfare through virgin forests. Mariah stood on a

sandbar, the slow current lapping at her fetlocks. When I
went back, I would be Carson the adult again, the child-
less mother, the alcoholic, the failed wife. It was with great
reluctance that I set Mariah on the trail home.

7

"Pass the corn bread, please, Mother," Dorry said. "No matter how I follow your recipe, mine isn't the same. Tommy says so, too."

"Dorry, your corn bread is perfectly fine, and stop trying to flatter me," Hannah Lynch, my mother, said, but a tiny pink blossom of pleasure crept into her cheeks.

"It is the best," I said, drawing three pairs of eyes my way. It was just the four of us for a five-thirty dinner at my mother's antique cherry table. Even though my father was an upper-middle-class pharmacist, my family had always kept the same hours as the community. We ate dinner on farm time, as if the family had worked hard in the fields all afternoon and needed sustenance.

"Mine is nothing like that flat corn bread your husband liked," Mama said to me. "I think it was made with water instead of milk."

I looked down at my plate. I'd been divorced from Daniel for a year. My parents had never liked him, had never allowed themselves to know him. He was too different. They'd never been able to see beyond his Latin appear-

ance and different mannerisms to *who* he was, I think
because he'd taken me away. Had we stayed in Mississippi,
they might have grown to love him. Instead, he would
always be an interloper and the guy who stole their
daughter, the man who'd kept them from really knowing
their granddaughter, a man with his heart in a foreign con-
tinent and culture.

"Mother, the pork chops are delicious, too." Dorry struggled to push the conversation over the bump. "I don't know
how you keep cooking like you do."

"I like to have you both here. My children." Her voice
faded.

There had been another child. My brother, Billy. I remembered him as a tall, lanky boy who drove the tractor
and was always followed around by at least six big dogs.
The dogs would smell him, then follow him slavishly for
the rest of their lives. Billy was ten years older than me,
and he was killed in Vietnam. The loss of a child should
have brought my mother and me closer together, but it
didn't. She blamed Dad for Billy and me for Annabelle.

"I'll put some coffee on," Dorry said. "Maybe Carson
will tell us about the killings on the coast. I saw it on the
late news yesterday. They found five bodies in a mass
grave last Thursday, and then last night a girl was killed
on a pier, right, Carson?"

Dorry meant well, but I could cheerfully have cut out
her tongue.

"Five bodies in one grave and a girl murdered!" Mama
put her hands on the table. "What is this world coming to?"

"The five bodies are almost twenty-five years old," I said.

"And you're writing about this?" Mama's voice was

suddenly strident. She hated what I did for a living. She thought it was ghoulish and adversarial. She called it "making trouble" for folks or "poking into other people's business."

"Yes," I said, rising from the table. "I'll help Dorry with the coffee." The cell phone in my purse rang. "Excuse me." I grabbed my purse and went into the bedroom that had been mine.

I closed the door, walked across the polished pine floor and the handwoven rag rug and sat on the chenille bedspread patterned with a smiling sun. I was momentarily taken aback by the black-and-white photographs on the wall. They were my first attempts at photography.

"Lynch," I said, because it could be nothing other than business.

"We identified the girl. Pamela Sparks. She has a four-year-old daughter." Avery Boudreaux's voice was flat. "Mitch told me I was supposed to call before six," he said.

"Shit." I was digging through my purse for a pen and paper. "Just a minute."

I took down the particulars as I asked Avery for details. He answered grudgingly, and I didn't blame him. He also confirmed the identity of four of the five bodies in the grave of the Gold Rush parking lot. As I'd thought, they were the girls who'd gone missing in '81. There still wasn't a line on the fifth body.

I hung up, dashed down some thoughts on my pad and called the newspaper. It was past the six-o'clock deadline for Sunday's paper, but I knew they were saving room for me on the front page. I'd talked with the weekend editor, and he knew the gist of what my story would be. The television had scooped us Saturday evening with the story on

the murdered girl, but we'd have the big story, identifying
Pamela Sparks and tying the five bodies to the Bridal Veil
Killer. I also had the identities of four of those girls confirmed. It was going to be a story that would have some of
the larger tabloids hovering on our doorsteps.

"My dad's got a computer. I could write the story and
e-mail it to you," I told the editor. That would allow me at
least a chance to polish it.

"You've got half an hour," Clive said. "Make it tight."

I went to the dining room, where everyone looked up.
Mother was clearly aggravated that the meal had been
disturbed by my work. Dorry was worried, and my father
was sad. "I have to write a story. Can I borrow your computer, Dad?"

"Sure," he said. When Mom started to protest, he waved
her to silence. "She's working, Hannah. She's taking her
job seriously. Can't you let that be enough for right now?"

I wanted to thank him, but it would only have made for
a scene. Instead, I went into his study and wrote the story
and e-mailed it in, then called to confirm that Clive had it.
When I returned to the dining room, they were finishing
their coffee and an Italian cream cake that Dorry had made
that morning. She loved to cook, and she was a fabulous
pastry chef. She could do it professionally if she chose.

"Cake?" Mama asked.

"No, thank you."

"You're too thin. Cake would be good for you," she
insisted, cutting a slice and putting it on the bone china that
had been her mother's.

I took the saucer and put it down at my place. She
passed me coffee.

"Was the call about the murdered girl?" Dorry asked.

I frowned at her. "Yes." I took a forkful of the cake I didn't want and put it in my mouth. Alcoholics seldom eat sweets. That's why my mother had insisted. I swallowed.

"Well?" Dorry leaned forward.

I started not to answer, but it seemed pointless. They'd read it in the paper the next day. I told them about seeing the girl on the dock, about the bridal veil, about the other girls and who they were and what little I knew about their deaths.

"That is the most gruesome thing I've heard," Mom said. She folded her napkin and pushed back her chair. "For the life of me, I don't understand why you want to live your life in that environment. It's ghoulish."

The cake on my saucer was a small mound of crumbs. I pushed them around with my fork, stopping when I realized how juvenile it was. She couldn't force me to eat it. I looked up. "I'm sorry you feel that way, Mom. It's my job."

"You could have been anything. A vet. A doctor. You were plenty smart."

"If you think journalism is gruesome, you should hear Tommy talk about some of the things he cuts out of people," Dorry said. "Last week he was removing this guy's gall bladder. It had ruptured, and he found gangrene all in his stomach. Now, that's gruesome."

Instead of a reprimand, Mom turned to Dorry. "Tommy sure is working hard. I worry for him. He has this compulsion to save everyone, and it's wearing him down."

I was glad the conversation had turned to Saint Tommy. If Dorry never did another thing in her life, it was enough that she'd snared Tommy Prichard, surgeon extraordinaire, breeder of magnificent specimens of children, witty conversationalist, humanitarian and, most important of all, Mississippi boy.

The courtship had been hotly contested. Tommy was born in McLain, a small town on the Chickasawhay River. He had "I'm getting out" written all over him. He was a superb athlete, a baseball player who could hit and catch. He played shortstop on the high school team, which was where Dorry met him when he was a senior. McLain played Leakesville, and on one sultry spring afternoon, Dorry and I went to watch the game.

Tommy got a scholarship to the University of Southern Mississippi, where Dorry decided she was going. She tried out for the college dance squad, the Dixie Darlings, and ensured herself a place in Tommy's line of sight. But there was another girl with the same idea. Lucinda Baker knew a good thing when she saw it, too.

Never one to act in haste, Tommy vacillated between the two girls for most of his college career. He'd date Dorry, until she got too demanding, then he'd switch to Lucinda for a while. When she disagreed with him or began to expect a certain kind of treatment, he dumped her and went back to Dorry.

As Tommy's college days at USM drew to a close, and it was certain he'd go to medical school in nearby Mobile, Alabama, on a very nice scholarship, Dorry gave up. She started dating a young man from Hattiesburg. Tommy proposed instantly. They were married within a semester of Dorry graduating from college. Instead of a college degree, she got pregnant with her first child.

"Tommy loves his work. He operates almost every day

now in Mobile. There's no one else who can perform the delicate surgeries that he does."

I drifted back into the conversation as Dorry gathered up the cake saucers, sweeping mine away before Mother could comment. "I thought he was opening a clinic here in Leakesville so he could spend more time with the kids."

"He's going to, as soon as he can find time," Dorry said, a hint of defensiveness in her tone.

"Tommy doesn't have the kind of career he can just drop," my mother said.

"What about some music, Dorry?" Dad asked. "The two of you. It's been a long time since I heard you play together."

The blood must have drained from my face. "I don't think Carson's up to it," Dorry said quickly.

"I haven't played…in a while." Not since Annabelle died. We'd played duets together, just as Dorry and I had done when we were children.

I stood up. "I'm really tired. I think I'll lie down for a while. Strange will be here early in the morning to trim the horses' hooves." I knew Strange Yoder didn't like to work on Sundays. He did it for my dad, who'd been good to his sick mother. Sundays were the days Strange liked to fill his ice chest with beer, get some luncheon meat and go to the river to fish in solitude.

"Good night," Dad said, effectively releasing me.

"Do you need Emily to help in the morning?" Dorry offered.

"No, I can handle it. I'd welcome the company if she's up."

"If she comes home from Susie's tonight, I'll tell her." Dorry went into the kitchen to help Mother wash up after the meal. Such an action exemplified her status as the perfect daughter. I went to my room and picked up an old paperback that I'd bought more than twenty-five years before. I couldn't believe Mom kept all my junk. I held the book and thought that at the time I was reading it, five girls were still alive on the Gulf Coast. Five women were probably dreaming the same dreams that I'd once had, of a future with a happy family and career. I'd tucked into my bed in Leakesville with a book, and they'd gone out for an errand or to meet a friend or to a party. They'd died. The randomness of life was inconceivably cruel.

8

Strange Yoder was a man of indeterminable age. When he bent or moved, he seemed young. He was thin, like a teenager, and he wore his hair long. Quick, alert eyes belied the lines in his face. He was older than me. I knew this only because I'd known him all my life. He had a gift when it came to horses' feet, and though he was one of the best farriers in the nation, he chose to stay in Greene County, where there were still long stretches of piney woods and the slow amble of the Leaf River.

Strange didn't talk a lot. Mostly he looked. He could watch a horse walk and know exactly how to trim a hoof or shoe it or what treatment to prescribe for thrush or founder. He did it not for the money, but because he liked to help animals. He'd been my brother Billy's best friend. He'd come back from Vietnam; Billy had not.

Morning light shafted into the old barn through cracks in the east wall, and I sat on a hay bale holding a slack lead rope. Strange crouched in the center of the aisle with Mariah's left rear leg resting on his thighs as he used nippers to trim off the overgrown hoof.

"She's lookin' good for an old girl," he said of Mariah.

"She seems to feel good. I don't see arthritis, but I've got her on some joint supplements anyway. I'm glad I didn't jump her too hard."

"She jumped what she wanted," he said. "You didn't push her and she knew what was right for herself. If more folks listened to their horses, there wouldn't be the trouble there is today." He shook his head. "Damn quarter horse people just about ruined ten generations of horse breeding for those little tiny feet. Like putting a fat woman in ballet toe shoes. Damn bastards."

Strange didn't earn his name because he was normal. He was opinionated, but about animals, which was the only thing he ever talked about. I could remember Strange when he was called Dustin and had a crooked smile and a twinkle in his eyes. He left those things, and his sense of humor, somewhere in the jungles of Vietnam. He'd held Billy as he bled out, unable to stop the flow of blood. Billy had been hit by a piece of shrapnel in the femoral artery. Had a medic arrived in time, my brother could have been saved. That was the midnight image that came to visit Strange when he slept—my brother, trying to smile and not panic as his blood soaked the jungle floor. Strange never talked about it after he'd told me this.

Strange trimmed Mariah all around and started on Hooligan. "Needs shoes on the front. His toes are chipped slam off," he said, going to his truck to get horseshoes. "I hate to shoe 'im. If he gets down in the back pasture with all them roots, he'll tear 'em off."

"I'll tell Dad to keep them up in the front for a few weeks." He nodded and went to work. Hooligan was half snoozing as Strange hammered the iron shoes to his two front feet and trimmed the back.

"Now for Bilbo." I got the gray pony, a cross between a Shetland and a Connemara. For Annabelle, Bilbo had been a dream pony. He didn't hold me in the same regard, but Bilbo was always good for Strange, saving his practical jokes and shenanigans for me. Mariah and Hooligan were snuffling at the last morsel of grain in their stalls. For the first time in months, I felt a shadow of peacefulness slip over me.

"This pony needs ridin'," Strange said. "He misses your daughter."

"I miss her, too," I said. With Strange, it was okay to talk about painful things.

"Maybe I could send someone over to ride him."

I hesitated, and though no word was spoken, Strange stopped his work, stood and looked at me.

"Your daughter wouldn't mind. She'd be glad someone was giving the pony attention."

"You're right," I said, trying not to tear up. "Please, if you know someone, ask him or her to come over. I'll tell Dad. I think he'll be relieved."

Strange finished the last foot and stood, arching backward to relieve the strain of his job. "This here pony won't ever forget your girl. She's a part of him, like she's a part of you. But he needs someone to love him now." He gathered his tools. "Animals got a lot more sense about dying than human folk. They know it's the cycle. Livin' and dyin', they're not so different, except for those of us left behind."

"I wish I could believe that," I said.

"It took me a while to get there, Carson. Maybe I believe

it 'cause I have to to survive. I can only say I'm a more peaceful man since I came to that way of thinkin'." He gave Bilbo's rump a gentle slap. "Turn 'em out now, and I'll be on my way."

I pulled money from my pocket.

He shook his head. "No, I won't take the money. When my mama was dying, Mr. Lynch mixed up her medicine special. When we didn't have the money, he mixed it for her anyway."

"The horses are my responsibility, not his."

He gave me his sharp blue gaze. "It's one and the same and you know it."

I was about to argue when I heard a vehicle pull up. I walked to the barn door and looked out, surprised to see Michael Batson walking toward me from his red vet truck.

"Carson!" he said, his face breaking into a wide smile. "What a surprise."

"Michael," I answered, knowing it was no surprise at all but my meddling mother. "What brings you here?"

"Spring vaccinations for the horses. Dorry implied you were having a conniption to get it done."

"I see." I realized that my sister now rivaled my mother in games of manipulation.

"Hey, Dustin, how's it going?" He held out his hand.

The men shook, then Strange gathered his tools. "I'm done here, Doc."

Michael glanced down at Bilbo's feet. "I wish you'd come over and work out of my clinic. Folks could come to you instead of you having to drive all over tarnation."

Strange shook his head. "I like drivin'. I like to look at the woods and think."

Michael nodded. "Well, the offer stands."

"Thanks, but I like it the way it is." Strange inclined his head, then he was gone, his slender frame slipping out the barn door and casting a long, thin shadow across the patch of dirt in front of the barn.

"You called him Dustin," I pointed out.

"I don't like the name Strange. Dustin's a little different, but if more people were like him, the world would be a better place." He took Bilbo's lead rope and moved him so he could feel in his mouth. "Dorry said I should float their teeth, too, if they need it."

"Dorry's mighty good at tending to everyone's business," I said.

He laughed. "I thought this might be a setup. She asked me to lunch, too." He released Bilbo's head and started toward his truck. "I brought a Biloxi paper. I figured you'd want to see the front-page splash you made."

"Don't take it in the house," I said.

"I wasn't going to." He walked out of the barn and returned in a few moments with three vaccinations and a stainless-steel bucket containing a rasp to file the sharp points down on the horses' back teeth. "This won't take long at all."

After we'd finished with the horses, Michael led Bilbo while I took Mariah and Hooligan out to the front pasture. We stopped at his truck and he handed me the newspaper.

Bridal Veil Killer Strikes After 24-Year Hiatus, the headline screamed across the top of the page. My stomach knotted. If I'd ever doubted Brandon's total disregard of responsibility, I didn't any longer. Right below the headline was my byline. Mitch and Avery would both know I had nothing to do with the way the story was played, but most people didn't understand that.

"You're making quite a name for yourself," Michael said.

There was no criticism in his tone. Michael wasn't a man prone to panic, so he didn't see the potential damage such an article could do.

"It's a frightening situation, but this—" I shook the paper "—isn't going to help. My boss is an idiot."

Michael put his equipment back in the truck. "I'm not staying for lunch, Carson."

"Mother and Dorry will be disappointed."

He touched my chin, a whisper of a caress. "I don't really care what they think."

"I figured you'd want to be home for lunch with Polly and your daughter." I held his hazel gaze.

"Polly's filed for divorce. She wants a husband who gets off at five and comes home smelling of aftershave and money instead of cow shit. I'm not the man for her."

I had a jolt of memory. Polly was standing in front of Elliot's Jewelry Store on Main Street. It was a hot summer afternoon. We were eighteen, just graduated and wondering what the next fall would bring for us.

"I'm going to marry a rich man," Polly had predicted. "Mama says you can love a man with money as easily as one without."

June Tierce had been with us. June's future was set. She'd gotten a full academic scholarship to Ole Miss. She claimed the school was filling a quota for black females, but I knew better. June was brilliant.

"Money doesn't have anything to do with happiness," June said to Polly.

"Of course it does," Polly said with a grown-up snap in her voice. "Try being without money if you think it's not important. It's the only thing my mom and dad fight about."

"Carson, are you okay?" Michael touched my arm, and I left the past to return to the barnyard and my former lover looking at me with open concern.

"I'm fine. I was just thinking of Polly."

"She's still a beautiful woman. She'll find someone who gives her what she wants." He shook his head. "I was foolish to think she'd—" He broke off. "Anyway, tell your folks I send my regrets. The truth is, I've got a herd of cows to vaccinate over in Vinegar Bend. It's going to be a long day so I'd better get after it."

I headed home before lunch, telling my parents that I had work. No one questioned me, but no one believed me, either. Greene County was dry. At one time my parents kept liquor in the house, amber and clear liquids for an afternoon highball or the frequent visitors who came to play cards or have dinner. It was only recently that the cut-glass decanters had been emptied and not refilled. I was the cause of that.

Almost home, I stopped at a small joint tucked away in the piney woods of Jackson County. The state blue laws had once dictated that liquor could not be sold until noon on a Sunday, but with the arrival of the casinos, times had changed for the Gulf Coast. I asked the bartender for a screwdriver, and she handed it over without even blinking.

When I got home, Mitch had called, tersely asking for a meeting Monday morning. There was also a message from Brandon, hyperventilating about the next big story.

The sound of his voice made me want to do something violent. The last call on my machine I returned.

"Jack," I said. "Those were good stories on the Dixie Mafia."

"It's easy to dredge up history. Your piece on the murders was well written and restrained."

"Except for the headline."

Jack barked a laugh. "You should've seen Hank and Brandon go at it."

I felt a twinge. Hank had a bad heart, and he had no business arguing with Brandon. I took what comfort I could in knowing that if it wasn't my story they fought over, it would be something else. "You said you needed a favor?"

"I'm in a little bit of a jam." Jack's voice was thin, as if he were having to force the words out. "Could I borrow five thousand dollars until Friday?"

"Sure." I didn't hesitate. Money was one thing I had. When Daniel and I had sold our property in Miami, we'd made a lot of money. Daniel had been more than generous. "Want me to run it by?"

"No!" He took in a deep breath. "I'll come get it now. Thanks, Carson."

"Don't worry about it, Jack." I could run up to the ATM and get some cash, since it sounded like a check wouldn't do. "Come on by."

The bank was only five minutes away, and I was sitting on my front porch when Jack pulled in. The fact that he wouldn't meet my gaze told me a lot. I put the envelope on the seat of a wicker chair.

"I'm glad to do this, Jack. It's the first time I've felt useful in a long time."

He still didn't look at me. "I'll pay you back."

"I know. Don't be in a rush about it."

He was a proud man, and whatever circumstances had forced him to borrow money from me was not my business unless he wanted to talk. Obviously he didn't. I stood up. "I'm going to make a drink. Would you care for one?"

"No."

I left the door open when I walked inside. His footsteps sounded on the porch, and then the screen door slammed. He was gone.

9

I got to the newspaper at 8:18 Monday morning. My arrival earned a sarcastic whistle from the police beat reporter, who rightly felt the Bridal Veil killings should have been his story. I ignored him as I walked by, but he couldn't let it go.

"What happened? They close the bars early last night?" he asked, pointedly looking at his watch.

I turned slowly to face him. "What happened to put you in such a nasty mood? Your wife refuse to let you wear her garter belt and stockings?" I understood his anger, but it was directed at the wrong person. Brandon should be his target, not me.

Jack gave a loud laugh and there were a few twitters around the newsroom. I was disliked because of Brandon's treatment of me. The police beat reporter was disliked because of how he treated others.

I lost interest in the newsroom when I saw my office door standing ajar. I'd left it locked.

"Nice comedy routine." I stepped into my office. Avery was sitting in the chair in front of my desk, and I had no idea how long he'd been waiting.

The Biloxi detective wore a black suit that was indistinguishable from his other black suits. Or, perhaps he had only one. It fit him well, the pants creased and sharp. His shirt was crisply ironed, his shoes polished. He was a detail man; it stood to reason he was good at his job. "I gather this isn't a social visit," I said, trying to disguise the fact that I was flustered. I didn't know Avery well, but I knew him well enough to know he wasn't in the habit of paying social visits to reporters. "How'd you get in?"

"Brandon opened the door with his master key." He didn't bother hiding his amusement at the heat that jumped into my face.

"He's such a jerk."

"Yeah, this business—" he waved a hand around my office "—seems replete with 'em."

"Why are you here?" I didn't want a fight.

"Mitch sent me. For some reason he wants you to be part of the investigation. He gave me some hogwash about how we needed the newspaper with us on this case."

"He's right," I said. "You have five bodies, four of them girls killed in 1981. The fifth is unidentified. And now you have a current body." I paused for effect. "Without any real leads. I'd say the newspaper could be a very powerful ally."

Avery didn't like being pressed into a corner, and it showed in his expression. "Mitch is the boss. If he wants you in on this, you're in." He stared into my eyes. "I'm just a little curious. Mitch has never felt the need to buddy up with the press before. Maybe he wants a date."

"Would you like some coffee?" I decided to ignore his misplaced antagonism. "I have some questions about the investigation."

He thought about it. "Sure. Black."

I went to the coffee kitty, put in a five-dollar bill and poured two cups of strong black coffee. When I got back to the office, Avery took his, and I closed the door.

Once I was settled at my desk, I opened my notebook and flipped through the pages. "I searched through the back issues of the paper. That's where I got the names of the missing girls. But there wasn't a fifth girl. At least not one that I found."

"There's not a missing-person report on the fifth victim, either."

That would save me some long hours of eye-straining work. Avery didn't want me in this investigation, but he was going to do what Mitch said. "Thanks for telling me that."

He shrugged. "Aside from the headline, your story Sunday was good. Accurate. Not blown out of proportion. Well written."

"Thanks." I was surprised. Avery had paid me a compliment. "So what do you have on the fifth body?"

He frowned. "We're checking missing-person reports from around the Southeast." He hesitated and his discomfort was clear. "Have you talked with Pamela Sparks's family?"

"I was going to do that today, and then follow up with an interview of the families of the other dead girls."

He nodded. "We sent a couple of officers over to the Sparkses', but the parents got upset. I went by there myself, but they won't talk to the police. Mitch said this was your forte—that you could get anyone to talk to you."

I leaned forward onto my desk. "Why won't the family talk to you?"

"Pamela's dad did a stretch in Parchman for a burglary he says he didn't do. He doesn't trust the police for any reason. He says he's going to find Pamela's murderer himself."

If Highway 90 is considered the Gulf Coast main drag, then d'Iberville is the backstreet. The homes fronting the beaches are lovely. Except for the blight of condo and fast-food development, there's no squalor or poverty. That can be found in d'Iberville.

Of course there are lovely neighborhoods in the Back Bay area, so called because of the way the Bay of Biloxi cuts west, creating an elongated inner waterway. It's a perfect natural harbor for the fishing vessels that were once the lifeblood of the coast.

Pamela Sparks's neighborhood was not one of the lovely ones. The land was low and had the smell of poor drainage, a nightmare for mothers during the summer when mosquitoes could savage an unprotected child in thirty seconds or less. Especially worrisome now with West Nile virus.

The address was a double-wide trailer in a park of some thirty other manufactured homes, as it was now politically correct to call them. Pamela had lived here with her parents, her four-year-old daughter and two younger siblings. I pulled in the drive and got out. The trailer and yard were neatly maintained. Latticework had been put up around the trailer, and there was a nice porch with steps and a railing surrounded by shrubs and well-tended flower beds. Yellow-and-white daffodils held center stage in the bed, but red tulips were budding.

A curtain at the door fluttered, and I knew I'd been spotted. When I knocked, the door was answered immediately. "We aren't talkin' to anyone," a woman with red, swollen eyes spoke through a small crack.

I introduced myself. "I'm sorry for your loss," I said, the words like dialogue off a cop show. Keep it impersonal, I warned myself. I didn't want her to see my pain. She carried enough.

Mary Sparks came out on the porch, pulling the door shut behind her. "My husband can't talk." Her own eyes filled and the tears spilled down her cheeks. "He can't stop crying. Pamela was his baby girl. The boys are younger, but Pamela was his girl."

"Where was Pamela going Friday night?" If I didn't get into the questions fast, Mrs. Sparks would fall apart. So might I.

"She said she had an errand. I figured she was going to buy some things for the party. Her friends were coming over Saturday to plan a shower for her. She was getting married in two weeks." She leaned against the porch rail, her back sagging and her head bowing. "This is too hard."

I wanted to comfort her, but I didn't touch her. It would have been wrong, somehow. False. I was there to get information, not act as a friend. "Her fiancé was…?"

"Joe Welford. He works up at M&N Motors. He's a mechanic." She shook her head. "He was over here Saturday, and I thought I'd have to bury my Bob and Joe both."

The muscles in my jaw tightened involuntarily. To get the story, I had to keep pushing. "Could you tell me the names of Pamela's friends?"

I wrote them all down, including addresses and phone numbers. Mary Sparks was a mother who knew the details of her daughter's life.

"Did Pamela have a bridal dress and veil?"

"No. She was gonna wear a regular dress. She said she'd rather save the money for a down payment on a house. When she was twelve, we lived in a normal house. That's when Bob got arrested for that burglary he didn't do. He went to jail, and we lost the house. Pamela wanted a real house so much."

"And the veil?" I prompted.

"No veil. I don't know where the one came from when she was—" She turned away and leaned against the trailer. "I can't talk anymore."

The trailer door cracked open and a young girl with blond hair and blue eyes came outside. She took Mary's limp hand and hid behind her leg.

"Memaw, when's Mama comin' back?" she asked.

My eyes burned and I had to fight to stabilize my voice. "Hello," I said to the child. "Who are you?"

"Megan." She didn't smile. There was a shadow in her blue eyes. "Where's Mama?"

"Go tell your uncle Timmy to get a video for you," Mary said. "I'll be inside in a minute."

"And Mama?" she asked, reluctantly going inside the door as Mary gently pushed her. She turned to look over her shoulder at me. "Do you know where Mama is?"

"I'll be there in a minute." Mary closed the door and faced me. "Megan doesn't understand that Pamela won't be back. We tell her, but she doesn't understand."

"I'll check the information you gave me. If I find anything, I'll let you know. One more thing, Mrs. Sparks. Who is Megan's father?"

"Pamela never said. She was eighteen." She took a long

breath and put her hand on the doorknob. "When Bob gets hisself together, he's going to find Pamela's killer. He might go to prison for murder, but it's what has to be."

I put my hand on her arm, in caution not comfort. "No, it doesn't. Please, Mrs. Sparks, don't do anything foolish. Megan needs both of you now." The words were ashy in my mouth. I'd heard them before, directed at me. Daniel had needed me, but I'd had nothing left to give him. Mary Sparks was only a few years older than me. Her face was worn and lined from hard work, but there was substance there. She wasn't going to cave. She would pull her family back together and do what was necessary.

My hands were shaking as I backed my truck out of the drive. Instead of going to the paper, I went to the Ruby Room, a small restaurant in the Back Bay run by Garnett Roper. Garnett was my age, unmarried and a fine Southern cook. Her menu varied from day to day, but she always had the best fried chicken, homegrown vegetables, iced tea and, on demand, alcohol. I ordered a Bloody Mary and sat at a table on the patio. She came out to serve me herself.

"You okay?" she asked, putting the drink in front of me and taking a chair.

It was only ten, too early for her lunch regulars, so the place was quiet. I looked at the still waters of Back Bay. The morning was undercut with the cawing of the gulls around the shrimp boats.

"Tough interview," I finally said. "The mother of the dead girl."

She put her hand on mine, and her fingers were warm. "I'm sorry, Carson. I know that brings up a lot of stuff."

Garnett Roper, née Dupree, was also from Leakesville.

We'd been friends since the first grade, when I'd punched Robby Caldwell for trying to steal Garnett's new box of eighty-four Crayola crayons.

"A lot of my customers knew Pamela one way or the other," Garnett said as she straightened the sugar packets. She had lovely hands, long and graceful. Even in grammar school her hands had fascinated me. They were never still.

"What's the talk?" I asked. Garnett's restaurant was the meeting place for almost every faction on the bay. The fishermen came in early for breakfast and a packed lunch for the day. The businessmen and housewives rolled in at lunch. If there was talk, Garnett would have heard it.

She frowned, the harsh cut between her eyebrows the only line on her lightly tanned face. "She made a mistake and got pregnant, but she had the baby. From what I hear, she never even told the father. He must have been someone from outside Back Bay. Anyway, she had the kid, stayed with her folks, worked to earn a nest egg and started going to junior college last year. She was engaged to be married."

"In two weeks," I added.

"Shit." Garnett's hands flattened on the table for two seconds, then busied themselves rearranging the condiments on the far corner.

"Do you know the guy? Joe Welford."

"Yeah. Joe comes in every Saturday morning with Pamela's dad. He's quiet, but in a shy way not a psycho way." She shook her head. "He didn't kill Pamela."

"People are capable of anything," I said, looking at the last swallow in my glass.

"You used to believe they were capable of kindness, too. And love." Garnett's brown eyes were sad.

"I used to believe in a lot of things." I drank the last swallow. "Heard any talk about the fifth body in the grave?"

"Lots of talk, nothing I'd consider to be even a half-cocked theory. Let's see, it's the killer's sister or mother, going with the assumption that she was the first victim and that she drove him to do the others. An Anthony Perkins kind of thing. And—"

"Wait a minute. So everyone is certain the victim is female and the killer male?"

"That's the consensus. Why? Do you think differently?"

"No, that's pretty much what I think. Maybe he killed someone in Louisiana or Alabama and brought the body here."

"I've heard that one, too, and that's the one I'd put my money on. The thing that's really got folks buzzing is Pamela's murder. I mean is it a copycat? Or is the guy back?"

"I wish I knew." I picked up my empty glass. "I think I'll have another."

"If you eat something first," she said in a tone that was more sister than friend.

Arguing with Garnett was like punching a tree. "Okay, a vegetable plate."

She took my order to the kitchen and returned with a heaping plate and a glass of iced tea. "You can have the drink after you eat."

"Yes, Mother," I said, taking a bite of the field peas and stewed okra. I was suddenly starving.

10

My plans to interview the families of the other dead girls had effectively been annihilated by Mary Sparks. I couldn't do it. I didn't have the grit to wade into more grief. That the girls had been killed twenty-four years before wouldn't lessen the horror of it. It just meant that four families had been living with hope for a quarter of a century, and that hope had been ripped from them.

I went back to the paper and realized I'd not been there for Mitch Rayburn's visit when I saw his note on my desk. I'd forgotten. I called him and agreed to see him at four. I'd just put the phone down when Brandon appeared in my doorway. I wanted to challenge him about having a key to my office, but he was the publisher. I supposed he had keys to everyone else's desk, too. He probably got his jollies with surveillance cameras in the restrooms.

"Carson! Did the Sparkses give you anything juicy?"

While I stared at him my brain played a film. In it I slapped him so hard that his fat earlobes jangled against his fat cheeks. Reality check. This was the only place that would give me a job. My reputation as a big-shot reporter had quickly given way to my reputation as a drunk. I was a walking liability, and I knew it. "Juicy?" I put as much scathing into the two syllables as I could.

"You know, was the girl wild or not?"

"The family is grief stricken. Their daughter seemed to be getting her life in order."

"She had an illegitimate child! There's bound to be something newsworthy in that."

"Brandon, she got pregnant. It's not like she took an Uzi into a classroom of children and killed them. She made a mistake."

"It can be played—"

I stood up. "You are not going to malign that dead girl."

He grew very still, staring at me. "I realize you've got some issues, Carson, but I'm the publisher."

"If you don't want to be the laughingstock of every news organization in the nation, you need to listen to me." It cost me to tone it down, but I did. What was at stake wasn't my pathetic career; it was Mary Sparks and her husband, Bob.

"This is the biggest story we've had in years and I intend to maximize it. I got a call from *Newsweek* this morning. They're interested in our coverage."

"Really. *Our* coverage?" I didn't have to say anything else. My reputation was shot to the point no one would hire me, but it didn't mean they wouldn't buy my work when it was good—and it was better than good. The *Morning Sun* could share in that glory, *if* I wrote the story.

Brandon and I stared each other down. Outside my office, the newsroom had grown uncharacteristically quiet. Brandon had left the door wide open when he came in.

I spoke first, and in a carefully neutral voice. "I thought we could play this as a real community newspaper, one that's concerned for the citizens. One of our daughters has been murdered. We want to catch the killer, and solve five other murders in the process. We can be a leader, Brandon, and one that comes out on top. We can be the good guys."

He was an ambitious man, but he wasn't stupid. "Okay. We'll do it your way. For now." He leaned closer so he could whisper. "Watch yourself, Carson. I dragged you out of the gutter and if I let go, you'll slide right back."

I started to tell him to shove it, but I didn't. If I was fired, I couldn't finish the story. And I wanted to. Badly.

He left my office and I walked over and closed my door, but not before I made eye contact with Hank, the city editor. His blue eyes behind his thick glasses were sparkling, and over the top of his computer screen he gave me a thumbs-up. I sat down and started writing, oblivious to everything except the story.

I'd just finished writing up the interview with Mary Sparks when Mitch tapped at my door. The fluorescent lighting of the building made everyone look either sallow or ruddy, but Mitch was blanched. His eyes were circled in darkness, and even his mustache seemed to droop.

"I'm worried, Carson." He took the chair Avery had occupied that morning.

"About?"

"How this thing is going to play. If we have the entire Gulf Coast convinced that a psycho killer is on the loose, we're going to start a panic. I got a call from the mayor, who's leaning hard on Chief Nelson, who's leaning hard on Riley and all the officers. There's talk of canceling the junior-senior proms that start next month. People are terrified already."

"Okay."

His eyes narrowed. "Okay?"

"I think I convinced Brandon to be a civic good guy, at least for Tuesday's edition."

He sighed and relaxed. "That's one worry down. Brandon can be reasonable, and I think he wants what's best for the community."

"I hope you're right."

Mitch smiled, and I wondered again why he wasn't married or at least in a permanent relationship. Fire had scarred both of us in terrible ways, but Mitch seemed to have recovered better than I had. Still, it was sometimes hard to see beneath the facade.

"Avery told me that Bob Sparks is going to conduct his own manhunt," he continued. "We can't have that."

I shrugged. There was little I could do to stop Bob Sparks. "He said that in anger and pain. He'll probably change his mind. His wife seems like a reasonable woman."

"I looked up his burglary conviction." He rubbed his eyebrows between his forefinger and thumb. "I think he got railroaded."

I sat forward. "Is this for print?"

"Yes. I want to go public with this. I'm going to ask that the police reopen the case. No conclusion, only that we'll be looking at Mr. Sparks's conviction with a fresh eye. If he was wrongly charged and convicted, I'll do my best to make it up to him. Personally and professionally."

A lot of things ran through my mind. First and foremost was that reopening that case would leave the police department wide open for a possible lawsuit. Mitch was eating Pamela Sparks's brutal murder for breakfast, lunch and dinner. The case was working him, and vindicating Pamela's father of a bum charge was obviously part of his view of justice. Some men would have been only too happy to let the past rest. That said a lot about Mitch's character.

"This'll make a great sidebar to the story I wrote on the Sparks family. Let me make a few notes." I asked him the routine questions—when was Bob Sparks convicted, who was D.A. at the time, who defended Sparks, what physical evidence did they have, who investigated, how much time did Sparks serve? The former D.A. had retired, and the investigating officer had quit the department under a cloud of suspicion. "Thanks, Mitch." I still had some facts to check. I started jotting a few notes.

"There's something else," he said.

I looked up. "What?"

"Have dinner with me tonight?"

Avery's words came back to me with a strange force. I hadn't even given it a thought that he might be right. "Why are you asking me to dinner?"

His smile only heightened his tiredness. "I haven't slept but a couple of hours in the last five days. I haven't eaten a decent meal in that same amount of time. I haven't jogged or worked out, and I feel myself slipping into the abyss."

"And you think I know my way around there," I said.

He smiled. "No, but you just gave the perfect example of why I'd like to have dinner with you. You make me laugh, and I need that right now."

The things I knew about Mitch were that he'd lost his entire family. He'd come up through the ranks of lawyer, assistant D.A., and finally D.A. in an election two years ago. By all accounts, he was as clean as any elected official could be. He'd never been married, but he wasn't a man who played the field a lot. He worked, and he jogged. He coached a Little League baseball team, and he sometimes went to his uncle's cattle farm in Stone County for a long weekend.

"Okay," I said.

"I'll pick you up at seven. How about the White House?"

"How about the Brown Raisin?" It was a soul-food joint way north of I-10 in the middle of pine forests. They served barbecued everything and raisin bread pudding to die for. They also had acoustic entertainment every night of the week. That would lessen the pressure on both of us to be so damn entertaining.

"It's a date."

There were other reasons I'd chosen the Brown Raisin, and I was aware of all of them as Mitch escorted me through the door. It was dark and located in neighboring Hancock County, away from the glitz and glamour of the casinos. Mitch was D.A. in Harrison County. At the Brown Raisin, folks minded their own business. We were given only a cursory glance as we walked in and were led to a table in the back.

We placed our drink orders—a vodka martini for me and a Jack Daniel's on the rocks for him. Mitch ordered an appetizer of marinated crab claws. When the drinks and appetizer were in front of him, his shoulders visibly relaxed.

"Good choice," he said, indicating the restaurant. "I've never eaten here."

"Used to serve a largely black clientele. Now that the

race war is at a truce, folks of all color who like good barbecue come here. I went to school with Junior Robicheaux, the cook. His daughter was friends with mine." I stared into my drink. I hadn't meant to call up the ghosts.

Mitch's hand touched my fingers. "I'm so sorry about your daughter."

I forced my gaze up to meet his. "And I'm sorry about your losses, Mitch."

"How old would your daughter be?"

"Annabelle would've been eleven this year."

"I can't imagine losing a child," Mitch said. "When I lost my brother, I thought I'd give up. The instinct to survive must be the strongest of all."

I didn't want to talk about Annabelle, but I wondered if Mitch needed to talk about Jeffrey. "How did you survive?" I asked, motioning the waiter for another drink.

"I buried myself in the law. I held on to the thought that if I got good enough, I could be what Jeffrey had once been to me. Someone who looked out for the weak."

It was strange that Mitch had ever considered himself to be weak, but he was the younger sibling, and from my experience with Dorry, I sometimes felt less than. He'd also explained his need to uphold justice for the underdog. "What was Jeffrey like?"

For a moment the strain left Mitch's face. "He could play baseball like nothing you've ever seen. He was stunning to watch. They have some video footage of him at the high school. I borrow it sometimes and play it on slow. It's like perfection in slow motion. He had a real talent."

"I heard he had scouts after him, and that after the fire

he turned down an athletic scholarship to State so he could stay around the coast with you."

He gave me a curious look. "That's true. Instead of going to college, Jeffrey took a job at the docks so we could stay on the coast. My folks had adequate insurance, so some local businessmen helped us arrange to buy a house in a good neighborhood. Jeffrey wanted a family more than he wanted to be a baseball star. How'd you come to know this?"

"I did a little research. By accident. When I was looking for information on the missing girls, there were also stories about Jeffrey."

The waiter brought my drink and Mitch asked for another. We placed orders for pulled pork, fried pickles, turnip greens, sweet-potato fritters and corn bread.

"Jeffrey was at a baseball clinic the night my parents died. A talent scout there had offered him a full scholarship not eight hours before the fire." He spread his hands on the table. "He gave up a lot for me."

"He must have been a wonderful brother."

"No one could ever begin to know the things he did for me. The way he protected me." He stopped talking, and I left him in his thoughts. At last he spoke. "You would have liked him, Carson."

"I wish I could have known him," I said, and meant it. Jeffrey Rayburn had obviously helped shape Mitch into the man he was.

Mitch sipped his drink, and the sadness in his eyes was clouded by pain. "He suffered a lot. When we were growing up, he took the blame for things that I did." He finished his drink. "Let's talk about something else."

On the stage in the other room, the band had begun to tune up. "Why are you asking to reopen the Sparks burglary conviction?"

"I examined the case, and I honestly believe Bob Sparks didn't do it. He served two years in state prison. An apology won't amount to much, but vindication may be something he can hold on to."

"You're really one of the good guys, aren't you?" I meant it sincerely.

He shook his head. "I don't believe in the good guys. We're all...fallible, Carson. We make mistakes. No one is totally good."

"What about the bad guys? Do you believe in them?"

"I believe we all suffer. Some more than others."

The band swung into a rendition of "The Thrill Is Gone." There was a small dance floor in front of the band. From our table we couldn't see, but I knew that in the darkness there were couples dancing. It was a slow, sensual song where belly and pelvis met and melded. The band moved on to some Bobby Blue Bland and more B. B. King.

We were both listening to the music as the waiter put our food on the table. I ordered another drink while Mitch asked for sweet tea. The pork was tangy and sweet, absolute perfection, but I was more interested in my drink. I kept glancing for the waiter as I forced myself to eat.

"Carson, there's a psychologist in Biloxi. He's good. He's had success with helping people stop drinking."

Anger was my first reaction, but I tamped it down. "I don't want to stop drinking," I said. "Alcohol blurs the edges enough that I can stand it. Why would I give that up?"

"You aren't a real drunk, at least not yet. You still take

responsibility for your actions. But you're killing yourself. It's just a really slow way to suicide."

"The biggest part of me died with Annabelle. I'm just trying to anesthetize the last quivering hunk."

His hand moved across the table and covered mine. "It won't do any good. As I said, the instinct to survive is too strong. Go ahead and decide to live, Carson."

When my drink arrived, I finished that one and didn't order another. We listened to the music and talked between songs. Mitch talked about running and his love of movement, of covering ground. I listened and realized that there was nothing in my life I loved more than drinking. For a moment, the abyss yawned before me. Fear, for myself and what I was doing, crept up my spine. "If you're ready, I'd like to go home," I said.

He didn't argue. He paid the tab, refusing my offer of Dutch. On the drive back to my house, he talked about the changes along the coast, keeping the conversation light and casual.

When he pulled in the drive, I didn't give him a chance to walk me to the door. I got out, thanked him for dinner and rushed up the steps. Once inside, I locked the door and leaned against it. I wasn't trying to lock Mitch out. I wasn't afraid of him, but he'd pulled off a scab, and my wound was bleeding. I hurried into the kitchen.

My hand was shaking as I reached for the bottle of vodka under the kitchen sink. When the phone rang, I yelped, causing the cats to scatter from around my feet.

I answered with a hello.

"Carson, are you okay?" Daniel's warm voice was like a familiar touch. Spanish had been his first language, yet his English was impeccable. He retained the rhythm of Nicaragua.

"I'm fine. I just got home." My heartbeat had quickened to the point that I sounded short of breath.

"I've called twice. I was getting worried."

I leaned against the counter. Chester twined between my legs, purring and demanding attention. Miss Vesta would not lower herself to such antics. She sat on the arm of the sofa watching me with golden-green eyes.

While I held the phone with one shoulder, I opened a can of their favorite cat food. I tried to follow the vet's instructions on dry food, but sometimes a treat was in order. Chester rewarded me with a lick on my ankle, and Vesta ignored me.

"I'm okay, Daniel. The job…it's been hectic."

"I heard about the murders."

I wondered if Dorry had called and told him, but I didn't ask. I hated it when I felt that they were talking about me behind my back. "I feel for the families."

"Is this a good idea?" he asked.

"I don't get to pick and choose what happens that I cover," I said, a little angry. "I'm working. That's a step up, right?"

"The story was excellent. Dorry faxed it to me."

"Yes, Dorry would do that. She can manage four children, keep a perfect house, bake cookies for the neighborhood's underprivileged, pacify Mother and tend to my business. She's amazing."

There was a silence. "You make it impossible for anyone to care about you, Carson. You drive us away."

My fingers closed around the neck of the vodka bottle. I gripped it so tightly my knuckles whitened. "Why are you calling?"

"I'm going to León for a few weeks. I didn't want you to try and call and not be able to find me."

The town he spoke of was on the Pacific side of Nicaragua. It was an old town with a beautiful cathedral. There were lavish homes with courtyards and servants. Clubs and restaurants lined the square, and at night the sweet breeze blew in off the ocean. León was a city of smiling white teeth, cigarettes, long hair blowing in the breeze and salsa. The things that were not available in León were reliable telephones or mail. Daniel would, effectively, be out of touch. The damage from years of war had been extensive, and there'd been no money to repair the infrastructure.

"How long will you be gone?" I felt him slipping away from me. Nicaragua was his heart home, the place he loved. Though Daniel had been born in Miami, he yearned for Nicaragua. He loved all of it—the volcanoes and coffee-bean plantations, the fields of rice and the pounding surf of the Pacific.

"Two weeks."

"It should be beautiful there now." March would be dry.

"I'll telephone you when I get back."

"Thanks for calling, Daniel." I wanted to beg him to come to me. If I asked, he would. All he needed was one word. I couldn't, though. I could not give him even a half measure of what he needed, what he deserved.

There was a long silence as we both thought about other goodbyes, ones where we'd clung to each other with whispered promises of reunions. I could almost feel his long fingers combing sensuously through my hair, feel his heartbeat beneath my ear as I pressed against him. He smelled of starch and sunshine. Parting had been physically painful, for both of us.

"Take care of yourself, Carson," he said and hung up.

The cats were finished eating. I took the vodka bottle to the sofa and sat holding it. It was round and solid in my hand, something permanent that was always available. I got up and put it under the sink and signaled the cats to bed with me.

11

That night I dreamed of slow drops of blood falling onto the weathered wood of a pier. The wood was thirsty. It drank and drank. I was the wood. I ached for more, focused only on the next falling drop and the pale, three-fingered hand from which it fell. And then the dream changed. I was walking in the meadow behind our home in Miami. It was a spring day. The azaleas that Daniel had insisted on planting along the white vinyl fence were blooming a vulgar fuchsia. Annabelle was hiding in the flowers, laughing. She ran from bush to bush, her laughter a ripple of merry notes. She loved the vibrant color of the flowers, and I teased her by saying they were too loud, too bright.

In the blink of an eye, she disappeared. My heart clutched with dread. Then I heard her giggle.

"Mama," she said. "Find me."

"Come on out, silly. We have treats for Bilbo. Let's go find him."

"Mama!" Annabelle's voice changed. There was fear in it. "Mama!"

I looked around the bush, but she wasn't there. I crawled

under it, now a huge, gnarled azalea with black branches and deep, leafy secrets. My daughter was gone.

"Mama! Please find me. I'm lost!"

I tore into the leaves and branches with my hands. I hurled my body into the shrub. "Annabelle!"

"Oh, Mama, I don't like it here. Come and get me."

"Annabelle!" I screamed her name. I fought against the shrub, but suddenly there was nothing. I clawed the air above my bed, and I awoke, panting and sobbing.

Moonlight streamed through the wooden blinds of the window, crossing the bed with bars of gentle light, yet no prison could be constructed of stronger bonds. I put my head in my hands and waited until I could stand. Then I got up and changed my T-shirt. It was soaked with sweat. Instead of going back to bed, I went to the screened porch and sat on the swing. Chester joined me, curling his warm yellow body against my bare thigh.

The night breeze was laden with wisteria. Olfactory melancholy. I was haunted by my dream. It was composed of different elements but contained the same emotion of many I'd had before. My daughter was lost and needed me, and I couldn't help her.

The swing creaked on the chains, and I pulled Chester into my lap. He was the more forgiving of the two cats. Vesta had rules, and they changed with each location. She could be stroked on the back in bed, but not in a chair. The swing was still undetermined territory. When she hopped up beside me, I risked running my hand down her spine and she purred.

"I can't drink enough anymore to stop the dreams," I told them. "Six drinks used to do it. My liver won't last another year at this rate, and I still won't be able to sleep."

Chester licked my hand with a rough tongue. I was sweaty from the dream, and I recalled that primitive man first caught deer by pissing on a rock. The deer came up to lick the salt from the dried urine, and the men jumped on them. Salt was necessary for the survival of all mammals. Alcohol for a number of others.

I thought about a drink, but it was getting close to dawn. The sky to the east was just faintly brightening. I curled on the swing and rocked with the cats, trying hard not to think of my daughter.

My porch faced south, the yard sloping down to the water. Big oaks shaded the centipede grass that looked like a gentle green swell in dawn's first light. At one time there had been picnic tables and party paraphernalia close to the water. Those had been cleared away after I bought the place. I wasn't exactly a party girl these days. I watched as the sun struck the first sparkles along the gray water, turning the bay to a sheet of silver. The sky awoke with a brush of peach overtones. Soon it would be a cloudless blue, pale and serene.

I had no near neighbors. The property I bought was ten acres, a rare tract on the water in booming Jackson County. My house was secluded, nestled in live oaks with limbs that stretched to the ground, inviting. How Annabelle would have loved them.

When the water was a cool slate and the sky blue, I got up, made some coffee and got ready for work. I was at my desk at seven-thirty, a fact that earned no remarks from anyone.

For two hours I organized my notes, typing up interviews in case I couldn't read my own brand of shorthand later. When it was closer to ten, I went out to talk to Hank.

"I'm headed to the bridal salons," I said. "The killer had to buy these veils somewhere."

"Pretty tough to describe a veil," Hank said. "I mean for a gal who never worked the society desk."

I smiled. It was a compliment of a sort. "I can stop by the PD and see if they'll let me photograph the one found with Pamela Sparks."

"Good idea. I'll let Brandon know what you're doing."

I refrained from rolling my eyes. "Whatever you think best." I walked out of the newsroom and for the first time saw a couple of reporters smile at me. Jack was right—I should have put money in the coffee kitty the first week.

The day was gorgeous. It was as if spring had jumped the coast overnight. Azaleas were everywhere in shades of pink, lavender, purple and white. Delicate white branches of bridal wreath laced the breeze, reminding me of the veil that Pamela Sparks wore. I was certain Avery was already on this, but it didn't matter. It wasn't a competition to solve the case.

I'd made a list of all the bridal salons along the coast. I used my cell to check with Avery before I left town. He had no new leads in the case, or so he said. He reluctantly agreed to let me take a Polaroid photo of the bridal veil taken from Pamela Sparks. His team had worked the salons with no results. He didn't seem to mind that I was following his footsteps.

With the photo in hand, I drove along Highway 90 to Waveland, the last Mississippi town before the Louisiana State line. The land was flatter here, the water a gentle shush against the beach. There was one bridal shop there, and the clerk said the veil looked too expensive for her to carry.

Driving east, I made Bay St. Louis my next stop. The

small downtown was situated on a series of bluffs. This was the place where artists and old hippies had settled, and there was a small bridal shop with an eclectic selection of gowns. Many women swooned at the confection of a bridal gown, but I felt nothing. White was never my color. The clerk was knowledgeable, though, and she examined the photograph for a long time.

"It's an imported lace," she said. "I doubt any of the bridal salons here will carry this. In fact, I haven't seen it around for quite some time. I'd say this was a special order, made for a particular bride because the pattern meant something to her. See, it's twining ivy, thistle and rose. Something Anglo-Scottish."

I studied what she pointed out and saw the different elements of the intricate pattern.

"This cost a pretty penny, and from the look of it, I'd say it's antique. It could have even been brought over to this country, an heirloom, from a mother to a new bride."

My heart sank, but I made the notes. "What about dressmakers?"

She smiled. "Rose McKay. Every bride on the coast with a specialty dress has used her. She's about eighty now, but she turns out a dress that no factory can rival."

I took down the dressmaker's address in Jackson County, thanked the shop owner and continued to work my way east.

The bridal shops in Long Beach, Gulfport and Biloxi offered no additional leads. I went to the office and called Rose McKay. She agreed to see me at three o'clock. I had time to write my story for the day.

Hank read over the piece I wrote on the history of bridal

garb and motioned me to his desk. "Brandon's gonna shit fireballs."

I laughed. "Good."

"This isn't the kind of story he expects from you."

"It's the total harvest of my labors." I shrugged. "There's nothing new on the case. To keep pounding on it would be sensationalism."

"Well, duh! What do you think you're getting paid for?"

I laughed out loud. The sound attracted the attention of the features editor and Deedee Bridges, the society editor. She was staring at my wrinkled slacks, which were covered in cat hair.

"I have a gut feeling the veil will turn out to be important." I leaned down and lowered my voice. "Tell Brandon I'm meeting with a wedding dressmaker this afternoon. That should add a little blue flame of Tabasco to his fireballs." Hank was laughing when I left the newsroom.

I hit school traffic before I got to Rose McKay's, so I was ten minutes late and walked up to the door of the old Victorian with two young girls about seven and nine. They wore the uniforms of parochial school. Mrs. McKay met them at the screened door, swinging it wide with a smile. The odor of peanut-butter cookies wafted out into the cool front porch.

She gave them big hugs. "Girls, there're cookies and milk in the kitchen. Do your homework." As the girls skittered away, laughing down a long, dark hallway, Rose turned to me. "May I help you?"

I obviously didn't look like bridal material, nor would I pass muster as a mother of the bride. "I'm Carson Lynch with the Biloxi *Morning Sun*."

She nodded and again held open the screen. "Come in. You're here about the bridal veil on that murdered girl."

I followed her into a large sewing room with a small turret containing a dressmaker's dummy and the most incredible gown. I made a sound of appreciation.

"It's beautiful, isn't it? And the bride is just as lovely. She couldn't have picked a more suitable dress." She walked to it and adjusted a tiny loop that was used to lace the sharply Veed back of the dress. "A lot of girls want dresses that outshine them. Lauren, though, can wear this dress and not be overwhelmed by it." She laughed softly. "I've gotten grumpy in my old age. If a dress doesn't suit, I just turn the business down. I'm not going to try to fit a bride with a dress that doesn't serve her."

I remembered then that Rose McKay was in her eighties, but I would have said sixty. She was erect and slender, her movements without the stiffness of old age.

"I've never seen a dress that lovely," I said, remembering Dorry's dress of sleek elegance and my, much bemoaned by my mother, choice, which didn't involve lace and pearls.

She looked at me, her gaze analyzing. "I'd say you didn't bother with a wedding dress at all. Too much fuss."

I nodded. "You'd be right. But how did you know I was married?"

"Unmarried women of a certain age have a look. Not a bad look, just different. Living with a man softens a woman. The art of compromise is what marriage is all about, and that changes a person, inside and out." Her gaze went to the dress and beyond, out to her front yard where a huge oak tree shaded the house. "I was married once, a long, long time ago. My husband died. I had four children to raise."

Rose motioned to an old desk with papers sticking out everywhere. She sat in one chair and indicated the other for me. When we were facing each other, she asked me a question. "What do you want to know?"

I pulled the photograph of the veil from my purse and held it out to her. She took it, adjusting her glasses. "I might have made that. Seems familiar. The lace…" Her voice drifted away as she studied the photo. "My memory isn't so good."

I saw the age then. She studied me, and for a second, she looked lost.

"Grandmama?"

I turned to the woman who had appeared so silently in the doorway. She assessed me in a split second and knew I wasn't there on wedding business.

I introduced myself and explained, and she said she was Rose's granddaughter, Lele. The two young girls were hers.

She took the picture from her grandmother's hand, studied it, then handed it back. "Grandmama, do you remember that veil?"

Rose studied the picture as if she were trying to memorize it. "I remember it, but I can't say when or who it was for. I can almost feel that lace."

"Do you keep photographs of your dresses?" I asked. "Maybe if we went through some records, a name would jog your memory."

"I never kept records. Once a dress was finished and the bride wore it down the aisle, it was just a memory for both of us."

She appeared upset. "It's okay," I said gently. I stood and thanked her for her help. Lele followed me to the door.

"Grandmama is slipping," she said. "She can still sew anything, but she forgets where she put things and when people are supposed to come by for appointments. She doesn't go out much anymore, so that's not a problem. But she loses time. Whole chunks of time. There's a chance she'll remember that veil. If she does, should I call you?"

I gave her my card and thanked her. I had nothing new for a story, and it was close enough to quitting time. When I pulled out of Rose's drive, I headed home, beating the traffic by half an hour.

Down the long, winding drive of my house, my own azaleas were blooming. I went outside and sat on an old bucket, my focus on the azaleas. They were huge, perhaps fifty years old, and a shade between purple and pink. Not the color of the azaleas in my dream, but close. They were quite beautiful in the fading spring dusk. I got down on my knees and looked beneath the branches. I don't know what I hoped to find there, but the gardener had been very thorough. Only old, dead leaves were piled around the base.

12

My hands were shaking as I steamed the wrinkles from a slate-blue blouse. The weight of the iron was unfamiliar, and I felt awkward and jerky. I'd ironed plenty in my day, but it had been a long time. In Miami, we'd had an endless supply of Daniel's cousins to help around the house, quiet young girls who were fleeing the hopelessness of Nicaragua. Many were probably no relations of Daniel, but I never asked. It didn't matter. The girls had no future in a country without a middle class. If they could get an education, they could become teachers or nurses, professions desperately needed back home. Or, they could marry an American. Several preferred that route.

We had a large house with a mother-in-law suite in the back where the girls stayed. They attended community college, where Daniel and I paid their way. They repaid us by doing light housework and babysitting Annabelle. My daughter had spoken Spanish like a native, and, more important, she was happy with her "big sisters" when I had to leave her for long stretches while I worked.

The still-warm blouse slipped over my skin with a light

sensuality that caught me unawares. As I put on the right sleeve, the silk glided onto my scar, bumping over the uneven texture. I glanced in the mirror, surprised by my reflection. My eyes were old, more brown than I remembered. I'd always considered them green.

In the kitchen the cats threaded my ankles crying for the shrimp I'd thawed. I tossed the pink flesh into the air for them to snag with a paw. It was just after seven when I drove to the office. To my surprise, Jack was there, and it looked as if he hadn't gone home. His shirt was rumpled and his tie thrown in a wad on his desk.

"Carson, about that money," he started to say.

"Forget it, Jack."

His face clouded with anger. "I'm going to pay you back."

I sat down on the edge of his desk. "Okay, you can. Educate me about the coast. Tell me the history. Who's who? Who's got power? Who wants power? That's something money can't buy."

Jack couldn't meet my gaze, and I felt such sudden kinship that I touched his shoulder. He was in some kind of trouble, and it wasn't any of my business if he didn't want to talk. "Tell me about Alvin Orley and the Gold Rush."

What he told me fleshed out the bare bones of what I already knew. Orley had been the center of prostitution along the Gulf Coast from the 1970s through the late '80s. He'd hosted illegal gambling in his nightclub, sold untaxed liquor and plotted the enforcement of the "neighborhood" protection plan, all while fronting as a civic-minded businessman—sure, his girls showed a little flesh as they performed, but it was all harmless fun. Orley had the best bands and even the church didn't object *too* strenuously, thanks to his large donations. Right on the beach, the Gold Rush was party central at that time. Everyone ended up there on a Saturday night.

"Orley was a French name, but Alvin's bloodline was mostly Yugoslavian," Jack continued. "They had a mob—these beefy guys who would visit a place of business and squeeze the owner for money so his place didn't get robbed or torn up. Of course, they were the vandals and robbers. Just like the Italians, but on a much smaller scale."

I thought about Orley and his pale blue eyes. I'd heard that he once cut a man's toes off, strung them on fishing line and made him wear them as a necklace. I mentioned the story to Jack.

"I heard that, too, but nobody's ever been able to confirm it. It suited Alvin's purpose to let folks believe that even if it isn't true. I know he didn't hesitate to work his girls over if they gave him any sass. There was some talk, too, that the CIA hit man who was actually involved in the Kennedy assassination in Dallas ended up working for Alvin. There's a house up the Little Biloxi, sort of on a peninsula. That's where he lived. It's a fortress."

Now, that was something I hadn't heard. "Could there be any truth to it?"

"If you don't believe Oswald alone killed Kennedy, there's always the possibility the CIA was behind it. Bunch of dirty bastards."

Jack didn't soften his opinions. It was another thing I liked about him. "Women, gambling, protection. Mississippi's Studio 54. Anything else?"

"Dope. Alvin sold weed, and a little coke. Back then, though, folks didn't do drugs like now. It was a kinder, gentler bunch of drug addicts." Jack smiled. "Why the big interest in Alvin?"

"It was just that photo of him, giving a check to a scholarship fund. And he made a comment about how he'd personally helped Mitch Rayburn through law school." I couldn't exactly say why that niggled at me.

"Like I said, Alvin did some civic-oriented stuff. He sponsored the Boys and Girls Ranch, did some fund-raisers for the sheriff's department. Of course, he contributed directly to some law-enforcement officers' salaries. A lot of police officers made ends meet by working nights as security for Alvin."

"What about the girls?"

"Alvin ran some dives where prostitution was flagrant, but the Gold Rush was something else. Some of the girls were real beauties. Exotic looking. They'd dance on the runway, or on stages that hydraulically moved up and down, that kind of thing. They were professionals worthy of a Vegas act."

He shrugged. "There were rumors they hooked out of the back. That gave Alvin a lot of muscle. Politicians from north Mississippi, Louisiana and Alabama would come over to spend some time with the girls. It was a little quieter than New Orleans, where a man might run into someone he knew. And Alvin kept clean girls. Besides, he knew how to keep his mouth shut, and it paid off handsomely for him. He had friends in high places."

Jack had given me plenty to think about as I went to my office and began to organize my notes.

Verda Coxwell was a ghost of a woman. Her hair was a colorless gray, like her eyes. Her lips were skin toned, and she wore a gray cardigan over a pale dress. She blinked against the sunlight as she stood in the doorway of her small house north of I-10 in the Woolmarket community. This was a rural area, a good place for kids to grow up with tree swings and dirt roads.

"I don't want to talk to the press," she said, her hand already swinging the door closed.

"Please, Mrs. Coxwell, the man who killed your daughter is still out there, and he may be killing again." I spoke as gently as I could. I knew what it felt like to be drained by grief, but it was important that she talk to me.

She sighed and stepped back from the door. "Come on in, I guess." She led me to the kitchen where a pot of coffee had just been brewed. She poured two cups and handed one to me. "Sugar's on the table. Cremora, too."

"Black is fine," I said. She was too defeated to even argue about talking to me.

"I'm not supposed to be home today," she said. "I'm supposed to be at work. I'm a clerk at Baby Power, over at Edgewater. I didn't feel well today, so I stayed home."

She was nervous. I sipped my coffee, trying to think of an approach to a subject that could only be painful. "I'm sorry about Audrey," I said.

Her eyes filled. "For twenty-four years, I've prayed every night that she would come home. All of that time, she was dead, lying in that ground under asphalt, cars parking on top of her like she was some kind of trash that didn't matter."

"I wish it had turned out differently."

"It's Nat's fault." She dared me to disagree. "It is. He was too hard on her. He wouldn't let her go out and be a teenager. He kept her home, saying her friends were wild. He made her pray and read the Bible for hours at night." She bit her lip, bringing the first bit of color to her face. "I should have stopped it. God forgive me, I should have. But I didn't."

"Hindsight has remarkable clarity," I said. "'If only' is a dangerous game to play, Mrs. Coxwell. You did the best you could, and I'm sure Audrey knew that. And knows it now."

She sat across the table from me, but the look she gave me was as solid as a touch. "You have regrets, too," she said. "I can see it."

"Everyone does." My regrets weren't part of the story. "Is your husband home?" I wanted to talk to both of them, if possible.

"He died. Two months ago." Her face held no sadness.

"I'm sorry."

"I'm not." Her tone was flat.

"Would you mind telling me about Audrey?"

She stirred her coffee. "She was going to be a bridesmaid in another girl's wedding. She was so excited. The dress was yellow chiffon, and I was going to hem it for her that weekend. It's still hanging in the closet. I should have given it away, but I just couldn't. She loved it so." She got up and went out of the room. In a moment she returned with a well-worn photo album. "Audrey was beautiful. See for yourself."

I thumbed through the photos, studying the smiling face of a girl who looked happy. She was beautiful, with long dark hair that hung straight, more the style of the '60s than the '80s. She was posed with stuffed toys, with her classmates, with her graduation hat and robe, with cats and dogs. But there were none of her with boys. "She was lovely," I said.

"She wanted to date. It was only normal. Nat wouldn't hear of it. He said she'd drop her panties and get pregnant and shame us all. He said that kids had gone wild and were smoking dope and screwing like rabbits. He said he wouldn't let them influence his daughter and turn her into a jezebel."

I made a note. I hadn't thought that the murders might be committed by someone with a fanatical religious streak, someone who saw young girls as potential temptresses. That might explain the severed ring finger—they weren't worthy of marriage.

"Nat saw God as his mission. He had a personal relationship with Him. He studied the Bible and interpreted it for me and Audrey. He was a domineering bully who punished us for the sake of our souls." A flush touched her cheeks and her pale eyes, giving them a spark. "He accomplished two things, though. I hate his God. And he killed his daughter."

Her face was suffused with anger. I wasn't certain if she meant what she said. "How did he kill Audrey?"

"She had to sneak around to do anything with her friends. She had to lie. That night she disappeared, she was supposed to go over to Sheila Picket's house to talk about plans for her friend's wedding. She didn't go there, though. She went somewhere else, somewhere where the killer saw her and got her. Nat's to blame because she couldn't act like a normal girl and just go out on a date."

"What were Audrey's habits?"

"The police have already asked me all of this." She wasn't complaining; she was just stating a fact.

"I have to make my own notes," I explained. "I can't use what you told them."

"Audrey was an honor student in high school. She played the flute in the band. She rode the bus there, and she came straight home. Nat wouldn't let her spend the night with anyone or anything like that. God forbid, they might have a brother who she would sleep with." The bitterness in her tone stung me.

"What about that Friday? If she didn't go visit—" I looked at my notes "—Sheila, where did she go?"

"I never found out. It doesn't matter now. She's dead. There's nothing that will change that."

And she was right. Saying I was sorry wouldn't change the facts. I gathered my notes. "Is there anything at all you can think of that might bear on who killed her? Did she ever mention someone was following her? Or bothering her?"

Verda Coxwell shook her head. "My sin is that Audrey couldn't confide in me. I was afraid of Nat. He'd make me kneel and lay across the bed and then whip me with a belt if he thought I went against him. He said women were children who had to be taught the right path. I didn't encourage Audrey to tell me things because I was afraid I'd blurt them out and get her in trouble."

Verda Coxwell had no information for me, only regrets. Blaming was the only action left in her life, and I wished I had something more to offer her. "Thanks, Mrs. Coxwell," I said, standing.

"Find the person who did this," she said. "I want to be there when they kill him."

She stood in the door and watched me get in my truck. I pulled out of her driveway, went down the street and parked in the shade of a live oak. I sat with my hands on the steering wheel of the truck and took a few deep breaths. Death had taken Verda's daughter, but it had also taken her life.

The clock on the dash showed eleven. I could justify lunch, or at least a Bloody Mary, but instead I drove to the Lopez home. I hadn't yet been able to locate an address for a relative of Charlotte Kyle, the second girl murdered, so I went on to the Lopez home downtown off Pass Road, one of the busiest streets along the coast.

A neat brick house was centered in a yard fenced with eight-foot-high chain-link. After I got out of the car I understood why. Four large dogs and five small children all ran over. The dogs barked frantically, and the children screamed. It was bedlam.

A middle-aged woman with dark hair and olive skin came up to the fence. She wore shorts and a long-sleeved shirt. Her face was etched with lines around her mouth and between her eyebrows. She yelled something in Spanish and the little children ran squealing back to the swing set. The dogs weren't so easily deterred. She had to clap her hands and lunge at them to get them to move.

"Sorry," she said, "I babysit my grandchildren while their parents work."

I introduced myself and watched the wariness creep over her face.

She turned away from me. "I have nothing to say."

"Mrs. Lopez, the more information the public has, the better their chances of keeping their daughters safe."

That stopped her in her tracks. "Come in." She unlocked the gate, let me in, then relocked it. "I can't leave the children alone."

As I followed her to a swing set, I wondered how often she'd said those words since Maria disappeared.

"What is it you want?" she asked when we were seated in two lawn chairs beside the swings.

"I'd like to know a little about Maria."

She turned her head away so I wouldn't see the pain, and I knew I'd walked across her scars. My hands had begun to shake, and I would have given a lot for a drink.

"Maria could make anyone laugh," she said. "Even when she was in trouble. She got away with a lot because she'd get her father laughing, and he'd forget why he was mad with her." She put a finger in her mouth and nibbled at the nail, forgetting for a moment that I was there. She put her hand down. "Carlos never got over losing her. The light died in his eyes. I should have been stricter with Maria."

"Where is your husband?"

"He's at work. At Keesler. He's a mechanic."

"Was Maria a good student?"

I took down the specifics of high school as Bonita Lopez talked. "Maria had just finished the tenth grade, but she looked older. The legal drinking age was eighteen, but Maria never had any trouble getting into bars. She liked to go to that place where the bodies were found." She swallowed. "She liked to dance. She'd start dancing in a group and everyone else would stop to watch her." She paused. "She had a big dream. She wanted to go to New York, to be in the Rockettes." She got up to check the children and returned. "She wasn't tall enough but I never told her that." Her voice thickened. "No one should steal a child's dreams."

"Was she seeing anyone?" I asked.

She shook her head. "She'd dated a couple of boys at

high school, but that had ended with the school year. Maria was a kind girl, really, even though she loved to play pranks." Mrs. Lopez's face took on softness. "That girl, she told her friends she was getting married and even went up to Gayfer's and registered herself as a bride. Picked out china and crystal patterns." She shook her head. "Two of her friends believed her and bought wedding presents. I made Maria return them, but she thought it was hilarious."

"You're certain she wasn't seeing anyone?"

She nodded. "Positive. Maria was in love with life. She wanted to laugh and dance, and it cost her her future."

"Why do you say that?"

"The Gold Rush always had a band. There were lots of men there, from the air base. She was just flirting, but I told her not to go there. The crowd was too old for her." She shook her head. "She didn't listen. That night she disappeared, she snuck out a window."

"How do you know she went dancing?"

"She took her favorite red dress and her dancing shoes with heels."

I asked her the same questions I'd asked Verda Coxwell about someone following Maria or wanting to hurt her.

"Maria was well liked. She had dozens of friends. Boys and girls. It wasn't someone she knew. I won't believe that. But I'll tell you what I think happened. She went to that club, she danced, she caught the eye of that murderer, and then when she went to leave, he snatched her up and killed her."

I thanked her and left. As I drove to lunch, I considered the bottom line of what both mothers had told me. It would be much harder to find a man who picked his victims at random.

13

The Vieux Marché was a business district in Biloxi designed to encourage tourists. The old brick road that ran in front of the shops, once the town's main street, was closed off to cars. There were quiet benches, palm trees among the oaks and bright flowers. I went there with a Subway sandwich and a Diet Coke. I ate what I could and fed the rest to the birds, a wild mixture of pigeons, seagulls, sparrows, blue jays, mockingbirds and one fat robin. Pedestrian traffic was slow, and I had plenty of solitude. I thought about Verda Coxwell and Bonita Lopez, shying away from their pain and clinging to detached reason. If I allowed myself to sympathize, it would ignite my own sorrow.

They both loved their daughters. The girls were bright and well liked in school, but without serious boyfriends. Or so their mothers thought. The wild card was Nat Coxwell. I would have given a lot to interview him. As it stood, the police would make more headway checking into his record. I flipped out my cell to call Avery to see what he'd uncovered on Nat and his religious obsession.

"He belonged to Mt. Sinai Primitive Baptist Church,"

Avery said. "We're checking there to see if any complaints were ever lodged against him. I think it's a dead end. I'm like you—any kind of fanaticism indicates mental instability, but the man has been dead two months. He didn't kill Pamela Sparks."

"Copycat?" I asked.

"I'm not going there, Carson."

"We're having a discussion, Avery, not an interview." I was annoyed. On and off the record were tricky things, unless firmly stated. My rule was not to print casual conversations unless I was specifically "on the record." Avery didn't know this about me, and even if I told him, he would still doubt me. "What do you have on the killer? And this is on the record."

There was a pause. "I'd rather not talk about this over the phone."

My pulse quickened. Did he have something, or was it the lack of leads that made him reticent? A cell phone wasn't a good idea either way. "Are you free this afternoon?"

"Tomorrow morning," Avery said. "Gotta go." He ended the call.

I calculated what I had for the Thursday edition, and the two interviews were enough. It kept the story alive, but it didn't sensationalize it. The interviews were legitimate journalism, although it would reiterate the fact that five, very likely six, girls were dead.

The unidentified body gnawed at me. Was some mother still waiting for her daughter to come home? Would Avery ever be able to identify the remains?

In the pattern of behavior I was trying to build around the victims, the only common elements I could find were that the girls were young and pretty. Only Pamela Sparks had been engaged. Audrey hadn't dated, and Maria was too young to be serious, or so their mothers thought.

I cleaned up my bag lunch, threw it in the trash and walked out by the sculpture of the fisherman casting his net. I loved the statue. Old Biloxi had relied on the fishermen. It was only fitting that they were honored.

Instead of going back to the office, I called in and got Jack to find Sheila Picket's address. It took him a few minutes to ferret out that she'd married Roscoe Bellington, a prominent divorce lawyer. I took down her address in a ritzy area on Back Bay and drove over, stopping at the wrought-iron fence to stare. The house was a muted coral Mediterranean with a red tile roof that covered at least five thousand square feet. The green back lawn sloped down to a boat slip, and from the driveway I could see the deck of a boat. The yard was manicured, the curve of the drive perfect, just like the date palms and the orange lilies that bloomed profusely.

When I knocked on the door, I was expecting a maid. Instead, a pretty blonde in designer shorts opened it. I introduced myself, gave her my card and watched her think through what I might want with her. Her life was far removed from dead girls on the beach.

"How can I help you?" she asked, shifting so that she blocked the door. Her body language told me not to expect entry to her home.

"Audrey Coxwell. You were friends with her, right?"

"Audrey." Her posture changed slightly. "I was horrified when I read that they'd found her body. I guess I always hoped that she'd run off with that airman."

This was more than I expected. "Could you tell me about him?"

"Let me see." She cocked a hip, frowning. "It's been a long time. I was a different person then."

"Did you grow up with Audrey?"

Wariness touched her face. "Yes." The answer was curt.

She didn't want to talk about her past. She'd left all of that behind, and any reminder would be unwelcome, especially one in the newspaper for all of her society friends to gossip about. Crossing the tracks was a hard task to pull off.

"This isn't for publication, Mrs. Bellington. But it might be useful."

"I'd have to have that in writing to believe it," she said.

"I only want to know about Audrey. If I quote you, I can merely say an old friend. I don't have to use your name."

She thought about it. "My husband doesn't need to be reminded that I was ever anyone except Mrs. Bellington. I wasn't a bad girl. Maybe a little wild, if you call drinking in the bars and dancing wild. Still, it's not an image my husband would be happy to see smeared in the paper."

"I'm not interested in making trouble for you."

She nodded. "Audrey was a good girl. She didn't have a choice. Her father—" she rolled her eyes "—was like some kind of psycho religious nut. She couldn't wear makeup, she had to wear dresses down to her ankles, she had to keep her hair long. Goodness, if he'd ever seen her in a pair of shorts, he would have whipped her to within an inch of her life."

"But she did wear shorts, right?" I thought I had a handle on their friendship.

"She did. Mine. She'd come over to my house, get out

of that frumpy dress, put on some shorts or one of my skirts, and we'd go out. If her father hadn't been such an asshole, she wouldn't have had to lie and sneak around. She was eighteen, for Christ's sake."

I didn't make any notes because I didn't want to spook her. "You said Audrey had a boyfriend. Can you tell me something about him?"

A look of distaste crossed her face. "Adrian. He was stationed at Keesler."

"You didn't like him?"

"It's not that. It was hard not to like Adrian. He was handsome and quick-witted. He liked to laugh and party. I think that's what attracted Audrey. She thought he was the exact opposite of her father, and she knew she didn't want any more of that."

"But…"

"But he had this edge. He was a tough guy. He liked to fight, and he'd start them. I saw him beat another man one night. If the bouncer at the Gold Rush hadn't pulled him off, he would have killed the man."

"Do you have a last name on Adrian?"

"Welsh." Her tone was reluctant. "Audrey met me and some girls up at the Gold Rush the night she disappeared. Adrian joined us up there. They got into a fight, and Audrey walked out."

"What happened to Adrian Welsh?" If Audrey was the first victim, as I suspected, then Adrian could have killed her and gone on with the series of murders. As far as I knew, he could have been transferred off the Gulf Coast and now returned after retirement.

"After Audrey disappeared, I don't know. I mean I never

saw him again in the clubs." A new look crept into her eyes. Guilt?

"Your friend disappeared and you didn't even talk to her boyfriend about where she might be?"

"I thought she might have married him and just decided not to ever tell her parents. I didn't want to know. I'm not a good liar, and if I knew, I was afraid they'd get it out of me."

It didn't ring true to me, but I let it go. "Was she serious enough about Adrian to marry him?"

"She had a ring, and they'd set a wedding date. They were going to elope right after she was the bridesmaid in her friend's wedding." She smiled slightly at a memory. "We were going to throw her a surprise party, so we took her up to Gayfer's and registered her as a bride. Back in the '80s the bridal registry was the be-all and end-all for a Gulf Coast girl. Literally a rite of passage. Every bride spent hours picking out china, crystal and silver patterns. It was Audrey's proof that her life was really about to change. I don't think I'd ever seen her so happy."

"Her parents didn't know anything about this?"

"No. She would never have told, and her parents would never have thought to check the bridal registry. If her father had even had a hint of it, he would have chained her in her room." She looked down. "I was sort of afraid that was what happened for the first week or so. I didn't call or ask any questions, because Mr. Coxwell didn't like me. I thought I'd make it worse on Audrey. And then I thought she'd run off with Adrian. I knew if that was true they were both in trouble. Him with the air force and her with her folks." She took a breath. "I was dating Roscoe by then. He would have dumped me if I'd gotten involved in a scandal."

I didn't say anything. She'd had no way of knowing her friend was dead. "Can you describe Welsh?"

"Tall, blond, hair cut real short, hard jaw, six-pack, about six foot two." She thought. "Blue eyes, a scar on his chin from a bicycle wreck, he said. Tattoo on his arm. Something to do with the air force." She shrugged. "He was handsome back then."

"Do you know where he was from?"

"Nebraska, originally. I kind of got the idea that his home life wasn't any better than Audrey's. I think that's one thing that drew them together."

"Thank you, Mrs. Bellington. This has been helpful."

She straightened and started to close the door, then stopped. "Please. My husband will be furious with me. He's worked hard to develop a certain…status."

"I won't use your name," I assured her.

An unusual pall had settled over the office when I walked in. It was normally a place of busy noise. Jack jerked his head, indicating that I should meet him in the coffee room. I walked back there wondering what new thing I'd done to offend my coworkers.

"The CEO of the Gannett newspaper chain just left," Jack said. "He made an offer to Brandon."

I felt my lungs tighten. "What kind of offer?"

Jack shrugged. "I only saw Brandon once since the guy left, and his face was grinning. He's been on the phone. Probably counting his money."

The *Morning Sun* was one of the few independent newspapers left. Brandon was publisher and owner. That had a downside, but working for one of the large chains had plenty of downsides. For example, a chain newspaper would never have hired me because of the liability factor. Brandon could take that risk with his paper.

"Do you think he'll take it?" I asked. It had never occurred to me that Brandon would sell the paper to anyone. It gave him power and prestige in the community.

"I don't know," Jack said. "If Gannett bought us out, we might have better insurance and retirement."

I nodded. Sometimes I forgot about the financial benefits that were important to the survival of the average person. Money couldn't buy happiness, but it could buy good doctors and a 401k.

"I don't want to work for a chain," Jack said. "I've never liked being part of an organization. Hell, I won't even eat at a chain."

He made me smile. "Brandon will do what he's going to do."

"Right. I just wanted you to know what was going on. The reporters are meeting at Baricev's tonight to talk. They asked me to ask you to come."

"Okay." It amused me that they'd send Jack as an emissary. I hoped I wasn't all that fearsome. "I'll be there."

14

Beer had never been my drink, but I ordered a Corona with lime and sat at a corner of the table and listened. None of the reporters were freaking out. They discussed the pros and cons of going with a chain. Ultimately, though, they realized that their fate would be determined by Brandon. Some saw it as a chance to move up through a corporate structure, others as the death of whatever small journalistic impulses still survived at the paper. I kept my opinions to myself, which seemed to work best. For most of them, the Biloxi paper was where they worked because Biloxi was where they lived. Lack of talent wasn't what held them there. They were rooted, and not even a hurricane could easily blow them away.

When the meeting broke up, I put my half-finished beer on the bar, considered a martini, but decided to go home to the cats. It was already seven. I'd eaten fried crab claws and a salad, so the evening meal was behind me. I could take a walk. I felt drained.

* * *

My trek took me down the shoreline and back to my own yard, where I sat on the old, upturned bucket. Darkness fell over the slope of the lawn and the undulating water with a gentleness that saddened me. Another day had closed. Time was endless in the passing, but change touched us each with pain. I went in the house and ran my bath.

I was about to step in the water when I realized I hadn't checked my phone messages. Normally, it was the first thing I did on returning home. But I had a cell, if anyone really needed to track me down.

The red light blinked, and a wild hope that Daniel had called made me pick up the receiver. There was one new message.

"Carson, it's Dorry. Tommy didn't come home from work this afternoon. He was supposed to get off early and be home by two. It's eight now." She spoke fast, stumbling over her words. "I haven't heard from him. He left the office at three. I tracked down one of his nurses and she told me he left right at three. I checked the hospital, but he isn't there." Her voice broke. "I'm afraid he's been in an accident. Could you check with your sources? I've called the highway patrol and the Mobile County sheriff's office, but no one will tell me anything."

I called the Biloxi PD and asked the desk sergeant to make a few calls. There was professional courtesy between law-enforcement agencies, and he could easily obtain the information. He didn't have to do it, but he did. He called me back within ten minutes.

"Ms. Lynch, there haven't been any reported accidents on Highway 98 in Mobile County or Highways 98 or 63 in Mississippi." I heard the click on the line that indicated someone else was calling me.

"Thank you, Sergeant," I said. "It was nice of you to do that for me. My sister will be relieved."

He hung up and I clicked over.

"Carson!" Dorry's voice fluttered with relief. "Tommy just drove up. He's fine. He was in surgery."

"Are you okay, Dorry?" I was more worried about her than Tommy at this point. Dorry never lost her cool, and she'd been on the verge of hysteria when she'd called. She wasn't one to jump to dire conclusions. I'd seen her wait up all night for her teenage son and never bat an eyelash.

"I'm fine. I called the hospital and they said he was off, but he was pulled into an emergency situation. Some child was stepped on by a horse and his thoracic cavity was crushed. They caught Tommy after he'd signed out. I guess no one even realized he was operating."

She was talking a mile a minute, probably from the rush of adrenaline still in her bloodstream. I let her talk, but I was wondering why Tommy couldn't have asked someone to give his wife a call when he realized he was going to be tied up for six hours.

"Tommy said the little boy still may not make it. Can you imagine? I never gave riding horses a thought until I had my own children. I'm glad Mother wasn't such a scaredy-cat."

"I'm glad Tommy's okay," I said. It was only nine o'clock, but I wanted a martini and the bed. Dorry's frantic energy only served to make me feel drained.

"You're coming home this weekend, aren't you?"

Dorry wanted me home. That much was clear. "Depends on the story," I lied. "I'll try."

"Carson, I know Mother stays on your raw side, but she's trying. She loves you. She just wants you to be happy."

"That's not true, Dorry. She wants me to be happy within the framework she provides. If I can't be happy within that, she doesn't care if I'm happy or not as long as I do what she wants."

There was a pause. "I'm not going to argue with you on the phone. I'm going to hang up, go make my husband a drink and then enjoy his company. But you're wrong about Mother. Good night, Carson. Thank you." She hung up softly.

I climbed in the still-warm tub with a double shot of vodka and the intention of preparing myself for a deep sleep. I wanted six hours without dreaming or panicking. It wasn't a lot to ask.

Avery was waiting outside my office Wednesday morning when I got there—on time. He gave me a critical look. "Change your makeup?"

"I got some sleep," I answered.

"Maybe you should try that more often. It looks good on you."

I pretended to lift my bottom jaw with my hand. "A compliment? Your wife must have been awfully good to you last night."

He laughed. "A jab below the belt. Ah, that's the exchange rate when you converse with a reporter."

We were both smiling, and I realized what a handsome man he was when he wasn't scowling disapproval at me. He had thick, dark, curly hair, an olive complexion and dark brown eyes that often looked black. His nose was sharp, aristocratic, and he dressed with care.

He walked in behind me, closed the door and took a seat in the interview chair. "We don't really have anything new." He held up a hand to halt my comments. "It would be nice if you didn't print that."

"This is what you didn't want to tell me over the phone?"

He nodded. My front-page story of my interviews with Verda Coxwell and Bonita Lopez was on his lap. He unfolded the paper to the sidebar of material I'd obtained from Sheila Picket Bellington. Her name was never used. "You've done some good stories without sensationalizing things. I know Sheila. You could have made it hard on her, and you didn't."

"I had no reason to use her name."

"You made Mrs. Lopez and Mrs. Coxwell sound like real people. You weren't making fun of them or using them."

"I don't use people."

"Is that a guarantee?"

"No more than you use people when you're gathering information."

He looked down at the paper for what seemed like a long time. "I'm going to tell you this because Mitch says we have to trust you. We've found nothing on the Sparks girl except rug fibers in her hair. She wasn't raped. There were no defensive wounds, no bruises or torture. It would seem the killer grabbed her or somehow got her in his vehicle without a struggle. The M.E. is still working on it. That would give us our best lead."

"Have the M.E. check for Thorazine, or something like that. A psychotropic."

He raised his eyebrows.

"When Annabelle died, I was suicidal. My family was

afraid my mind would snap." I looked at him with a steady gaze. "My husband was desperate. He called a doctor friend who prescribed Thorazine for me, just to tide me over through the funeral and relocating. I was a walking zombie. Someone could take my elbow and I would stand and shuffle after him. If they sat me in a chair, I'd stay there without moving. It's a very effective drug on the mentally unstable prone to violence. It would make Pamela manageable, unable to defend herself, but still mobile."

He listened with as cool a stare as mine. Not a shred of pity flickered in his eyes, and that was good, or I would have hated him.

"I'll check it out. That's a good lead, Carson. If the M.E. can screen for a particular type of drug, it makes it so much quicker."

"Pamela's funeral is today." I wasn't going regardless of what Brandon said. "I think Jack will be there."

"Jack's done a lot of that kind of duty." He stood up. "My wife is wondering if you're going to write your column here."

"I don't know," I said, surprised that anyone even knew about the weekly column that covered Miami's politics and the cultural mishmash of the city I loved so much.

"Mitch downloaded a whole bunch of them from the Internet, and Celeste and my daughter, Jill, read them all. They even made me read a few." He gave a wry smile and leaned just a hint closer. "I told you Mitch had a crush on you. I foresee a very cozy relationship between the police and the newspaper in the future." He stood up and left my office without ever looking back, so he missed the gesture of my middle finger.

* * *

Sarah Weaver was the fourth and final victim I could find record of in the 1981 killing spree. In the search for her family, I found myself driving down the tree-shaded lane of the Veteran's Administration Hospital just off Pass Road. The VA system was something I'd heard horror stories about—men who'd served their country honorably given minimal medical care. In Miami, one veteran had shown me scars where deep, cyst-like tumors had been excised from his back without anesthesia. There had been no money for local anesthesia. The result had been another series of stories that had won enemies for me. The government hadn't torched my house, though. That had been done by Charlie Sebring, a Miami contractor who'd erected multimillion-dollar public buildings that didn't meet the hurricane code. I'd nailed him in the newspaper—along with the politicians who subsidized him—and he'd murdered my daughter. That I'd been the intended victim didn't matter.

I pushed the past back and focused on my job. Royce Weaver was in a ward, his bed curtained off, but his rasping breath could be clearly heard ten beds away. I steeled myself against a wave of emotion as I stood outside the curtain. He was very sick and had been in the hospital for three months, without a single visitor. He'd raised Sarah alone. He was divorced, and his ex-wife was long gone, hadn't been seen in at least thirty years.

I cleared my throat to announce my presence, then stepped around the curtain. He should have been in his late sixties, but he looked ninety. Death was camping in the room, waiting. He struggled for oxygen, even though he had a tube in his nose. He took my card in trembling hands and examined it.

"I hope you're here to do a story on this. Agent Orange. I hope you've come to make the fucking government pay." He panted for breath. "They poisoned me while I was doing their fucking dirty work on the Cong."

"Don't exert yourself," I cautioned, afraid for a moment that my mere presence would overexcite him. "I'm here about Sarah, your daughter."

The tears were instant, and I fought back my own. This man was dying, alone, because his daughter had been stolen from him. "I'm glad she never saw this." He panted. "I wasn't always this way."

I stood by the bed and told him why I was there and what I wanted. I did most of the talking to save him.

He told me, in spurts and gasps, that Sarah had just broken up with her boyfriend, a twenty-year-old named Eddie Banks. They'd been engaged, but they'd argued, and she'd returned the ring because she'd caught him cheating on her. Sarah was angry and hurt, and she and some friends went out to some clubs, the Gold Rush being one of them. Clubbing was something she didn't normally do, but her pride was wounded and she wasn't going to sit at home and cry about Eddie. At 2:00 a.m., when she hadn't returned home, Royce had called her friends and then the police, but he'd been told to wait twenty-four hours. Sarah was nineteen, old enough to stay out if she chose.

"I knew she was dead," he said, too weak to even try to control the tears. "All this time, I knew. Now I can't even visit her grave."

The pressure of tears stung my own eyes, but crying wasn't professional, and it certainly wouldn't help Royce Weaver for me to stand over his bed, sobbing. Tears seldom achieved anything except difficulty breathing. I was pretty certain of that.

"Do you think Eddie Banks could have hurt your daughter?" I asked.

He shook his head. "Eddie cheated on her, but he wasn't violent. He hurt her because he was weak. He didn't kill her."

I nodded, made a note, then thought of my last question. "Did Sarah have a wedding gown and veil selected?"

"She did. I kept it for years and finally gave it to Goodwill. I'm dying. I wanted to sort through her things myself. Cleaning out her clothes was the last thing I did, because I knew I wasn't going back home. I'm ready to die, Ms. Lynch. Ready, willing and able."

I left the VA thinking about Sarah's closeness with her dad. She'd been engaged and hurt. I hadn't pressed Royce Weaver to give me details of her high school social life or friends. He hadn't the breath or emotional reserve. Finding Eddie Banks was the solution to that.

I also had to locate Charlotte Kyle's family. My efforts so far had yielded little, but I simply hadn't searched hard enough.

Since I'd determined to make a conscious effort to eat better, I stopped at the Ruby Room for some fresh vegetables. As I ate, I scanned the restaurant. The lunch crowd was a mixed bag. There were lawyers from the courthouse, fishermen, secretaries and tourists. The chatter of the clientele was somehow soothing, and I sipped my tea.

My cell phone rang, a rude violation in a restaurant. I got up and took the call outside.

"Carson?"

I recognized the voice, but couldn't place it immediately. "Yes?"

"It's Michael. I have to ride up to Poplarville this evening to check some mares. I thought you'd enjoy the drive. We could have dinner with the owners of the Lazy Q."

My automatic response was to refuse, but I didn't. "Sure. That sounds like it would be nice." I think I was as surprised as Michael.

"I'll pick you up about five-thirty?"

"My address is—"

"I know." He chuckled softly. "You have no secrets where your family is concerned."

"I suppose you know my ovulation schedule, too."

He laughed hard. "Your mama didn't lay much finish on you, did she, girl?"

"Not from lack of trying."

"As you remember, horse people are casual."

"I won't embarrass you by being overdressed." I hung up and returned to my meal with the strangest sensation, as if I had a secret. A good one.

15

My jeans were worn, the waistband nothing but threads in one place and the cuffs a ragged white. No pair I'd ever bought fit better, so I continued to wear them, even though my mother would have banished them to the trash. To offset the jeans, I wore a green silk blouse. I even ironed it, and touched my eyes with liner and mascara and my lips with a hint of lipstick. The summer humidity hadn't set in yet and my hair was straight, a heavy mass of dark blond. When appearances had been important to me, I'd kept it highlighted. Stress had taken care of that for me. I already had clumps of gray, not the salt-and-pepper sprinkling of Dorry's, but heavier ropes of silver.

Michael was on time, a feat for a veterinarian who was often waylaid by illness and emergency. He came up the sidewalk through the gathering dusk with a long, country-boy stride. It was the gait of a man who'd walked many a field in search of a cow or horse that was down or missing. Michael's love of animals had been a source of teasing in high school, when he refused to hunt with the other boys. He didn't make an issue of not hunting, but when asked, he'd simply said that killing gave him no pleasure.

"Do you want to use my shower?" I asked from the darkness of the porch. I could only imagine where he'd been and what he'd been up to.

"Muley Phillips has one in his barn. I cleaned up before I drove over." He came up the steps and I smelled cologne and soap. He wore jeans, a cotton snap shirt and a straw hat.

"If they retire the Marlboro man, you could fill in," I said. He was handsome in the lean economy of an Old West cowboy.

"Smoking's bad for you." He wasn't biting. "I don't think they do that ad anymore. Politically incorrect."

"The money that man made posing on a billboard would be mighty tempting. I never even saw him with a cigarette in his mouth."

"It's hard to believe a man can make a living by posing for pictures," he said, smiling. "You look good, Carson. I guess it's just a lifetime habit with you."

His words opened the door of the past, that long-ago time when he'd greeted me with a smile that said I belonged to him. "You look good," was always the first thing he'd say. Instead of making me uncomfortable, it gave me the smallest connection to the girl I'd once been.

"I'm ready whenever you are," I said. I was holding my purse, suddenly eager to go.

"At your service." He tucked my hand through his arm as he escorted me to the truck. Michael had learned a little suavity since our high school days.

The night had turned crisp, and Michael put the heater on low as we drove north to the rural stretches. He kept the truck at a steady seventy-five, and I recalled that even as a teenager he hadn't been one to speed. He'd never been reckless or careless.

"I've been reading your stories," he said. "You won't be here long, Carson. Soon the big time will be knocking on your door again."

"If I can get my drinking under control." I said it without bitterness.

"Everybody has something they have to master. If you want my two cents' worth, I'd say you don't have a problem with alcohol." He hesitated. "You have a problem with living."

If anyone else had lectured me, I would have gotten angry. Then I realized that wasn't true. Mitch Rayburn had offered help. Mitch was practically a stranger, and Michael was someone I'd once known intimately. I allowed them to counsel me, though I refused tenderness or concern from my husband or family. I couldn't have said why.

The silence in the truck had grown lengthy. "I can't sleep. I drink because I can't sleep. I can't take any more sleeping pills. They make me feel drugged and dead, and it's too hard to come back from that." In the gentle rocking of the truck, it seemed like an intimate confession.

"Nightmares?"

"Yeah." The word was raw. My emotions were always so close to the surface. It shamed me.

"I've talked a little with Dustin Yoder about his dreams. He suffers."

"I know." I'd seen my fate in Strange's desperate need for solitude. He didn't drink. He just lived alone, letting nature offer solace and companionship because he couldn't trust that offered by man.

"Dustin can recount how every man in his company died. He carried them out, sometimes in pieces, but it was Billy that undid him. He couldn't save your brother, and he can't stop blaming himself. He just relives that day over and over again in his dreams. I'm not sure if he's hoping for a different outcome or if he's punishing himself."

I'd revealed as much as I dared. "Speaking of a drink." I pulled a pint of Jack Daniel's from my purse. "On the night of my high school graduation, you came home from Auburn to help me celebrate. Remember?"

In the light of the dash, I could see that he was smiling. "I remember. You wanted to climb the water tower and spray paint your initials."

"You wouldn't let me."

"I brought you liquor, but I did have a little common sense."

A silence fell between us. We'd drunk the bourbon straight from the bottle and gone skinny-dipping in Bluff Creek. Then Michael had asked me to marry him. Both of us naked and shivering, he'd dropped to one knee in the white sand of the creek bank and offered me the ring.

"You made the right decision," he said, as if he was able to hear my thoughts.

"Did I?" Since Annabelle's death, I'd often wondered if I'd ever made a single right decision. Our conversation was about to flounder in deep emotion. "The decision now is, do you want a drink?" I'd meant the pint to be celebratory, not a reminder of a past that couldn't be reclaimed.

He took the bottle, held it a moment, then passed it back to me. "I've still got work to do."

I hit it lightly, screwed the cap on and put it on the seat

between us. Jack Daniel's had more burn than the vodka I usually drank. It felt good.

"Are these people we're going to visit friends of yours and Polly's?" I wanted to know the terrain.

"They know Polly, but I wouldn't say they were friends. Stephanie Jennings is the horsewoman. She's very bright, and gutsy. You'll like her. Richard is a doctor. It's a nice combination because no matter how hard Stephanie works, she isn't going to make a fortune with horses. Not here."

"Would Polly be upset about this visit?"

He considered it. "Yes, probably so, but not because she cares about me." He paused for at least a minute. "I was in Ocean Springs because I saw a lawyer. Polly knows this. She wants to believe I'm the cause. The easiest thing to do would be to blame me for cheating on her, which I haven't. But you'd be a perfect scapegoat if she knew about this. Then she'd never have to think about her role in what went wrong."

Michael wasn't being hard on his wife. I'd known Polly since first grade. She'd never been one to take the blame for her actions. "What about your daughter?"

"The truth is, I work too much. She'll be better off with her mother. Polly's a devoted mother. It's for the best."

I glanced at Michael furtively, studying his mouth. He would give Polly everything and start over. Money had never mattered to him. "I'm sorry, Michael."

"Penny will be sixteen next October. She's almost grown, Carson. She's on the phone 24-7. She's so boy crazy it scares me. She wants parties and fun. Polly will give her that."

He was right, of course. It still didn't make it easy. I snapped on the radio and found a country station with more music than chatter. We drove in silence for a while, the crescent moon guiding our way. The farther we got from the coast, the more the traffic thinned until we stopped passing other vehicles. The trees crowded close to the two-lane, and I was reminded of another time, when I was a teenager and Michael and I had driven into the woods at every chance to park and make love. I could remember it well, but it seemed a borrowed memory. Surely I had never been that young and carefree.

We drove into Poplarville and then through it. When we came to what seemed like a two-mile stretch of white vinyl fencing over pastures that looked inky-green in the truck lights, I knew we were at the Lazy Q. The barn was huge and lit like a cruise ship. When we got out, we were met by four Mexican workers and a woman in riding jeans, Western boots and a burgundy velour top that hugged her body. She was lithe and fit, and she held out her hand for a shake as she walked toward me.

"Stephanie Jennings," she said. "I've been reading your stories. I'm impressed."

"Thanks." I shook her hand.

She turned to Michael. "Let's finish with these mares. Carson, if you'd rather wait at the house, Richard has made a pitcher of martinis."

"I'll wait here." I'd seen horses checked for pregnancy, and I took a seat on a hay bale and waited as Michael examined three beautiful mares, all with positive results. The barn was immaculate. Fluffy shavings filled each of the twenty stalls. Horses with alert eyes and refined heads looked back at me. Gleaming leather halters hung in front of each door, which held a nameplate for the horse. Doc's Best Babe, Little Lulu Bar—I read the names.

"Do you race?" I asked Stephanie.

"No, we breed for competitive events and cow work. These mares are cow bred. Their foals from four years ago are taking top honors now in cutting. I could run through the bloodlines." She grinned.

I shook my head. "Sorry, it would be Greek to me."

"Michael said you ride."

"Just for pleasure."

"You'll have to come out sometime. We have a lot of trails and plenty of horses."

It was a kind and generous offer to a stranger.

"Thanks, I'd like that."

Michael washed up in a bathroom with hot water, and we walked up to the house, a trio chattering about horses and riding. The doctor met us on the patio with the promised pitcher of martinis. They were chilled to perfection and I sipped mine with pleasure. The night was magnificent. Stars glittered like fairy-tossed silver in a sky undimmed by the pollution of city lights.

"This is lovely," I said. "I grew up in the country and I miss it. My work often keeps me in a city, but this is where I feel I belong."

"We love it," Stephanie answered. "Richard has a long drive to New Orleans, where he practices, but he only goes in three times a week."

"You're not a surgeon, then?" I half stated.

"No, psychiatrist," he said. His smile was wry. "You know what they say, the people who go into psychiatry are there because they're crazy."

I laughed, but I cut my eyes at Michael. It occurred to me that this was a setup. Then I knew better. Michael didn't deal from the bottom of the deck. Not even for my own good. He would never sandbag me.

"What kind of practice do you have?" I asked.

"Primarily pediatric. A lot of mental and emotional disturbances present themselves at puberty, but the conditions actually start in early childhood."

He didn't seem reluctant to talk about his work, and I was curious. A maid came out with a tray of canapés. Everyone was looking at me, so I took a small pastry topped with pâté and black currants. It was rich and delicious, a nice contrast to the dry martini.

"Would you mind if I asked some theoretical questions about a story I'm working on?" I asked him.

"Heavens, please ask him," Stephanie said, laughing. "When Michael is here, Richard has to listen to our endless jabber about horses. No one ever asks him about his work."

Richard laughed easily. "She's right."

I was serious. "You've read about the murders on the coast?"

He nodded. "Terrible. I feel for those families."

"What would make someone stop killing for twenty-four years and then resume?"

He thought about it, his gray eyes unfocused behind his glasses. "Remember, I specialize in children. This would fall more in the realm of criminal psychiatry. With that said, I'll make an educated guess. I'd say that either the killer had moved away and was continuing to kill elsewhere, because this type of killer doesn't stop, or else he was confined so that he couldn't kill. Prison or a mental institution."

"What if the discovery of the bodies prompted him to begin killing again?"

Richard paced the patio, the olives bobbing in his drink. "My understanding of the pathology of this kind of killer is that they can't stop or control it. To have a dry spell of twenty-four years indicates fairly disciplined control. That's virtually unheard of."

Richard cocked his head as he thought, an owlish man trained to follow the twisted thoughts of the insane. "I'd say it's far more likely that this last murder was committed by a copycat."

"But how would a copycat have known about the missing ring fingers?" Too late I realized I'd spoken out of turn. "I'm sorry. That was privileged information. Please don't repeat it."

"So, the killer cuts off the ring finger of each victim. He takes a trophy." Richard considered. "If he is a copycat, he has inside knowledge of the crime. He's a police officer, member of the media, relative or close associate of the original killer."

"Can you tell me anything else about this killer?" I asked, casting a furtive glance at Michael. He and Stephanie were deep in a conversation about horses.

"I'd say this killer has an issue with the mother figure. I'm sure you've heard of men who suffer from the Madonna-whore complex. They love sexy women until they marry, then they want their women to act like virgins. There's something triggered in a man by matrimony that can change the dynamics of a relationship drastically."

"But these girls weren't married."

"No, but judging from the photos in the paper, they're

all of marriageable age. They're young and ripe and ready to marry and reproduce. It's their potential to become wives and mothers that offends him. If I had to make a guess, I'd say the killer's mother abused him. He viewed her as his protector, and she turned on him, either by neglect or by action. She warped the wife-mother role for him forever. It's not a sexual thing as much as it was a parental failure in his eyes. If I'm right about this, the girls were not raped."

"Pamela Sparks wasn't. We can't say about the others."

"This isn't about sex or power or control. This is about betrayal. And there will be a trigger. Something that sends him back to childhood, which would be a place he views as a living hell."

I felt cold. "Would the copycat suffer from the same set of issues?"

"Doubtful. If it is a copycat, I believe his motive would be fame. He'd be proud of his cleverness and ability to bring fear to a community. It would be about power."

"Thank you, Richard."

"Remember, this is a conversation of theories. I'm not a specialist in this field."

Michael came over and put his arm around me. "Dinner's ready."

"Please, keep the business about the fingers—"

"Confidential," Richard said, patting my shoulder. "I'll bury it along with all of the other secrets I play host to."

16

The fragrance of pine trees filled my dreams, a pungent smell, clean and filled with varied pleasures. The scent triggered a panorama of scenes, dark pine forests with a carpet of brown needles underfoot, woodland vales where crooked limbs dipped over a creek just perfect for dangling feet on a hot summer day and soft fronds of feathery wild ferns crushed into a perfect cushion. I was young, a teenage girl, and I was lying in the soft embrace of the green earth. Sunlight dappled my skin, my perfect skin, unblemished by scars or time or disappointment. I heard laughter coming from the pine trees, and I rose up on my elbows to greet my lover, greedy for his touch.

A figure stepped out of the trees, a slender man with casual grace. I couldn't see his face with the sun at his back. His body was fringed in golden light. He was beautiful, Adonis, a gift from the gods.

He came toward me, dropping to his knees beside me, and I felt his hand on my thigh.

"Daniel?" I was confused. I had thought it was someone else, but I couldn't think who.

"Mi amore," he whispered in my ear, his words generating a torrent of passion. His hand slid up my thigh as his other hand stroked my breast. If I had not recognized his voice, I would have known his touch. "I've come such a far way to see you, my love," he said. I could only moan, my need consuming thought and reason.

He bent to kiss me, but before our lips could meet, a shadow fell over us. Night had suddenly fallen, and the woods were now sinister. Daniel disappeared.

"Mama!"

I sat up, alone, deep in the woods. But I wasn't alone. My daughter was there, and she sounded frightened. "Annabelle!" But there was only the echo of her voice, her single cry for my help and protection.

I realized I was sitting up in bed. I turned on the light and checked the clock. It was nearly 2:00 a.m. I wouldn't sleep again, so I got up and went to the kitchen.

Before I'd moved into my house, I'd had walls removed, windows replaced, the hardwood floors refinished and all the curtains removed. I'd gutted the house and opened it up. I'd thrown myself into the renovation, hoping that it would spark something inside me. It hadn't, but I did enjoy the feelings of not being closed in. When it was day, sunlight filtered through the trees and shrubs and vines that acted as my curtains. It was a greenish light that gave me a sense of peace. At night, though, the openness was different. I felt exposed.

The cats jumped up on my lap, and I stroked their arching backs. I picked up the phone. Nicaragua was in the same time zone. I dialed, hearing the foreign two rings of the phone. Often the lines were down and took weeks, sometimes months, to repair. But the phone was ringing somewhere. I couldn't guarantee that it was my ex-husband's extension, though.

"Hola."

Daniel's voice was wide-awake. Relief rushed over me, and desire. Remnants of the dream were hiding in the shadows of my heart. "It's me," I said, willing my voice not to shake.

"Are you okay?" Instant concern.

"Yes." I had to force myself to continue. "I had a dream. I miss you."

There was a long pause. His hand covered the telephone and he said something in Spanish I couldn't hear. A chill slipped over me. Nicaragua was a very social country. Parties of the upper class moved from hacienda to beach house to mountain dwelling without ever breaking up. Business was conducted, but it was often mingled with pleasure. Daniel could have a business associate with him at two in the morning. It was possible, but I knew better. He was a divorced man, free to do what he chose.

"I'm sorry, Daniel," I said when he came back on the line. "Call me when you have time. I'm fine, just a little shaken."

The silence told me he was considering his options. "Tell me about the dream," he requested.

There had once been a time when I shared everything with my husband. But now he was no longer my husband, and I had no right.

"Same old, same old," I said. "I feel much better now. I'm so sorry I called at this hour." I made my voice strong, wryly aware of my foolishness.

"You said you missed me."

There it was. Daniel's love for me was banked. He hadn't walked away from our marriage, even when it consisted of hauling me out of bars so drunk I'd lost my shoes and couldn't stand up alone. He'd held my head when I was sick, and he'd never censured me or tried to make me feel ashamed. He didn't have to. I was dying from guilt and shame. I'd left him, telling him that I needed a clean break from everything in the past. But I'd learned I couldn't leave my guilt behind. I had to leave him, because I could never risk another child, and he deserved the family he so desperately wanted.

"My work is going well," I said, changing the subject. I could not lie to him. If he'd found someone to share his early mornings, I didn't want to interfere.

"Good. You sound…"

"Sober," I supplied. "I am."

"I'll be home Sunday. My trip has been cut short. I have to get back to Miami to take care of some problems. I'll call you Sunday evening."

"Daniel, are you okay?" I realized it had been a long time since I'd asked him that question.

"Yes, Carson. I am good." The flowing cadence of his accent made the words roll like a gentle wave.

I realized I wanted to know about his companion, but I couldn't ask. We were divorced. Daniel would tell me everything I needed to know to keep from being hurt. When the time came.

"Sleep well," he said.

I heard the echo of the past. *"Mi amore."* But it was only in my head. The line buzzed empty. For a long time I sat in the darkness, trying to sort through my emotions. I didn't make any progress, except in admitting that I had feelings. But they were all jumbled and knotted. I'd done the right thing in letting Daniel go. My head was so messed up that I might never be able to find the love we'd once shared so effortlessly. Sure, he could still make me tingle with desire, but life and marriage were beyond those blurred moments of sensation.

I thought about Michael and Mitch, one man I'd known, and one who seemed to offer a new chance. My therapist had told me, before I fired her, that life would return to me whether I wanted it or not. If I didn't kill myself with alcohol, new emotions would grow. How I dealt with them would depend largely on how I resolved my guilt over Annabelle's death. She said this with a large measure of trepidation. She was right, which was why I fired her. So I sat alone in the darkness and wondered if I would ever be able to love anyone again.

I'd been searching the area for almost a week for members of the Kyle family, and at last I'd found Ammon Kyle, a man without a phone or credit cards. Actually, Avery told me where to look. In a strange coincidence, Ammon worked with Joe Welford, Pamela Sparks's fiancé, at M&N Motors. Coincidence is rarely that. I felt the rush of excitement as I drove to the garage.

I hadn't bothered going into the office. Exhausted, I'd fallen asleep at five and slept until Miss Vesta licked my left eyelid open at ten o'clock. I'd called Hank and told him I'd overslept and that I was going straight to M&N Motors.

The sky was overcast, a gunmetal-gray that promised torrential rain and bolts of lightning that felled huge oaks, zapped televisions, microwaves and computers, and occasionally quick-fried a golfer. M&N Motors was off Hospital Road in Ocean Springs, not ten minutes from my house. Once a pleasant rural road, it was now a shortcut to the interstate.

The sign out front had been freshly painted, and cars jammed the parking lot. Four work bays were filled. When I walked over to a man in blue overalls with grease stains, he directed me to the office. "Tell the girl what's wrong, and she'll set up an appointment."

"I need to see Ammon Kyle," I said.

The man frowned. "Ammon!" He turned on his heel. "Ammon!"

A slender man with a balding head rolled out from under a minivan. He wore thick glasses, and he came toward me with an expectant smile. "Can I help you?"

"I'm sorry to trouble you at work." I should have done this after he finished his job, I realized. He was busy. I told him who I was. "I'm here to talk about your sister, if you have a moment."

"Charlotte," he said, wiping grease or something from beneath the lens of his glasses. "I've been thinking about her a lot lately. I've waited a long time to give her a proper burial." He looked at the man who'd called him. "Just a minute. I'm due a break." He walked over, conversed with the man, then came back. "Let's go in the break room. Joe's working beside me, and I don't want him to hear it. He's having a hard enough time."

One of my questions was already answered. I followed him into a room with two Formica tables stained with grease. The floor was concrete, also stained. There was a

Coke machine and a refrigerator with black fingerprints all over the handle. I took the chair across from him.

"Would you care for some coffee?"

I could see that it was thick and might possibly be the culprit making all the stains instead of grease. "No, thanks. I've had my quota."

He sat down, folding his hands on top of the table. "What do you want to know?"

My basic theory was that all of the girls had something in common—their engagement, real or otherwise. "Was your sister seeing anyone seriously?" I asked.

"She had a fella." He looked down at his hands. "She was in love with him. Charlie King. After she disappeared, I thought maybe he was involved, but he wasn't."

"How can you be certain?"

"When Charlotte didn't come home that night, I was desperate. See, things were tough. She and I were the oldest, and when our folks up and disappeared one day, we were left with the little ones. There were five of us altogether. Charlotte did the cooking and cleaning and such, and I quit school and got a job. We worked as a team. Charlotte wasn't the kind of girl to skip out on the young-uns, so that next morning I had a long talk with Charlie." He rubbed at a grease spot on his hands. "He didn't hurt her. The way she disappeared, it's like it killed him, too. He died in a car wreck not a week later."

I jotted a few notes. "Your parents left?"

"Here one morning when we left for school, gone when we got back. No note. Nothing."

"Did you call the police?" I wondered if the fifth body could be one of the parents.

"No. If I'd done that, child welfare would have come and taken my brothers and sisters. Besides, my folks just left. They took all the food in the refrigerator and the car. It was an old rag heap, but it was all we had to get around in. They didn't care." His voice had gotten harder. "But we stayed together. We were a family."

"How old were you when they abandoned you?"

"Sixteen. Charlotte was fifteen. For seven years, we held the family together. She was twenty-two when she died. Jim was in tenth grade. He was the last. Charlotte was getting ready to have her own life, and I made her feel bad about it. All she wanted was to marry Charlie and have a little house of her own, a portion of life for herself. I made her feel bad for wanting that."

Some wounds never healed. Finding Charlotte's body had ripped Ammon's wide open. "The night she disappeared, do you know where she was going?"

"It was a Friday night. She was going out to meet some of her friends." A painful smile touched his face. "She was excited. I remember that. She'd bought a new blouse. She had on that pink blouse and lipstick that matched." He shook his head. "I almost asked her to stay home, but I didn't. She'd stayed home so many Friday nights. I knew she needed her own life. It was past time. So I didn't say anything except to be careful, and I watched her walk out the door and get in a car with some of her girlfriends. They tooted the horn and laughed as they drove away. They were planning the wedding. Charlotte had a dress set aside, and the bridesmaids were all picked out. The wedding was all she talked about."

"Where did they go?"

"Charlotte loved to dance. She'd dance with the younger kids in the kitchen while she was cooking."

"Did she go to the Gold Rush?"

"Yeah. That place had the best band. All the young people liked to go there. The shows were fancy back then, with the dancers and all. Then the band would crank up and everybody had a good time."

"She was with her friends. What happened?"

He rubbed at the spot on his finger. "Her friends said she got hot dancing. She went outside for some air and didn't come back in. Charlie was supposed to meet them, so they thought maybe she'd left with him. She didn't have much time alone with him, and they figured she'd taken advantage of a few hours together." His hands finally rested on the table. One knuckle had been skinned slightly.

"I'm sorry, Mr. Kyle. What happened after that?"

"In the morning, when Charlie showed up looking for her and I realized she was gone, I couldn't take it. I drank for a while. The truth is, I drank for months. I was a mean drunk. I haven't spoken to my brothers or sisters in over twenty years. Charlotte sacrificed it all for family, and now they're scattered like dust in the wind."

"Do you remember her friends?"

He shook his head. "When they found the bodies in that grave, the police came around, and I tried to remember." He shook his head. "I was working two jobs. I'd come home tired and sleep, then get up and go to work. I didn't pay attention to Charlotte's girlfriends. The last thing I needed to do was get sweet on a girl, so I ignored all of 'em."

"If you think of anything, would you call me?" I gave him my card. "One last thing. What kind of man is Joe Welford?"

He looked at me, immediately catching what my interest was. "He's a man in mortal pain. He loved Pamela Sparks and don't get ideas that he'd hurt her. You stay away from him with your questions and inferences. He got enough of that from the police."

I nodded. I had stories to write back at the office, and I'd had all the pain I could take for one day. Joe Welford was safe from me.

17

I was absorbed in my work when my phone rang. I'd just sent the copy to the desk, and I was surprised to hear Avery Boudreaux's voice.

"We got the tests on Pamela Sparks's blood. She was drugged, and you were right. She'd been given Thorazine." There was a pause, and I hoped he wasn't remembering what I'd said at the time. "Carson, we need to keep this information quiet. It's a good lead. One of our few."

Avery called because he had a favor to ask. He wanted me to hold information again, and he realized that if I got the facts on my own, I could print them or not. If he gave them to me, I might feel that I owed him.

"Did you check the drugstores I suggested?"

"Every pill they've sold is accounted for. This had to come from somewhere else."

"Stolen?"

"We're looking into it. Once we find the source, I'll tell you." There was a pause. "I can't believe I'm going to ask you this, but I promised my wife. Our daughter thinks she wants to be a journalist." There was actual pain in his voice—a father torn about accommodating his daughter's wishes when she wanted something he disdained. "Would you consider talking with Jill? She's read all of your stories. She thinks you're 'wicked cool.' That's a direct quote. My wife said I wouldn't receive any marital pleasures until I got a yes from you."

I'd never met Avery's wife, but I liked her. "Just understand that the last budding journalist I spoke with immediately grew a forked tail and belched fire."

"Ah, that's a relief. I thought it would be worse."

We laughed, and I agreed to meet with Jill the following morning at 9:00 a.m.

I checked my messages at home while I waited for Hank's corrections. I watched him read the story while the phone messages played in my ear. I sat up a little at the sound of Mitch Rayburn's voice. I'd deliberately not thought about whether he would call or not, but I realized I'd subconsciously wondered.

"Sorry the week has gone by," he said. "I had a good time at the Brown Raisin. Good enough that I'd like to do it again. How about dinner tonight? This time I pick."

Fridays were my night to go to Lissa's Lounge for martinis, karaoke and cigarettes. I didn't want to share that with Mitch or anyone else. Saturday evening I was obligated to go to Leakesville. I'd worried my parents nearly to death. The least I could do was show up and dance a few choruses to my mother's tune. "Rush Limbaugh has already booked me, but I'll cancel him."

"I'll pick you up at eight."

I hung up. Out in the newsroom, Hank gave me a thumbs-up, effectively releasing me for the rest of the day. I picked up my purse and stopped at his desk. "That fifth body. I just can't leave it alone. I have a hunch I'm going after."

"The cops are at a dead end, huh?"

If they had something real, they weren't sharing with me. Of course, dinner with Mitch might be more about work than pleasure. "I talked with Avery. He says they have nothing new except the toxicology on Pamela, which he asked me not to print. There was Thorazine in her blood. I said I'd hold off on printing it while they try to track down where it came from." I didn't tell him that I'd suggested they screen for that substance. In a larger crime lab, such a test would have been automatic. Biloxi, though, wasn't a den of murder. Such blood tests weren't always mandatory.

Hank's eyebrows rose. "You're being awful accommodating to the local law."

I was. But I had my reasons. "I'm trying to act as a counterbalance to Brandon. On the whole, Avery has been very forthcoming with me."

"And Mitch? Has he been sharing a little pillow talk?"

I had to smile. Hank had some excellent sources, obviously. "I'm afraid I haven't lured him into bed so that I could later blackmail the story out of him. But that's on my to-do list."

"My advice is to fuck him so hard he yells out everything you want to know. Blackmail is so tedious, and it takes too long."

I laughed and blushed. "That's grounds for a sexual-harassment suit."

He made a concerned face. "And I thought it was a compliment." He grew serious. "You're looking better, Carson. Got some pink in those cheeks. Must have slipped down from your eyes because they're clear." His hand moved across his desk and touched mine. "Get out of here before I assign you more work."

I frowned. "I haven't seen Brandon today."

"He's been at the country club with the bigwigs from the newspaper chain. Negotiating."

I could see the worry on Hank's face, but I had nothing reassuring to offer him. Chances were that Brandon would sell. Everyone else had. Running an independent paper was hard work and expensive. The larger chains could homogenize the news and distribute it over their own wire services, pander to politicians to gain favors and reduce lawsuits and overhead by printing pabulum designed to inform and offend no one. It was the way of the world, or so I'd been told.

"I'll see you later."

"You turned in an excellent story, Carson. It goes beyond reporting to show the horror of those murders. The repercussions continue to damage those families. You have a real talent."

"Thanks," I said, glad that I was facing out of the newsroom and giving the curious only my back.

The storm clouds that had gathered earlier in the day were massed to the west. I ran to my truck and considered going home to change clothes. I'd be a lot more comfortable in jeans and boots, so I drove east. Lightning forked to the north, and the smell of rain was heavy and mingled with the slightly brackish scent of the Sound. The rain hadn't begun to fall, but it was imminent as I hurried in my side door.

The cats were dozing in preparation for night, when I would want to sleep and they would want me not to. I

roused them by rubbing their bellies. I put on my favorite
old jeans, a cotton sweater and some black cowgirl boots.
Daniel called them roach stompers because the pointed
toes were perfect for corners and other tight places where
bugs loved to hide. Florida had waged a campaign to refer
to the disgusting black insects as palmetto bugs—a more
socially acceptable sounding term. Right. They were huge,
flying roaches that could live a week with their heads
severed. I was the unofficial death squad.

The traffic had thinned by the time I got back on
Highway 90 and headed across Biloxi Bay to Barnacle
Bill's. It was one of the few pre-casino bars left along the
water, and it had a loyal clientele. I was looking for
someone. I wasn't sure who, but if anyone could help me,
it would be the crowd at B.B.'s, as it was fondly called.

B.B.'s was a shack on stilts that jutted out into the Sound
and was a thumbed nose at the neon and grandiose design
of the casinos. The parking lot was jammed at all hours,
and just as I got out of the truck, the sky opened up. I made
a dash for it but was thoroughly soaked by the time I got
to the door. I walked in and felt a dozen eyes on my
clinging sweater. I had two options; one was going home
and I wasn't leaving.

The barkeep was too young and too handsome. He
handed me some towels and I dried the pictures I'd protected in my purse and then my wet hair and face. There
was nothing to be done about my clothes. I ordered a
martini and the barkeep's gaze dropped down to the photographs of Pamela Sparks and the four girls killed in 1981.

"Are you a cop?" he asked.

"Reporter."

He nodded. "I wasn't born when those girls disappeared. Even if I had been, I would have been stuck on a farm in Nebraska."

"What about this one?" I pointed to Pamela.

He shook his head. "Most of the crowd here is older. Boat people, those who lived here before the casinos. They talk about how good it used to be all the time."

"Boring, huh?"

"Things change. That's progress." He shrugged and pulled a beer for a customer. "No point clinging to what's gone."

I studied him, seeing the lack of pain in his handsome face. He'd yet to lose anything worth clinging to. I had no desire to warn him of the road ahead. Besides, he wouldn't listen. Youth was wonderful in that way.

"I'm looking for some of those old-timers. Maybe folks talking about the Gold Rush bar."

He mixed a tray of cocktails before he had time to answer. "See that woman in the red dress?" He nodded to a pretty brunette who was in deep conversation with a man.

"Yeah."

"Her name's Babette. Ask her. I've heard her talk about that bar and how they had dancers, drugs and other things."

"Thanks," I said, leaving a twenty on the bar to pay for my drink and the information. I approached Babette's table with caution. The conversation looked intense and personal, and not all that happy. The brunette looked up with a frown—the man with curiosity.

"Excuse me." I introduced myself. I was holding the photos in my hand.

The woman reached up for them, an eager look on her face. "Yeah, I saw them in the newspaper. That was awful.

I used to hang out at the Gold Rush." She glanced at her friend.

"Do you recognize any of the girls?" I'd put Pamela's photo back in my purse. The Gold Rush had been razed by the time she was killed.

She looked at the photos closely. "That one." She pointed at Maria Lopez. "I remember her because she could really dance. She was underage, I'm pretty sure, but nobody cared. They didn't bust places back then like they do now. Alvin Orley ran the club and he either paid off the cops or had something on them so they left him alone." She shrugged. "It was a different time. Now they'll put you in jail for driving home from a bar. Pigs." The last word was uttered under her breath, causing me to wonder how many DUIs she'd acquired.

"Do you recognize any of the others?"

She looked again. "I can't be sure. We were all that age back then, young and full of life." She handed the pictures back, turning to her companion in an abrupt dismissal of my questions.

"Excuse me one more time," I said. "If you remember the Gold Rush, would you remember anyone who worked there?"

"What are you implying?" she asked hotly. She started to stand but the man touched her arm.

"I'm not implying anything." I suddenly understood her antagonism. She'd worked at the Gold Rush, and not as a bartender. "I thought maybe you knew someone who worked behind the bar or a musician. Like that."

Her ruffled feathers were slightly soothed. "Everyone knows Stella Blue. She's still around. She danced there, did some bartending. She was the most beautiful woman on the coast back then."

"Do you know where I might find her?"

"Try McBeth's. It's off Thirteenth Avenue in Gulfport. It opens at noon. It's a bartenders' bar, but Stella is there at three. Business interests."

"Thanks," I said, heading for the door. I had a lot of time to kill, and I didn't want to do it sitting at a bar. One thing I'd promised myself was that I'd never work drunk. Hungover, maybe, but not drunk going into an interview. There had to be some standards, even if they were minimal.

The rain had let up and the heat from my own body had begun to dry my clothes. Leaping mud puddles, I made my way across the parking lot. The casinos had put in little trolleys to haul suckers from one casino to the next, and I hopped one and rode the half mile to the Grand. It was a huge building with bright colors and a small theater that semiresuscitated the careers of aging performers. It wasn't uncommon to see shows by Michael Bolton, David Allen Coe, Tom Jones and even a couple of the famous tenors.

My parents had been to a few of the shows, and it was good for them to get dressed up and go out. The casinos had raised the level of entertainment, and even made it affordable. They'd also perfected the art of spinning dreams from dust. Trouble was, dust returned to dust.

I walked into the deafening roar of the slot machines and human jubilation or defeat. People milled everywhere. Some looked lost and others on a mission from God. Banks of slot machines were against every wall and in stands. A swiveling red stool was in front of each machine. It wasn't uncommon to see someone playing three machines at once. To approach was a declaration of war.

A thick haze of smoke hung over the room, even though it was well ventilated. The craving for a cigarette was instantaneous. My fingers curled at the need for another drink but I brushed that back. I was working. I had to hang on to that thought.

I moved down the brightly colored carpet, taking in the gaiety and desperation that marked such places. When I'd first heard that Las Vegas casinos were coming to the coast, I'd had a mental image of James Bond, the real one—Sean Connery—in a tuxedo with a pair of dice in his hands. Reality was a bitter draught. This was Club Corpulent in khakis and polyester.

Stopping at the blackjack tables, I watched a few hands. It was a simple game, if you could count cards and calculate odds in a matter of seconds. Most people played with the hope that Lady Luck would see them through.

I'd heard the buffet in the Grand was delicious, and I decided to eat a snack to absorb the alcohol. I got in the long line and inched forward with everyone else. If the glitz and glamour of the casinos was hollow, the buffet was replete. There was enough food to feed a Third World country, which used to be what Mississippi was considered.

I got a tray of food and sat down. Instead of grace, I thanked my lucky stars that gaming wasn't my vice, or I'd be sunk. The casinos didn't bring gambling to the Gulf Coast. They just legalized it and turned it into entertainment.

The chicken was crisp and moist. I ate slowly, knowing I had lots of time to kill. I drank my tea, and the waitress came around and refilled it. When I finished my meal, I ordered coffee and scanned the faces of those involved in their food. I had once known a lot of people on the Gulf Coast. I didn't recognize anyone in the vast room.

"Carson Lynch!"

I looked behind me to see Justina Cooley, a girl with whom I'd gone to high school. She looked tired and very much alone. "Would you like to join me?"

She took the chair and pushed her tray aside. To my surprise, she blinked back tears.

"Justina, what's wrong?"

"Mama has cancer. Your brother-in-law operated on her two weeks ago. They called him in because it had spread from her ovaries to her liver."

I swallowed. I knew the prognosis. "I'm sorry."

"It's about to kill me. I guess you don't know that Gary and I divorced. My son is over here staying with his dad. I'm supposed to get him later. I didn't have anything else to do, and I thought if I came here with all these people I couldn't fall apart. It's, uh, not working as well as I planned." She sniffed.

"Can I do anything?" Her mother was near the same age as mine, in her mid-sixties. It seemed impossible. I remembered Mrs. Cooley in black slacks and bright sweaters with her slender feet in flats with jewels across the vamp. She'd been the epitome of style in 1980s Leakesville. Fear spiked through me.

Justina pulled herself together with grim determination. "I'm sorry, Carson. I heard you had enough grief of your own."

"There's plenty for everyone." I sipped my coffee.

"Tommy did everything he could do for her. It's a good

thing Dorry married him and got him to stay in this part of the country. I've heard he's had offers from Cedars of Sinai and Johns Hopkins, but Dorry said no. We've had a real problem keeping good doctors around. The income just isn't there."

"Neither are the lawsuits," I said. "Folks around here still view those in the medical profession as lesser gods."

She stared at me, trying to read the underlying tone of my words. "Are things okay with Tommy and Dorry?"

"You tell me," I said. Justina looked down at the table. "If you know something, please share."

"There's a nurse. She just made me…uncomfortable. She was sort of proprietary, if you know what I mean."

I did. I'd seen it before. The good doctor's little helper who turns adoring eyes on him at every occasion and wins his attention, then has to be sure that no one else ousts her. Tommy had an ego. A big one. He was as prone to eager adoration as any other egomaniac. But he got plenty of it at home.

"How uncomfortable did it make you?" I asked.

"Pretty much. She was brushing her ass against him at every chance, and he wasn't backing away."

"Thanks, Justina. Did you get her name?"

"I didn't. She was a surgical nurse, though, because I haven't seen her since Mama was taken off the surgery floor." She rearranged her napkin for the tenth time. "Don't tell this to Dorry. I don't have anything conclusive, and this kind of rumor can ruin a marriage."

"I wouldn't dare go home with a nasty tale about Tommy. No one would believe me if I had pictures."

Justina smiled sadly. "Your mother picked him out for Dorry. I remember when they were both at college and he dumped Dorry for that other Dixie Darling. He'd go with one for a while and once she started pressuring him, he'd dump her and go back to the other."

"Dorry should have left him then," I said, remembering my sister's face streaked with tears. "She married him and dropped out of college. That was what he wanted, a stay-at-home wife to provide comforts while he was in medical school. Dorry's youngest is only nine." Dorry was effectively stuck.

"Have you seen Gary since you've been on the coast?" She didn't look too eager as she asked.

"No. I doubt our paths would cross." I remembered her husband as a golfer who liked mahogany bars with waiters in white jackets.

"I hear Gary's out every night when he doesn't have our son." She smiled, a tired attempt at being blasé. "I just don't have it in me to get dressed up to go out."

"I haven't seen Gary, but I have seen Michael."

She grinned, and I saw the teenage girl who'd encouraged me to date Michael Batson. "He's a good man," she said. "Polly's a fool. He always loved you, anyway. Wouldn't it be something if—?"

"We can't go back to prom night," I said, regret edging my voice. Sometimes it was so easy to slip the bonds of time and float in the free space of youth.

"Few people get a second chance, Carson. I never knew your husband, but from what I hear he was a fine man."

My skin was suddenly warm. "He is."

She studied me. "You still love him, don't you?"

"Probably."

She reached across the table and patted my hand.

"When did everything become so complicated? One minute Gary and I were in love, and the next, it was like we'd shut down those feelings. We didn't dislike each other. There just wasn't any passion there. When we decided to divorce, it was simply exhausting. I couldn't even work up the energy to get angry. I just wanted it over. That was four years ago."

"Are you seeing anyone?" I asked.

She shrugged, her gaze falling on the plate of food she hadn't touched. "I date, but it's like something inside me has died. I can't work up enthusiasm for anyone. I don't blame Gary—I think it's me."

"Sometimes your body goes numb to protect itself."

"My life is slipping away from me, and I'm in some twilight state." She shook her head. "I owe my boy more than that."

"What about a rest?" I asked. "Maybe a spa or someplace where you could go and be tended to. I suspect it's been a while since anyone met your needs in that way."

"A long while," she said. "But I can't now. I'm sitting with Mother at the hospital during the day. She's in a lot of pain."

I didn't know what to say. I couldn't imagine sitting with someone I loved and watching him or her suffer and die. "You should eat," I said, nodding at her plate.

"I'm not really hungry."

"I've heard that," I said. "But you should eat something, anyway."

She took a bite of her vegetables. "How is it at the paper?"

"It feels good to be writing again."

"Those murders have been awful," she said. "Those girls were being abducted and killed, and we were running around Leakesville gossiping about our first kiss. That killer could have been in Leakesville as easily as Biloxi."

What she said was true, and a door opened in my mind. Why were the girls taken from the Biloxi area? What was the killer doing here in 1981? What job brought him to town and what took him away? At least it was a lead, something to look into.

"Carson? Are you okay?"

"I was thinking about the killer and the Gulf Coast and why this location."

"Keesler brought in a lot of strangers. Remember, back in Leakesville everyone knew everyone else. Our parents knew every boy we dated or even talked to. Strangers just didn't come to town and talk to the local girls."

What she said was true. Of course there were bars, legal or illegal, as Greene County went wet and then dry again. But these were places where everyone knew everyone else. Strangers were closely watched.

"How different could the coast have been?" I asked.

"Some. It drew tourists. Strangers were welcomed instead of suspected. Add the airmen to that, and you had a fair mix of people who weren't natives. There were the college kids, too. They'd come to the coast for the weekend from Hattiesburg or New Orleans. Biloxi and Gulfport had that kind of allure. Folks remembered when Jayne Mansfield was decapitated."

I'd forgotten that story. The actress had been riding on the back of a convertible when there had been an accident. It had happened back in the '50s, but it was still legend, though the details were now disputed. Peculiar what events become tourist attractions. Tragedy is a big draw.

Justina pushed her plate away. "I guess I'll go get my son. We have a bit of a drive back to Leakesville."

"I hope things improve." It was an empty statement.

"Thank you." She stood and leaned down to hug me, the light fragrance of perfume in her hair. "Come see me, Carson. When this is over, maybe we could go to that spa together. Drink margaritas and paint our toenails cherry-red."

"Sure," I said, and then watched her walk out the dining room and slowly disappear on the escalator. I walked out after her and stood in the parking lot, deliberating my next move. I pulled out my cell phone and dialed Kevin Graves at home, knowing I could leave a message. Instead of a machine, I got him.

"Kevin, are you still doing PI work on the side?" I asked.

"Sure. It pays better than police work."

"I need to hire you. A surveillance case."

"Sure." He was curious. "Who, where and when?"

"Dr. Tommy Pritchard. I'll check his schedule and see what time he's supposed to get off today. It would be good if you could do this tonight."

"What do you suspect Dr. Pritchard of doing?" he asked.

"Cheating on his wife."

"I'm sorry, Carson. I have to tell you, though, Dorry's not going to appreciate you meddling in this. If he is screwing around on her, she probably knows already. She won't want to hear it coming from you."

"I may not tell her. I just want to know the score myself."

"Okay, sure." He sounded dubious, and with good cause. Kev had gone to high school with Dorry. They'd dated their junior year, before she became infatuated with Tommy. Kev knew the rivalry between me and my sister.

"I'll mail a check, just tell me how much. Or I can drive over to Mobile and deliver it."

"Don't worry about it until we have something to show for our efforts. Any idea where he might be going when he isn't headed home?"

"I understand he's very friendly with a nurse."

"Must be those sexy white stockings and shoes."

I had to laugh. Kev had a way of putting things in perspective. "I'll call you back and leave the particulars."

"I don't want to be around when you tell Dorry."

"Right." Kevin would do an excellent job, and he would be discreet. Tommy would never know he was being followed.

I called the University of South Alabama Medical Center and was switched to the surgical ward when I said I was Tommy's wife. I got a nurse to tell me that Dr. Pritchard had finished surgery at ten and had gone to his office to see patients. I called his office and was told that I couldn't speak to him. He was with a patient—and would be until he finished at four. His nurse would return his calls then.

"Actually, I need to speak with his surgical nurse," I said sweetly. "My mother had surgery two weeks ago and I have a question. I don't want to bother the doctor. I'm sure the nurse can help me."

"She'll call you this evening or in the morning."

"Is her name Susan?"

"No. It's Debbie Leigh."

"Please ask her to call when she has time. I know how busy she is," I said, sounding suitably cowed and in awe of the power of a surgical nurse. I left a fake number and hung up. Getting to talk to the president of the United States was easier than getting Tommy on the line. He had a barricade of women, and they would sacrifice themselves to keep him away from his patients. No wonder doctors were sued all the time.

I called Kev back and gave him what I had.

"I'll check in when I have something."

"Thanks." I hung up feeling only a little sick. My mother and sister thought nothing of butting into my life. Why was I suddenly nauseous at my own ability to interfere? Because if I found out something definite, I'd have to take action. I thought of what Justina Cooley had told me. I wasn't the kind of person to sit around and let my sister be abused by an egomaniac husband and a bitch with an itchy ass.

18

Of all the coastal cities, Gulfport's downtown was the largest with several blocks of multistory brick buildings. McBeth's was located on the ground floor of what had once been a mercantile. I entered and took a seat at the bar. My order of a Diet Coke was met without curiosity. A bartender's bar was one place where a nondrinker wasn't an oddity. Plenty of bartenders drank, but plenty didn't.

I recognized Stella Blue the instant she walked in. She was only a few years older than me, but she looked like a million dollars. Babette had called her the prettiest woman on the coast back in the '80s. I wasn't sure she didn't still hold the title. She had thick blond hair cut in a straight shag and Tina Turner legs that were well displayed in a slit cocktail dress that spoke of a time when elegance was expected. Her waist couldn't have been larger than twenty-two inches, and her hips and bosom swelled with a lushness that made every man in the bar swallow hard.

She saw me looking at her and walked over. "You're the reporter, aren't you?"

I introduced myself. "Babette called to warn you?"

"That's what friends are for, sugar baby."

"She tell you I was going to ask about those dead girls?"

"Yep." She took the drink the bartender handed her, a Harvey Wallbanger. "So, ask."

"Do you remember them?" I pulled out the pictures.

"That one for sure." She, too, pointed to Maria. "And those two." Charlotte and Audrey. "Can't say, but the other looks familiar. You have to understand, I was a little busy back then. I had choreographed some dance numbers that required a lot of concentration." She had blue eyes that crinkled at the corner with good humor.

"Do you remember any men who hung around these girls?"

She didn't blow off the question. She thought a moment. "That one—" she pointed at Audrey "—had a regular guy. The only reason I remember is because he always tipped me with a ten-dollar bill. He said his fiancée sent it to me, then he'd point at her. He was a looker, too. Hard body, short hair, classic pinger. You know, Keesler airman."

"Do you remember ever seeing him after Audrey disappeared?"

She shook her head. "I don't." She put the picture on the bar and sipped her drink. "He was trouble, I can tell you that. He liked to fight. But I never got the idea that he was anything other than devoted to his fiancée."

"Why would you remember that?"

"In that job I saw a lot of couples, and I got where I'd make bets with myself about how long they'd last. I got pretty good at it, and I remember thinking that they were mismatched, but that they'd make it for the long haul. There was something in the way he looked at her. Fierce and protective, like she was the most special thing he'd ever seen. That's the only kind of love will hold a guy like that."

"Do you remember anyone who set your teeth on edge?"

"Other than Alvin's buddies who thought they could grab and fondle me?"

"Maybe one of them."

She shook her head. "None of them killed those girls. They were old, fat white men who liked to cop a feel, but they weren't into killing girls." She eased down on the bar stool beside me. "Let me think about it. Since no bodies were found I guess I wanted to assume those missing girls had simply left. I wasn't thinking about a killer. There were some strangers at the bar, geeks and losers, guys who had to pay for a look at a pair of tits. But a killer?" She frowned. "I'll have to think. Did you talk to Alvin?"

"He wasn't very helpful."

"I'll bet if you could get his sentence reduced he'd have a better memory."

Mitch would have to work that angle. "There's a good chance the killer targeted each of those girls at the Gold Rush. While you're dredging up memories, you might try to remember another girl that would be like these four. The police haven't identified the fifth body yet."

"It could be one of a thousand girls. Rich girls, Yankee girls, sorority girls or ones that came in wearing their one good dress like Cinderellas praying Prince Charming would find them."

I nodded. "Just think about it."

"Why are you so certain those girls were taken at the Gold Rush?"

"Just a hunch," I said. "I could be wrong."

"Beats me how Alvin didn't notice someone was digging in his parking lot. Five bodies buried there, you'd think someone would have caught on."

Stella was nobody's fool, and we shared that sentiment. Alvin might have turned a blind eye, and he might not know what someone was burying in his parking lot, but he knew something was going on. He was guilty, but to what degree we'd probably never know. "Do you remember anything about that?"

"Most of the time Alvin sent a car to get me. They'd let me out right at the back door so I could get into my costume. I was the featured dancer then." She smiled a slow, lazy smile. "I was a star. I made two grand a week working two hours a night. That's not counting another grand in unreported tips."

"I heard you were good."

"I could make men want me to the point that they didn't care about money. I studied the Vegas acts and created my own costumes. Feathers, balloons, you name it."

Sex appeal was indeed a talent. Stella still had a lot of it left if she chose to use it. "I'm not trying to be rude or imply anything, but did any of the gentlemen ever request anything odd?"

"Like I should wear a bridal veil?" she asked. "No. I didn't date after the show. A lot of the girls who danced did, but I didn't. I made that clear with Alvin before I took the job. Whorin' wasn't my thing, and I was making a lot of money dancing. I had a steady man, and he was plenty for me. I knew I had something waitin' at home and nothing hanging in that club could compare." Her smile revealed strong white teeth. "Sugar, when you got the candy man, you don't go lookin' for a gumdrop."

I couldn't help laughing. "Are you still with him?"

"No, he played the blues, and that kind of life depends on travel and sadness. I'm basically a happy person, so I didn't want to stay sad. That man could fuck the kinks out of me, but he never learned to laugh. I heard he died last year. Alcohol."

Death was all around me, tapping the shoulders of everyone I talked with. "Did any of the other girls talk about a kinky guy?"

"No, and they would have said something about a guy with a bride fetish. I mean there were the normal requests for a three-way or domination or a little slap and tickle, but nothing like bridal veils. Tell you what, though, I'll make a few calls."

"Thanks, Ms. Blue," I said.

"Sure, but call me Stella. And remember, you can't use any names if some of the girls do talk. We're older now. That was a long time ago. Most everybody has family."

"No problem," I said, giving her my card. "Just give me a call."

Hank had ordered me home, but it was pointless. I couldn't relax. The phone was in my hand and I called Mitch.

"Any luck with the fifth body?"

"No," he said. "We know it's a female, and she's a real mystery. We just don't have anything to check her against because there were no other missing girls. Our regional check hasn't produced anything that matches her dental records. We'll broaden our scope to a national hunt, but the records from 1981 are going to be sketchy to say the least. Anything else?"

"Have there been any convicts released lately with records of the type of violent criminal past that would lend themselves to these murders?"

"Two. Avery has already checked them out and they have alibis the night Pamela Sparks was killed. Solid alibis. Avery said he believes them, which is rare. He seldom believes anyone."

"Wow. I'm impressed." And I wasn't being sarcastic. "The Thorazine. Has any been reported stolen?"

"Not from the coast. We're checking the Jackson area and over in New Orleans. It's a long shot, but we have to try it."

I thought of the things that Dr. Richard Jennings had told me. "What about mental institutions? Has anyone gone missing?"

There was a pause. "Avery doesn't have any reports locally, but we're still checking."

"I guess that's everything I have to ask right now. Thanks, Mitch. See you later." I hung up and realized I was smiling. I'd never really considered that I might enjoy dating the district attorney, but it was hard not to like Mitch Rayburn.

I drove back to the office and typed up the answers I'd gotten from Mitch for a brief story updating the investigation. Then I wrote a story about Stella Blue, and a time when the coast was a place where girls in sequins and feathers dancing on a runway seemed like a scandal. I set the scene for the last place I believed the five young women were seen alive, and then I got on the phone and began tracking down Adrian Welsh and Eddie Banks.

Captain Adrian Welsh wasn't that hard to find. He was stationed in Colorado Springs, Colorado, a career military man working with the air force weather station there. It took three phone calls and several transfers before I got him on the line. It was only nine o'clock there.

This was a part of my job that I hated. I asked if he'd spoken with the Biloxi police recently, and when he said he hadn't, I could hear in his voice that he knew.

"It's Audrey, isn't it?" he asked. "They found her."

"Yes, I'm afraid she's dead."

"She never disappeared—she was killed, wasn't she?"

"Yes. Probably the night she disappeared. I'm sorry to have to tell you this."

There was a pause. "My God, you can't imagine the times I've thought about her. I called her parents again and again and again. They hated me. They blamed me. Saw me as the bad influence. They told me she'd gone away to school and never wanted to see me again. I knew they were lying, but I couldn't find out anything. Then they reported her missing in the newspaper and I knew something terrible had happened. I called the police, but nothing ever came of it."

I made a note to check the old police records to see if Adrian really had called. If those records still existed.

"Do you have any idea who might have killed her?"

"I have some thoughts," he said. "I had five years or so to think about it before I finally gave up on hearing from her. I sort of always hoped that she'd call me one day, maybe saying that her folks had locked her in her room and wouldn't let her use the phone, but that she'd finally escaped. It didn't happen."

Most people live on improbable dreams and fantasy, and Adrian Welsh, career military man, was no exception.

"I understand from her friend Sheila that she went outside for some air the night she went missing. Can you tell me what happened?"

He took a deep breath. "It's my fault."

"How do you figure that?"

"I was putting pressure on her to wear my ring. She'd agreed to marry me, and accepted the engagement ring, but she'd only wear it when she was away from home. She didn't want to tell her parents. She wanted to run off, you know, elope. But I thought that lacked honor. I wanted her to tell them so I could confront them and prove that I was going to be a good husband. I loved her to the point of desperation."

"Why wouldn't she tell her parents?"

"She was afraid her father would lock her in her room. Really. He was like that. But I wanted her to break the hold he had over her and her mother. I should have eloped with her and done it her way. Everything would be different now. My life would be so different."

Adrian spoke like a man who'd let a lot slip through his fingers. "So that night, you were arguing," I prompted.

"About the engagement. She'd signed herself up at some bridal registry. It was a big deal to her to do that. She said she was taking it one step at a time, and when it was right she'd tell her folks. When I got angry because it wasn't enough, she said she was going to get some air. It was smoky in the Gold Rush and I was pissed off. She walked outside and I went to the bar and got a beer. I guess about fifteen minutes went by before I got concerned. I went outside to check for her, but she wasn't there. Her friends were worried, too. Sheila went looking for her and we hunted all over the parking lot. We asked the security guy, but he hadn't seen anything. So we all went home. Sheila was afraid to call the Coxwells, because if Audrey was in trouble, it would only make it worse. Sometimes Mr. Coxwell would beat Audrey with a leather strap."

There was a silence on the line. "What did you do?"

"I called the Coxwells about forty times. Her dad hung up on me, until he finally told me that she'd gone away to school and never wanted to see me again. I went over there and pounded on the door, and he called the police on me. They told me at Keesler that if I went back to the Coxwells' I'd be arrested and discharged. I didn't have another career to go to."

"You never heard anything else?"

"Only the stories in the paper where they were offering a reward for information. I knew something awful had happened. I spent the next four months going to every bar, looking for her, asking questions, showing her picture. But no one had seen her. When the other girls disappeared, I knew someone was killing them. I went to the police again, but they just laughed at me and told me to mind my business at Keesler. Then I was transferred to Germany. I married while I was over there."

"You were right, as it happened," I told him. "Those girls were killed. All four of them. And there's a fifth body, too. One that hasn't been identified."

"How was Audrey killed?" he asked.

Based on what happened to Pamela Sparks, Audrey's throat had been cut. But I had no evidence of that, and no need to leave him with that image in his mind. "The police don't know for certain. They believe it was a quick death."

"Shit." It was a terse whisper. "She was such a sweet girl. Who would kill her?"

"That's something we'd all like to know. Where were you last Friday night?" I asked.

"Me? Friday night? Why?" He put it together fast. "There's been another girl taken?"

"Where were you?"

"Here, at the base. I teach geographic weather and some other weather-related courses. Has someone else been hurt?"

"Do you have anyone who can validate your alibi?"

"Of course. It's a military base. Everything is documented. Besides, I have thirty students. Tell me what's happened."

His alibi would be easy to check out, and besides, I believed him. "Another young girl was taken and murdered. The police feel the MO is the same as that used when Audrey was killed."

"Do the police know who it is?"

"They have some leads, but no one has been arrested."

"The bastard who killed Audrey is still out there, killing again?" His voice was hard with fury and I remember what Sheila Picket Bellington had said about him, how he liked violence.

"You can help by trying to remember the night Audrey disappeared. Was there anyone watching her, someone who paid particular attention to her?"

He took a moment to collect himself, and I knew what such restraint must have cost him. "There was a guy," he said. "I remember, because he was looking at Audrey. We were arguing, and she got angry and was pulling at the engagement ring. It was tight and she was having trouble getting it off. She was crying and yelling at me, saying she wasn't going to let me browbeat her after she'd lived her whole life with her father dominating her." His voice broke. "God, I'm so ashamed. I *was* bullying her. I thought I was loving her."

"Captain Welsh, you were doing what you thought best, trying to get her to break free of her parents."

"I saw that guy staring at her. He was sitting by himself at the bar, with a drink. But he was staring at her like he was afraid of her. It pissed me off so bad, I smacked him."

"You hit him?"

"Slapped him. That really set Audrey off. She screamed at me and threw the ring. The guy flipped out. He jumped down from the stool and ran out the door. Audrey yelled at me again and went outside to cool off."

My heart was pounding. "Can you describe the man?"

"He was dark haired. Dark eyes, I think. About six feet tall. He was strong looking, but he didn't fight back. He just sort of cowered, then ran. I thought that was odd because he looked like he could hold his own in a fight. I mean he wasn't a pussy. I didn't go around hitting ninety-pound weaklings, you know."

"Is there anything distinctive about him that you can remember?"

"Man, it was dark in the bar. I didn't get a good look at him. I was blinded by anger. You think he took Audrey because I hit him?" His voice rose high on the last word.

"No, I think he took her because she was convenient."

"You think that man could be the killer?"

"I think there's a chance. I'm going to call Detective Avery Boudreaux of the Biloxi Police Department. He may ask you to work with a police sketch artist. Would you do that?"

"If I have to, I can fly back to Keesler."

I was nodding as I made quick notes. "Detective Boudreaux will be in touch, Captain. Thank you." I hung up and called Avery. There was no time to consider if I was pimping for the police. I didn't care. What mattered was that Adrian Welsh might actually have seen the man who'd killed five, maybe six young women. I felt the dragnet beginning to tighten at last.

19

The newsroom was quiet when I went to get a cup of coffee. As I walked across the room, I was greeted by at least three smiles, and to my surprise, I smiled back. I went into my office, closed the door and dialed the number I'd dug up for Eddie Banks. It was a branch of the Ohio National Bank in a town called, unbelievably, Metropolis. Eddie was assistant bank manager. He came on the phone quickly, and when I told him who I was, he already knew why I was calling. Someone had sent him clippings of the newspaper stories about the dead girls.

"It's just impossible to believe that Sarah is dead," he said. He'd been in the Midwest long enough to tame his accent, but it wasn't completely gone. If he was upset over his ex-fiancée's death, he was handling it.

"Where were you last Friday night?" I asked.

"Home, with the wife and kids. We have five. The youngest is eleven. Martha's a good bit younger than me, you see. I guess you could say we got a late start on the family."

He seemed to have lost touch with the fact that a young girl who'd once been in love with him was dead. She'd never been married or had a chance to have a child. She'd been buried under a parking lot instead.

"Congratulations on your ability to reproduce," I said, regretting the sarcasm the minute it was out of my mouth.

"Yeah, I guess that wasn't very thoughtful. It was just such a long time ago with Sarah. And we'd broken up and everything."

"Because you were cheating on her."

There was a pause. "Yeah. I cheated on her. I was twenty. I was too young to settle down, but Sarah wouldn't consider having sex unless we were going to be married."

From the little I knew of Sarah Weaver, she'd deserved a lot better than Eddie Banks. "So you lied to her and told her you wanted to marry her." I was bearing down on him hard, and he began to rationalize his actions.

"Guys do it all the time. Girls are supposed to know that. It's just how it works."

"Right. So your wife will corroborate your alibi for last Friday."

"My wife and my neighbors. They came over for some venison stew my wife cooked up. I can give you their names."

I took them down. "When you were dating Sarah, do you ever remember anyone watching her, paying special attention to her, something like that?"

"I saw her the night she disappeared." There was a pause. "She was a pretty girl. Guys looked at her all the time, but she didn't look back at them. She was shy."

"Where did you see her?"

"At a bar called Lobos. And then she went to the Gold Rush." He paused. "I followed her. I was thinking about making up with her, but I didn't. She was with some friends, and I knew they'd give me a world of grief if I tried to talk to her."

"You didn't talk to her at all?"

"Not in the bar. She went outside to get something out of the car, and I followed her. I tried to talk to her. She just screamed at me and told me to leave. So I did. I didn't want trouble with the law, and she was acting like I was trying to kill her."

"She was loud."

"Loud? Like a cat yowling in a fight."

"What did she yell at you?"

"She called me a creep and a liar. What do you think? She was mad at me."

Eddie Banks wasn't my idea of a prize, but he sounded as if he was telling the truth.

"You left then?"

"I was a little hot under the collar. Sarah made me feel…guilty. I was mad at her. So I went to Spider's, a bar down the highway, and had a few beers. I stayed out most of the night, and when I got home, there was a call on my answering machine from her friend, Peggy Adams. She wanted to know if Sarah had left the bar with me."

"Did you talk to the police?"

"I did, but folks had seen me at Spider's and later at the Jungle Room, and then later at Sambo's for breakfast. I was with a couple of friends. My time was accounted for, and I guess the police didn't realize something bad had happened to Sarah."

"Is that what you figured?"

"I knew something bad had happened to her, but I didn't know what to do about it."

I could only pray that my fate would never rest in the hands of someone like Eddie Banks. "Thanks, Mr. Banks." I hung up.

I wrote my copy and turned it in. To my surprise, Brandon wasn't hovering over my desk prodding me to put a dash of sensationalism in my stories. When Hank walked into my office and closed the door, I looked up with concern.

"The stories are fine. I just got a call from Brandon. He's bringing the CEO of the chain in Monday morning. He wants us all to spiff up a bit."

"Did he direct that at me personally?" I asked.

"Yes." Hank grinned. "Wear your Daisy Dukes and carry a bottle."

"Right. I'm so employable already."

His smile faded. "Will you stay if they buy us out?"

"I don't know. I don't know if they'll have me."

"You've done some terrific stories."

I shook my head. "Don't go out on a limb for me, Hank. I'll be fine, whatever happens. You need this job. You have a wife and responsibilities."

"I need my self-respect more."

He spoke quietly and I gave him a weak smile. "What about Jack? Has he said anything?" Jack had been noticeably absent from the office. He'd rush in, write his story and fly out the door.

"I'm worried. Something's not right with Jack, but he won't talk about it."

There it was again. I suspected, but it wasn't my place to speculate. "I'll try to run him down this weekend and talk to him away from here."

"Thanks, Carson. What do you have going on the social calendar?"

I couldn't be certain if he somehow knew, but I wasn't going to lie. "I'm going to dinner with Mitch tonight."

His grin was puckish. "Who's bait and who's the fisherman? That's all I want to know."

"I'm not sure," I said, laughing. "Maybe we're just two lonely adults who want someone to drink with."

"Maybe you should learn to lie better."

"I'm gone, anyway."

"Yeah, spruce up for your date, and be on time Monday. If Brandon sells, I want you to stay on. You're the only good thing about working here."

I was underdressed for the Cloister, a lovely old restaurant in one of the antebellum homes of Pass Christian. Pass Christian was old money, culture, the highest waterfront property and Old World class. Highway 90 along the coast was a promenade of beautiful homes and landscaping. The ride in Mitch's convertible had whipped my hair into a tangle, and my mascara was blurred with tears brought on by the cold wind. It was magnificent, and we walked, smiling, into the elegance of chandeliers and candles.

He'd reserved a table in a small private dining room, and I was impressed. I'd gone to the Brown Raisin for anonymity; his choice was one of the coast's favorite dining establishments.

When we both had drinks in front of us, he cleared his throat. "I know I said no business, but I have to thank you for calling Avery about Captain Welsh."

"You're welcome." I sipped my martini. "I'm not the

enemy of the police. I'm not even an adversary. It sounded as if Welsh might have seen the killer. I wasn't about to surprise Avery and the investigation by sitting on that until the paper ran it."

"It was good work. Avery's team should have been there before you, though."

"It isn't a competition," I said. "Let's just hope you get a good likeness of the killer from the captain."

"Do you think he really saw the killer?"

I ate the last olive in my drink. "He's the best lead we have," I said. "He saw someone watching Audrey."

"And he said Audrey was angry and verbally abusive?"

"Obviously, you can't wait until tomorrow's paper for the details."

"I'm sorry." He sipped his drink. "We can talk about something else."

"The captain said he and Audrey were arguing loudly. She was upset with him because he was pressuring her to confront her family and tell them she was engaged. She wanted to elope, sort of sneak away. He's more of a confrontational kind of guy. He felt slighted that she wouldn't stand up and say she loved him."

Mitch nodded. "And the guy he saw in the bar, what did he look like?"

"The description we're running in the paper isn't very specific. Dark hair, brown eyes, nice build. That describes a lot of men on the coast."

"Including me," he said, a frown marring his forehead. "Or at least I had lots of dark hair back then. Now it's getting gray."

"Does your department have that computer that progressively ages a photograph or drawing?"

"We have access to one."

"As soon as you get the composite, I'd like to run it, along with the one that's been aged. Maybe for Sunday's paper." That would give me the best excuse possible not to go to Leakesville.

"Captain Welsh is flying in here tonight. They may have something by tomorrow. I promise to call you. In this instance, I think Avery will agree that the media can help us more than anyone else."

"If you give it to the television station Saturday, I'll skin you alive." I wasn't kidding. "Hold it for them until Sunday after the paper comes out."

"They'll accuse me of playing favorites."

"You wouldn't have that lead if it wasn't for me."

"You drive a hard bargain, Carson, but you have my word."

"I never doubted I'd get it." I grinned. It was nice to have someone I couldn't run over, yet I could trust Mitch to do the right thing. So far.

"Enough shop. I hear you have a fan in Jill Boudreaux. She's a great kid. She gives her father a rough time." He laughed. "She's beautiful and smart and headstrong."

"Sounds like great journalism material to me."

"Avery is certain that it's some kind of karmic boomerang from another life. He thinks he may have been Attila the Hun, and Jill going into journalism is his payback."

I laughed out loud. "Life has a funny way of sending us exactly what we need. Avery has such a dim view of journalists, maybe if his daughter becomes one, he'll have to change his thinking."

"You're already changing his thinking. He actually likes you, and it's killing him. He's developed a new interest in my social life since he found out we've been on a couple of dates. He'll probably be sitting on my doorstep when I get home for a rehash of the night."

"I'm glad to know that," I said. "I don't kiss and tell, and I certainly don't want the police involved in my social life."

Mitch grinned. "I can just make it up to suit me, you know. I am a lawyer, after all. In the surveys I've seen, lawyers tied with journalists for the title of professional liar."

"Just remember, my mama lives right down the road, and she still thinks I'm a lady."

We ordered and ate, chatting about the coast and a couple of his cases that had been in the paper. When my cell phone rang, I almost didn't answer it, but it was Dorry. Concern about my dad's heart shot through me. She didn't even give me a chance to say hello.

"Carson, you are coming to Emily's birthday party Sunday, aren't you? She's counting on you. We're having a tea party at the Crazy Lady Tea Shop. Emily will die if you aren't there."

I felt Mitch's gaze on me as I tried to frame an excuse. "I'm really busy, Dorry. I—"

"Emily loves you, Carson. She wants you there. I know it must be difficult. I look at her and think about Annabelle…"

"Dorry, I'm having dinner."

"Then say you'll be there. At eleven."

"I'll be there." By the time I hung up, Mitch had paid the check.

He drove me back to Ocean Springs with the top still down. I snuggled into my leather jacket and enjoyed the smell of the water and the glitter of the stars. Even the neon was crisply beautiful as we passed the casinos. Progress was inevitable. Gambling, in many ways, was the cleanest industry Mississippi could have gotten. Across the state line, Mobile sweltered with chemical plants and oil refineries. The environmental damage would take decades to undo. Sure, pawnshops had come, hanging on to the coattails of the casinos. And drugs. And the desperation of those who were perpetually drawn by the promise of a big win. But desperation wasn't the calling card of only the casinos. It had always been a way of life in a state that was perpetually on the bottom economic-educational rung.

"I had a good time," I said when Mitch stopped in my driveway. We were surrounded by azalea bushes that towered above the car, a magic tunnel of vivid flowers interspaced with the fragile wands of the white bridal wreath. The flowers reminded me of the dead girls. "Thank you, Mitch." I got out of the car and closed the door.

"You're not going to invite me in for coffee?"

"No." My emotions were too unstable to move from a public good time to a private one. And, I'd limited myself to three martinis. I wasn't drunk enough to rush a jump.

"I had a good time, too, Carson. Thank you. It's enjoyable to spend time with a bright woman."

"There are so few of us," I said drolly.

"I didn't mean that. I just haven't had a lot of time to date."

"I'll keep you honest, and politically correct," I teased him. Leaning over the door of the BMW, I brushed a kiss across his cheek. "Good night."

I'd turned to walk into the house when I heard his cell phone ring. It was almost midnight, and I paused, caught by instant curiosity and a whisper of dread.

"What?" he asked, his voice revealing shock. "I'm on my way."

Before he could protest, I was back in the passenger seat. "I'm going," I said. "You'll have to drag me out of this car before you leave me."

"Carson!" He was exasperated. "This is official business."

"How well I know. I'm going."

He backed out of the driveway without another word and sped back across the bridge toward the purple-and-orange neon of Biloxi.

20

Spanish moss draped the spreading limbs of the oak trees and cast eerie shadows over the white-shell cemetery road. I would have thought it was a joke except for the flashing of the red lights up ahead. Mitch didn't waste his breath telling me to stay in the car. As soon as he stopped, I hopped out and followed at a discreet ten paces. It looked bad for him—bringing his date to a crime scene, especially his reporter date. I couldn't help it. I wasn't about to miss a story, and I already knew, in my heart, that we had another dead girl.

I stopped short of the crime-scene tape when I saw the body. She was propped against the headstone, her bare legs extended in front of her, arms at her side, her naked torso covered in the blood that had gushed from the slash in her neck. Long brunette hair fluttered against the folds of a bridal veil. Her pale eyes gazed at nothing.

"Shit." I whispered the word.

Mitch had gone up to a knot of police officers. From among them Avery Boudreaux gave me a hard glance, daring me to try to get any closer. I was close enough. This crime scene might actually yield physical evidence. Unlike the public pier, which had contained thousands of finger-prints, a tomb was relatively private. Chances were only the caretakers, the family and the murderer had been in this area in recent weeks.

I knew I should call the newspaper photographers, but instead I reached into my purse and turned my cell phone off. I had no heart to see this mutilated young girl on the front page of the paper. I got out my notebook and began jotting down details. The picture I painted with words would be bad enough.

Avery approached me, scowling. "I see a serious conflict of interest."

"It could be worse," I said. "He could have been out to dinner with Mimi Goldcrest from the television station. Do you think she'd hesitate to call a crew out here right this minute?"

He growled something I didn't catch. "Just to prevent you from trying to get closer, I'll tell you that her ring finger is severed. That's not for publication."

So far, I'd been able to hold back that information on all of the bodies. The time would come, though, when it would have to be printed. "Any luck with the air force captain?"

"He's with a sketch artist now."

I nodded. "Have you identified the girl?"

"She didn't have anything on her. Looks like she walked in here on her own. There are footprints. I'm sure she was drugged, like Pamela." He spoke with some bitterness, and I realized he was blaming himself.

"You couldn't have prevented this, Avery."

"I could have if I'd caught the freaking pervert last week."

"Good plan, if you'd had something to go on."

"Tell it to the corpse. I'm sure she's sympathetic to the difficulties of my job."

Whatever I said, Avery was going to take this murder very personally. I understood. Stories became personal to me, too. Justice was important to both of us.

"Ballpark on how long she's been dead?" It was after midnight now.

"Not more than a few hours."

"How'd you find her?"

"Couple of kids parking."

He was protective of the kids. He wanted a chance to talk to them first, at length, and away from the gruesome crime scene so they might calm down and remember something important. I would have done the same thing.

"They stumbled on the body?"

"Right. They had a cell phone and called 911. I got here and called Mitch."

I had the sequence of events, even in minimalist form. "Did the kids see anything?"

"I can't be sure. They may have heard something."

I made a note. If I didn't use their names, I could say they might have evidence without putting them in the line of fire. I looked up to find Avery watching me.

"They're kids, Carson. I don't want them in any danger. Even if you find out who they are, don't print the names."

Sometimes Avery could push it too far. After delivering his edict, he left me and went back to talk to the forensics team. I heard some commotion at the gate to the cemetery and looked up to see the television van trying to

drive past two patrolmen. Avery was going to have his
hands full now. He'd soon discover that I was a far different kettle of fish.

"Damn it all to hell. Where did they come from?" He
headed toward them like a pit bull after a poodle.

The television crew probably heard it on a scanner, or
they could have a tipster in the police station. At least this
was one area where Avery couldn't suspect me.

I reached in my purse and pulled out my pack of cigarettes. It was, after all, Friday night. Though I'd given up
Lissa's and my date with the karaoke boys, I needed a cigarette. I lit up and blew a spiral of hazy smoke against the
reflection of the still-whirling red lights. I sat back to watch
the battle between the police and the fourth estate.

The television camera was only allowed inside the
cemetery gate, but Tate Luckett, the reporter, walked up to
stand beside me. "Good God," he said, his voice shaking.
"This is sick. What a shot! Dead girl on a tomb with a bridal
veil. We don't have a lens long enough to get it, though."

"It would be a sensational shot," I agreed. The nicotine
had calmed my shaking hands. Now I was simply cold.
And needing a drink. The scene throbbed in the whirl of
the red lights, hellish and cruel. Tate Luckett's face re-
flected only ambition, and I wondered if I'd ever looked
that way. Probably.

"My camera guy can't get a damn thing from back there."

"Could be for the best," I said.

He looked at me. I obviously wasn't the hotshot reporter
he'd heard I was. "It's not my place to decide what's best
for the viewer. I'm just supposed to get as much as I can."

"There'll come a day when you realize it is up to you

to decide," I said slowly. I didn't buy into the pass-the-buck defense.

"I wondered why you'd work for a paper like the *Morning Sun.* Now I know."

"Fuck you, Tate," I said. It wasn't the witty rejoinder I'd hoped for, but I was weary and cold. A young girl's life had ended some fifty yards in front of me. My reputation with the likes of Tate Luckett wasn't important.

Mitch was busy talking with the M.E. and a forensics team. The last thing he needed was to tell me good-night in front of everyone. I slipped away into the darkness, letting the moss-draped shadows fall over me until I was lost to his view. When I'd made it to the road where the TV camera crew huffed and fumed, I called a taxi. I smoked three more cigarettes while I waited.

When I got home, I made a pitcher of martinis and took my cigarettes out to the porch. There was no wind on this protected side of the house, and the smoke from my cigarette curled lazily up. I finished one martini and poured another. I intended to get very, very drunk, and if I was lucky, the image of that dead girl would blur behind a haze of vodka.

"Carson."

I thought I was imagining things. "Who is it?"

"It's Michael. Are you okay?"

"Where the hell are you?" My words slurred out of control.

He stepped out from beside the tall azaleas and came up the narrow steps to the screened door. I stumbled toward it, unlatched it and let him in.

"I called several times this evening. When you didn't call me back, I got concerned."

"I'm too tough to kill." My pronunciation was interesting. The words tumbled into each other.

He sat down on the wicker sofa beside me and I caught the scent of his cologne, something gentle and clean, like I remembered him.

"I'm tired," I said. "He killed another girl."

His arm slipped around my shoulder and I leaned against him. He was warm and I burrowed closer. "You're okay," he said, his hand rubbing my arm as he would a frightened horse. "The things you've had to see in your life."

It had been such a long, long time since I'd allowed anyone to comfort me in any way. "Talk to me, please." His voice was solid, something that connected me to a fragment of my old self that was still strong and unbroken.

"I had a day today," he said, his hand rubbing, his voice soothing. "Old man Windom had four cows down. I lost two and saved two, but I tell you, Carson, I came as close as I ever have to striking a man. Sometimes I just don't understand the cruelty in this world."

I understood then that as solid as Michael was, he, too, saw horrors that he couldn't correct. I lifted my chin and kissed him. His mouth covered mine in a way I remembered, firm and wanting. I turned in his arms and was in his lap, clinging to him, kissing him with a passion that was partly liquor and mostly wild need.

"Carson," his said, his voice shaking. "Are you—?"

I ripped his shirt open, buttons flying. I kissed him hard, my hands tugging at his clothes, demanding.

He stood up, lifting me with him, kicked the door open to my bedroom and carried me inside. Instead of putting me on the bed, he eased me to my feet. His hands held my shoulders. Eye to eye, he began to unbutton my blouse.

Long ago, we'd made love with youthful passion, unaware of the consequences of life and loving. We both knew now how much it cost to care. There would be a price. There always was. His hands began to slide the blouse off my shoulders, his palms tracing my skin. When he felt the scar tissue, he halted. He knew what it was. I saw it in his eyes. He was a man of medicine, after all. He could feel the ripples and puckers of burns.

I stepped back from him, pulling my blouse around me. "I was late getting home from work. Annabelle was home alone when the fire started. They meant to kill me, but I worked late. When I got there I ran inside. A beam fell on me. The house was burning and I had to get Annabelle. The firemen pulled me out and wouldn't let me go back inside."

He didn't say anything else. He just pulled me to him and held me, rocking slightly, pressing me to him as if he meant to meld us together.

I woke in darkness, alone, my heart pounding from the vodka and emotions. There was a note on my bedside table written in Michael's loping script. "Call me tomorrow." I took my cigarettes out to the porch. It was Saturday, technically, but I didn't care if I broke a few more rules. The cats came with me, tumbling and mock-fighting. I watched them, feeling a calm settle over me. They were independent and proud creatures, yet able to play and give affection. I'd lost that balance in my life. Pride was what I had left.

Chester climbed on the sofa and came to lick my cheek. Then he was gone, chasing Miss Vesta's black-tipped tail.

It was good that we'd let Annabelle have both of them. They were company for each other while I was gone. There were times, though, that I found one or the other of them sniffing the boxes in the closet where I'd put some of Annabelle's favorite things. They could smell her, and I know they wondered where she'd gone. I wondered, too.

I finished my cigarette, took four aspirin and went back to sleep. I dreamed my daughter was standing beside my bed. She was so beautiful, her hair falling over her shoulders in curls. Her eyelashes were thick and fanned across her cheeks when she closed her eyes. Her pink lips curled with childish mischief as she opened her eyes and looked at me.

"Mama, I'm always here," she said, laughing at me. "I watch you all the time. The cats know."

"Annabelle." I couldn't move. My body wouldn't respond to any order I gave it. I wanted to touch her, to grab her to me and kiss her. I longed for the feel of my baby in my arms.

"I'll stay as long as you need me," she said.

There was the slightest green cast of light over her, and I shifted my head to see if dawn had broken through the window. It was still dark. The light came from Annabelle.

"I love you," I told her.

"Of course." She laughed. "I'm watching." And she was gone.

I woke up but stayed still in the bed. Miss Vesta was on my pillow, staring at the exact spot Annabelle had been. I drifted back to sleep and woke up to the ringing telephone.

"Ms. Lynch?" The voice was young. "It's Jill Boudreaux—Detective Boudreaux's daughter."

I glanced at the bedside clock. It was eight. "What's up?"

"Mom and I are going to New Orleans today, but could we meet next week?"

"Sure," I said.

"I hope I didn't wake you."

"No, I have a story I should write this morning."

"It's the dead girl, isn't it?"

I wondered how much Avery told his family about the gruesome details of his work. In my experience, policemen seldom discussed a case with their loved ones. A "boys in blue" mentality developed that created a sense of isolation in a cop. My therapist had cautioned me against developing such an attitude. She'd never understood that reporters were observers, not participants. That was the real danger—to always view life from the outside.

"Yes. That's the story."

"Dad was upset when he came home."

"It's terrible to see someone dead, especially a young person."

"Dad said the killer lives here."

I closed my eyes and held the phone as a war of ethics suddenly raged in my brain. Could I legitimately pump Avery's daughter for details? "I wonder why he thinks that?"

"He didn't say. He just said he thought it was personal. He said something about the cemetery but I didn't catch all of it. He was angry."

"Jill, your dad might not like you repeating what he tells you in private."

There was a tiny pause. "You're right. He'd be mad." She felt the pinch of her chosen profession, and I realized that no conversation I had with her could ever teach her more.

"I won't mention any of this, okay?" She was an eighteen-year-old kid. She shouldn't have to spend her Saturday wondering if she'd end up in print.

"Will you still talk with me?"

"Absolutely."

"I'm going to get Mom to call and invite you to dinner. She wants to meet you, too. She says you're the best thing that could happen to the coast."

I smiled. "You two must make Avery's life a living hell."

"Only when he needs it."

This time I laughed. "Call me when you have time to meet."

"I will. And thanks."

I replaced the receiver and was about to get up to put coffee on when the phone rang again.

"Carson Lynch?"

"Stella?"

"How about brunch? Mary Mahoney's in thirty minutes?"

"Forty. I have to shower."

"You're on," she said.

I hung up and got busy. The day had already become very interesting.

21

The drive to Mary Mahoney's, a Biloxi landmark, could have been ordered up for a Cecil B. DeMille production. The sky was Wedgwood and the flowers a blaze of vivid Easter colors. Whitecaps frothed on the shallow waters of the Sound, kissing the shore with the last promises of cool weather. Even the traffic was negligible as I took Highway 90 to my destination.

Stella was seated at an outdoor table, a Bloody Mary in front of her and one at my place. Her red slacks matched a red-and-white-striped nautical blouse. She was casual elegance.

"What's going on?" I asked as I sat down. I drank half the Bloody Mary. Hair of the dog and all.

"You tell me," Stella said. "I saw the news."

I closed my eyes, but the images of the night before were still there. "I wish I knew something."

"This killer's not going to stop, is he?" She was a woman who didn't fidget.

"I can't figure out what he's been doing for twenty-four years," I said.

"I remembered who was working security for Alvin back in 1981." She waited until she had my full attention. "Jimmy Riley."

"Deputy Chief Jimmy Riley?"

"That's him."

I thought about it a minute. "I'm sure Avery must have talked to him already. Do you think he knows something?"

She shrugged. "Back then, police made about twelve thousand a year. A lot of cops worked private-security jobs to make ends meet. Jimmy worked for Alvin. I was just wondering, if he was walking that parking lot like he was paid to do, why he didn't notice someone was digging it up and burying girls there?"

"Good point." There was a tightness in my stomach that indicated I was on to something. I tried not to let my excitement show. "What kind of guy was Riley?"

"Nuts. You know his daddy was CIA, or that's what he said. He'd come in the bar before his shift started and he'd have a free drink and talk to the girls. He led a wild life, to hear him tell it. He grew up all over the place, and when he was a teenager his father disappeared in the jungles of Panama. Jimmy and his mother were living in the Riverview Arms along the Back Bay. They were poor and she had one way to support herself." The ice had melted in her drink and she twirled her celery stick in the glass. "I think Jimmy had a lot to prove."

I hardly knew Riley except by name, but I was surprised that he'd ever been involved with the likes of Alvin Orley. Stella was right, though. Back in the '70s and '80s, police officers did a lot of side security jobs to supplement thin paychecks. Protecting citizens in a parking lot, even for Alvin Orley, was a long way from anything illegal or unethical. But how could he have missed those graves?

"Are you going to talk to him?" Stella asked.

"First thing Monday morning."

"Please don't tell him you spoke with me. I always had the impression that the one thing Jimmy could do well was carry a grudge. He has a lot of power now."

"I won't say where I heard any of this."

"I talked with some of the girls, but they don't remember any more than I did. There were so many men in that bar, and they all looked at the young girls." She sighed. "We never believed we'd get older. Life has a way of slipping through your fingers."

"I know."

She finished her drink. "If you're out on the town some night, give me a call."

"Thanks, Stella. I'd like to do that."

She stood up. "Gotta go. My friend and I are driving over to New Orleans for the weekend." She picked up her purse and started to pull out some money.

"My treat," I said. "You can get it next time."

"Thanks." She went down the steps and out toward her car. Even the waiters stopped long enough to watch her walk. The woman didn't have to dance. Walking was enough.

I finished my drink and went to the office. I wanted to call Avery, check to see what he'd learned about the dead girl, get the composite that Captain Welsh had helped create and write up my story for the Sunday paper. My cell phone rang when I was halfway there.

"Carson." Mitch's voice was tired, and instead of the

guilt I expected, the sound of it triggered only concern. "I apologize for not getting you home last night."

"I'm a resourceful woman, Mitch. You were busy and I didn't want to interrupt."

"Thanks."

"Did you identify the girl?"

"No. There hasn't been a missing-person report on anyone her age."

That wasn't good. I hadn't watched the television news, but I was certain the discovery of an unidentified female body had been played big. Panic along the coast would be reaching a fever pitch by this evening. "Will you let me know?"

"Yes. I will." He fumbled with some papers. "I'm going to send someone from my office over to the paper with the composite drawing we did based on Captain Welsh's description. Could you run that Sunday?"

"Sure."

"We've got to find this man. It's not going to end until we do. Carson, I—" He broke off. "This has to end."

There was such desperation in his voice that I tried to think of something comforting to say. "I'm on my way to the office now," was the best I could come up with. "Did you get any fingerprints?"

"He's too smart for that."

"Murder weapon?"

"No. Whatever he used was sharp and curved, and he took it with him, same as Pamela."

"Toxicology?"

"Not back yet, but she wasn't sexually assaulted."

"No surprise there," I said. "It's not about sex. It's about power, maybe, or fear." I remembered what Dr. Richard

Jennings had said, and I wondered how much of it I should share with Mitch.

"How do you figure fear?" Mitch opened that door for me to continue.

"Just a guess," I said. "A friend of mine suggested that this killer has some issues with women of marriageable age. You know, they represent matrimony and motherhood, but the killer is somehow screwed up about his mother." I felt silly even saying it.

"Who told you this?" He sounded angry.

"A friend. I'm not going to print any of it."

"That would be totally irresponsible. A story like that— some psychobabble—could start a stampede. Folks would be hunting the coast with pitchforks and torches."

He was pissing me off, but I held my temper in check. He had a lot on his plate. "Take it easy, Mitch. I said I wasn't going to print it."

There was silence on his end of the line. I broke it. "What's your take on the killer?" I asked.

He must have heard the note of anger in my voice. "I'm sorry, Carson. I'm frustrated, and I'm taking it out on you. This whole thing could blow up, and a speculative story about a lunatic killer could be the fuse. But I know you wouldn't print something like that."

"Forget it. Look, I'm going to do a story. It's going to be fairly explicit, but nothing the television hasn't already covered. The only thing is the kids. I know they heard something. I want to know what. I've been more than responsible in my past stories." I didn't move into the territory of threat. I hoped I wouldn't have to. Mitch had said he wanted to work with me, but it wasn't all a one-way street.

"Leave out the psychobabble, please. Maybe by Monday we'll have the girl identified, and we can hold the panic to a modified roar. Shit, you'd think someone would miss their daughter or wife or fiancée."

He was really in a hole with another body and no physical evidence or leads. Stella Blue had given me a good lead about Riley, but I didn't mention it. Neither Avery nor Mitch had mentioned to me that Riley had once worked security at the Gold Rush, and I figured they both had to know. "I've held back a lot of stuff. We come clean on Monday."

"You've got it."

I hung up and ten minutes later pulled into the parking lot of the newspaper. It was ten o'clock, and Jack Evans's car was parked beneath an old mimosa tree that had showered it with faded pink blossoms. I walked over and touched the cool hood. It had been there for a while. Probably overnight, judging from the layer of dead flowers. I felt a pang of concern and hurried in through the janitor's door.

I saw Jack, slumped over his desk. My heart stopped. It pounded again with a painful thump, and I started running. I was almost at him when he sat up blearily and looked at me.

"What?" he demanded.

"Are you okay?"

"What's wrong?" His eyes were red and his face dull. He reeked of bourbon.

"Jack." I looked around. It was one thing to be discreetly tipsy, but Jack was falling-over drunk. I put a hand under his elbow and lifted him to his feet. "Men's room. Now."

We only hit two desks and a trash can before we made it down the narrow hall to the men's room. I went in with

Revenant 217

him and started running some hot water. I went to my desk and got a hand towel out of an emergency gym bag I kept in my drawer. When I went back to the bathroom, Jack was slanted against the wall.

"Sorry," he said. "I'membarrassed."

His words were a messy blur. "Try this." I soaked the towel in hot water and draped it over his head. There was a muffled roar of disapproval. I took it off, soaked it in cold water and did the same.

"Shit! Carson! Stop it!" He batted feebly with his hands, but I ignored him. After ten minutes there was color in his face and fire in his eyes.

"Drink some water," I told him. "And comb your hair. You have to walk out of here, and my guess is that by now there are folks in the newsroom."

"I don't give a shit."

"You'd better." I propped him against the sink. "Drink water, and I mean it."

He started sipping out of his cupped hand and I went to the snack room and brought back a steaming cup of black coffee and five Little Debbie oatmeal cookies. I gave him the coffee.

"Thanks." He blew on it and sipped.

He looked a little better, but he had a way to go. I retrieved the Little Debbie cakes. They were pure sugar, fast fuel to burn off the liquor. He ate two and then begged off.

"Okay, but only if you let me buy you breakfast."

"Look, I need to go home."

I tried to gauge how intoxicated he still was. He seemed better, but any drunk worth his salt could imitate sobriety for at least a while.

"I'll drive you home."

He searched my face. "Why are you doing this?"

"Because you're drunk?" I asked.

"Why?"

"You could kill someone. You could go to prison. You could ruin your life."

"I see." He looked down at the floor. "It won't do any good to argue."

"Nope." I straightened his shirt and told him to tuck it in. "I'll wait outside."

Two reporters had come into the newsroom, as well as the Saturday editor. If they noticed me coming out of the men's room, they didn't say anything. I retrieved my purse and walked out, picking Jack up on my way to the door. He lived in an apartment complex on Pass Road, and I drove him there. He got out at the curb. "I'll get my car later." He was sober enough to be embarrassed.

"Forget it, Jack. Get something to eat, take four aspirin and sleep a few hours. You'll be fine. Call me and I'll come get you."

He nodded and stumbled across the lawn to his door. I waited until he was inside before I pulled away. I drove back to the paper, slowing only when I heard the sirens as I turned off Highway 90. I realized they were in the parking lot of the newspaper. It took me a few seconds to realize that Jack Evans's car was on fire. Someone had torched it.

22

After the commotion in the parking lot settled down, I sat at my desk and listened halfheartedly to Clive, the Saturday editor, persuade Brandon that the newspaper had to cover the story of Jack's burning car. Brandon was showing a loyalty to Jack that left me flabbergasted. I called Jack and left a message on his answering machine telling him to take his phone off the hook, in case other media had hold of the story. In his state, he'd only make matters worse for himself.

As I hung up the phone, a police officer tapped on my door and handed me a manila envelope. I tore into it. The drawing Mitch had sent over of the possible suspect was strangely familiar, yet it could have been almost any handsome man with regular features. His nose was perhaps a little too thin, the skin around his brown eyes feathered with lines that didn't come from laughing. Aside from the strange tension the artist had captured, there was nothing extraordinary about the face. I gave the composite drawing to Clive.

The entire front page of Sunday's paper would be devoted to coverage of the murders. We had a shot of the cemetery where the unidentified girl had died. The body had been removed before Joey took the shot, but the ground was soaked with her blood. I hoped it wouldn't reproduce so graphically in the paper. We'd run the composite drawing beside that, along with my story detailing the latest murder and recapping the other murders. The Sunday edition was going to pack a hard punch, but it wasn't irresponsible. There was no speculation in my story. No mention of mother complexes or attempts to explain the motivations of a serial killer. I quoted Mitch and Avery liberally in their efforts to calm coastal residents.

When Clive signaled me that my story was okay, I put in a call to the Biloxi PD. Jimmy Riley didn't work on Saturday. I called his home and got an answering machine. Instead of leaving a message, I decided to drive by.

Riley's home was impressive for a police officer. It was nestled in a private neighborhood on a lake, a split-level house with a pool and a boat dock, which was empty. I knocked on the door, but no one answered. Chances were Riley was out at Chandelier Island running the red fish. I'd heard he was an avid sports fisherman.

There were no other leads to follow, so I drove home. The cats greeted me at the door, and I petted my way into the house. I'd come to rely on the felines. They needed me, and it gave me pleasure to meet their demands. Out of the corner of my eye, I saw the blinking red light of my answering machine. While the cats ate a can of high-end food, I checked my messages. Kev Graves was first, and he sounded tense. There was also a call from Dorry, telling me that Mother had bought a pork roast because she knew it was my favorite. They wanted to go to Foley, Alabama, to the outlet stores Saturday afternoon. Tommy was on call

all weekend at the hospital, and the kids were busy so she was free to shop if I had time.

The very idea was terrifying. I'd been with Dorry on a shopping spree. There was a certain point where plastic could actually produce enough friction to combust.

I called Kev back first.

"You were right," he said. "The good doctor is playing doctor with that nurse."

"Can we get photos?"

"Are you sure, Carson?"

"Yes. Never go into a fight with an unloaded gun."

"Okay. I should have photos and video by Monday morning."

"Yeah, Tommy's on call all weekend, or so he told Dorry." I hesitated, then asked anyway. "Why do you think he'd be with this woman? I mean over Dorry? Is she prettier?"

"She's not as pretty as Dorry. She's younger." He sighed. "It's not a choice of either-or," Kev said. "He has Dorry. I don't think he has any intention of divorcing his wife. This is just a piece on the side. You know, he'll buy this girl a car or a pool or some big-ticket item that she couldn't really afford on her own. He'll fuck her silly for about five months, and then he'll ease out of the relationship and wait for the next pretty nurse who makes him feel *muy macho*."

"Why do men do this?" I didn't understand this behavior. Loss, not adultery, had killed my marriage.

"The honest truth?" Kev asked, not bothering to hide his anger. "That little nurse comes without baggage. She can pretend that Tommy Prichard is the most wonderful man in the world. She makes him feel special and virile. He meets all of her expectations and then some. A real relationship doesn't work that way."

There were men in all professions who lived that life, but medicine created a stratified society—the gods and the minions. Gods, as everyone knew, took what they wanted. Minions supplied it. Dorry was just another minion, and one without even the courtesy of a professional title. Mother and wife didn't carry a lot of respect in a world where doctors had the power of life and death.

"Nail him, Kev. If Dorry does decide to divorce him, I want to clean him out."

"You got it."

I hung up and called Dorry. My intention was to beg off the weekend, but when she answered, I could hear in her voice that she was pushing hard to be her perky self. Pity made me concede to a trip home.

"I want to talk to Daddy," she said. "About going back to school."

"To college?"

"Yes." She was instantly defensive, a tip as to how low her self-esteem had sunk. "Daddy was saying the other day that he'd pay your bills if you wanted to go to pharmacy school. It's not too late for me."

"Of course it's not too late," I said. "I was just surprised. I think college would be a good choice for you." Dorry wasn't blind. She was positioning herself for change.

"The kids are old enough, and Tommy is working a lot."

"What would you study?"

"Maybe midwifery."

That was a shock. Dorry had once been squeamish around blood, but fingers in car doors, falls, broken bones and knocked-out teeth of four children had toughened her. "I think you'd be wonderful as a midwife."

"You always support me. That means a lot."

I heard the emotion in her voice. "See you for dinner. No shopping, but I'll come for dinner." I hung up.

My last call was to Michael. Acting on impulse, I thought I'd invite him to dinner in Leakesville. The clinic was closed, but an answering service patched me through to his cell phone.

"Batson Veterinary," a female voice answered.

"Polly?" I was shocked, and it showed.

"Who is this?"

"Carson Lynch. I was calling for Michael."

"Mike is busy. The clinic is closed on Saturday afternoon except for emergencies. He needs some time with his family, don't you think?"

"This isn't an emergency," I said quickly. "But please ask him to call me Monday when he reopens."

"I'm not his secretary. You can call back then."

I started to say something else, but the line was buzzing. She'd hung up.

If I had to drive to Leakesville, I had the perfect day. I left the windows down and played a station of country oldies. I took a lot of back roads, meandering through stands of pines, ugly subdivisions on clear-cut acreage and bottoms where the smell of a free-running stream reminded me of my childhood.

I stopped at Brushy Creek and took off my shoes. The water was icy, and I remembered the days when Mother brought us to the creek with a watermelon to chill in the shallows and have a picnic lunch. Dorry and I had hunted

Indian relics in the sandy clay bluffs of the creek. We'd found arrowheads and shards of pottery. I'd taken a lot of them to Miss Lizzie, an elderly black woman who was said to be a conjurer. She'd told me stories of a time and people left behind in the past.

The water was bitingly cold, and I waded for only a few minutes before numbness made me slosh out to the bank. I drank a Diet Coke while my feet dried in the sun. Then I put on my shoes and continued to Leakesville.

Dad was still at the store, and I was left alone with Mother in the kitchen. The smell of the pork roast made my mouth water. The thought of spending an hour or two alone with her made me think of the pint of bourbon tucked in my truck.

"You look better," Mama said, her pale gray eyes examining me. I'd seen them warm when she looked at Dorry, or pictures of Billy. But never for me.

"I'm sleeping a little better."

"You never were a good sleeper. Not like Dorry. She'd go to bed and be in the same position until I woke her the next morning. I was as likely to find you out walking in the moonlight as tucked up in bed."

"I must have worried you a lot." It was actually a revelation. I'd never considered that my nocturnal searches for fairies would worry anyone. There had never been a time when I'd felt unsafe in the woods around my house.

"I was always concerned that you'd make it to the river and fall in and drown."

"You should have gotten one of those child harnesses and hooked me up."

She laughed at the idea. "You were a wanderer."

"I loved the woods. I was thinking of Miss Lizzie today when I was driving over."

"She asks whenever I see her. You were her favorite. I always wondered what it was you two talked about. I felt like you'd rather be with her than with me."

Again I felt a pang of revelation. "That was never true. It was just that Miss Lizzie…" How far could I take this? I decided to try. "Accepted me."

"And I didn't. I was critical." The sharp edge of disapproval that I knew so well had crept into my mother's voice.

"You were only trying to protect me," I said, hoping to mollify her. I didn't want my father to come home to tension. I didn't want to spend an evening sitting poker stiff around a table of food I couldn't swallow.

"You'd take off after school and I wouldn't see or hear from you until it was time for bed. I'd be frantic when you finally came dragging home."

"I'm sorry, Mother. I never realized how much I worried you."

She turned her back on me and began chopping the celery for potato salad.

"Can I help?" I asked.

"You never liked to cook."

"I'd like to help now." There was such bitterness between us. It felt hopeless, but somehow I had to make it through dinner. How was it that my mother and Dorry could laugh and carry on and enjoy being with one another? I brought up only bad memories and bitter emotion.

She put a chopping board in front of me with an onion, pickles and hard-boiled eggs. She continued to work on the celery as I chopped the other ingredients. She liked things chopped fine, and I tried to make them uniform, the way she liked them. I'd never been able to perform the simplest task to her specifications.

When everything was diced, she took the ingredients without comment and mixed the potato salad. When she turned with a spoonful for me to taste, I was surprised.

"Delicious," I said, "as always. Dorry is right. There are some things that never taste as good as the way you make it."

"That's imagination," she said, but she was pleased.

"I guess it's association with a time and place where everything seemed good."

She put her hand on my shoulder and gave a light squeeze. When I didn't stiffen or pull away, she gave a tentative smile. I'd done my share of damage to her. That was something I hadn't understood until recently.

"Hannah, honey, I'm home."

My father's voice brought a full smile to our faces. We both moved to give him a hug, and then Dorry arrived. The shadow of Billy entered the room. Maybe I was the only one who saw him; maybe the others had simply learned to live with the absence of my dead brother more easily than I had.

"Do I have time for a ride before dinner? Dorry, want to come?" I asked.

Mom looked at her Bulova wristwatch with the thin, double-stranded, black, silk band. It had been her mother's and Mama had worn it every day since I could remember. "For an hour. Dorry, are you going to ride?"

"Are you kidding? I wouldn't be able to walk for a week. I'll stay here. I want to make some cream puffs for Emily's party tomorrow. The tearoom provides everything, but Emily really wanted homemade cream puffs."

"You're a bad influence," I said, teasing her. But I was halfway out the door.

* * *

There is no finer time in the Mississippi pine barrens than the spring. Wild dogwoods scatter the woods with delicate white blossoms. Clumps of black-eyed Susans bloom in the most unlikely places. Where the soil is sandy and damp, pitcher plants and buttercups lure insects to their deaths, and the mayhaw trees are laden with berries that make the best jelly in the world.

Mariah was too old to gallop through the woods as I'd done as a young adult, but then so was I. Even so, her muscle tone was good. Emily was doing a great job keeping her in shape. We headed down the river trail at an eager walk.

My offer had been sincere, but I was glad Dorry had decided not to come. I needed the solitude of the ride. I didn't want to be distracted from the beauty of the woods by chatter or the need to focus on another person. I wanted to be with Mariah. We'd been friends for a long time.

The trail wound through the woods and along the Chickasawhay River, a slow-moving, brown stream with white sandbars that invited swimmers and picnickers. There were treacherous currents, though, especially farther downriver where the Leaf joined the Chickasawhay to form the Pascagoula. Merrill had once been the thriving river town at the fork of the river. Miss Lizzie had told me stories of gambling, prostitution, hangings and cutthroat outlaws. It had been a real Old West boomtown in spirit, if not location.

Beneath the canopy of limbs, Miss Lizzie's green house was almost undetectable. The grass path that led to it off Beaver Dam Road was choked with weeds, and for a moment I felt panic zing through me. Then I saw her in the yard, her apron full of feed for the chickens. She scattered it about, clucking to the birds that provided her with fresh yard eggs.

Mariah and I stood perfectly still, but Miss Lizzie's face lifted and she stared right at me, waving one hand slowly in a gesture of welcome that I remembered.

I rode down the bluff to her yard, slid off Mariah and gave her a hug.

"Why, Carson Lynch, you've grown yourself into a woman."

The past three years had changed me greatly, but not Miss Lizzie. Her face was smooth, and her gray hair pulled back in a bun, just like the first time I'd seen her thirty years before.

"I've got some spring turnips cooking, and some corn bread. Come in and eat."

"Mama's cooking dinner," I said. "She'd be upset if I ate here."

She gave me a critical eye. "You could stand to eat both places. Open your mouth."

I obliged and let her examine me.

"You need you a tonic, and I don't mean the kind you can buy at the liquor store. Your gums are pieted."

I knew that was her word for showing poor color, splotchy. Miss Lizzie was a conjure woman of the medicinal type. She'd delivered three hundred babies and diagnosed a lot of illnesses, later confirmed by "real" doctors.

"Dorry says she may study to be a midwife. I think you've influenced her."

Miss Lizzie nodded as she began to broadcast the chicken feed again. "That would be a good thing. I'm getting too old for sitting up all night with wailing women."

She shook out her apron and started to the house. "I haven't seen much of Dorry these last years."

"She's been busy with her family."

"She used to come when she first married. She was happy then."

It was pointless to try and hide anything from Miss Lizzie. She saw straight to the soul. But Dorry's business was not mine to discuss.

"How are you doing? Is Jimmya taking good care of you?"

"He's a good boy. Got seven children of his own now."

"Seven?"

She laughed. "I told him I was going to have to fix him where he couldn't make Vanessa pregnant again. He stayed gone about two weeks. I think I scared him."

Her son was my age, and I'd gone to high school with him. As close as I was to Miss Lizzie, Jimmya had never allowed me to become his friend. His friends were black.

We took our customary seats on the front porch. I'd taken Mariah's bridle off, and she grazed along the grass path. Miss Lizzie's old Lincoln was under a shed, and it sparkled with a new wax job. She didn't drive often, but when she did she went in style.

"Tell me how you are," she said, reaching across the short distance between us and touching my heart, "in there."

"Angry," I answered. It was pointless to lie.

She nodded. "You lost your baby girl. A part of you is dead forever, and there's no way to change that."

Instead of making me angry, her words brought the fresh start of tears.

"How is your husband?"

"We're divorced."

She nodded. "I'm sorry. He's a good man." She looked off the porch. "Sometimes, when you lose so much, you have to let go of everything."

"I know."

"Did you come for some thoughts on the future?"

I considered her offer. There had been times in the past when Miss Lizzie had offered a glimpse of what would be. Or what could be, because she felt that nothing seen in the future was absolute. Free will could change anything.

"No," I said. "The truth is, I can hardly face the day at times. If I knew the future, I might have to give it up altogether."

"That doesn't sound like the girl I knew who wanted to see how soon she'd conquer the world."

"That girl is gone." I wasn't sorry for myself. It was just the truth.

She touched her fingers to my cheek, the tips smooth and dry. "Carson, she's not gone, but you have to help her heal. Nothing you do to yourself will bring your baby back."

I sighed and looked out at Mariah. She grazed, and I suddenly wondered if I'd been cruel in never letting her have a foal. We controlled the lives of our animals without a thought. We sold their babies as if we had the right.

"Tell me the news," I said to break the chain of unpleasant and unproductive thoughts.

"Ole man Joe Bill Tom died this year."

"I'm sorry, Miss Lizzie." Joe Bill Tom had been her friend. He'd gathered roots and berries for her tonics. He claimed to be a descendant of the Chickasaw Indians who had once roamed the area, but most white people thought he was a black man with delusions of grandeur. I'd talked to him and listened to his stories. I believed him.

"He's one of the very last who remember," she said. "Soon, a way of life will be forgotten in this part of the world."

"Some people have written it down."

She shook her head. "It's the living who hold the true memories. All times pass away, Carson. That's not a bad thing. What's left is a haze. There are a lucky few who can walk into the haze and see the past. At one time, my grandfather was a slave. Life had a very different rhythm then. Those times are gone and trying to hold on to that misery is a trap. The past can be an instrument of instruction or it can be a weight of grief."

Her message was to me. I nodded. "How does one leave the past behind?"

"By tending to yourself now, here, in this moment. Heal in this moment and you will heal the past."

I didn't disagree with her; I just didn't know how.

"You'll figure it out," she said, patting my knee. "You'd best head home for dinner. You know Miss Hannah gets all worked up when you stay here too late."

I stood up and bent to kiss her cheek. She smiled and waved me home as I bridled Mariah and jumped lightly onto her bare back. We headed home at an easy jog, Mariah ready for her dinner even if I was not.

Dorry met me in the barn, a knowing smile on her face. "I didn't want to start this in front of Mom, but what do you have going with Mitch Rayburn?"

I tried to hide my reaction, but I'd never been very good at lying. "We've gone to dinner a time or two. These murders have drawn us together."

"That's really unpleasant. But if that's what works as an aphrodisiac for the two of you, who am I to judge?"

I brushed Mariah's golden hide, trying not to let Dorry get under my skin. She was trying to be my big sister. "There's nothing going on, Dorry. Our careers put us together."

"I disagree. You like him. I can tell." She picked up a comb and began to work out a few snarls in Mariah's tail. "I miss the horses. Tommy was afraid I'd get hurt, and with the kids and all, I needed to be well." She brushed for a moment. "Mitch Rayburn has an upstanding reputation. You could do a lot worse."

"From what I've seen, he's a good man." I checked Mariah's feet, eager to get finished and out of the barn.

"He's helped some of the young people in Harrison County. Kids that got in trouble with drugs. He didn't prosecute them. Instead, he helped get them into programs. He's done a lot to raise money for summer programs for kids all over the coast, even here in Greene County."

"Did he hire you to handle his PR?" I kept it light. "He's a nice guy, Dorry. I concede that. But I don't really know him, and he certainly doesn't know me. Can we just leave it at the fact that he's a nice guy?"

"Sure." She put the comb down and put her arm around my shoulders. "Bring him to Emily's party tomorrow, if you want. Now let's go eat before the food gets cold and Mama has a conniption."

23

Driving back to Ocean Springs, I thought about the offer my father made at the dinner table—a chance to start over in another career. Dorry was ready to turn in her apron and spatula. I, on the other hand, had never wanted to be anything except a journalist. Wife had been a surprise avocation, mother an unexpected joy. But journalism was my rock. There were ideals and principles that anchored me in a way that no other profession could.

I had grown beyond the youthful belief that writing the truth could change anything. Change was no longer my goal. I had no goal when it came to writing a story. I simply wanted to tell what had happened in a responsible way. Maybe I'd lost my fire. Or maybe I'd grown up. I didn't know.

When I left the dry counties of Greene and George behind and entered north Jackson County, it was only midnight. I stopped at a small bar that did a surprising business on such an empty stretch of highway. I knew if I sat there long enough, I'd see plenty of people I recognized. Many voted against alcohol in their own counties. Still, they bought it and drank it.

I settled on a bar stool and ordered a screwdriver. I'd have one drink and finish the drive home. There were at least two dozen people in the bar, men and women, old and young. They were country folk, dressed in clean jeans and shirts, hair pouffed up or slicked back. They wore boots or tennis shoes, and several couples danced belly to belly in one corner where a jukebox played.

"Care to dance?" I swung around, surprised by the voice and the hand on my shoulder. Michael.

"Last time I saw you, there were two of you." I met his gaze and didn't flinch. I'd been very drunk. Our seduction scene had been a failure. Thank God it was blurred by vodka.

"Last time I saw you—" he touched my cheek in a way that sent a shiver through me "—I may have made a mistake."

"Chivalry was always your trademark."

"Maybe I should take up something else." He eased down on the stool next to me. "I remember a famous quote. 'He who hesitates is lost.' Have I lost again, Carson?"

This wasn't a moment for a flip answer. "I don't even know who I am anymore, Michael. Sometimes, when I'm with you, I almost feel like Carson Lynch, girl reporter. Then I blink and I lose her again."

He motioned the bartender for another drink for me and a soft drink for himself. "Polly said you called. I must have left my cell phone on the table when I stopped by to visit my daughter."

"Polly was pissed off. She acts like you're still married."

"Yeah, but only on the phone to other women. She instantly jumped to the conclusion that we were sleeping together, and that you'd called to rub it in."

"I'm sorry."

"She only thought that because that's what she'd do. Don't be sorry. The papers are signed. This thing just has to grind its way to the finish."

"What are you doing here?" Michael didn't hang out in places like the Back Room. At least he hadn't way back when.

"I saw your truck. I was on an emergency in Hurley and was driving by."

"And they told me high school was over for us."

He laughed. "We could go back to your place."

I was surprised, and it must have shown.

"Not a good idea, huh?"

"It's not that. I'm just trying to figure out why you put me to bed alone last night, and now you're suggesting that we go home together."

"Carson, you were drunk then. I didn't want to take advantage of you. When you pulled away from me, I didn't want to push it. You've been through hell and back, and I'm not going to add to your worries."

I thought of the nickname he'd been given in high school. St. Michael. He was waiting for my answer. "I don't know what I feel for you."

"That makes us even, I guess."

"This isn't the best basis for jumping into the sack together." I took a breath. "I haven't slept with anyone since the divorce." And not before that, for a while.

"We've made love before." His eyes were clear, hungry.

"I was a different person then. It's almost a bigger risk now. What if I disappoint you? What if I disappoint myself? There was a time when making love with you was like breathing. What if it's not like that, and I end up without even the memory?"

He stood up and signaled the waiter for a check. "Come on," he said, grabbing my hand.

I started to balk; this was a Michael I didn't know. I followed him outside, and he put me in the passenger seat of his truck.

"Okay," he said, "there's only two rules."

"What?" Gone was his hesitation. This was a man who took action.

"You can't drink any more until we finish, and I drive you home afterward. I won't stay."

I frowned at him. "What's going on?"

"No questions allowed. It's a simple yes or no."

"Yes." My curiosity would have killed me if I'd said no.

He got behind the wheel and headed north, taking some of the old farm-to-market roads that were narrow and unlined. We passed fields of soybeans and stands of pines, until we came to a narrow gravel road. He turned onto it and cut his headlights.

"What are—?"

"No questions, remember?"

I closed my mouth and waited until the truck pulled up under the Salter community water tower.

"Let's go," he said, pulling a can of spray paint out from under the seat.

"No!" I was shocked.

"Yes, sir. Out of the truck and up that tower. I was marking fence posts this afternoon and have just enough paint left to do the job you didn't finish."

I slid to the ground and walked to the rickety ladder that

led up the side of the water tank. I was surprised there wasn't an electric fence around it, but it was unprotected. I looked up. Back when I was in high school, it hadn't seemed so tall. I felt a tiny knot of excitement. I was way too old for such foolishness. I'd outgrown the high school rite of passage, but that was the point.

"Go on," he said, trying not to laugh. "I'll be the lookout. Unless you're scared."

I grabbed the paint can, stuffed it in the back pocket of my jeans and began to climb. I was winded by the time I got to the top. It was dark, and I couldn't see the tower well, but I sprayed what I hoped was a big *C* and *L* on the shiny aluminum skin of the tank. That high above the pines, a stiff breeze whipped the air, and though I knew Michael couldn't see me, I spread my arms wide and yelled, "I'm the king of the world!"

Applause floated up to me.

"Thank you. Thank you very much," I said, laughing at myself and the foolish exhilaration I felt. Below me, lights scattered among the trees for at least a mile around. I took a deep breath, tucked the paint can in my pocket and climbed down.

Michael's arms caught me and I turned into his body, my face lifted for his kiss. I thought I'd never forget his kisses, but this was new and different. He'd changed, too. That was part of the equation I hadn't considered.

"We can't ever go back, Carson," he whispered into my hair. "But it's okay, because we can go forward."

I lifted my lips again, but he kissed my forehead. "I'm taking you home, like I promised."

"St. Michael," I said, remembering too late that his nickname had galled him.

"Not a saint, just a man of his word." He put me in the truck and closed my door. In another minute, we were turned around and headed to Ocean Springs, the night making me feel both cold and alive.

"You can take me to my truck," I said. "I'm okay to drive."

"You are, aren't you?" he said.

"Another challenge is met and conquered." I found his hand on the truck seat and gave it a squeeze. "Thanks."

"No thanks necessary. That was simply unfinished business."

"I'd like to cook dinner for you one day next week."

He hesitated only a moment. "I didn't think you cooked."

I laughed at his teasing. "I can, when I choose to."

"Sounds great. You know I'm sometimes late."

"Sure. I'll cook something that doesn't matter."

He squeezed my fingers. "I'm glad you're back in my life, Carson. I'm sorry for the way you got here."

"I never expected to be back in Mississippi, but here I am."

When we got to the Back Room, I leaned over for a soft kiss good-night. He started to get out of the truck, but I stopped him. "Go on," I said. "It's late."

He waited until I'd gotten in my truck, started it and began to move away. I watched his taillights disappear down the highway as we drove in separate directions.

Sunday morning the phone rang at dawn. I checked the caller ID and reluctantly answered.

"The whole coast is buzzing about your stories, Carson. Congratulations."

"Brandon, it's hardly six o'clock. What do you want?"

"Saul Grotowitz wants to have breakfast with you this morning at eleven."

Saul Grotowitz was a big cheese with the Gannett chain of newspapers. "It's five hours until eleven. Why are you calling now?"

"To make sure you're up and presentable."

I wondered what angle Brandon was playing. He wasn't doing me a favor—that was for sure. "I'm sorry, I've already committed myself for this morning." I didn't want a private meeting with Saul Grotowitz.

"Break it." There was iron in Brandon's voice. He'd forgotten that I didn't care if he fired me. I was surprised to discover that I did.

"No," I said. "I'll meet him with the rest of the staff. Tomorrow."

"Carson, you need to meet him today, and you need to be sober. You have problems the other staffers don't. At least some of them don't."

I was momentarily stunned into silence. It seemed Brandon was trying to look out for me. "I'm sorry, Brandon, I can't. It's my niece's birthday party, and let's just say I haven't been the best aunt lately."

The silence was so brittle I thought the telephone might shatter in my hand. "You're self-destructive, Carson. And your priorities suck."

"I've given my word," I said softly. "That's all there is to it."

"I'll speak with you later." He hung up and I put the phone down. I made some coffee and thought about my morning. Emily would have a bevy of girls her age, but she also enjoyed the company of adults, specifically my company. She was an extraordinary girl, and one I was afraid to get too close to.

When I realized I had no gift for her, I went online and ordered a gift certificate for the movie theater. I put the printout in a large cardboard box and dug through the closet until I found some wrapping paper. I had a vast selection, because Annabelle had loved to wrap gifts.

I pushed that thought aside and went into the kitchen to fry bacon and scramble an egg. I'd had a dreamless sleep, and I felt good. I finished breakfast and took a cup of coffee out on the porch to watch the spring day come alive. My yard was so beautiful. How could there be such beauty and such pain in the same world?

Determined not to fall into the abyss, I went back inside, took a shower and dressed. It was after nine, and I knew Dorry and Emily would be putting up decorations at the tearoom. I wanted to surprise them by showing up to help.

Grabbing my gift, I drove through the quiet Sunday streets of my small town. A few restaurants were open. From the bakery, the smell of fresh bread wafted beneath the live oak trees that canopied the main street, and I slowed to sniff the air. Behind me a van rode my bumper.

Ocean Springs was the most beautiful of the coastal towns, and I wasn't about to let anyone rush me in my appreciation. The van eased back a respectful distance, as if the driver understood. When I got to the restaurant that catered to private parties for young girls of a certain age, I saw Dorry's SUV there. I'd begun to think the van carried a guest, but as soon as I pulled over, it drove past at an angry speed. Too bad. This wasn't a morning for ill tempers.

At the front door, I clutched my gift and took a deep breath. The first squeal of girlish laughter was like an unexpected slap. There was an excited babble of voices, all young girls. My mouth went dry and my stomach knotted around the breakfast I'd been so proud of myself for eating. Suddenly, I couldn't breathe. I leaned against the balustrade and tried to steady myself. I hadn't had a panic attack in over a year. My hands were trembling so much that I put the package down and gripped the handrail. I was acting like a fool. It was only Emily and her friends, laughing. It was a party. What did I think, that they would sit in chairs and sip tea?

I tried to make myself ring the doorbell, but I couldn't do it. I looked in the window where the lacy curtains fluttered, and I saw Emily. She was taller than Annabelle, paler, but the resemblance was uncanny. She was laughing with three of her friends, young girls on the verge of being teens. They were hanging streamers. So beautiful. So alive. I turned and fled, leaving the package on the steps.

As I was pulling out of the drive, the front door opened. Dorry stepped into the sunshine. She put a hand to her brow to block the sun as she watched me drive away. I couldn't help it. It wasn't that I didn't want to share Emily with her; it was that I couldn't. Not yet. Maybe not for a long while.

By the time I reached Jack Evans's Biloxi apartment complex, I'd quit shaking. I rang his doorbell, and when I started to knock, the door swung open.

"Jack!" I had a very bad feeling. "Jack!" I stepped inside and pushed the door open wide. The place had been trashed. Furniture was broken and I stepped on shards of crockery as I moved into the apartment. My first impulse was to call the police, but I had to see if Jack was hurt.

I found him in the bathroom, crumpled in the bathtub. Blood bubbled at his lips.

"Jack!" I pulled out my phone and called 911 for an ambulance.

"Go 'way," he urged, and it wasn't liquor that slurred his words. His teeth were gone. I saw one on the porcelain of the tub and felt a rush of nausea.

"Who did this?"

"Go 'way!" He flapped a useless hand. "They'll hurt you if you in'fere. I owe 'em money."

One leg looked at an odd angle. I was afraid to try to move him. I squatted on the floor beside him and touched his hand. "Help is coming."

He closed his eyes. "Let me die."

"Jack, whoever did this is going to pay." I didn't know if he should talk or stay quiet.

"Stay out of it."

Wise words, but an unlikely course of action. It was impossible to see someone with the shit beat out of them and just brush it off.

He looked at me. "Stay out of it. I brought this on myself. Gambling." He was more forceful, and that made me feel a little relieved.

"We'll talk when you feel better. Is there someone I should call? Your son?"

"No!"

"Okay, take it easy." I started to put my phone away when I heard something at the door. I got up and walked into the floodlights of a television camera. Tate Luckett was standing in the middle of Jack's trashed living room.

"We heard the 911 call," Tate said. "What happened?"

"Tate, this is a private residence. Leave."

"But you're here," he said.

"I'm not working, okay? Now leave." The worst thing I could do would be to lose my cool. I gave the cameraman a pointed look and he backed out the door. Tate was not so easily intimidated.

"Jack Evans lives here, doesn't he? Is this retribution for some story he's working on?"

"Tate, for the last time, please leave."

"Can I get a few comments from Jack?" Tate was trying to step around me but I blocked him, daring him to try and push past. We stood like that until the door opened for the paramedics and three police officers.

"Leave or I'll have the officers remove you," I said.

"I've heard you were cozy with the district attorney." His smile held distaste. "I guess you do what you have to do to get a job." He walked out, and I knew he'd be waiting so he could get a shot of Jack.

Jack didn't scream when the paramedics put him on the stretcher, but I saw his leg fall and knew it was badly broken. When they were ready to take him out the door, I threw his windbreaker over his face to hide the damage. Tate could speculate that it was Jack, but he couldn't document it. Instead of riding in the ambulance, I followed, wondering just how much worse my Sunday morning could get.

Two hours later I knew. Jack's spleen had burst and he was in emergency surgery for that and to set his broken leg. His teeth had been knocked out, and his wrist, three ribs and his jaw were broken, as well. He was in critical condition because one of the ribs had punctured his lung, which had collapsed. Had I not found him, he would have been dead in another few hours.

The story would be on the television news, so I called Hank Richey at home and told him what had happened.

"So he owes someone money." Hank's voice was speculative, and I wondered how much he knew about Jack's problems.

"Does Jack have any relatives nearby?" I asked. I knew he had a son in Seattle, but he was too far away to be of practical help.

"He has a daughter in Pass Christian." Hank seemed reluctant to say more.

"I'll call her," I said.

"They don't have a good relationship," Hank said.

So he knew something I didn't. "She should still know about this. Jack could die."

"She won't appreciate the call."

"She can do whatever she wants, but I'll tell her." I hung up and got her number and called. I barely got as far as saying I worked with her father when she lit into me.

"I don't have any money. If he owes you, that's your hard luck. Even if I had money I wouldn't bail him out. Why don't you ask him how many times he was around to pay my doctor's bills or buy me shoes when I was a kid? Ask him that. How dare he give you my number to call."

"Jack didn't give me the number. He's in surgery. He can't talk."

That slowed her down, at least long enough for me to tell her what had happened. She was too quiet, and I knew beneath the pain and anger there was some soft emotion for her father.

"He's at Biloxi General."

"I'm not going—"

"I don't care. I just wanted you to have the information." I hung up with a throbbing headache. My cell rang almost instantly, and I considered not answering it.

"I heard you were asking questions about my past."

I didn't recognize the voice and unknown number that appeared on the ID panel of my cell phone. "Who is this?"

"Deputy Chief Jimmy Riley. Why don't you meet me at Bebop's Bar?"

Something about the call made me hesitate. "I've been meaning to talk to you, but why are you calling me now?"

"Do you want to talk or not?"

"When?" I asked.

"Three o'clock."

"Sure," I said, making up my mind to take the bait. "I'll be there."

24

There were no vehicles at Bebop's, which wasn't surprising since it was early afternoon. The bar was a late place for serious drinking. Located between a junkyard for old cars and the back of an abandoned Wal-Mart in a rundown neighborhood just south of I-10, the bar was hidden from view from the road. Seedy didn't begin to cover the potholes filled with oily water, rusted tin roof and general air of trouble that hung over the place like a black cloud. I felt a ripple of concern as I started toward the front door. The whole thing screamed setup, but I had to see who was inside.

The door was weathered and worn and hadn't been cleaned since it was hung. When I pulled it open, the hinges screeched and stale cigarette smoke made my eyes water. Stepping from the bright sunlight, I was momentarily blinded. Once my eyes adjusted, though, I realized the place was empty. This was not good. Folks didn't leave the door of a place stocked with liquor unlocked.

At home I had a gun and a stun gun, but I normally didn't carry them in the car. Now I wished I'd taken the precaution. Instead of going inside, I eased back, checking the area around the building. There were numerous junked vehicles, many nearly covered by weeds and kudzu, but my heart skipped for a second when I saw an old blue van. Like the one that had been behind me in Ocean Springs. Taking a deep breath, I moved toward it, hiding behind the old junkers. When I got close enough, I was relieved to see it had long been abandoned. There were no seats in it, and the hood hung at an odd angle. It wasn't the same vehicle, but it was a clue that my paranoia was hard at work.

I went back to the bar, pushed open the door and moved cautiously into the room so I could face the door that closed behind me on a spring. Riley had called me for this meeting. There would be phone records. He was a cop. He was too smart to do something stupid.

"Hello!" It was pointless to try to be clandestine. The screeching door had signaled my arrival.

"Hey! Anybody here!" My voice echoed in the emptiness. At the bar, I stopped. There was a white envelope with my name on it. Beside it was an old-fashioned box of matches. One match had been stuck in the top of the box, another leaned against it. Both had been lit, resulting in a strange curl of burned matchstick, a duo united in death. At first I couldn't believe what I was looking at, but then the full impact hit me with the force of a physical blow. My stomach churned.

Spinning around, I looked for whoever had done this cruel thing. My impulse was to lash back, to hurt the person responsible. The bar was empty. Whoever had done this was long gone.

I retrieved the envelope and opened it. There was a

single note. "The wrong questions get dangerous answers," was written inside.

Jimmy Riley wasn't going to meet me. The bartender wasn't coming in to work. The place had been left open for one reason—so I could receive my message.

Using a napkin from the bar I carefully picked up the matches. I'd already touched the envelope. Nonetheless, I took all of it out of the bar, my legs unsteady and my breathing harsh in my own ears.

It wasn't until I was in my truck, the engine running and the doors locked, that the anger set in hard. "You cheap bastard," I whispered. "I'll have your ass in a sling." Jimmy Riley might be deputy chief of the Biloxi police, but he was in for a tragic surprise.

Two years ago I'd received warnings to back off a story. When I didn't, my house had been torched. I'd survived, but my daughter had died. No figure could have been more appropriate than those matchsticks, curled and blackened. Jimmy Riley was a sick, psycho bastard, and he was going to pay. The blue van was gone, and I sat in my truck until the shaking stopped and I could drive.

My first inclination was to go to a bar, but I went to the hospital. Jack had survived surgery and was in intensive care. I needed to talk to him, but instead I watched him sleep through the glass window of his room. Whom did he owe money to, and how much? Unless he volunteered the information and this was resolved, they'd beat him again. Violent images turned me toward the elevators. Passing a large window in the hallway, I looked down on the parking lot. A blue van with darkened windows was parked near the emergency entrance, and I reversed back to the nurses' station.

I walked up to the desk and stood a moment. There were two nurses there, but neither of them would look at me.

"Has anyone been by to see Jack?" I asked. A bank of monitors beeped behind the nurses. They were sharing a pizza and one of them passed the box to the other. She dug out a huge slice and they put the box down.

"Excuse me, has anyone—?"

"No." The younger one answered but didn't look up from the pizza slice she held in her hand.

"Mr. Evans may be in danger," I said.

"No kidding." Her look contained only boredom.

My adrenaline was still pumping. I reached down to the desk and flipped the pizza box onto the floor. Pepperoni and tomato sauce spattered on the linoleum tile. "Someone may try to hurt my friend again. I'd like for you to make sure no one goes into his room except medical staff you recognize."

The girl was frozen in her chair. The other nurse reached for the telephone. I put my hand on it, and she leaned back, eyes darting to her right where there was another phone.

"I'm simply asking you to do your job," I said softly. "If anyone tries to see Jack, call Detective Avery Boudreaux. And call me." I wrote the numbers down. "Because if anything untoward happens to my friend, I'll put enough heat on this hospital to broil both of you."

I waited to be sure they read the phone numbers and then walked away. As I turned the corner, I heard the mad scramble for the phone. They would call security, but it would be too late. I'd already be gone. Later I might feel bad about bullying the nurses, but at the moment I was still too angry.

Once at my truck, I had to make a decision. If I took the

matches and envelope to the Biloxi PD for fingerprinting, I risked the chance of running into Jimmy Riley or one of his henchmen. Riley had political connections or he would never have risen so high. That made it difficult to know whom to trust. There were independent sources where I could get the matches and note card fingerprinted. As an officer, Riley's prints were on file, but I wasn't sure which files were accessible by private companies. I headed east, noting that the van was still parked, and pulled my cell phone from my purse.

"Carson." Avery was surprised. "What's going on?"

"Did you question Jimmy Riley in regard to his job at the Gold Rush?"

"Why are you asking this?" There was an edge to his voice that matched my own.

"Damn it, Avery, I've been up front with you about everything. What did Riley say?"

"We're not going any further with this until you tell me what's going on."

Avery was stubborn, but he was no match for me. "I'm worried about Jack Evans. I'm beginning to think the beating Jack took has something to do with these murdered girls and a not-so-pretty past of a Biloxi police officer." I wasn't about to tell him about the threat to me.

"You think Riley is involved in Jack's beating?"

"Maybe." I didn't, but if Riley was involved in the murders of the girls, Avery might be compromised. One good cop couldn't fight corruption that came from the top. "Riley worked at the Gold Rush, and Jack's been working background on the murders. Maybe he dug something up, something Riley knew."

"Did Jack tell you anything?"

"Jack hasn't woken up yet. I'm speculating, and it occurred to me that Jimmy Riley was one good suspect. He was there, he failed to notice graves that had been dug in the parking lot he was being paid to guard and he's been on the coast for all the murders."

"Except Riley doesn't look anything like the composite Adrian Welsh gave us."

"The man Welsh described was a patron of the Gold Rush. Welsh never saw him do anything except sit at the bar. Riley was there, too, but no one noticed him because he was supposed to be there."

"Why would Riley stop killing and suddenly start again?" Avery changed tactics.

"Maybe because five bodies have been recently exhumed. I don't have the goddamn answers." My temper flared. "Why are you protecting him? All I want to know is what he said when you interviewed him. Or maybe you didn't interview him."

The implication in my voice was ugly, and I didn't care. Jimmy Riley had threatened me by bringing up my dead child. He'd used the thing most painful to me as a goad. If Avery wanted to protect his superior, then I would just have to trample them all down.

"I questioned Riley about his work at the Gold Rush right after we found the bodies there. He told me his job entailed walking the parking lot and making sure young women got safely to their cars. He busted up a few fights and took car keys away from people too drunk to drive. He said he mostly sat in the back shed and smoked."

"And you believed him?" I tried not to color my question.

"I had no reason not to. His story was the same as the other two police officers' who worked for Alvin. Carson, we questioned all three of them."

"And not a single one noticed that five bodies were buried at the Gold Rush."

"If you've uncovered something, you should tell me."

"What about the night Pamela Sparks was killed? Where was Riley and what was he doing?"

"He says he was on his boat. Alone. His wife had gone to the delta to visit her family."

So he actually had no alibi. "And this past Friday night?"

"He was out in the gulf fishing."

"You have his alibi confirmed?"

"Riley pulled out of the harbor, and he didn't come back until Saturday evening."

"Riley could have docked anywhere along the coast and doubled back to Biloxi."

"I don't need tips on how to run an investigation. If you know something, tell me." His patience was gone.

My anger won out over my common sense. "Read tomorrow's paper."

There was the click of the line in my ear. He'd hung up. A vein pounded in my temple. The fragile relationship that I'd been building with Avery was severed. From his point of view, I'd called him up and acted like a total ass. From my point of view, I'd seen too many cases where the boys in blue protected one of their own.

I used directory service to get an address on Stella Blue. Her house was on my way home, and I stopped there, catching her just as she returned from New Orleans.

She paused in her yard, her short shorts showing tanned

and toned legs. I got out of my truck and started across the well-maintained lawn.

If Stella was surprised to see me, she was too cool to show it. She waved me into the house and put a glass of merlot in my hand.

"I don't keep the hard stuff. Too tempting." She adjusted the blinds. "I saw the drawing of the suspect in the paper. If you came to ask, I saw guys that looked like that in the Gold Rush, but none that stuck out. I wish I could be more help."

I sipped the wine. "You can help me. Jimmy Riley. Tell me everything you know."

She sat on the arm of her sofa and thought for a minute. "Jimmy was quiet most of the time, but he liked to talk big, especially about his old man. He was something of a rogue agent for the CIA. Jimmy would talk about how his father would be sent on these secret missions into the jungle. I was never really clear who they were supporting, and I don't think Jimmy or the agents really knew. As far as I could tell by the stories, those spooks had a license to torture and kill anyone who crossed them. He told one story about how his daddy came walking out of the jungle with a guy's head in a burlap sack to take back to CIA headquarters."

"Did Jimmy believe the stories?" I was beginning to wonder if maybe the deputy chief was delusional.

"He seemed to believe everything he said. He loved to talk about his father. Of course, his old man was never around." She shrugged. "Maybe Jimmy needed to think his dad was doing something heroic to explain his absence." Her expression shifted to disgust. "Jimmy had this necklace made of human ears. I saw that."

I felt the tightening of my lungs. "Human ears?"

"Absolutely. He said his dad gave it to him. He said when his dad caught some of the rebels, he'd chop off one ear and then if they didn't talk, he'd cut off the other ear and string them on that necklace right in front of them. Must have been twenty ears, all shriveled up. It was pretty gross."

"Did he ever talk about his mother?"

She shook her head. "Not really. But one time his mom came to the club. I thought he was going to hit her. He pushed her back in her car and told her not to ever come there again. He was ashamed of her. He always referred to her as 'that fat cow.' Like if she were more attractive, his father would've stayed home."

Jimmy Riley was shaping up to be a close fit for Dr. Richard Jennings' profile. "When Riley worked at the Gold Rush, did he seem to take a particular interest in any of the girls?"

She shook her head. "He liked to talk to me and a couple of the others. He never tried to date us. He was engaged. We figured maybe he was one of the few men who took his pledge seriously."

I put the wine down on the coffee table. "Would you say his conduct was abnormal?"

She laughed. "It's a shame when you have to label a man who doesn't come on to you as abnormal. Let's just say the girls preferred Jimmy to the other security guards. They were always ass-grabbing and saying things they thought were funny and weren't."

"Was he normal?"

"A couple of girls figured he had some problems. You know, couldn't get it up." She stood. "He didn't seem interested in the dancers or the girls. But like I said, he had a fiancée."

"Did you ever meet her?"

She shook her head. "She never came to the Gold Rush. She was attached. It was a party place for single women."

I rose. "Stella, do you think Jimmy could hurt anyone?"

She thought about it. "Maybe. When he talked about the things his father did, he seemed to get a rush, you know. Like chopping those ears or torturing people got him off." The look that crossed her face was telling. "Like hurting people was sexually exciting for him. Honestly, he was a little creepy."

25

Once I was home, I put the matchbox on the kitchen table and stared at it. The blackened matches reminded me of two dancers, one holding the other in a graceful arc. I was mostly over my anger. What was left was a cold desire for revenge. Jimmy Riley had something to hide or he wouldn't have tried to frighten me off the story. Now I'd discover his secret, by means fair or foul. He'd chosen the rules of the game, and I was more than ready to play.

After Annabelle's death I'd broken. Guilt and shame and loss had dropped me to my knees. By the time I was strong enough to seek revenge, the trail was cold. Arson investigators had established that the fire was deliberate. The men I knew to be responsible had presented airtight alibis. Certainly they hadn't struck the match, but they'd paid an arsonist. They'd killed a nine-year-old girl, my beautiful daughter, without a single charge brought against them. There was no physical evidence linking them to the fire. That I knew they were guilty counted for nothing.

Rage is too weak a word to describe the emotion that

swept over me. Jimmy Riley had made the biggest mistake of his life.

My message light was blinking, but I ignored it, picked up the phone and called Kev Graves.

"Hey, Carson, glad you called me back. I have the photos and video. It's pretty explicit and there's no mistaking the doctor."

"Good work, Kev. I'll drive over and pick it up."

"No point in that—I can mail it."

"I have something I'd like for you to run through the Mobile PD for prints. Can you manage that?"

He hesitated. Kev took his job seriously. Sometimes the line between right and just was too narrow. This was one of those times. He knew I'd never ask unless it was important.

"Someone threatened me today," I said. "They used matches. There was a note telling me my questions were dangerous. A lot like the note I got before Annabelle was killed."

"Shit." His breathing was harsh. "Bring it in. I'll run it for you."

"This could come back on a high-ranking official in the Biloxi PD."

"I don't care if it's St. Peter. If he's threatening you with a fire, I'll break the bastard's neck myself."

Kev took his job seriously, but he took his friendships seriously, too. "I expect this will come back clean, but I have to know, and I can't trust the cops here."

"Whatever you need."

"I'll drive it over this evening," I said. "What do I owe you, Kevin?"

"The promise that you won't show this tape to Dorry unless you have no other choice."

"That goes without saying. Now how much?"

"I won't take money, Carson. But if you decide to confront this prick of a husband, let me know. I want the pleasure of holding him for you."

"You're the best, Kev. Will seven be okay?"

"I'll be waiting."

I hung up and went straight to my answering machine. There were three new messages. I hit Rewind and played them back.

"Hello, Carson." My breath caught at the sound of Daniel's voice, and I missed him so suddenly and so intensely that I felt sick. "I'm home in Miami. I think we should talk. In person. I'm coming to Biloxi this week. Call me and let's find a good time."

To say that I longed for him would be accurate, but the tenor of his message gave me warning. This was "the talk." He'd found someone he was interested in. He was coming to tell me face-to-face, as honor dictated. I knew it as certainly as I knew my name. With this talk, he would sever himself from me forever, and I wouldn't stop him. I loved him enough to cut him loose.

The second call was from Kev, letting me know he had the photos.

The third message was unexpected. The male voice sounded hesitant, afraid. "Uh, Ms. Lynch. The dead girl is Tammy Newcomb. Please. Find out who killed her." The caller hung up.

I replayed the message four times, listening hard for something in the voice or the background noises that would give me a clue as to the caller's identity. I didn't think it was the killer, but I couldn't be sure. I knew for certain it wasn't Jimmy Riley.

I picked up the phone to call Avery, then put it down. Instead, I got the phone book. There were seven Newcombs listed. One was T. Newcomb on Lavender Road just off Biloxi Beach. The address was an apartment complex, Woodland Vale. Right. They'd bulldozed all the trees when they built the complex. I drove back across the bay to Biloxi.

At the manager's desk I pretended to be a friend of Tammy's from out of town. He told me she was in 133 in Block D. I found it without trouble and tapped on the door. My hope was that a young woman would answer and tell me that she was Tammy Newcomb and that she was perfectly fine.

No one answered my knock. When I tried the doorknob, it opened. I stepped inside.

The windows of the apartment had been left open, and a gentle breeze lifted the sheers in the living room. In the semidarkness, they looked like ghosts hovering near the walls. The apartment was so silent that I could hear the beating of my own heart. I had the sense that someone lurked in the shadows. I took two steps inside and the door creaked closed behind me of its own volition.

I knew by looking at the furnishings that Tammy was young, and she was just starting out on her own. There was an innocence about the place that touched me. A photo on an end table caught my eye, and I picked it up. A cute young woman and a man were posed together. He held her hand, which sported an engagement ring. It was obviously the photo that had run in the newspaper announcing their impending marriage. I knew then that Tammy Newcomb was dead.

As I started to put the picture back I saw her answering machine had at least one message. Using a pencil to tap the buttons, I rewound the tape and played it.

There was a beep and the recorded voice of the machine. "One new call, 10:45 p.m., Friday." Static and background noise blurred over the tape. At first, I thought there was no message, but then I realized someone was whispering. I rewound the tape, turned up the volume and listened more closely.

"You'll make a lovely bride until innocence turns into deceit." The last word was almost hissed and it lingered in the stillness of the apartment.

Behind me, something crashed to the ground. I dropped and rolled, banging into the sofa as I scrabbled to regain my feet and look behind me. It took a few seconds to realize the curtains had blown into a vase of flowers. Water dripped onto the floor.

My hands shook as I rewound the tape and played it again, writing the exact words on a pad. I had to call Avery. There was no choice, but I was certainly going to get everything I could first. I could no longer act on the belief that the Biloxi Police Department was investigating this case in an unbiased way.

I checked the tape again to be sure there were no other messages from previous calls that might tell me a little more about Tammy Newcomb. There was nothing. I punched the machine off. The voice had been smooth, confident, chilling. I wondered if this was the last message Tammy Newcomb had heard before she died, or if she was already out Friday night and had never heard any of it. Was it the voice of the young man in the photo with her? Her fiancé? It didn't seem to fit him. This voice was rich, low, experienced with life…and death. The young man in the photo was callow and youthful.

My legal obligation was to call the police, except I'd found myself in a situation where the cards were stacked. I'd have one chance and one chance only to find out what I could before anyone else.

I knocked on the door of apartment 135 and listened to the rustling of papers before the door cracked open on the face of an older woman. She had a chain on the door, and she peered through the crack.

I told her who I was, showed her my business card and talked through the crack for a few minutes before she felt comfortable enough to open the door. Her name was Gladys and she'd lived beside Tammy ever since the young woman had moved there from Kansas.

"Why are you interested in Tammy?" she asked, worry touching her face. "She's a lovely young girl. Down here on her own, too. No family or anything. Just her fiancé."

Gladys was going to be a gold mine of information. I just had to take it slow and let her talk. Sweat trickled down the back of my shirt and into my slacks. Time was the one thing I didn't have. My anonymous caller may have called the police, too.

"Do you know her fiancé?" I asked, trying to keep my tone light and casually interested.

"Oh, yes, Harvey is a nice young man. Of course, we don't really like it that he's a blackjack dealer over at the Grand, but at least he has a job. Nowadays young folks have to take what they can get. Jobs don't grow on trees."

"That's true." I smiled. "Have they set a date for the wedding?"

"That's why Tammy is down here. Her folks didn't want her to come until after the wedding, but she wanted to get a job herself, and they've been looking for a house to rent together. Both of them in apartments is draining them financially, but Tammy won't move in with Harvey until she has that wedding band on her finger. That's a smart girl."

The image that leaped into my mind must have shown on my face.

"Is something wrong with Tammy?" Gladys asked. "She's not hurt, is she?"

"I don't know," I said.

"Why are you here asking all these questions?" She put it together. "That dead girl they found, is it Tammy?" Her voice rose high, and I heard furniture moving in the apartment. A male voice from behind Gladys asked what was wrong.

"There's a reporter here asking questions about Tammy." Gladys's voice rose higher and higher. Horror played across her features as she contemplated what might have happened to the neighbor she'd grown to like.

The door opened wider and a burly man in his mid-fifties wearing a white T-shirt stepped forward. "Can I help you?"

I introduced myself again and explained that I was trying to find Tammy's fiancé and any information I could about Tammy.

"I'm calling the police," he said. "If there're questions to be asked, they should be doing the asking."

"What's Harvey's last name?" I asked Gladys since I knew her husband wasn't going to tell me another thing. I'd upset his wife and he didn't like it.

"Bailey," she said. "Harvey Bailey. He's from up around Tupelo, Mississippi. Or at least that's what he said." She was trembling. "Harvey wouldn't hurt a fly, though. And certainly not Tammy. He loves her." The last sentence became a wail. She turned into her husband's broad chest.

"I'm calling the cops," he said again before he slammed the door.

Good, I thought as I left Block D and headed back to the apartment complex office. If they called the police, I wouldn't have to.

The young man behind the counter was fairly easy to intimidate. I normally preferred the soft approach, but at any minute I'd hear the sirens. I wanted to be gone from the scene, on the off chance that Avery would try to arrest me. I didn't have time to waste in jail.

The clerk tried to hold firm, but between the pressure I applied and his desire to have his name in the paper as part of a big story, I got Tammy Newcomb's information, including her parents' names and address in Paradise, Kansas, and the fact that she worked as a graphic designer at a small public relations firm in Gulfport. Tammy had turned twenty a few weeks before, and she was a quiet girl who paid her rent on time.

I checked my watch. It was after four. As I was leaving, I heard the sirens. I went out the back exit. Using my cell phone, I called the Grand Casino. Harvey Bailey was on the floor. His shift was over at nine, but I didn't have time to wait. He was my most likely suspect as the man who'd called and left me an anonymous message.

It took about twenty minutes to drive to the casino and park. I found Harvey dealing at a table. I watched him from behind a bank of slot machines for a while. He was courteous to the players but subdued, a man who kept looking at his watch and then scanning the crowded floor of the casino. He was expecting trouble, and it would no doubt arrive. I walked over and took an empty place.

"Hi, I'm Carson Lynch," I said. His hand on the cards froze. We stared at each other for a moment.

"Excuse me," he said to the man and woman who were ready to play, "I have to close this table."

"Hey, I'm on a streak," the man complained.

"I apologize. I'm feeling ill," Harvey said, and he looked as if he might be sick at any second.

He stepped out of the pit and I followed him through the maze of clinking, blaring, whirring machines to the employee lounge. He leaned against a wall. "I can't lose this job," he said, unable to look at me. "My fiancée is dead, and I'm having to deal cards to assholes because I can't lose this job."

"Why are you so sure it's Tammy?" I asked. There was no doubt he was my caller. I recognized his voice.

"She didn't call me Friday night. Or yesterday. Or today. She's not like that. She's not that kind of person. I knew something terrible had happened to her, and then I heard some folks talking about a dead girl, Saturday. When I read the paper today, I knew it was her."

"Why didn't you call the police?" I asked.

He turned to me, his expression tense. "I have a record in Tupelo. I got into some trouble. To get this job, I had to lie. If the police go snooping around, I'll be in real trouble."

"I'm afraid it's too late for that," I said, feeling both pity and revulsion. "You should have contacted them when she went missing Friday."

"I know," he said. "I kept thinking that she'd show up and say her folks had gotten sick or something." He shook his head and I saw tears in his eyes. "My life changed when I met Tammy. I'd made a lot of bad choices, but it was going to be okay with her."

"I didn't call the police, but I'm sure her neighbors did. I think it would be best if you went and talked to the casino management now." He was only a kid, and he had suffered a terrible loss. I hardened my heart and stuck to business. "Then I'd put in a call to the police. They're probably on their way, but it will make it look better."

He nodded, using the heel of his hand to dash his tears away.

"What were Tammy's plans Friday night?" If I could figure out where she'd been, I might be able to determine where she'd been abducted from.

"I didn't get off until midnight, and she was supposed to meet me at my apartment. She got off at five, and she was going to go shopping for some things for our house. Her mother and sister were coming down to give her a shower." His voice trembled, but it didn't break. "She was going to look at dishes and things. At Edgewater Mall."

"By herself?"

"She hadn't had a chance to make a lot of girlfriends. She liked her neighbors, but they were older. We were both working as hard as we could to save some money for a honeymoon. We were getting married in June."

His shoulders dropped another notch. "How am I going to get along without her?" he asked.

I handed him my cell phone to call the police because I didn't have an answer.

26

When a loved one was murdered, the repercussions were endless. Trust shriveled. My truck was parked a hundred yards down the road from Jimmy Riley's house, but I was across the street in a dense azalea bush that offered an advantageous view of Riley's front door and his boat slip, where a large craft bobbed at the dock. After all my years in Miami, I still didn't know one boat from another. That didn't matter. I only needed to make sure no one was home so I could board the boat and have a look around.

Since Riley had become a suspect in the murders, I'd had several revelations. I'd wondered how someone had walked Pamela Sparks out to the end of the public pier, especially since the gate on the beach had been locked at 10:00 p.m. in an attempt to keep stupid tourists or drugged teenagers from falling in the Sound and drowning. There were ways around the locked gate, but the most obvious conclusion was that Pamela had been brought to the pier by boat. Until recently, I hadn't considered that possibility.

My mind was speeding along when the front door of

Riley's house opened and a slender woman stepped outside. She came down her front walk to the sidewalk and turned left.

The front door of the house opened again, and Riley stepped out. "Where are you goin'?" he yelled, his words slurred by drink. He must have been half-crocked when he called me, yet he'd sounded sober.

The woman I recognized as Yvonne Riley, his wife, stopped. "I was planning on taking a walk, but your bellowing has probably stirred up the whole neighborhood." She returned to the house, brushed past Riley and went inside. The door slammed. For a long moment, Riley swayed on his front porch. At last he turned slowly and entered.

Dusk had slipped over me from the east. As night began to fall, I inhaled the odor of damp earth and leaves from beneath the azalea. A light flicked on in a front upstairs window of the Riley house. As drunk as Riley was, he'd probably passed out by now. If I was going to search the boat, I had to take a risk and do it while there was still a little light in the sky.

The grass was thick, lush, as I ran across the backyard. The short wooden pier announced my footsteps as I ran down it to the boat. I didn't have the tools or expertise to do an in-depth search, but if there was something obvious—like bloodstains or clothes belonging to the dead girls—I might be able to find that. Besides, I couldn't count on anyone else to even look.

Riley was a drunk, and chances were that he was a careless drunk. There was nothing more important in an alcoholic's day than a drink. It was a long shot, but I might get lucky.

The galley was the first place to start. The tiny kitchen was surprisingly spotless. I went through the drawers. The

knives were neatly placed in their slots. The cooking gear
was stowed away, and the floors and counters scrubbed.
My take was that Riley didn't cook a lot.

The boat rocked gently in a westerly breeze, the tie
lines complaining. Or was it something else? Had someone
slipped down the pier and stepped onto the deck? I held
myself perfectly still.

I'd been careful to make sure I wasn't followed to the
neighborhood. The blue van still troubled me, but I hadn't
seen it. Even though I told myself there were hundreds of
blue panel vans on the coast, I still felt apprehensive.

After a long minute of waiting without additional noises
coming up the deck, I continued in my search. The tiny
bedroom was a repeat of the kitchen. The bed was neatly
made, nothing out of place. Riley's clothes were folded in
the drawers of the built-in dresser. Even the head was clean
and orderly. Not so much as a bottle of headache medicine
was there. Disappointed, I moved to the stairs.

The boat had been a long shot and a waste of time. I was
climbing out of the cabin when I heard footsteps on the
wooden dock. Before I could duck back down, a beam of
light swung over the deck and caught me full in the face,
blinding me. The boat shifted as someone boarded. In a
moment, light flooded the companionway where I stood.

Yvonne Riley was standing on the deck over the
stairs, a flashlight and a pistol pointed at me. "Come up
here," she said.

I eased up the short flight of stairs, my eye on the gun
and the silhouette of the woman who held it. She didn't
seem nervous or upset.

"What are you doing here?" she asked.

"I'm Carson Lynch, a—"

"I know who you are. What are you doing here?"

I decided to risk the truth. "Looking for evidence."

"Of what?"

There was no easy way to say I suspected her husband of murder. "Mrs. Riley, does your husband go fishing alone often?"

She was a smart lady. She lowered the gun but kept the flashlight beam on my face.

"Jimmy has a temper, but he didn't kill those girls." She spoke in a monotone. "Believe me, I'd love to divorce him, but not by seeing him charged with a crime he didn't commit. He was fishing last Friday night."

"Are you sure?"

"Yes," she said simply. "I am."

"He called me today and asked me to meet him at a bar at three o'clock. When I got there, the bar was empty, but he left a message for me. A threat."

"Jimmy couldn't have called you," she said. "He was asleep on the sofa all afternoon, from about eleven o'clock until just a few minutes ago."

She sounded so sure, but I didn't hide my incredulity.

"Look, even if he did call you," she said, "he didn't kill those girls." She clicked off the light. "Now get off our property. I'm going to sit here and count to twenty. If you aren't gone by the time I finish, I'm going to call the police and charge you with criminal trespassing."

"Carson!" Kev stood up from his desk and scooped me against his chest. Though I was tall, he made me feel petite. "You look good."

"You, too," I said, and he did. Kev had put on forty pounds from his lean high school days, but it was muscle he carried, not fat. I looked around his home office and saw that he had a simple but very professional operation. I turned my focus back to him. His hair was close-cropped and bore a sprinkling of gray, but his blue eyes were as intensely curious as I remembered. He'd been the high school football jock who'd also excelled at science. He'd hung around the house, talking to my father about a career in pharmacy. I realized suddenly that it had never been pharmacy school that interested him.

"How's Dorry?" he asked.

"She's a fool," I said slowly, "and me, too."

His smile was slightly embarrassed. "I was so in love with her that I couldn't see straight when she was near, but I played it so cool."

"She never suspected you really cared, Kev."

"I was never very good at telling folks how I felt. And once she met Tommy Prichard, she never knew there was anyone else around. I'm glad she didn't suspect my feelings because then she would have been uncomfortable around me."

I sighed and tried not to think of what Dorry's life might have been like with Kev. She would have finished college and had a career. "Had I realized your feelings, I wouldn't have asked you to do this surveillance."

"I have to say, my first impulse was to break the door in and beat the shit out of the good doctor."

My lopsided grin told him how much I liked that scenario. "But you did the right thing."

He sat on the edge of his desk. "Did I?" From the desk

beside him, he pulled a manila envelope of photos and a VCR tape. "The good doctor is a little on the kinky side."

I felt shame for my sister as I took the items he held out to me. I wouldn't further embarrass myself or Kev by looking at them now.

"I'm sure this is a pattern of behavior," Kev said. "This nurse is one of a long line. I'm not cynical—I've just seen it so many times before. He'll screw her for a while, dump her, then move on to a fresh face."

"Do you think he'll ever stop?"

He shrugged. "Depends on whether his self-interest kicks in and he realizes that the consequences are greater than the pleasures." He frowned. "I doubt this has anything to do with whether he loves Dorry or not. This is all about his ego."

"Fuck his ego. He could give my sister a disease."

"He's a doctor. Let's hope he has some common sense."

"He's a doctor with his dick in charge of his life. Excuse me if I don't put a lot of faith in his common sense."

Kev sighed. "It's a shame I was so infatuated with Dorry. I think I overlooked a diamond in the rough. You talk like one of the guys."

I finally laughed. "Flattery will get you nowhere, Graves."

"What did you bring me?"

"It's in the truck." I went out and got the matchbox and the note. When I put it on his desk, he bagged them and marked them. "I'll run them. If I get a match, I'll call you right away, but these things are probably clean."

I nodded. "I have to try."

"You want to talk about your suspicions?"

I considered it. If anything happened to me, Jimmy Riley might actually get away with it. "Riley wants me to stop asking questions, presumably about his past. Maybe because he killed those girls. Maybe for another reason." I also told Kevin about my trip to Tammy Newcomb's apartment. I could tell I'd worried him.

"Carson, you've stomped all over a serious police investigation. They have a right to arrest you and they can make the charges stick."

"It'll make excellent copy."

I could see that remark flew all over him. Police officers hated to be reminded of the power of the press. "Appreciate my situation, Kev. I'm not dealing with you—I'm working with police officers I don't know. My past experience tells me that it's as easy for a cop to be a crook as an accountant or a banker or a schoolteacher. And this particular cop is the deputy chief."

"And my experience tells me that it's real easy for a reporter to go off half-cocked and use the power of the press for the wrong reason." His face was red and his eyes a hard blue.

"I know you're not that kind of cop, and you know I'm not that kind of reporter." I spoke gently, trying to move away from the cliff of hard feelings we were both about to step over.

His features softened, but only slightly. "Carson, the Miami police did everything they could when Annabelle was killed. I talked with the investigating officer several times. They had absolutely nothing to go on, except your suspicions. Sure, they could have arrested Charlie Sebring and his cohorts, but they couldn't have held them. There was no evidence." The last was spoken very clearly.

What he said was true, but that didn't lessen the sudden wave of rage that swept over me. "That bastard hired someone to burn my house and kill me. They killed Annabelle instead."

"I don't doubt it. But the police can't arrest someone without evidence. You know this. Remember the '60s and '70s? For God's sake, remember when your friend's father was arrested and died in the jail? That's what happens when cops decide to be the judge and jury. You know that can't happen again. Not ever. Not even if some criminals get away."

I was finding it difficult to breathe. "You wouldn't say that if it had been your daughter who burned to death in her bedroom." The tears started and I couldn't stop them. "She thought she was safe. She was sleeping." I was panting. "They waited until Daniel was out of town on business. They planned this because I was supposed to be home, but I was late. They didn't care that they killed my little girl."

"There is absolutely nothing I can say that will ever make this any different for you. I won't try. But the Miami police were not corrupt. They tried, Carson. I know that. And you have to believe it."

I swallowed a bitter lump of anger. "The horrible truth is that I do believe you, Kev. I know they tried. They just couldn't do anything, and Charlie Sebring is still building shoddy schools, and the next big storm that comes through, more innocent people will die. Probably children."

He stood up and walked over to me. His large hands held my shoulders and he squeezed tightly. "He'll screw up, Carson. One day, he'll screw up. And he'll pay."

"My daughter is dead. She paid with her life two years ago and she was innocent."

He hugged me against his chest and held me tightly. "This isn't over, Carson. I promise you that. It isn't over."

For just a moment I leaned against him and drew from his strength. I would feel ashamed later, but now I needed him. His hands stroked my back, giving comfort. It was a luxury I hadn't allowed myself in a long time. Strange that I could accept it from this man, a high school friend who was in love with my sister.

When he felt me begin to straighten, he released me and stepped back. He was smart enough to change the subject and quickly. "On the Jimmy Riley thing. Do you have any physical evidence that he's the killer? For that matter, do you have any evidence that he actually left those matches and note for you?"

It was good to meet the logical wall of Kev's thinking. Emotions played no role. I was back in control. "The fingerprints will be evidence. I'll check his phone records."

"The fingerprints *may* be evidence," he emphasized, "*if* we get them. The phone record would be helpful."

I nodded. In my years of reporting, I'd learned that the worst type of investigator, be it a writer or a police officer, was the one who jumped to a conclusion and then saw only the evidence that fit the conclusion. "I'm not going to print anything."

"I've been following your stories," Kev said. "From what I can tell, the police have very little to work with. Whoever is killing these girls is smart and they know police procedure."

"There are things that I haven't put in the paper."

"Like?"

"The ring finger of each girl has been severed. On the bodies in the grave and the two recent dead girls. The police aren't sure if this is the same killer or a copycat. If it is a copycat, it would have to be someone with privileged information, like a police officer. I'm the only reporter who knows about the ring fingers."

He took a breath. I could only imagine what he'd seen and heard in his years of law enforcement, but it was never easy to visualize the things one human could do to another.

"This Riley guy could fit the profile of a sexual killer," he conceded. "The necklace of ears, the taking of trophies. But *could be* is a long leap to *is*."

I nodded again.

"Carson, don't corner him."

His words tripped the danger switch in my brain. I felt the tingle of fear. "I don't intend to. I won't write a story unless the police charge him."

"I don't care what you write. I care about what you do. You forget that I knew the seventeen-year-old girl who snuck into Hubie Kittrell's barn to see if he was cooking mash."

"I was right."

"And you nearly got your head blown off by an irate bootlegger."

"That was a long time ago." My sudden flush of memory turned bitter. "I'm not that girl anymore."

Kev stood up and walked over to me, lifting my chin. "Oh, yes, you are. You had the stuffing kicked out of you, but you're still there. Maybe a little older and wiser." He smiled. "I can only hope."

"I've gotta go, Kev. I have a story to write for tomorrow's paper."

He nodded. "Call me if you need me for anything. I can hold 'em while you kick 'em."

It was an old joke between us, and it touched me. "I wish—" I broke it off.

"Wish what?"

"Nothing," I said, because my wishes were so conflicted. I wished Dorry had married Kev. I wished he'd been on the police force in Miami. I wished I had been home when the fire that killed Annabelle started. But mostly I wished I could be the strong, fearless girl that Kev remembered.

27

It was shortly after nine when I returned to Biloxi. I put in a call to a very angry Avery Boudreaux. He curtly told me that Tammy Newcomb's family had been notified. Harvey Bailey had identified her body in the morgue, and he was now being questioned.

"I thought we had an understanding, Carson," Avery said.

"Things have changed."

"You bet they have. Mitch can play up to you however he wishes, but you violated my trust when you went in that apartment and didn't call me."

"I don't have to justify my actions to you." He could play wounded and indignant all he wanted. If I found out I'd misjudged him, I'd apologize at a later date.

"You're smart enough to know I can have you arrested."

That statement told me he wasn't going to. "Have you checked into Jimmy Riley's whereabouts the nights Tammy Newcomb and Pamela Sparks were murdered?" I asked.

There was a pause. "You really think Riley is the murderer?"

"It wouldn't be the first time a cop hid behind his badge."

"You're wrong on this, Carson."

"Prove it to me."

He sighed. "This explains a few things, but it doesn't make them right."

"Set up a meeting with Riley. Me, you and him. No one else." This was the course of action I'd decided to take. I was going to confront Riley head-on, but with a witness.

"I'm a little busy to be scheduling tea parties."

"I was straight with you, Avery. I held information out of the newspaper, and I told you everything I found. I gave you my leads before I wrote them. You didn't tell me jack about your interview with Riley. Is he a suspect?"

There was a pause. "I can't trust you, Carson."

"I know the feeling. Set up the meeting." I hung up. I had the information that I needed to write my story. The Newcomb family in Kansas had been notified that their daughter was dead. I was free to use her name in the paper, but I wouldn't harass them for a quote. That could wait until Monday.

Clive was on the desk, and he told me to go home before he even edited the story. He said he'd call if there were questions. I left, feeling ten years older than I had the day before.

Driving home, I thought of some of the things Kev had said. I'd been six when my friend's father disappeared from his home. We were in first grade, and it was right before Christmas. She didn't come to school one day, but I thought maybe she'd gone shopping. It was only after I got home that I heard my mother talking on the phone. She was whispering, unaware that I'd even come in the house. I stood in the small back den where she kept a television playing her afternoon shows and eavesdropped, caught by the panic and fear that threaded my mother's normally reserved voice.

"Do you really think they killed him?" she'd asked. The words were branded in my mind. There had been a pause and she'd caught her breath. "Dear God. I have to call right now. John Tierce didn't hang himself. Those men killed him."

She'd put the phone down and turned to see me standing there. She'd shooed me out of the house and for the only time I could remember, she locked the door so I couldn't come back in. I'd sat on the back steps, wondering who would hurt my friend's daddy, a big man who never smiled but who'd taught me how to cut a whistle from bamboo cane.

It was only later, in junior high school, that June had told me the rest of the details. Some men with white masks had come and taken her father. He'd struggled, and they'd beaten him. June's mother had jumped on them and they hit and kicked her until she was unconscious. June had clung to her father's leg, but they'd pulled her off and tossed her out of the way as if she were a doll. They'd dragged John out of the house. Two days later, he was found, severely beaten, hanging in a county jail cell. His death was ruled a suicide. He'd been charged with attempted burglary of a backwoods service station.

Those were the excesses Avery was speaking about when cops became judge and jury. I understood. But there was also the other extreme, where police officers protected their own from punishment. Neither course of action was acceptable.

At last I pulled into my driveway, a haven of foliage. I parked under the portico and got out, stretching. As I started to unlock the door, I realized there was a light on in the den. My fingers held the key in the lock, but I didn't turn it. When I'd left the house, no lights had been turned on. I was positive of it. Someone had been in my home, and they were either very careless or they wanted me to know it.

Anger was my first reaction. Someone had violated my home. My gun was in my bedroom, in a drawer. I kept it cleaned and loaded, and I went to the firing range at least every six months to practice. After Annabelle was murdered, handling the gun became a passion. I was a damn good shot, and put to the test, I'd pull the trigger without hesitation. I had to be careful, though. Whoever had broken in might still be there.

I removed my key quietly and slipped around to the screened porch that led to my bedroom. Using the small penknife on my key ring, I sliced the screen, unlatched the door and entered the porch. I unlocked my bedroom door and slipped into the darkness of the house. Standing in my bedroom, I listened, but nothing seemed out of order, except the cats hadn't acknowledged my arrival.

At the thought that someone had hurt them, I felt my chest constrict. In a moment, the gun was in my hand. Moving silently through my bedroom, I slipped down the hall to the den. If someone was there, I wanted the element of surprise and the authority of a .38.

As I stepped into the doorway of the den, I saw him. He was sitting in a comfortable leather chair, the reading lamp focused over his shoulder on a sheaf of paperwork he held. I lowered the gun and drew in a long breath.

"Daniel," I said, the relief so sweet. "You scared the bejesus out of me." The cats looked up at me from his lap.

His expression went from startled to electric. He put his papers aside and slowly stood, the cats jumping to the floor.

"My God, Carson, you look like an avenger. If I ever doubted you can take care of yourself, I don't anymore." He stepped toward me. "Please, put the gun down."

I set it on a table, too keenly aware of every physical move and sensation. In the past two years, my husband hadn't seen me alive. I'd been numbed by drugs and grief and alcohol. Now I hummed with adrenaline.

We stood for a moment, staring at each other. Daniel was standing in the pool of light cast by the lamp, his face half lit, half shadowed, revealing the angles I knew so well. He was a handsome man with classic features, a rare blend of his Nicaraguan heritage on his mother's side and some combination of Nordic blood in his father's line. His brown hair was long, curling more than he liked, though I preferred it that way. He'd lost weight, accentuating his tall, lean frame. My mouth was dry and I licked my lips.

His presence was so unexpected that I didn't know what to do. When he stepped toward me, though, I met him halfway. I was in his arms, on fire with his kisses. In the recesses of my brain, I knew that I was making a mistake. I didn't care. I'd been dead for so long, had never expected to feel alive again. Daniel was the man who knew me best, the man who held my heart.

His hands tore at my clothes. I fumbled with his belt, jerking at the button and zipper of his pants. This was all familiar now. In our marriage, our passion had never been slaked. I loved his touch. I craved the sensations he aroused in me with the tiniest kiss, the whisper of his breath on my skin. From the first time I'd made love with Daniel, we'd been totally compatible.

We made it to the bedroom, mostly naked, and I pulled him onto the bed with me. There was nothing but the need for his touch, for the joining. We had no time for whispers or the slow seduction that he was such a master of. We made love hard and fast and with a desperation that sent us both into climax. We were left panting and spent, covered in nothing but a sheen of sweat.

He put his hand on my stomach, a light touch of possession and love. "I'm glad to see you, Carson," he whispered into my damp hair. "I gather you're glad to see me, too."

I kissed him. I'd missed him more than I would ever tell him. In the morning, things would become complicated. This night, though, I claimed the intimacy and love of the man who would always claim a portion of my heart. He was an unexpected gift I didn't have the strength to refuse.

As if he sensed my thoughts, his hand moved lower. I turned to him and kissed him with such intensity that he groaned.

"I've missed you, Carson," he said.

But I didn't want gentleness or declarations of love. I was too hungry. We made love until we fell asleep, exhausted and tangled in the sheets. I awoke once in the night to find Miss Vesta and Chester keeping watch over us from the safety of the chaise beside the window.

28

A hazy gauze of sunlight filtered through the bedroom window, casting the features of the man asleep in my bed in soft light. Daniel's tousled hair was a soft, golden brown against the sage sheets. His bronzed skin was a shade so beautiful that I wanted simply to stroke my hand across his face. When I sat on the edge of the bed, his eyes opened. He always awoke with a smile, and it was one of the things I loved best about him.

"Good morning," he said as he pushed up on the pillows and took the cup of coffee I'd brought him. His fingers brushed mine and the spark was totally sexual.

"We didn't get much of a chance to talk last night," I said. I thought I might feel guilty, but I didn't. Instead, I felt alive.

"Sometimes words are a hindrance." He sipped the coffee, but his gaze slid from mine. Though I was prepared for loss, the first stab of pain was brutal. Daniel was feeling guilty. I hadn't been prepared for that.

"We've never been less than totally honest," I said, wishing that we could be spared this conversation for a day, or a week, or the rest of my life. But Daniel had come to tell me something. The past had climbed out of the grave and bound us together. But like all stories of the night, it disappeared in the light of the sun. "I know you've found someone. It's okay. I know that's what you came to tell me. Last night doesn't change anything."

He looked up at me, the pain clear in his eyes. "Doesn't it?" he asked. "Doesn't it change everything? I thought you were dead to me, Carson. Last night proves otherwise. Yes, I've found someone. I care for her. I could have a marriage with her, and children. But what I feel for her is a pale imitation of last night. Last night changed everything."

The last words were spoken with bitterness. When I didn't respond, he continued.

"When Annabelle died, you lost your daughter." He threw back the sheet and got out of bed. He found his clothes and began to dress. "I lost Annabelle and you. Except you weren't dead. You were right there in front of me. I could touch you and talk to you, but it did no good. Each day you drifted a little further from me. And I was helpless to stop you. I lost you in degrees."

My eyes burned with a dryness worse than tears, but I didn't interrupt him. He jerked on his shirt and turned to me.

"You let me go. I wasn't worth hanging on to. And now, you toss me my freedom again, as if it were of no consequence to you. You tell me that nothing has been changed by last night. I'm just a convenient fuck, I suppose. A novel substitute for the bottle you normally sleep with."

"Daniel, I didn't mean that." He was too angry to listen

to anything I said, and I didn't blame him. "I only meant to give you a chance to find happiness."

"A happiness that doesn't include you. Correct?"

I took a slow breath, trying to think. "I'm getting better. I am. I'm…stronger. But I have a long way to go. I'm not ready to offer the things I know you want."

"You're not the only one who's changed." He tucked in his shirt and slipped on his shoes. "Goodbye, Carson. I'll telephone when I've calmed down."

"Daniel, please don't leave like this." In the past two years I'd seen him despondent and angry, but I'd never felt the lash of his fury. Perhaps I deserved it, but maybe not. I hadn't held a gun to his head to get him into my bed.

"Do you even know what you want?" His hazel eyes sparked.

"Yes."

My answer stalled him. "What?"

"I want you to be happy."

It took several seconds for the anger to leave him, but when it did, he walked toward me. "Sometimes I forget who you are. Nothing is ever simple with you."

"I don't mean to hurt you. After Annabelle died, I couldn't help it. I did what I had to do to survive. But now, last night, I didn't mean to do anything that would harm either of us."

"Even though you knew I came here to tell you I'd found another woman?"

"I knew when I called you. She was there. With you."

"And you didn't care?"

"That would not be an accurate statement. I care. Deeply. But I know how much you want a family. I know that you want another child. Not to replace Annabelle, but to love for who and what that child is. You've never hidden your passion for family, Daniel. And I want that for you, even if I can't give it to you."

He came and sat down on the bed. His hand gathered mine and held it. "I don't know if you're crazy or simply the most generous woman I know. Last night tells me that you still love me."

"I do."

"My love…" He hesitated as he sought the right words. "My love is not so generous. The idea of you with another man is like a raw wound filled with salt. I dream about you with someone else and I wake up wanting to fight. How can you love me and want me to be with someone else? I don't understand this."

I wondered if I understood. I had to try. "I think that I'm broken, Daniel. Last night caught me by surprise. I didn't have time to raise my defenses. But I'm afraid that if I began to love you every day, I'd wall off those feelings so I can't be hurt."

He thought about it for a moment. "Before Annabelle, you loved me unconditionally."

"Before Annabelle, I loved myself."

"You still blame yourself." It was a bleak statement of fact.

"I'm getting better, but it's a long road. I'm forty-one. There's no time to heal and have a child. You need a younger wife."

"It's that simple for you."

What did he want from me? "Science doesn't always dovetail with emotion."

Daniel picked up his tie from the floor and wadded it

into his pocket. "All these years I thought you were your father's daughter. Now I see you were created from the mold of your mother."

He walked out of the bedroom and I heard the front door slam. It was only then that I wondered how he'd gotten to my house without a car. I called a taxi for him to be picked up on Washington Avenue. He'd go to the Gulfport airport and wait for a flight to Miami.

Daniel had left me numb, and I did nothing to try and awaken my senses. I was late for work, but surprisingly no one had called to dog me about it. I remembered then that Brandon was bringing the prospective buyers, in all likelihood my new bosses. I cursed a blue streak as I showered and dug through my closet for clean slacks, a blouse and a blazer to hide the wrinkles in my blouse.

On the drive I turned on the radio, focusing on the WKIS report of the coast murders. To my surprise, the newscaster credited my story in the paper as his source. I pulled into the parking lot and hurried to the office.

The newsroom was busy. Reporters typed away at their computers, focused on their work. It was a model place of employment with no dirty coffee cups or feet propped on desks and no chitchat. Standing outside Brandon's office was a short man with a huge nose and big ears. He looked like a caricature of a certain former independent candidate for the U.S. presidency. He was watching me as I came in, and he said something to Brandon, who turned around and glared at me. The two men began to approach as I ducked into my office.

"Ms. Lynch," the short man said as he came into my office and extended his hand. "Saul Grotowitz."

"Good to meet you," I said, ignoring Brandon, who seemed to want to kill me with his gaze.

"Excellent story in this morning's newspaper. I remember your column from Miami. That was before you were fired."

"Yes," I said calmly.

"Brandon tells me that you're considering doing a column here."

That was news to me. "I'm interested," I said, keeping it vague. I had no idea what Brandon might have said, and though I had no inclination to save his bacon, I wasn't averse to doing another column.

"You're aware that Gannett has a policy against hiring reporters with drinking problems."

"I'm aware that every newspaper has such a policy." I needed a job, but I wasn't going to beg for it.

He stared at me. "Are you in a treatment program?"

"No, and I don't intend to be. I'm not a twelve-step kind of person."

"You have to make some effort, Ms. Lynch. I'm trying to meet you halfway."

"Carson has done a story a day for the past two weeks," Brandon said. "She's on top of every lead and she follows up. If she's drinking, it doesn't show. Except for the fact that she can't seem to make it to work on time."

"I worked Saturday and Sunday," I said calmly. "I'm not a child and I won't be treated like one. I do my job when it takes sixty hours a week and I won't be kept on a leash like some pet."

Saul Grotowitz turned away to hide his smile. When he faced me again, he was serious. "I'm not sure you'll fit into the structure of our system," he said.

"I'm not sure I want to." I could see this was coming to a bad end. As much as I'd begun to care about this job, I couldn't conform. I wasn't strong enough or certain enough of myself to let someone box me in.

"You're a talented writer, Ms. Lynch. I wish you the best of luck," Saul Grotowitz said as he indicated to Brandon that he was ready to move on.

Brandon cast one surprised look over his shoulder as they exited and he closed my office door.

I sat down at my desk. In the space of two hours I'd lost my ex-husband and my job. I was batting a thousand.

The telephone rang and, figuring it would be Avery, I readied myself for the third ream job of the day. Might as well get it over with.

"Lynch," I said.

"Carson, it's Avery. Can you meet me for lunch?"

"Sure," I said, a little confused by his abrupt change in attitude. "Where and when?"

"Bucky's Bistro, at noon. I'll reserve a table."

"I'll be there." Now I only had to occupy myself for another two hours before lunch. I picked up the phone to check on Jack at the hospital.

He was actually able to talk, but what I had to tell him called for a personal visit. Since I'd already ruined my chances with the big cheese from Gannett, I left the office and drove to the hospital.

Jack looked amazingly chipper for a man who'd been beaten to a bloody pulp. He'd been moved from intensive care to a private room, and a policeman sat in a chair outside his door reading the newspaper. He ignored me as I tapped on the door and entered at Jack's request.

"I've decided to take up smoking again as soon as I get out of here."

Jack's first words made me smile. "Good plan. Now that you know how it feels not to be able to breathe, you should go for that sensation on a permanent basis."

"Carson, I would have died if you hadn't come along." He was suddenly serious.

"But you didn't. Jack, do you know who did this to you?"

"He was a professional. He knew exactly how to work it." He winced. "The maximum pain for the least amount of effort."

"Do you owe someone money?"

"Yeah, a lot. I'm in way over my head. They got tired of my excuses."

I sat in the Naugahyde chair beside the bed. "Are you sure it was about your debt?"

"These guys take their loans seriously."

He was embarrassed, and now wasn't the time to push an offer of help on him. "Tell me what you know about Jimmy Riley."

Jack's face was still swollen, his words a little slurred by the gauze wadded in his mouth. "What's Riley got to do with anything?"

"That's what I intend to find out." I told him the facts I had.

"Carson, I've known this guy for years. He's not a good cop, but I don't think he's a serial killer. And he wasn't involved with this beating. This is only about my gambling and my debt."

"He's an asshole." I told him about the threat with the matches.

"Can you prove he did it?"

"Who else? No one else knew I was meeting him, and he called and set the place we were to meet."

"Something isn't right here. That's too obvious, don't you think?"

I respected Jack's opinion, but I also had to respect my gut instinct. "I'm just saying we should follow the lead, play it out, see where it goes. I've asked for a meeting with him and Avery Boudreaux."

"Riley is going to resent the hell out of your suspicions. He's touchy to begin with. I doubt he'll ever forgive you."

"I don't give a damn about his forgiveness. I want the truth."

"Just be careful. Riley may not be a killer but he can certainly hold a grudge. He could make your life miserable if he chose to."

"And I can do it right back." I didn't mention that I probably would be unemployed within the next month. If that was the case, I'd be moving on anyway.

"I wish I could be with you," Jack said.

"You've got to handle your own problems." I couldn't offer Jack more money, and I knew he wouldn't ask. But there was the possibility of a bank loan. "My banker—"

"Stop it." He grimaced as a sudden pain struck. "I already owe you money."

"I was going to suggest a loan."

"No banker in his right mind will loan me anything. That's not your problem, Carson. Let's keep it that way."

"Okay." There was nothing else to say. "I'll be back to check on you." I leaned over and kissed his cheek. I think it surprised him as much as it did me. I winked. "You owe me a dinner when you get out."

"Only if you drive."

An orderly appeared with a lunch tray, and I left. I drove to Bucky's Bistro and into the society lunch crowd of tennis ladies and a scattering of men in polo shirts and slacks. This wasn't my scene, and I would never have suspected it was a hangout of Avery's, but he'd done the choosing.

He wasn't in sight so I went to the hostess. "I'm meeting Avery Boudreaux."

"Yes," she said, her flawless face revealing nothing. "The back room."

I followed her to a white wooden door. She opened it and stepped aside. I walked into the room and stopped. Avery was nowhere in sight, but Jimmy Riley was sitting at the only table in the room watching me with distaste.

29

Riley had once been a handsome man, but liquor had taken its toll. Ruptured blood vessels in his nose and cheeks gave his flesh a bluish tone. Pale eyes were nearly covered in swollen folds of skin, and his neck bulged over his shirt collar. He was sixty pounds overweight and unhealthy.

"Where's Avery?" I asked from the doorway. I had no intention of meeting with Riley alone. I hadn't even brought a tape recorder.

"He'll be along directly." He frowned. "Where's that waiter? I need a beer."

He had a plate of raw oysters in front of him and he'd worked through half of them. He picked one up on a fork, dipped it in sauce and swallowed it whole.

"Avery said you wanted to talk to me." He swallowed another oyster, wiping the cocktail sauce from his chin with a crumpled napkin. "Something about back when I worked security." He pushed the oysters back, leaving two uneaten. "I don't mind talking about the Gold Rush, but folks associate a lot of negative things with Alvin Orley."

"Things like murder."

"Yeah. Things like that." He waved at a chair. "Are you gonna sit down and eat or just stand there? Don't get the oysters. They aren't the freshest around."

I couldn't figure Riley out. Either he was an incredible actor or dumb as a post. Either way, he'd piqued my curiosity. I walked to the table and eased into a chair. I'd planned on an interview with a backup witness, but I sensed it was now or never. I didn't have time to wait for Avery. Riley picked up the menu and studied it.

"I was at Bebop's at three, as *you* requested," I said again.

He lowered the menu. "What are you talking about? The place don't open till four."

"You said three, and I was there."

"I never said anything to you. This is the first time I've talked to you, and I can tell you it wouldn't be happening now if Avery hadn't asked as a personal favor." He looked at the empty doorway. "Where the hell is he?"

I decided to try another tactic. "I got the present you left for me."

"I didn't leave anything for you."

"At Bebop's," I insisted.

"What is this about that bar? I never told you to go there, and I haven't been there in weeks."

I had to give the man credit. He was convincing, but I wasn't ready to let it drop. "I don't normally accept such intimate gifts, but I'll make an exception this time."

A frown passed over his face. "I don't know what you're talking about. Where's that damn waiter?" He slammed his empty water glass on the table. "Look, either eat or get on with your questions. I told Avery I'd talk to you, but I haven't got all afternoon to hold your hand."

He was insulting and not even aware of it. Or maybe he truly didn't care. "How long did you work for Alvin Orley?"

"From around 1979 through 1983. I worked there about four nights a week, patrolling the parking lot and making sure the girls got in their cars without being hassled by the drunks. It was a pretty simple job and it paid well."

"You were a patrolman then?"

"Yeah, a rookie. I'd just signed on to the police department. A policing career pretty much meant starvation. My fiancée had expensive taste, and I wanted to be able save so one day my kids would go to college. So I worked a second job. So what?"

"I hear your father was CIA."

That stopped him. "My father doesn't really figure into this."

"Was he CIA?"

"I don't have a certificate to prove it, but that's what he said. Is there a point to these questions?"

There was, but I wasn't ready to reveal it. "Were you working the nights those girls disappeared?"

He shook his head. "I couldn't say. I rotated with two other guys, so we never worked regular nights. Sometimes I worked the weekends, sometimes during the week. I could've been there, or not."

"Surely there are pay records."

He stared at me. "Alvin paid us cash. He didn't keep records and he didn't care who was there as long as some muscle appeared if he needed it."

"That's very convenient."

The redness in his cheeks intensified. "I don't have to sit here and listen to your insinuations. I'm here because

Avery Boudreaux asked me to talk to you, but I don't have to take shit from you." He put his napkin down, and the corner of his right eye twitched uncontrollably.

I'd hit a nerve. "Did you walk the parking lots during your shift?"

"Naw. There wasn't a need for that. Alvin had this storage room where he put us a coffeepot and a desk. We could sit there and look out the window to the front door of the club. When a woman came out alone, I got up and went out to escort her to her car. Other than that, I stayed mostly in the shack. It had a little heater and a window air conditioner, and Alvin didn't want us running off his business, if you get my drift. We were there strictly to watch out for the girls. Otherwise, we kept out of the way."

"Do you remember anyone suspicious, a man who seemed to lurk around the club?"

"Like the man in the drawing?" He laughed. "Only about two thousand of them. Guys were at that club every night. Those young men from Keesler, hell, they were nineteen and horny. They were like dogs sniffing after the girls. I didn't necessarily consider it suspicious."

"Were you after any of the girls?" My question was spoken softly.

He leaned forward suddenly. "That is none of your damn business. I was engaged. Happily engaged and looking forward to a good life with Yvonne. I didn't need to chase women. I had all I could handle in my own bed."

I wondered exactly how much Riley could actually handle. "You had a necklace back then. Human ears."

His eyes narrowed and he grew very still. "Who have you been talking to?"

"Folks don't forget something like that, Riley. Most people don't have souvenirs made of human body parts."

"That belonged to my father."

"But you kept it, and you showed it around like it was something special."

"I was young and trying to impress folks. It was stupid, a dumb kid thing to do."

"Where is that necklace?"

"I haven't seen it in years."

"You know about the fingers severed from those girls." I saw in his face that he did. "Someone is taking trophies. Fingers, ears, do you see a pattern here?"

He dropped the menu and pushed back his chair. For a large man he moved quickly. He was on his feet in an instant and he leaned over the table. "You put that shit in the paper and I'll sue you for everything you ever dreamed of owning. And Brandon, too. He won't have a chance to sell the paper before I run him into the ground."

"You patrolled a parking lot where five bodies were buried," I said, unflinching. "Did you simply not notice five graves?"

He was breathing through his mouth. "I didn't go in the back of the lot. Back then, that area was full of thick bamboo and weeds and snakes. Alvin made it clear that my job was in the front of the lot escorting young women to their cars. Not killing them. I was a police officer at the time. If I'd had any idea someone was killing those girls and burying them there, I would have done something about it then."

"I guess I have your word on that."

The sarcasm was too much. I thought for a moment

he might have a stroke. "Print anything close to that and I'll own you."

"Where were you Friday night?" My heart was pounding, but I wasn't going to show him I was afraid of him.

"On my boat. At Chandelier Island."

"Can anyone corroborate your whereabouts? And the night Pamela Sparks was killed? You were on the boat that night, too? And I'll bet you were all alone."

He stood up straight. "I'm finished answering your questions."

"I don't have any more questions, but I do have a word of advice. Don't ever try to use my past to intimidate me. It doesn't work. It only pisses me off."

"I don't have a clue what Rayburn sees in you. Everyone in town knows you're a washed-up drunk, but he keeps harping on how we need to develop a relationship with you." His lip curled. "I'm not playing any more games so he can jump in your pants." He slammed a twenty on the table. "Maybe you aren't as smart as you think you are."

He walked out of the private room. I waited a few minutes and followed him. When I stepped into the main dining area, no one was talking and everyone was looking at me. I walked through the tables, leaving a wake of silence behind me.

Sitting in the parking lot of a local souvenir store with a door that opened through a huge shark's mouth, I used a reporter's first tool, the phone. Avery wasn't in his office, and he didn't answer his cell phone. I didn't blame him. Riley felt set up and so did I. Avery had pulled a fast one, but he had made his point. He didn't believe Riley was a killer, and I'd begun to doubt it, too. Riley wasn't smart enough.

But had he set me up at Bebop's? And if so, why?

I called my home answering machine and retrieved a message from Kev Graves. The matchbox and note had come back with only my prints on them. I was disappointed but not surprised. There were no other calls, and though I hadn't expected to hear from Daniel, I couldn't help the sense of loss that settled over me.

I drove down the beach, thinking how I ought to call Dorry and apologize about Emily's birthday, but I didn't. I couldn't. I stopped along the beach. Once the windows were down I turned the radio to a country station and leaned back against the seat, my eyes closed. The waves broke gently on the shore, creating a soothing background for my troubled thoughts on the case.

I'd been so positive Riley was the murderer. Now I had to rethink the situation. Avery had made his point by setting up the interview, which had accomplished nothing except making an enemy of Riley.

I put the truck in drive and headed for the office. The impulse to go to a bar was strong, but I fought it. Someone had left me a very personal message in Bebop's, and I intended to find out who.

30

My cell phone rang just as I was pulling into the parking lot of the newspaper. Since I wasn't eager to enter the building and bump into Brandon, I welcomed the possible distraction. A soft voice with a black accent asked for me.

"This is Lele, Rose McKay's granddaughter," she said. "Grandmama remembered the veil."

I couldn't believe it. "Will she talk to me?"

"She's tired," Lele said. "She got upset once she remembered. I made her go to bed, but she said I should call you. She said it could be important."

"Who did the veil belong to?"

"Alana Williams. She drowned right after she was married. Grandmama went to the wedding. She didn't normally do that, but she said Alana was a special girl."

I was momentarily unbalanced. Of all the answers I'd expected, Alana Williams had never occurred to me. I'd been certain the veil would somehow connect to the family of one of the murdered girls. "Lele, did your grandmother have any idea how the killer might have gotten hold of Alana's veil?"

"She was upset, Ms. Lynch. She said the last time she saw that veil, Alana was wearing it at the wedding. She doesn't know anything else—I'm sure of it."

I thanked Lele and hung up. Someone who knew Alana Williams and had access to her things had killed Pamela Sparks. Who had access to those things? My next call was to Mitch, but I got only his answering machine. "I need to talk to you," I said. I found myself unwilling to say more. "Call me."

A couple of reporters came out of the building and went to their cars. They were either on assignment, headed for a late lunch or simply evacuating a sinking ship. I almost didn't care. Instead of going in, I telephoned the desk and told Hank I was working on a lead.

"Brandon is sitting in your office waiting for you to come in," Hank said.

"He can freeze there for all I care."

"I don't think freezing is an option."

"Hank, can you check the phone book for Alana Williams's parents' address? If they're still alive."

"Sure." He was gone for almost a minute. "Brewster and Eloise Williams. The residence is 5151 Palmetto Drive. That's off Pop's Ferry Road. What's going on?"

"I'm not certain, but I'll check back with you."

The address was a neat cottage set on a well-maintained, one-acre yard. I pulled into the gravel drive and walked to the front door.

My knock was answered by a woman in her seventies. She wore a pink housedress and slippers. Her silvery hair was in need of a perm and cut, but she smiled when she saw me.

"May I ask you some questions about Alana?" I asked.

"Are you a friend of hers?" Her face softened.

"I'm sorry, I didn't know your daughter."

"I wish some of her friends would come by." She turned and walked away, leaving me standing in the open door.

I stepped into the house and closed the door behind me. I told her who I was and handed her a business card. She glanced at it and put it on an end table by the sofa.

"The only person who ever talks about Alana now is Mitch. He comes by on Sunday mornings. Folks think talking about the dead is morbid, but it keeps her alive for me. Are you sure you didn't know her?"

A sense of foreboding touched my spine. "No, ma'am, I didn't know her. Is your husband home?" She was an old woman, frail and hanging on to the memory of her dead child. I needed someone more substantial to question.

"Brewster is dead. Five years now. Come on in the kitchen, and I'll make us some coffee. I like to have some in the afternoon. Doctor says the caffeine is bad for my heart, but he doesn't have a clue about the things that are bad for a heart. Try having your daughter drowned. Now, that's bad for the heart."

I followed her into the kitchen. "Do you live alone?" I asked.

"I'm the last of my family. It's hard to be the last. There should have been grandchildren."

"Was Alana your only child?"

"Yes. We wanted another baby, but I couldn't carry to term. When Alana and Jeffrey got together, he was like our son. Mitch, too. Those boys were over here more than they were at home. Jeffrey raised Mitch, you know. He gave up all his ambitions to play professional ball to care for his little brother."

I took a seat at the kitchen table. Mrs. Williams put the coffee on and slid a Tupperware cake container across the counter. She got saucers and cut two huge slices of coconut cake.

"I made this Saturday," she said. "Mitch loves coconut cake. I always make one for his birthday. He's like me, the last of his family. There's no one to remember the special days."

She put the cake in front of me and I picked up a fork. I took a bite and let the coconut flavor saturate my mouth. Eloise Williams sat down across from me while the coffee brewed.

"Why are you here?" she asked. She was old and hadn't kept herself up, but her mind was still alert.

"I wanted to ask you some questions about Alana's wedding, if you feel up to talking about it."

"That's a happy memory. I'll be glad to tell you about it. I try to remember that day and how much hope and joy we all had." She stared at the table but saw another time. "Jeffrey was so in love with my girl. He thought she hung the moon. He got down on one knee in front of all of us and held her hand like he was clinging to a rock. He said he'd made mistakes in his life, but that Alana had saved him. He said she was his gift of redemption."

"Do you have any pictures of the wedding?"

"I was hoping you'd ask. Let me get them." She left the room and returned with a huge album and put it on the table beside me. "I had every single photo printed up." She poured two cups of coffee, set them on the table and scooted her chair so we could look together. "I started the album at the very beginning, when Jeffrey asked her for her hand. He did it right in the living room."

She flipped the album open and I saw a photo of a handsome man on one knee, sliding an engagement ring on the finger of a young woman with a brilliant smile. She was a girl really, maybe twenty, but with all the freshness and hope of a child.

"Do you remember when Jeffrey proposed?" I asked.

"It was a Thursday night, the last one in June. I remember because Mitch was over for dinner. He'd just come home for the rest of the summer. He made some jokes about how Jeffrey should have asked sooner so there could have been a June wedding."

We went through photos of bridal showers where a bevy of young women laughed and held up gifts and ribbons, and at last came to the wedding day. Alana was magnificent. Her gown was a work of art, and I touched the photo of her coming down the aisle on her father's arm, her face framed in an exquisite lace veil.

"She's beautiful."

"Yes, she is. I love to look at her in this picture. Alana had just gotten a job with the local television station. She was an assistant producer for the news."

"She should have been in front of the camera, not behind it." The camera would have loved her face.

"I told her that, too, but Jeffrey didn't want her on camera."

"And Alana agreed to stay behind the scenes?" I was curious that a woman would give up a career at the request of her husband.

"She loved Jeffrey more than any job. And she understood that he had lived so much of his life in the public eye. His father was a well-known defense attorney, sort of a celebrity in his day, and the tragedy of the fire put both those boys on public display. The limelight can get very tiring."

"Yes, it can." The next photo showed Jeffrey surrounded by his groomsmen, including Mitch. Jeffrey was smiling, but his eyes were sad, as if he carried some tragic secret. The next photo was of Mitch and Jeffrey. The love between the two brothers was obvious, but that wasn't what I focused on. Two men stood in the background. Jimmy Riley and Alvin Orley. They weren't together. There was space between them, but they both had sought the back wall, part of the celebration but only as fringe spectators.

"Mrs. Williams, do you know these men?" My finger identified them.

"Friends of the groom. Jeffrey said something about how Mr. Orley had helped Mitch get into law school. Harry Rayburn had helped Mr. Orley with some legal problems, and after the fire, Mr. Orley and his civic group helped Jeffrey and Mitch. They collected the insurance money and helped the boys buy a house. Jeffrey said he'd been a good friend, so we didn't want to exclude him just because he had an unsavory reputation. As I recall, Mr. Orley didn't make it to the reception. Turn the page," Mrs. Williams directed. "The next one is beautiful."

I slowly flipped the page and looked at a photo of Alana holding her bridal bouquet of red roses. "Her gown is lovely. Mrs. Williams, what happened to Alana's wedding gown and veil?"

"I couldn't tell you. She and Jeffrey had rented a house. They were going to live over in Gulfport when they got back from their honeymoon. After they drowned, Mitch closed up the house. I guess he got rid of all the wedding stuff. I was too upset to care what happened to those things."

"I've never seen a gown so beautiful," I prompted.

"A local dressmaker, Rose McKay, made it for her. The lace for the veil was an heirloom."

She had moved to the topic I wanted to discuss. "It's a lovely veil. What kind of heirloom?"

"There's a story woven in the lace. The twining ivy and the roses are symbols of love and need. The thistle is the trials of life. You can't see it clearly in the photo, but in the lace, the ivy clings to the rose. Jeffrey said that Alana was the rose, and he the ivy. Alana thought it was very romantic, and it meant so much to Jeffrey for her to use the lace. I remember this clearly because Rose had to make two veils. The first one wasn't long enough so she made a second."

I was confused. "The lace came from Jeffrey?"

"From the Rayburn family. It's a long, sad story. Jeffrey's mother had ordered the lace from Ireland, from a shop run by some of her distant family. She was to have it for her wedding veil, but she and Harry eloped before the lace arrived. I think she was pregnant with Jeffrey and just couldn't wait." She paused. "Marilyn never got to use the lace, and since she didn't have a daughter, she had no girl to pass it on to."

"I was under the impression that the Rayburn house burned to the ground," I said.

"That's true. The lace was somehow salvaged. I've never asked Mitch, but it had to be out of that house before it caught fire because there was nothing else left. Those boys had so few good memories, I was glad Jeffrey had something of his family to include in the wedding. That wasn't a happy household."

"It's just odd that, of all the things they could've saved, the boys would save lace." Something was very wrong here. I was suddenly glad I hadn't told Mitch more in my phone call. "You don't remember how the lace escaped?"

"No, I don't remember the details. I know it was sentimental to Jeffrey. And Alana loved the story." Mrs. Williams put down her fork. She began nervously rubbing her hands together.

"You said the Rayburn household wasn't happy. How was it unhappy?"

"I may have spoken out of turn. Harry was a hot-tempered man. He was very successful, and he held the boys and his wife to a high standard. Those boys were driven to succeed. That's all I meant." She pulled the photo album closer to her.

"When you say hot tempered, what do you mean?"

"It does no good to speak ill of the dead, Ms. Lynch. Harry and Marilyn are buried. It's best to let rumors and suspicions die with them. I never knew anything for certain. Neither Jeffrey nor Mitch was one to talk about things that couldn't be undone."

"Mrs. Williams, this could be very important." I was remembering my conversation with Dr. Richard Jennings, and a real sense of dread colored my voice. "Do you think Mitch and Jeffrey were abused by their father?"

"Why is this important? What good can it do now?" She was upset.

"I'm sorry." I tried to soothe her. "I'm worried about Mitch." I'd gained control of my tone, but she was still looking at me with apprehension.

"Why did you come here? Alana's been dead a long time. Jeffrey, too. Why are you asking these questions now?"

I reached across the table and caught her nervous hands. "Two young women were murdered in the last few days. I want to stop the person responsible. I think you may be able to help me. Will you?"

She didn't say anything. She sat motionless, her gaze fixed on me.

"Were Jeffrey and Mitch abused?" I asked again.

"I didn't really know them when Mr. Rayburn was alive, but there were scars."

"What kind of scars?" I kept my voice calm.

"I saw it mostly in Mitch. He stuck to Jeffrey like glue. Even when he was in college, he called Jeffrey all the time. One time when he was here, Brewster and I got into an argument." She paused. "It was just a normal disagreement but it upset him terribly."

She closed the album and stood up. "I don't think I should talk to you anymore. Please leave."

31

After Mrs. Williams closed the door behind me, she locked it. I went to the truck and used my cell phone to call the paper. I got a terse Hank.

"Brandon is pissed," he said. "He's still waiting for you."

"When he sells the paper, I don't have a job anyway. Can you give me Mitch Rayburn's old address? When he lived with his parents." Disbelief had given way to dread. I remembered Mitch's face on the dock, staring at Pamela Sparks's dead body, the veil fluttering in the wind. His face had registered shock and horror. He'd never mentioned that he recognized the veil.

"Carson, you have to tell me what you're up to." Hank's demanding voice tugged me back to the present.

"I will, when I have something solid. I'm not going to have anything for Tuesday's paper, but if this pans out, I could have a big story for Wednesday. Just get me that address."

Hank put me on hold while he looked up the address in an old city directory.

"It's 135 Pelican Lane. The house is gone, though. I don't think anything was ever built there. The property is listed as still belonging to Mitch."

"Thanks, Hank." I hung up before he could ask any more questions. My cell phone battery was running low, but I called Jack at the hospital. He answered in a muffled voice, and I winced as I remembered his broken teeth.

"Jack, what do you recall about Harry Rayburn?"

"Carson, what are you up to?"

"Did you ever hear rumors that Rayburn was abusive to his boys?"

There was a pause long enough for me to travel two blocks in rather heavy traffic. School had let out, and I'd miscalculated my route, ending up in a slow crawl by an elementary school.

"Harry Rayburn was a bigger-than-life man. I never cared for him. He was always full of himself, the kind of guy who didn't bother to acknowledge the little people. When he died in that fire, I heard talk."

"What kind of talk?"

"That he beat the boys and wasn't shy about slapping his wife around. It was just talk. Nothing conclusive."

"Thanks, Jack. I'll be in touch." I broke the connection and put my cell phone down on the seat as I saw a break in the traffic and aimed the truck toward freedom.

The Pelican Lane address was nothing but an empty lot. All remnants of the fire had been erased by time. Trees and brush had grown up around the foundation of the house. I walked through the tall grass and found a few bricks and what had once been a walkway. Nature had done her work on the rest.

The neighborhood was an older one with solid houses and mature oak trees lining the road. I walked next door and knocked at a neat clapboard house that was flanked with blooming flower beds. A woman about ten years older than myself answered my knock.

Her name was Nan Baker, and she'd grown up on the street. Her mother had lived in the house until she died. Nan had moved back into it ten years before, when she'd divorced. She was talkative and seemed glad for the company. She invited me in and put on a kettle for tea.

"I remember the Rayburn family," she said as she arranged cups and saucers on her kitchen table. They were a fine old china pattern. Nan looked out the window at the empty lot where the Rayburn house once stood not twenty yards away. "I'm glad to see Mitch has done well. He was always a good kid. I felt sorry for him."

"Why was that?"

"Mr. Rayburn was a cruel man. An evil man, I'd say." She poured the tea and offered sugar and lemon.

"That's pretty harsh."

"He beat those boys. There were times when Jeffrey would come over here with black-and-purple bruises on his face. One time, Mom saw his back. He'd been savagely beaten. He said he got the bruises and welts playing ball, but I know differently. Mitch was in middle school then, and he'd show up with the same kinds of marks."

"Were you friends with the two boys?"

"I was older than both of them, so we weren't close friends, but I'd talk to them. They came over to the house after school almost every day. Mom would have cookies and treats for them. They didn't want to go home." She shook her head. "Jeffrey played the role of the daddy. He looked after Mitch, and several of their conversations led me to believe that Jeffrey took beatings for him."

"Didn't anyone call the police?"

"Once. My mother did. All it resulted in was Jeffrey coming over here and begging Mom not to do it again. Harry paid us a visit, too. He said he would sue us. That same night Marilyn Rayburn was rushed to the hospital."

"Did she press charges?"

"Marilyn Rayburn was extraordinarily clumsy." Her look was sarcastic. "She had broken arms, broken ribs, broken fingers. She ran into a door at least once a month for a black eye. It was tragic. Mom would watch for her, and if Marilyn didn't come out of the house for a few days, Mom would go over when Mr. Rayburn was at work. Just to make sure Marilyn wasn't dead. As I said, Harry Rayburn was evil. He abused his family on a regular basis."

"Surely the schools—"

"Wouldn't have touched it with a ten-foot pole. Harry Rayburn was a powerful man."

I thought about what life was like then. June Tierce's father had been murdered and it had been ruled a suicide. It wasn't inconceivable that a man of political power could beat his wife and children and never pay the price.

"Are you okay?" Nan asked. Her kind brown eyes showed concern.

"I'm fine." But I wasn't.

"Why is a newspaper reporter so interested in something that happened so long ago?"

"Do you recall the date your mother reported the abuse?"

"No, not specifically. But it was in the winter before the house burned. I was in college then, so I wasn't around. Mom said the most bizarre part of it was that she never heard arguing or screaming and yelling. Whatever went on in that house was done in total silence."

I pushed back my half-finished tea. "Thanks for your time." I had a few more facts to check and the day was drawing to a close.

"I hope I was helpful," she said. "If you talk to Mitch, please tell him I said hi. I'd love for him to come by for a visit."

I didn't say anything to that as I hurried past her bright beds of tulips and the sweet, sad smell of the blooming hyacinths.

It was four-thirty when I pulled up at the Biloxi Police Department. My request was routine, and I was shown to a small room until the desk sergeant found the records. Nan's mother had filed her report of suspected abuse in February 1974. The house fire that had killed Harry and Marilyn Rayburn had occurred in April 1974.

A cool sweat broke out on my forehead, and nausea knotted my stomach. I sat in the uncomfortable metal chair and tried to stop the buildup of saliva in my mouth. I didn't want to be sick in the police station.

I walked down the hall to the water fountain and drank. There were police officers all around me, young men who ignored me. They all knew Mitch. I wondered if they realized that he'd killed his parents and seven women, maybe more.

Miss Vesta was having one of her rare moments of docility. She sat, eyes half-closed, in my lap as I got Dr. Richard Jennings's phone number from information. An empty martini glass was beside the telephone cradle. The option of automatic dialing seemed nice, so I waited for the phone company to make the connection. As I suspected, the psychiatrist wasn't in, but his cell phone number was on his answering machine message. I had to dial that one myself.

Night had fallen, and I turned on a lamp as I counted the rings. I was about to hang up when Dr. Jennings answered.

He was surprised to hear from me, but when I explained what I needed, he agreed to talk.

"This is all hypothetical," I said, effectively letting him off the hook. "Say there were two brothers, both of whom were horribly abused by their father, a man who could never be satisfied with anything they did. The mother was abused also. Then the parents were killed in a house fire. Would—?"

"An accidental fire?" he asked.

"It was ruled accidental, but I'm not so sure, based on things I've learned now." The only piece I couldn't make fit was how a teenage boy could have set such a fire. It was possible Mitch had never been at Scout camp. There weren't records of such things. The picture I was getting of Jeffrey was a brother who would lie or do anything to protect his younger sibling. A younger brother who might possibly be a cold-blooded killer.

"Both parents died?" Richard asked.

"Yes."

"It would be more common for one of the boys to kill the father. Then again, the Menendez case comes to mind where the mother was allegedly killed because she failed to protect her children from the father. How old were the boys when the house burned?"

"One would have been around thirteen or fourteen and the other eighteen. Both had alibis."

"If the fire was deliberately set by one or both of the boys, then it indicates there was blame placed on the mother, as well as the father. What type of abuse are we talking about?"

"Beatings, that kind of thing. The only strange element is that there was never any arguing. At least not that the neighbors heard. No screaming or ranting."

"Could be a control issue on the part of the abuser. To keep his victims from making noise as he abused them would be ultimate control."

The picture Dr. Jennings was painting of Harry Rayburn was an ugly one. What he'd possibly turned one of his children into was even uglier.

"What type of person do you think these boys would grow up to be?" I asked.

"They'd probably go one of two ways, either become very successful, a classic overachiever, or else start abusing drugs and/or alcohol, and perhaps become a recluse or homeless person. Understand we're talking hypothetically here. Real life is seldom this clear-cut."

"Hypothetically, could one of the boys become a serial killer?"

"It's possible for the victim to become the offender. It's not unheard of."

"If one of these boys is our serial killer, can you tell me why he kills?" An even better question was why he'd stopped for twenty-four years, but I'd get around to that.

"Well, based on what I know of these killings, I'd say the murders reflect hatred toward the mother for her failure to protect the boys. It could even be as twisted as the mother somehow caused her sons to be beaten, either to save herself from a beating or because that was the only power she had in the family."

"And the girls, the victims?"

"All girls of marriageable age. But there had to be some way he selected them. Engagement announcements in the newspaper or something. I'd say the killer has a terribly conflicted view of women—he doesn't have a problem with them until they become brides, or wives. Once they cross that threshold, they change from desirable to dangerous. He has to kill them before that transformation takes place."

"We're back to the twenty-four-year hiatus." My fingers stroked Miss Vesta's hair, finding comfort in the contact with the purring cat.

"Something happened to stop the killings. Something traumatic. And I'd have to say that the recovery of the five bodies was likely what prompted the killings to start again."

"The death of his brother might be traumatic enough to stop the killings," I said it more to myself than Richard Jennings.

"What did you say?" he asked.

"What if the incident that stopped the killings was the death of his brother?"

"That would do it," the psychiatrist said. "Did the younger brother die?"

"No, the older one. He drowned while on the sailboat of the younger brother. The older brother and his new bride both drowned during a storm."

"That might possibly explain the gap in the killings," Richard said. "The younger brother might see the death of his older brother as some sort of retribution. You say he drowned with his new bride?"

"That's correct."

"An act of God somehow, a final vengeance. God took his brother away because of his sins. Now that the bodies have been uncovered, the killer might believe it's another sign from God to continue killing. Or is it possible that he killed his brother and sister-in-law?"

Mitch's handsome face filled my mind. He was a good D.A., a man with a moral conscience. A man who talked of his dead brother with such love.

I contrasted the man I knew with the man who could slit a woman's throat and leave her to bleed out, dressed in the accoutrements of a bride. It didn't seem possible that in the dead of night Mitch Rayburn turned into a monster, a murderer of young women.

"I don't know the answer to that question. Dr. Jennings, would it be possible for the killer to be unaware of his actions?"

"A psychotic split?"

I heard the incredulity in his voice. "Something like that. I don't know the psychiatric term. But this man maintains a prominent public image. He's involved in the investigations of the murders. I've seen him at the crime scenes, and he seems disturbed by the killings."

"Carson, this sounds dangerous and not hypothetical at all. I think you should talk to the police."

I thought of Avery. It would be a relief to talk to him, but I couldn't. "I'm going to," I lied. "I just want to be sure that I have my ducks in a row. This is a powerful man I'm about to accuse of murder."

"Let me just say that I personally doubt he's totally unaware of his actions. I don't buy the Dr. Jekyll-Mr. Hyde defense. Is this man married?"

"No. Never married." That, too, was incriminating, though I'd never thought of it.

"That would fit the pattern. It's hard for a person to lead a double life if they share space with someone else. Does he date?"

"I went out with him a couple of times. I haven't heard of any serious relationships."

"Forgive my questions, Carson, but it will help me think this through. Did this man make any sexual advances toward you?"

"No." I hadn't found it unusual at the time. Mitch and I were both adults. We weren't randy teenagers who couldn't keep our hands off each other. Mitch was a man with political ambitions; he had to use caution in his relationships. Even as I was trying to rationalize Mitch's conduct, I remembered the night I'd spent with Daniel.

"Would you say he's asexual?" Richard asked.

"I don't know."

"You should be very careful, Carson."

"I've heard that most people who commit this type of crime want to confess. They want to be caught and stopped."

"A word of caution, Carson. Don't corner this person. If this man feels helpless, he'll do whatever it takes to protect himself."

"Thanks, Richard."

"What are you going to do?" His voice was threaded with worry.

"Nothing rash."

"Do I have your word on that?"

"Absolutely."

32

I made another martini and sat in my favorite chair. No matter how I turned the clues over, I still came up with Mitch Rayburn as the answer.

A bold knock at my door startled me. Miss Vesta jumped off my lap and ran toward the bedroom. The door swung open and Dorry stepped into the room. Her face was splotched with the aftereffects of crying. For a moment I thought she'd gone off the deep end over my missing Emily's party.

"Carson, will you help me?" she asked.

I got up and went to the kitchen to put the kettle on for tea. Dorry had long ago given up coffee, though it was what I would have preferred. "Come sit down," I called to her.

She came into the kitchen and slumped into a chair. She put her face in her hands and rocked back and forth, not making a sound.

"What's wrong?" I asked. This was more than disappointment at my conduct. I stepped behind her and hesitated before I put a hand on her shoulder. Dorry had never been one to accept my offers of comfort. Even as I thought it, I realized I had no memory of attempting to comfort her. My fingers gently kneaded her tight muscles.

"Tommy didn't come home last night. I haven't heard from him today. When I went to the hospital this evening, they said he wasn't there."

I thought of the videotape and the pictures lying on the desk in my home office. They were only fifty feet away. All I had to do was hand them to Dorry. I continued to rub her shoulders. "There could be a reasonable explanation."

"Like what? The phones in Mobile quit working? Or maybe he went to a doctors' conference and forgot to tell me. Could be that he's flown to Africa to volunteer his surgical skills for the wretched poor." Her voice had risen to a near shout. "The problem is, any of those things could be true. Tommy never talks to me anymore. He never touches me except as an obligation. It's like we're strangers condemned to serve out a sentence together."

Her shoulders were so rigid I stopped rubbing them. "Divorce him," I said.

"He's my whole life."

"Dorry, that's not true. You're complete without him. You could be anything you want to be."

"That's easy for you to say." She jerked out from under my hands and turned so that she could look at me. Her face was white with anger. "You live alone. You can't even put a kid like Emily in front of your own needs. But I'm not like you. I need someone to share my life with."

"And you really think I don't?" I wasn't angry; I was shocked.

"You don't need people the way most of us do."

Her words were an accusation. The kettle began to

scream, and I went to the stove and turned it off. I could feel Dorry's hot, angry glare in my back. I thought of handing her the pictures of her husband in bed with the little red-headed nurse with the big ass. Dorry had always assumed a position of superiority to me. Even now, she thought she felt more—hurt more. It was always more when it came to Dorry. I got two cups from the cupboard and put them on the counter, then grabbed tea bags from the shelf.

"I want a drink," she said.

I pulled a bottle of vodka out of the refrigerator. I made a vodka tonic and handed it to her. The anger was gone from her face, and her gaze slid away from mine. She was ashamed.

"I'm sorry, Carson," she said. "I came here to ask for your help, not to insult you."

I finished making a cup of tea for myself and sat down at the table with her. "What do you want?"

"Can you find out what Tommy's doing?"

"Are you sure you want to know?" My attempts at comfort were over.

"Yes."

"Why do you want to know?"

"You're not my fucking analyst," she snapped. She took a long drink of the vodka and stared at the glass when she set it back on the table. "I need to know so I can make a reasonable decision."

"Will you leave him if he's cheating on you?" I asked.

"Yes."

She spoke so quickly that I knew she was lying. She'd use the photos to gig him, to threaten him with financial disaster. But she wouldn't leave him. Not yet.

"I'll check into it," I said.

She took a deep breath. "Thank you, Carson." She looked down at her drink. "Mother would be so disappointed if I screwed this up. She adores Tommy. When you—" She stopped, aware that she was about to be too honest.

"She was disappointed that her daughter's marriage failed," I said. "But be truthful, wasn't she a little glad? She never cared for Daniel. Now he's out of the way."

She swallowed and met my gaze. "Mother isn't the way you see her. She cares about you, Carson. She only wants what's best for you. Daniel wasn't right for you. It was bound to end in divorce."

There was no point arguing with Dorry. She lived in a world of three-story houses with gingerbread trim and was the envy of all her neighbors for a marriage that was only a husk.

"I'll check into it," I said again. I glanced at my watch. It was only eight o'clock. Plenty of time left. "Go home, Dorry. The kids will be wondering where you are and what you're doing."

She stood up. "You're right." She started toward the door and then turned back. "Thank you, Carson. You'll tell me what you find out, won't you?"

"Sure," I said, the lie not even bitter on my tongue.

I waited ten minutes until I was sure she'd made it out of town. Then I got in my truck and drove to Mobile. I found the house where the redheaded nurse lived. Tommy's Porsche was in the garage.

Instead of knocking on the door, I hit it with the lug wrench from the boot of my truck. The wood splintered. I hit it again and again, taking chunks out of it.

"What the fuck do you want?" a woman shrilled from behind the door. "I'm calling the cops."

I hit the door again. "Tommy!"

There was a pause. I hit the door harder, feeling the strain in my shoulder and back. My scar burned as if it were on fire again.

There was the sound of locks being turned. The door opened a crack, the chain still on it. Tommy peered out. "Carson?" He sounded as if he'd just been awakened from a long sleep.

"I need to talk to you," I said, my voice calm and reasonable.

"How about ten o'clock tomorrow?"

I hit the door only a few inches from his face. He jumped back, and I leaned forward, speaking into the crack. "How about now?"

"How did you find me?" he asked from several feet away.

"Open this fucking door or I'm going to knock it off the hinges," I said softly.

The door shut and the chain rattled. Then it swung open. Tommy stepped back. The redheaded nurse was hiding behind him, peering over his shoulder with wide, brown eyes. They both looked startled, but they also moved in slow motion. Demerol? Codeine? I wondered what narcotic Tommy had gotten from his closet full of samples.

"You're going to jail." Tommy shifted, easing across the room. The nurse clung to him, staying behind him as if the lug wrench had turned into a gun and I could shoot her from ten feet away. Tommy reached for the telephone. "I'm calling the police."

"Do that," I said.

My reaction stopped him. He frowned, trying to think it through. His mouth opened but no words came out.

"Listen, Tommy, I have a business proposition to make," I said. I didn't recognize my own voice. "Keep your dick in your pants and go home to your wife or divorce Dorry. One or the other. I don't care which. But if you divorce her, you give her everything she wants." I pulled the pictures out of my jacket and threw them on the floor. Tommy and the nurse looked down at them, their expressions shifting to consternation that was almost comic.

"Has Dorry seen these?" he asked.

I wondered how I'd ever thought him good-looking. His face was slack, his eyes vacant. "No. She doesn't know. Yet." I toed the photos, spreading them out. "I'll send copies to the hospitals where you work. If you move, I'll send them to the next hospital you go to. It shouldn't take a lot of effort to run down your patient list, too."

Life leaped into his eyes. "You can't do this—"

"Don't tempt me. If you hurt my sister, I'll make it my life's goal to follow you wherever you go. I'll ruin you."

He stepped away from the nurse. When she tried to slip behind him, he pushed her away.

"Tommy!" She glared at him. "What—"

"Get the fuck away from me," he said.

"Don't piss her off, Tommy," I said softly. "Give her whatever she wants. Pay her."

She looked from me to him, realizing that the time for negotiation was now. "You promised me a car and a swimming pool."

When he didn't say anything, I did. "You'll get what he

promised, but if you ever do anything to hurt my sister, I'll make sure you regret it."

"Get your clothes and get out of my house," she said to Tommy. "You get out, too." She spoke nicer to me.

"I'll wait for you outside," I said to Tommy before I walked out the front door.

"You're going to have to get me a new door, too," the nurse was saying. "And the pool has to be twenty by forty. Not one of those little ones. With a slide and a diving board. And a red Mustang convertible, like you promised. With white interior…"

Her voice faded as I continued down the sidewalk to my truck. I got in it and put a Rosanne Cash tape in the player.

Tommy came out of the house ten minutes later, his clothes looking as if he'd been caught in a hurricane. Whatever drug he'd taken was wearing off, and he walked with authority. He came to my window, his face a mask of hatred.

"You think you're smart, don't you?" He didn't expect an answer.

"What are you going to do, Tommy?" I asked. More than anything I wanted him to say he would divorce Dorry.

"I'm not giving up everything I worked for."

"That's your choice." Rosanne sang softly about the need to be loved by someone who'd already walked away. "If you hurt Dorry, if you give her any kind of disease, I'll make you wish you were dead. That's a promise."

"Who appointed you the vigilante committee?" he asked. "Did your mother send you here?"

"I appointed myself. No one in the family knows about this, and I want it to stay that way." A gentle breeze brought the sweet smell of wisteria to me, and I thought of the long spring afternoons when Dorry had sat with me in a china-berry tree and planned her life. She hadn't made room for a husband who cheated on her.

"You won't tell anyone?" He sounded hopeful.

"Keep in mind, Tommy, that you'll never know who's looking over your shoulder. For as long as you're with my sister, you'll always have to wonder who I've hired to keep tabs on you."

"You're a bitch."

"Yeah," I said, starting the truck. "I am." I hit the switch to roll up the window. The glass slid between us as we stared at each other. I drove away.

33

The newsroom fell completely silent when I arrived Tuesday morning. Brandon was sitting in Hank's chair at the city desk, and he watched me as I walked to my office. I heard his footsteps behind me, and I thought of fate and how none of us could avoid it.

"Where the hell have you been?" he asked. "I left four messages at your house last night."

I didn't have to feign surprise. "I didn't check my messages. My sister had an emergency and I had to go to Mobile."

"We have an emergency here, Carson."

"Look, I realize Saul Grotowitz is going to fire me. I didn't realize you'd be so concerned about my welfare." Brandon had sold the *Morning Sun*, and I took it as a personal betrayal.

"I didn't sell the paper."

I must have looked slow or mentally deficient. Brandon enjoyed it far too much.

"What?" I might still have a job.

"I decided not to sell." Brandon's self-satisfaction made me want to slap him. He waved a hand, ushering me into my office. He closed the door behind us. "Which is why I'm here. I had to get another reporter to do a story for this morning's paper. She did some lame interview with Rayburn, which said all of nothing. I need a knuckle-biter for tomorrow. Hank said you had something. What is it?"

I had no intention of telling Brandon anything until I had all the facts hammered down. "Where's Hank?"

"He went to pick up Jack from the hospital. They're releasing him. He'll be back at work Friday. I've made arrangements to help with his financial difficulties."

Jack, like me, had nothing else to do but work. Brandon was throwing him a lifeline. "That's great news."

"What's the story?"

"I have some more work to do. When I have everything I need, I'll write the story."

"I don't have time for this bullshit, Carson. Tell me what you've got."

I forced myself to smile. Amazing the dance steps one could perform when something important was at stake. "I will tell you this much—if I get the facts, this story will put the paper in line for a Pulitzer." That possibility was as effective as a drug.

"I'm going to trust you on this, Carson."

I refrained from asking what else he could do. "If I'm right, it'll be a bang-up story."

He left my office, and I went to the phone directory. Dillard's was the largest department store at Edgewater Mall. More importantly, it had been the bridal center of the Gulf Coast in 1981, when it was still called Gayfer's. I called the number only to discover that the store didn't open until ten. I had a little over an hour to wait.

I called my home phone to retrieve my messages. Brandon hadn't lied. He'd left four calls, ranging from businesslike to Napoleonesque. There was also a call from Mitch Rayburn asking me to get in touch with him.

I concentrated on breathing normally as I dialed Mitch's number. "What's going on?" I asked after we were connected.

Silence stretched between us. He broke it at last. "Carson, will you meet me after work? I'd like to talk to you. There are some important things I need to tell you." He paused. "I need your help."

"My help?"

"You may be the only person who can help me at this point." His voice was strained.

"Sure," I said. My heart rate had accelerated. "How about the Ruby Room?"

"Come by my place. I'd rather be alone. This is difficult."

His words chilled me. Fighting to keep my tone casual, I asked, "Can I bring anything?"

"No. Make it about seven. I'll be finished at the gym by then."

"I'll be there." I hung up, air hissing through my teeth. From my desk drawer I pulled the small tape recorder I seldom used. I checked the batteries to make sure they were charged and dropped the recorder into my purse.

The day was crisp, the air gusting off the gulf with a tang of salt. I drove to Dillard's and was the first customer in the china department. The sales clerk, a woman in her sixties, was disgruntled at the idea of looking up old records. She refused, and I insisted. She called a store manager. It took ten minutes of badgering, but they both finally went to look up the names of the six brides I gave them.

When they returned, they were pale and more cooperative. They carried several sheets of paper in their hands. They gave them to me and I looked at the names of the brides. Audrey Coxwell, Charlotte Kyle, Maria Lopez and Sarah Weaver were all listed as brides in 1981. Pamela Sparks and Tammy Newcomb were recent additions to the Dillard's bridal registry. I looked over the lists. Each girl had selected fine china, an everyday pattern, crystal and flatware.

Dr. Jennings had been correct in his assumption that the killer had selected his victims because of their impending nuptials. They hadn't been selected from the newspaper, though, but from the bridal registry at Dillard's. Back in 1981, when the police force was mostly male, no officer had thought to check the bridal registry. Not all of the girls had run engagement announcements in the newspaper, so the wedding link was never made. One of the victims, Maria, wasn't even really engaged.

The store manager made photocopies of the lists. I took them back to the newspaper, closed the door to my office and sat down to go over them.

Maria Lopez's list showed only three gifts. She'd registered herself as a bride for a joke, and it had cost her her life. I studied the names on the list. F. Ryan had bought a cup and saucer in Maria's fine-china pattern. S. Merced had bought a plate. The last gift, a gravy boat, was purchased by an R. Roland.

I scanned the longer list for Audrey Coxwell and stopped. R. Roland had purchased a gravy boat for her, too. My fingers fumbled as I clutched at the other pages. R. Roland had bought a gravy boat for Charlotte Kyle. The same for Sarah Weaver. My hand was shaking as I traced down the gifts for Pamela Sparks. Another gravy boat, a gift from R. Roland. And Tammy Newcomb, too.

The pages rattled in my hands as I held them a moment, afraid to believe I'd actually found a common link to all six girls. I dialed the store, white-knuckling the phone when the operator transferred me to fine china. The same clerk was there. She didn't grouse about going through the transactions for the more recent gifts for Tammy Newcomb's and Pamela Sparks's weddings. In both cases, R. Roland had paid for each gift with cash. The clerk had no recollection of the man who'd bought the wedding gifts, but she promised to ask the other sales personnel when they came in.

I hung up and called Angola prison. After a lengthy discussion with the deputy warden, I was allowed to talk to Alvin Orley on the phone. I doubted that I could trust anything he told me, but I had to ask.

"Tell me about Mitch Rayburn and his bad luck," I requested when he was on the line.

"Yeah, that boy seems to have a black cloud over his head."

"Expand on that."

"His parents burned to death, his brother drowned during a hurricane. That's fire, water and air. Seems earth is the only element that hasn't betrayed him." He let seconds tick by. "Yet."

"What about the bodies in the parking lot?"

"I told you I don't know anything about any bodies."

"Somehow I don't believe you, Alvin. I think you knew about the bodies, and I think you knew who put them there."

"And who would that be?" His voice was lazy.

"You knew the Rayburn boys were severely abused, didn't you? So abused that Mitch was pushed right over the edge."

"You're making a serious mistake here, Ms. Lynch." His tone was amused.

"You made a serious mistake by killing that man in Louisiana," I said. "You should have stayed on the coast, where someone was watching your back. Had you not screwed up, your life would have been plush with a future D.A. in your pocket."

"Crimes of passion don't always pick a convenient location."

He was toying with me. He would neither confirm nor deny my suspicions that he'd allowed Mitch to bury the dead girls in the parking lot as leverage against future prosecutions.

"Harry Rayburn was your lawyer and he took good care of you, right?"

"Harry watched my back. He was the best damn defense lawyer in a five-state region because he was a ruthless bastard."

"And you felt a debt of obligation, so you helped Mitch and Jeffrey."

"I handled the finances when they bought a house. Got them a real good deal, you know. And when the welfare department snooped around, talking about foster care for Mitch, I put the kibosh on that. That's what I did."

"Did Mitch frequent your club a lot during the '80s?" I asked.

"He was there some. He had a normal curiosity about a good time. Ole Jeffrey would come in there and drag him out before he got in trouble. Jeffrey was a real bulldog when it came to keeping Mitch out of trouble." He laughed softly. "Jeffrey took a lot of heat for Mitch."

"Why don't you tell me about the bodies?" I asked. "Did you know they were there?"

"Let me ask you a question, Ms. Lynch. If I knew about those bodies, why would I have let a bulldozer dig them up?"

He was laughing as he broke the connection.

I went home for the afternoon, telling Hank that I didn't feel well. I must have looked convincing because even Brandon didn't question me.

The cats wound through my legs as I got the vodka from the freezer and made a martini. I drank it slowly while I smoked three cigarettes on the porch swing. Mississippi had few real days of spring, but this was one of them. There was no humidity, and the air had a bright quality of light that made colors pop and sizzle. I pumped the swing with one foot and half closed my eyes, letting the colors of the azaleas, the green grass and blue sky bleed into a whirl of color as I swung back and forth.

I napped for a while and then made another martini and called Dorry. I could hear her banging pots in the kitchen as she talked. She'd regained her composure and her energy.

"Emily wants to spend next weekend with you," she said. "She was really disappointed about her birthday party, but I lied for you. I told her you were called in to work. Tommy doesn't really like it, but he said we could bring her over Saturday morning. We're going on to New Orleans."

"Sure," I agreed. For the past two years, Dorry hadn't trusted me with her daughter. "So things are better with Tommy?"

"Did you talk to him?" she asked.

"No," I lied.

"I got upset over nothing. He was working, and today he was home at three. He said he's tired of working all the time. He's going to spend more time with his family."

"That's great, Dorry."

"We're going to Cancun next month. Sort of a second honeymoon."

"That sounds wonderful."

"And Tommy's going to help me set up my own interior-design business. He's going to talk to some of his friends who need their medical offices redone."

"What about school?"

"Don't get that tone in your voice," she said, and I knew that fear fueled her anger. "I have real talent as an interior designer. Tommy says that going to school would be a waste of time when I can start making money right away."

Using his friends as a client list. Tommy wasn't about to lose control of his wife. "Do you need more money?" I asked.

"Why do you hate Tommy so much?" Dorry asked. "He warned me that you'd try to put a damper on my ideas. He said you'd disapprove."

"Did he?" I'd underestimated Tommy.

"He said you were a control freak. That's why you haven't been able to recover from what happened to you. Because you lost control."

"I didn't realize Tommy had gotten a degree in psychology." There was an edge in my voice.

"Carson, I hope one day you find happiness like I have."

"Dorry, I hope I'm never that deluded." I hung up before she could respond.

I made another martini and my angry fingers jabbed the

number for my mother. By the time she answered, though, I'd gained control. My intention had been to tell her exactly what the wonderful Tommy had been up to, but instead I asked how Dad was doing.

"He'd be doing better if you came home more often."

"I will, Mom." There was no point arguing. All of the will to fight had left me. "Is Dad around now?" I wanted to hear his voice.

"He's at work, Carson. You know your father keeps the pharmacy open to give folks a chance to stop by after work."

"I lost track of time."

"That was a trait I hoped you'd outgrow."

I wondered if my mother realized that everything she said to me was a criticism. Then again, when would I realize that I was old enough that I didn't have to listen to it?

"Mom, I have to go."

"I hope you have a date."

"I still love Daniel."

That, at least, gave her pause, and it gave me a chance to say goodbye and hang up.

It was five o'clock, which would be six in Miami. I called Daniel. I wasn't surprised when I got his answering machine with a simple message that said he was unavailable. His voice was rich, sensual, and I was slow on the mark leaving my message.

"Daniel, I love you. I wish it was enough." I hung up, thinking it was better that I hadn't talked to him.

My next call was to Michael. He wasn't home, either, and I left a message saying I'd call later in the evening.

My last call was to Jack. I knew he'd end up back at his apartment. He sounded better, more alert. "Listen, I'm meeting with Mitch tonight. If it goes wrong, I may need some help."

"Mitch Rayburn?" Jack was incredulous. "What could go wrong?"

"There are too many things that come back to Mitch," I said. "The bridal veil on Pamela Sparks—" I waited while he followed me "—it originally belonged to Alana Williams. It was made from lace belonging to Mitch's mother. Lace that should have burned up in the fire that destroyed their home."

There was a moment of silence. "Holy shit," Jack finally said. "Are you sure? That would mean Mitch or Jeffrey took the lace out of the house *before* the fire. As if they *knew* there was going to be a fire."

"Right. I need you to do something for me. Call the Biloxi PD and find out if there have been any arrests of an R. Roland."

"Who's that?"

"I'm not sure, but I think it's the alias Mitch used to buy wedding presents for the girls he killed."

"Carson, I'm having a hard time buying into this. I've known Mitch for twenty years. He's not a killer."

"Think how much he looked like the guy in the drawing that Adrian Welsh gave the newspaper."

"That doesn't mean anything. I can think of at least five dozen guys who look vaguely like that."

"The bodies were buried at the Gold Rush," I continued. "Alvin Orley was instrumental in helping Mitch and Jeffrey because of their father. Alvin failed to see a grave on his property, and he's somehow managed to evade being prosecuted for anything serious in Biloxi."

"That doesn't prove anything."

Jack was almost as stubborn as I was. "Both Jeffrey and Mitch were severely abused by their father. Their mother, too. A psychiatrist I spoke with said that such abuse could lead children to hate both parents. That hatred could be extended to women in general, particularly women who are about to marry, about to become wives and possibly abusive mothers."

"That doesn't make a lick of sense. The boys would have hated their father. The mother was as much a victim as they were."

"Yes, but mothers are supposed to protect their children."

Jack sighed. "I'm still having trouble with this."

"If I'm wrong, then nothing will come of it. I'll talk with Mitch and come home."

"And if you're right?"

"I want to try to get him to confess."

"Carson, that's insane. If this is all true and he tells you, he'll have no choice but to kill you."

"That's why I'm talking to you, Jack. I'm going to have your number dialed into my cell phone. If something goes wrong, I'll hit the send button. Then you'll know to call the cops."

"I'd feel a lot better if you had some kind of backup. Have you talked with Avery?"

"No, and I don't intend to. Avery and Mitch are too close."

"You need backup."

"You're my backup. Jack, this could be the story that gives me a second chance at a career. If Mitch will talk to me, then I'll have an exclusive that will put me back on top." And there was the slim chance that I could talk Mitch into surrendering, but I wasn't about to confess that to Jack.

"You can end up dead, too."

"There are worse things than being dead. I need this chance."

I waited while he made his decision. "Okay."

After I hung up, I went in the kitchen and looked at the vodka bottle sitting on the ceramic counter. There were at least two inches in the bottle. The jar of jalapeño-stuffed queen olives was open on the counter. The ice had melted in my glass. I put it in the sink and walked away.

Dark had fallen over the house. In my bedroom I found a jacket from the closet and slipped it on. From the bedside table I retrieved my pistol. It was loaded, and I got a box of shells from my lingerie drawer and slipped them into my right pocket, the gun in my left. I was about to leave when I remembered the stun gun Daniel had bought for me. It was in the top shelf of the closet. I'd given it up for the Smith & Wesson. It might come in handy. Stunning Mitch would be far preferable to shooting him. The stun gun came with a little leather holster, and I clipped it onto my belt. Glancing in the mirror, I made sure it was hidden by my jacket.

I walked outside into the smell of rain. Clouds blew like shadows across a half-moon. I could hear the sound of water lapping gently at the shore and the call of a night bird. I turned back to look at my house. Miss Vesta's white face watched me from the window. Her green eyes didn't blink as I got in my truck and drove away.

34

Half an hour early for my appointment with Mitch, I parked down the block beneath the low-hanging branches of a tallow tree. I wanted to scope out the area, see if anyone came and went. It was an older residential area of Biloxi, where the houses sat back on large lawns. Dappled shadows swayed across the window of the truck as the wind moved the tree limbs beneath a streetlight. The street was quiet. No traffic. A dozen vehicles were parked at the curb in front of houses, but there was no evidence of a blue van.

Mitch's house was brightly lit, as if he were having a party. Avery Boudreaux's unmarked police car was in the drive, blocking Mitch's convertible. I'd been parked only a few minutes when Avery came out the front door. He and Mitch were framed in the doorway. They talked for a moment before Avery drove away, turning right with his tires squealing, his headlights never sweeping my secluded parking space.

As soon as Mitch closed the door, I eased out of the truck and hurried down his driveway. There was a separate garage. If the van was there, I'd have what I needed to

convince myself that a man who'd spent his career uphold-
ing the law was actually a killer.

Camellias grew thick around the garage, and I had to
fight to get through them to a small window. The beam of
the flashlight illuminated a room full of old furniture and
boxes. The garage was full.

My cell phone vibrated, and I answered it in a whisper
as I went back to my truck.

"I found R. Roland," Jack said. Excitement elevated his
voice.

"Who is he?"

"He was charged with killing his wife in 1974. Roland
was found innocent of that crime and later convicted of
killing four prostitutes in Louisiana. He was sentenced to
life at Angola in 1976. He died there in 1998."

I couldn't find the connection I sought to Mitch.

Jack's next statement gave me the link. "Harry Rayburn
was Roland's attorney on the original charge of murder-
ing his wife. It was a nasty trial. Harry pulled out all the
stops, bringing in witnesses to say the wife was sleeping
with other men, taking prescription drugs, teaching the
two daughters to lie and steal and cheat. In other words,
Harry Rayburn successfully tried the victim and won."

"Thanks." Instead of satisfied, I felt empty. I didn't want
to know how Mitch had come to identify with a man who'd
killed his wife and four young women. I couldn't help but
wonder about the things Harry Rayburn had told his family
as he'd beaten them to a pulp.

"Carson, be careful." The skepticism was gone from
Jack's voice.

"I will." I checked my pistol, the stun gun and the tape

recorder before I walked up the sidewalk to Mitch's house. He answered my knock with a frown, as if he'd forgotten he'd invited me over. He stepped outside onto the small porch, easing the door closed behind him. His gaze swept the street.

"Is this a bad time?" I asked, uncertain what I hoped his answer would be.

"Carson, it's important that I talk to you, but not tonight. Something has come up." He glanced over his shoulder at the door as if something dreadful waited behind it. Gooseflesh rippled down my arms. I sensed it, too. Danger.

"I can wait while you finish what you're doing," I said, careful to keep it casual, easy. "I don't mind. I'm just glad not to be working tonight."

"I'm really sorry, but I have to change my plans. Can we get together tomorrow?" The skin around his eyes was white with tension.

"What's going on, Mitch?" I asked.

"Call me tomorrow," he said. "I need to talk with you, but I can't do it now. I do need your help, but right now it would be best if you went home."

"I'd be glad to help." He was frantic to get rid of me, which made me determined to stay. "What's going on?"

He rubbed his forehead. "You'll find out soon enough, I suppose. Another girl is missing. Brittany Jacks. She was the lead in a community theater production. She's twenty-one, and her wedding is set for next month. I know this girl, Carson. I've known her all her life." He clenched his fists. "She finished rehearsals this evening and never showed up at her parents' home for dinner."

I felt as if I'd dropped down the steep incline of a roller coaster. "Did someone see the abduction?"

"We don't have all the details, and we aren't even certain the girl has been taken. Avery just stopped by to tell me that her parents are at the station. They're beside themselves. They believe the killer has her." He was jittery with tension. "I have to go. This can't continue, Carson. I have to do something to make this stop." He started back inside, his hand already closing the door.

I grabbed his sleeve. "What do you believe? Do you think the Bridal Veil Killer has taken another victim?"

The look he gave me was anguished and filled with guilt. "Yes. I believe he has her."

"Do you think she may still be alive?" I'd never been able to determine from the police reports if the killer held the girls for any length of time.

"I hope so. God, I hope so."

"Let me help." I took a small step forward, but he held up a hand to block me. Our gazes locked, and I read desperation in his eyes. He knew something. Something that was eating him alive.

"I'm the one who can make this stop. Go home, Carson. Go home and be safe." He closed the door, and I heard the lock turn.

I walked slowly back to the truck almost hidden in the drooping tree branches, but instead of leaving, I waited. It wasn't ten minutes before Mitch's car pulled out of the driveway. He drove right past and never saw me, his focus on the road ahead and his profile that of a man in torment.

I waited until he'd turned left at the end of the block before I started the truck, did a U-turn in the street and followed him. I made certain no one was tailing me. The blue van had spooked me, but now I wondered if it was my imagination.

Traffic through the residential neighborhood was light, and I hung back. Jack's number was already dialed into my phone. I hit Send, and he answered before it had even finished the first ring.

"Another girl is missing," I said. "Brittany Jacks. Does community theater."

"I'll get on it. Where are you?"

"Following Mitch." I paused. "He's deep in this, Jack."

"Carson, if you're right about this…" He let the sentence fade.

"I'll be okay." I had to make him believe it. "Mitch said the girl might be alive. Is that because he knows she's alive and he's going there now? I can't lose him. It may be the victim's only hope."

"Where's he going?"

"I'm not sure. I'll call back and update you."

"I'm too old to sit around and worry. Keep me posted."

"I will." I put the phone down and focused on Mitch. When he turned on Pass Road, I was able to ease closer, not so obvious among the other vehicles that cruised the area. He continued through another residential area and finally turned through the wrought-iron gates of the cemetery where Tammy Newcomb's body had been found.

Too close on his tail to make the turn, I drove on, taking the next street. Live oaks canopied the street, blocking out the scattered streetlights. The houses on this street were abandoned, and I searched my mind for a reason. New development project, strip mall or bad drainage and flooding—it could be any of the above. I couldn't remember the details, but the empty houses were creepy. Across the street, a black wrought-iron fence corralled the dead. I called Jack.

"I'm at the d'Iberville Cemetery."

"Shit, Carson. That's where that girl was found murdered."

"I know." Fog was rolling in off the Sound and settling into the low areas. My windshield was beaded with moisture, the visibility zero. "He may have the missing girl here."

"I'm calling—"

"Don't call anyone!" I meant it. "He might kill the girl."

"You can't stop him from doing that. You need professionals to deal with this."

"He said he needed my help, Jack. He said that twice. I think he wants to explain why he does these things. If I listen, maybe I can talk him into letting the girl go. He knows this one."

Jack thought about it, but I didn't have time for him to come to the right conclusion.

"I have to go. Don't call the police. Not yet. If I need them, I'll call you and hang up."

"I think this is a mistake."

"Bye, Jack."

I got out of the truck, feeling the moisture that hung in the air. The moon was blanketed by heavy drifts of fog, and I could taste the approaching rain in the air. A storm was brewing over the gulf waters and moving my way.

I didn't stop to question what I was doing. A young girl was missing, and I had no doubt I'd find her in the cemetery. I could only hope that she was still alive.

I climbed the fence and ran among the headstones. Tammy Newcomb's body had been found in the northeastern corner of the large cemetery, and I'd parked on the western side. Without the moon to guide me, I'd have to cross the entire cemetery and angle north, trusting gut instinct. I didn't have time to waste, so I couldn't afford a wrong turn.

Mitch had returned to the scene of his last crime. The possible reason for that eluded me, but so many things didn't make sense. Mitch was a decent, caring man—by day. I thought of Dr. Jennings's refutation of the Dr. Jekyll-Mr. Hyde split personality. He didn't believe such a split existed. I was about to find out for myself.

I pushed forward through the tombstones, each noise or the brush of a wet tree branch across my face making me feel as if Death gripped me. Mitch had to be here, somewhere. I only had to see him before he saw me.

When I came upon his car, parked on one of the narrow roads that wound among the graves, I dropped to my hands and knees and began to crawl from one headstone to the next. I listened, the darkness clogging my senses. In the distance crickets sang. To my left, when a bird broke cover from a cedar tree, wings whirring, my heart stopped for a long tick of time.

Thunder rumbled over the gulf, and heat lightning flushed the sky with a throb of white, revealing pale tombstones like jagged teeth. The storm was moving in fast.

I crept slowly forward, the St. Augustine grass wet beneath my palms and knees. I had to find Mitch and the girl before it was too late. The pistol banged against my thigh as it swung in my coat pocket, and I felt to be sure the stun gun was on my belt.

Soft moans came from in front of me. I stopped and listened, praying for another jolt of lightning. After a long minute I had to accept that whatever I'd heard was gone. There was only the chirring crickets and total darkness. The dead didn't need lights to sleep safely.

I was about to crawl deeper into the cemetery when I heard moaning again. I froze, listening. The sky fused white with electricity, and over the top of a headstone not twenty feet away, I saw the gauzy flutter of a bridal veil.

35

The moan came again, soft and muffled. I didn't have to see the girl to know she was drugged and possibly gagged. The chemicals in her bloodstream had rendered her unable to act upon the basic survival instinct of flight. She wouldn't be able to help me, or even herself. In my mind, I saw her leaning against the grave marker waiting for Mitch to draw the knife across her throat. He would do that before he cut off her finger.

When another pulse of lightning lit the sky, I searched for Mitch, but I didn't see him. He was somewhere nearby, waiting to finish the girl. I began to slowly circle toward her. I was ten feet away when I heard him.

"You don't have to do this." His voice was a chilling whisper. "I know you don't want to hurt this girl. She's innocent. She's done nothing wrong."

The idea that Mitch was standing in the middle of the cemetery trying to argue himself out of another murder was one of the most terrifying things I'd ever heard. I grasped the edge of a four-foot marker and peeped over it, waiting for the next burst of lightning. Mitch's face, as pale as the marble of the headstones, appeared in profile to my left. He was about eight feet away. If he'd been looking in my direction, he could have easily seen me, but his gaze was locked on something in the darkness to my right.

Beyond Mitch, Brittany was propped against a headstone, just as I'd imagined. She was naked except for the bridal veil, and her body seemed lifeless, or maybe paralyzed by drugs. As far as I could tell in the brief illumination of the lightning, her throat wasn't cut.

I rested my forehead against the back side of the cold stone and eased the gun from my pocket. I rose to a crouch, my head and arms lifting above the stone, the pistol extended in front of me. I aimed, waiting for the lightning.

Mitch whispered to the darkness as if someone hid from him, as if he were playing some sick game of hide-and-go-seek with a killer. I knew then he was hopelessly insane, and I would pull the trigger to save the girl.

"Don't hurt her." Mitch continued talking. He spoke softly, as if he intended to charm the night. "This isn't necessary. I know you didn't mean to hurt the others. We can make this okay. I promise. I'll never let anyone hurt you." I could tell by his voice that he was turning slowly as he spoke, casting his words in all directions. He was addressing an audience of tombstones.

When the next surge of lightning lit the scene, he was staring straight at me. It took him a second to recognize me and register the gun in my hand. His face showed shock that quickly turned to horror.

"Put your hands over your head," I told him. Night had fallen over us again. I couldn't be certain, but Mitch's hands had looked empty.

"Carson! Run! Get out of here. You don't understand."

"It's over, Mitch." Lightning illuminated the cemetery once again, and I saw him rushing toward me. I leveled the gun. "Stop!" My finger caught the trigger, but the lightning flash was gone and I couldn't be certain of Mitch's location.

His voice came from my left. "Jeffrey, no!" he shouted. "No."

A hand clutched my throat from behind. The fingers dug into my flesh, instantly choking off my air. Lightning popped and I saw Mitch still five feet away from me. Too late, I realized he hadn't been talking to himself. Someone else, someone very strong, was in the cemetery with us, and he had me by the throat. The fingers clenched tighter, cutting off my oxygen. I heard myself making an awful choking sound. I dropped the gun and put my hands up to try to tear the pressure from my windpipe.

Lightning sizzled again. "Don't scream!" Mitch said, his voice a buzzing whisper. "Whatever you do, don't scream or talk loudly." He was much closer. Darkness fell, but he kept talking. "Jeffrey, don't hurt her. She's a friend of mine."

"She's a deceitful bitch. Like all the others."

"No, she's a friend. A reporter. She can help us."

"You want to marry her, don't you?" the man holding my throat in a death grip whispered, his words raw. "You want to make her your wife, don't you? So you can have your family and leave me behind."

"No," Mitch said. There was a low rumble of distant thunder. "I'll always take care of you, just like you took care of me."

Jeffrey Rayburn, the man I thought dead for the past twenty-four years, tightened his grip. With another ounce of pressure, he'd cut off the blood to my brain. Even now I felt dizziness at the fringes of my mind. My fingers crept to my belt.

Jeffrey brought the blade of the knife to my throat. He still held me in a viselike grip with his other hand. "Don't talk," he whispered in my ear. He pushed me forward, moving me closer to Mitch. "The storm is coming. I don't want to hear the thunder. Make it stop. Make it stop now, Mitch."

"Don't hurt her," Mitch said. "Please, Jeffrey. She's the only person who can help us. If she reports the story, like it really is, people will understand. Let's go sit in your van and talk about this. We won't be able to hear the thunder in your van."

"She's been writing about me, and it hasn't been very nice." Jeffrey pressed the cold blade to my chest. "The Bridal Veil Killer. She doesn't understand. She can't."

The blade nicked my skin with a sharp sting. I suppressed the scream that rose in my chest as warm blood trickled down between my breasts.

"Jeffrey, I talked to her. She's going to write a story explaining why those girls had to die. She wants to help us."

I nodded slowly and felt the blade ease off my skin and his grip release a fraction. Relief made my legs shaky, but I didn't move.

"She understands?" Jeffrey whispered, his breath ruffling my hair. It was a voice I'd heard before, on the tape recorder in Tammy Newcomb's apartment.

"She does. She knows how you've suffered, Jeffrey. She's going to write about it so that everyone else understands, too."

I moved my head slowly up and down.

Jeffrey moved me forward again. The sky lit up, and from the corner of my eye I could see the naked body of the young woman. Her eyes were wide with fear or drugs. The sky strobed again, showing the name Alana Williams carved in the cold stone above her head.

At last I fully understood. The stone marked an empty grave. Just as Jeffrey Rayburn's grave was empty. The fifth body in the grave at the Gold Rush was that of Alana Williams. She hadn't drowned. She'd been murdered. The entire drowning had been concocted to cover up the fact that Jeffrey had murdered his bride.

She was the last victim in his killing spree back in 1981.

"Jeffrey, don't hurt Carson. We need her. We have to make everyone else understand, and we need her to write the story."

Jeffrey's grip on my throat relaxed even more. He was holding me so close against his body that I could feel the muscles move in his thighs. My fingers touched the stun gun on my belt. I worked it free of the holster and palmed it in my hand.

"Jeffrey, put down the knife." Mitch's voice was firm but calm, his words spoken in a low voice.

"She has to die," Jeffrey said. "She has to die before she hurts her children."

I prayed that Mitch would keep him talking. I had the stun gun positioned in my hand, and I flipped the switch that turned it on with my thumb.

"Turn Carson loose," Mitch said. "She needs to make notes while she talks to us."

Instead of freeing me, Jeffrey's grip tightened. The blood pounded in my ears, and I felt the blade of his knife bite into my throat.

With every bit of strength I had, I jammed the stun gun against his inner thigh. He jerked when the voltage went through him. The knife sliced deeply into my neck. Blood gushed down my jacket, but I managed to twist free of him. I turned with him and hit him with the gun again, this time on the chest. He arced backward and fell to the ground. Lightning webbed the sky, and I looked at the anguished face of Jeffrey Rayburn as he writhed on the ground.

"Hold it!" Avery's voice cut through the night. Three flashlights jumped to life, blinding me.

Hands grabbed me, and someone wrapped something around my neck as I was lowered into a sitting position on the ground.

"Call an ambulance," Avery said. He leaned down so that I could feel his warm breath on my face. "You're one stubborn ass, Carson Lynch."

I didn't have the strength to argue with him. Nor with the paramedics when they arrived. I let them load me onto a stretcher and carry me to the ambulance without a whimper of protest. I felt the sting of a needle in my arm, and then I remembered only a gentle rocking motion as the ambulance sped out of the cemetery and into the night.

My fingers traced the layers of gauze that covered my throat as I focused on the dull green wall and blind-covered window of my hospital room. It was morning. I could tell by the light that slipped into the room. I'd slept the night away. I had to get going because I had a story to write. As soon as I started to swing my feet over the side of the bed, I realized I wasn't alone.

Mitch Rayburn got out of the chair in the corner and

offered his hand. I took it and let him pull me up so I could sit on the side of the bed. My neck hurt like a son of a bitch.

"Brittany Jacks is going to be okay. He didn't hurt her," Mitch said before I could even ask a question. "He drugged her, but he didn't do anything else."

I looked at his handsome profile. He did resemble his brother. "Are you okay?" My voice was scratchy.

"Yes." He stared into my eyes, unflinching. "Avery's gone for a cup of coffee. I wanted to be here when you woke up."

"Why?"

"To explain."

I thought of the girl. Brittany. She'd survived, but there were seven dead girls. "Can you?"

"Some of it, at least. I had no idea Jeffrey was alive, until three weeks ago. He was found, homeless and disoriented, in New Orleans." His eyes lost their focus. "All of these years, I thought he was dead. He was my big brother, Carson. He taught me to play ball and he defended me, even when it cost him." He shook his head as if he could throw off the past. "The police had picked him up down in the Quarter for public drunkenness. He was harassing some of the young tourists. Anyway, he told them his name, and when they checked and discovered he was using the name of a dead man, the NOPD contacted me. I drove over and identified him."

"That must have been a terrible shock." I could only imagine a brother risen from the grave.

"He was pitiful. I put him in a mental institution for evaluation. I didn't tell anyone because he was so broken, and I knew the media attention would make it worse. I had this crazy idea that with medication and professional help, my big brother would emerge. At first the doctors thought he might have suffered amnesia from a severe blow to the head, but the deeper they looked, the more complex the problem was. When Jeffrey realized he was being detained, he grew violent and aggressive."

"So they put him on Thorazine?" I guessed. "Which he then gave to those girls."

He nodded. "He didn't take his dosage, he pretended to. When he'd capture his intended victim, he'd keep her for a couple of hours, lecturing her on the responsibilities of a mother and why she'd fail. Then he'd drug her and ultimately kill her."

"He got away with this seven times over a span of nearly a quarter of a century." It seemed impossible that a crazy man could complete such a killing spree.

"He's smart. Completely insane, yet smart." Mitch sat with his elbows on his knees, his head hanging. "They thought he was so heavily drugged that they didn't have to watch him closely. Everyone assumed he was what he looked like—a homeless man with no ability to connect to reality. The only peculiar thing they noted in his chart was his obsession with the evening news. He watched the local New Orleans station religiously."

"Why did he kill Alana and those girls? Does he even know what he's done?" I pushed the pillows behind me to prop me up. Though I was weak, lying flat would make me feel vulnerable.

Mitch took a deep breath. "Last night, he showed up at my house. He'd escaped from the institution, stolen a van and come back to the coast. He told me that he and Alana had got in a fight, on the boat, because he wouldn't turn back with the storm coming. He couldn't take being yelled at. Any loud noise sets him off. He said Alana was supposed to save him. She was his bride, his wife." His voice cracked.

"Sarah, Charlotte, Maria and Audrey were already dead. Did he kill anyone else in the years he's been missing?"

"We aren't certain yet. Avery is checking nationwide to see if we can match disappearances or murders with his MO."

The idea was more than depressing, but it would have to be checked. "Do you think he did?"

"Jeffrey's reasoning was very specific, and it may have extended only to this location, but I can't say that for sure. I do know he killed those other girls because he thought they would marry and hurt their children. Alana was the talisman that broke the spell for him. When he married her, he didn't have to kill anymore. Then he hurt her, and he lost all hope of saving himself. The tenuous hold he had on reality snapped. After he killed Alana, he abandoned the boat and swam to the barrier islands. It's a miracle he made it in that weather, but he had a life preserver, and later, a Vietnamese shrimper picked him up."

I wanted to go to Mitch, to offer support, but I didn't have the strength to get out of bed. "Where has he been all this time?" My eyes burned with emotion. Not for Jeffrey, but for Mitch. Mitch clearly loved his brother, yet he couldn't protect him.

"New Orleans and along the coast to Texas. Living in homeless shelters or wherever he could manage." He cleared his throat. "He was so close, all this time."

"Why did he start killing again?"

"The story you broke on the bodies being exhumed at the Gold Rush made it onto the New Orleans news. He thought it was a sign that he had to start again."

I felt a little dizzy and leaned back. Mitch was at my side in an instant. He settled the pillows behind me.

"You have to rest, Carson. You almost died."

I nodded my agreement.

Mitch paced the small room. "I'm not trying to justify anything, but I want you to know this. Jeffrey isn't a monster, or at least he wasn't always. When we were younger, Dad would punish us severely if we talked above a whisper. Even when he beat us, the house had to be perfectly quiet. God forbid if we dropped something by accident, or if the phone rang. He punished us for talking at the table, and for being dull and stupid and not talking. He beat us for staying in the house and for going outside to play. My father was a cruel and abusive man, and it took the biggest toll on Jeffrey."

I swallowed, unable to think of anything comforting to say. Mitch had lived a nightmare. "When did you realize he'd escaped from the institution?"

"They didn't let me know right away. I guess they hoped to cover their ass and find him. They called after Pamela Sparks was murdered, but I didn't put it together. I figured Jeffrey had gone back to the streets. He'd managed for twenty-four years. It never occurred to me that he was home and killing young women." He turned slowly and faced me. "I had no idea that Alana had been murdered. Not until he told me."

I believed him. "Why did you ask me to stop by your house?"

"By last night, I'd put most of it together, and I needed your help. You could write the story and do it justice. I didn't want him hurt. Then he took Brittany, and it spun out of control."

"Where is he now?"

"In jail. They'll transfer him to the state mental institution at Whitfield for a psychiatric evaluation. He won't last six months." He looked at me and I saw the horror of his childhood in his eyes.

"Why did he bury the girls at the Gold Rush?"

Mitch shrugged. "Alvin will never tell me the truth, but he must have known. There was heavy equipment in the parking lot all that summer. Alvin had the sewer lines reworked and some other projects going. Jeffrey liked to hang out there. I think it was convenient and he had access to a backhoe on the premises. He could slip up there in the early morning hours when the club was closed and bury the woman he killed in a matter of minutes. Alvin wasn't going to report the disturbances of that secluded part of the parking lot."

All along, Alvin had known. I'd seen it in his face when I interviewed him. He'd kept quiet about Jeffrey, waiting for Mitch's star to rise. Were he not in Angola prison, he'd be putting the screws to Mitch in a blackmail scheme right now.

Restless, Mitch paced to the window. "Alana was such a lovely, sweet girl. All these years, I can still hear her laughter. I'll always be haunted by her."

"Mitch, you didn't know." My words were as ineffective as throwing pebbles at a tornado. "You can't blame yourself. You didn't know."

"I should have known."

"You were a kid. A college kid. You'd finally gotten away from the horrors of your family and—" The question demanded an answer. I hated to ask but I had to. "The fire that killed your parents?"

"It was ruled accidental. I was at a Boy Scout campout, and Jeffrey was supposed to be at a baseball clinic." When he faced me I saw the doubt on his face.

"Do you think Jeffrey set the fire?"

"Yes. I'm certain he did. I think Alvin helped cover it up with that official ruling of faulty electrical wiring. Alvin was always a man with long-range plans."

Something else troubled me. "What about the fingers?"

"They're all buried in Alana's grave. Each one in a gravy boat. Avery and a forensics team recovered them."

"I found the bridal gift lists for the girls, and every single one included a gravy boat. I don't get the significance."

He looked down at the floor for a moment. "The worst beating Jeffrey ever got was over my mother's gravy boat. Dad almost killed him. He broke all the fingers on his left hand." He looked into my eyes. "I was the one who broke the dish. Mother was furious, and she knew what would happen if she told Dad—she told him anyway."

I tried to sit up, but Mitch came to the bed and took my hand. "Take it easy, Carson. There's nothing else to be done." A tiny smile lifted the corners of his mustache. "You almost got yourself killed, but you probably saved that young woman."

He walked to the door, turning for a last remark. "Riley has been fired. He confessed to the note and the matches. He tried to scare you off because he didn't want his wife to know about his mistress. He got involved with one of Alvin's dancers years ago and she has three kids by him. That's what he was hiding."

"Thanks, Mitch."

"Don't thank me. When Avery found out what Riley had done, trying to intimidate you, Avery threatened to go to the press. Chief Nelson fired Riley on the spot."

"Avery was going to the press. Who would have thought?"

"I guess everyone has something to hide. Some dreadful secret that we all fear will be unearthed."

I nodded because it was true.

"There's someone else you should thank," Mitch said. "Jack. He called Avery and sent him out to the cemetery."

"I'll thank him when I see him."

"Get some rest." He left the room, closing the door behind him. I gave him ten seconds, then rang the nurse. I needed a laptop and a phone line. I had a story to write.

Before I could begin, I had a couple of additional questions. I dialed Avery.

"Well, if it isn't the ace reporter," Avery said when he heard my voice. "I'd hoped to get at least a day's rest before you started calling."

"Very funny. If the gate to the pier was locked, how did Jeffrey get Pamela Sparks out there?"

"Bolt cutters."

"The chain was cut?" I ran through the scene in my mind. I'd gone past the gate, but I hadn't noticed because it was dark. "If you'd told me that, I would never have suspected Riley took her there in a boat."

"And Riley might still be deputy chief. Something good came of it."

I wanted to rap him upside the head with my knuckles, but there was no point getting angry. Avery had his job and I had mine. They wouldn't always flow parallel to each other. "So what about the bridal veils? Where did Jeffrey get them?"

There was a moment's hesitation on the line. "I guess it doesn't matter now. From thrift shops and used-clothing stores, all except for Pamela Sparks's. That was Alana's veil. Jeffrey must have stored it somewhere after the wedding. He brought it out after the dead girls were exhumed and began killing again.

"There's one more thing." Now it was me who hesitated. "Do you think Mitch will be okay?"

"Yeah. It won't be easy. He's losing his brother a second time, and in tragic circumstances. In some ways, Jeffrey died a long time ago. At least the brother Mitch loved. He'll come to see that."

I hoped so. I looked out the window and saw the angle of the sunlight. "I have to go. I'm on deadline."

"You're tough, Carson. I think you and Mitch both will do just fine."

The coffeepot had just started dripping when I heard the thud of the newspaper against the front porch. The morning was chilly, a rare occurrence for late March. I tied the yellow chenille robe more tightly around me and slipped on the ridiculous pink flamingo slippers Avery and his wife had brought as a get-well present. Jill, their daughter, was helping with the cats in exchange for advice on a career in journalism. I shuffled to the front porch for the paper.

The tall man standing on my porch caught me by surprise. I smiled as I held the door open for Michael. "Come in."

He gave me a long look. "You look wonderful," he said.

I laughed. The robe was at least twenty years old and Miss Vesta and Chester had pulled it to pieces with their claws. The slippers made me walk like a pregnant woman. "Right."

"I came to look at your wound. I heard that you haven't been tending it properly."

I hadn't gone back to the doctor, but the cuts had been merely flesh wounds. The stitches would come out in another six days, leaving a hairline scar.

"My neck is fine."

"Let me see," he said as he led me to the kitchen, sat me down at the table and began to unwrap the dressing.

"Who told you I wasn't taking care of myself?" I asked.

"Detective Boudreaux."

"Oh, really? Avery has become very good at poking his nose in my business."

"Yes, when I met him at the hospital, he and I both agreed you need someone to keep you safe."

I got cups and poured coffee for both of us, ignoring his comment. When I felt his hands on my shoulders, I turned into his arms.

He held me pressed against his chest. "Carson, I know you're still in love with Daniel."

I didn't deny his words. I couldn't. Daniel had called me every day. He'd offered to come and stay with me. He'd also been very angry that, once again, I'd put myself in danger. It was that very thing that had claimed our daughter's life.

Michael stroked my hair softly. "Until my divorce is complete, I'm not going to pressure you. After that, it's going to be an open playing field. I don't want to lose you twice, Carson."

I closed my eyes and leaned against him. He was solid, a man who honored his word. "I can't make any promises about anything," I whispered into his shoulder.

"I'm not asking for any promises." He kissed the top of my head, then led me back to the kitchen chair, where he finished examining my neck. He looked at the incision. "The doc did a pretty good job. I have to say I'm a little better at stitching than he is. Looks like I can take those out in a few days, though."

"You're going to take my stitches out?"

"That's another reason you need to keep me around. If you're going to continue with your career, you're going to be in harm's way. You need someone who can patch you up."

I thought about what he was offering and the lack of censure in his voice. "No promises. Not now."

He kissed the curve of my jaw. "We'll let nature take its course."

New York Times Bestselling Author

ERICA SPINDLER

Five years ago, three young victims were found murdered, posed like little angels. No witnesses, no evidence left behind. The case nearly destroyed homicide detective Kitt Lundgren's career—because she let the killer get away.

Now the Sleeping Angel Killer is back.

But Kitt notices something different about this new rash of killings—a tiny variation that suggests a copycat killer may be re-creating the original "perfect crimes." Then the unthinkable happens. The Sleeping Angel Killer himself approaches Kitt with a bizarre offer: he will help her catch his copycat....

"[A] bloodcurdling romantic thriller."
—Publishers Weekly

COPYcat

The chilling tale of a parent's worst nightmare, by acclaimed author

CHRIS JORDAN
taken

No parent believes it can happen to them—their child taken from a suburban schoolyard in the gentle hours of dusk. But, as widowed mother Kate Bickford discovers, everything can change in the blink of an eye.

Opening the door to her Connecticut home, hoping to find her son, Kate comes face-to-face with her son's abductor. He wants money. All she has. And if she doesn't follow something he calls The Method, the consequences will be gruesome....

"Jordan's full-throttle style makes this an emotionally rewarding thriller that moves like lightning."
—*Publishers Weekly*

Available the first week of August 2007 wherever paperbacks are sold!

MIRA®

74 Seaside Avenue

New York Times Bestselling Author

DEBBIE MACOMBER

Dear Reader:

I'm living a life I couldn't even have dreamed of a few years ago. I'm married to Bobby Polgar now, and we've got this beautiful house with a view of Puget Sound.

Lately something's been worrying Bobby, though. When I asked, he said he was "protecting his queen"—and I got the oddest feeling he wasn't talking about chess but about me. He wouldn't say anything else.

Do you remember Get Nailed, the beauty salon in Cedar Cove? I still work there. I'll tell you about my friend Rachel, and I'll let you in on what I've heard about Linnette McAfee. Come in soon for a manicure and a chat, okay?

Teri (Miller) Polgar

"Those who enjoy good-spirited, gossipy writing will be hooked."
—*Publishers Weekly* on *6 Rainier Drive*

Available the first week of September 2007, wherever paperbacks are sold!

REQUEST YOUR FREE BOOKS!

2 FREE NOVELS FROM THE ROMANCE/SUSPENSE COLLECTION PLUS 2 FREE GIFTS!

YES! Please send me 2 FREE novels from the Romance/Suspense Collection and my 2 FREE gifts. After receiving them, if I don't wish to receive any more books, I can return the shipping statement marked "cancel." If I don't cancel, I will receive 4 brand-new novels every month and be billed just $5.49 per book in the U.S., or $5.99 per book in Canada, plus 25¢ shipping and handling per book plus applicable taxes, if any*. That's a savings of at least 20% off the cover price! I understand that accepting the 2 free books and gifts places me under no obligation to buy anything. I can always return a shipment and cancel at any time. Even if I never buy another book from the Reader Service, the two free books and gifts are mine to keep forever.

185 MDN EF5Y 385 MDN EF6C

Name _____ (PLEASE PRINT) _____

Address _____ Apt. # _____

City _____ State/Prov. _____ Zip/Postal Code _____

Signature (if under 18, a parent or guardian must sign)

Mail to **The Reader Service:**
IN U.S.A.: P.O. Box 1867, Buffalo, NY 14240-1867
IN CANADA: P.O. Box 609, Fort Erie, Ontario L2A 5X3

Not valid to current subscribers to the Romance Collection,
the Suspense Collection or the Romance/Suspense Collection.

Want to try two free books from another line?
Call 1-800-873-8635 or visit www.morefreebooks.com.

* Terms and prices subject to change without notice. NY residents add applicable sales tax. Canadian residents will be charged applicable provincial taxes and GST. This offer is limited to one order per household. All orders subject to approval. Credit or debit balances in a customer's account(s) may be offset by any other outstanding balance owed by or to the customer. Please allow 4 to 6 weeks for delivery.

Your Privacy: Harlequin is committed to protecting your privacy. Our Privacy Policy is available online at www.eHarlequin.com or upon request from the Reader Service. From time to time we make our lists of customers available to reputable firms who may have a product or service of interest to you. If you would prefer we not share your name and address, please check here. ☐

BOB07